Praise for the novels of
New York Times and *USA TODAY*
bestselling author Kristan Higgins

MY ONE AND ONLY

"A funny, poignant romance....
Readers will be cheering for Harper all the way."
—*Publishers Weekly,* starred review

ALL I EVER WANTED

"Higgins has a special talent
for creating characters readers love....
Fun, charming and heartfelt."
—*RT Book Reviews,* 4½ stars

THE NEXT BEST THING

"A heartwarming, multi-generational tale of lost love,
broken hearts and second chances."
—*BookPage*

"I felt all of the emotions and was
drawn into the story as if I was there."
—*Publishers Weekly*

TOO GOOD TO BE TRUE

Winner—2010 Romance Writers of America RITA® Award

"Cheeky, cute, and satisfying, Higgins's romance
is perfect entertainment for a girl's night in."
—*Booklist*

"Kristan Higgins proves that she is emerging as one of the
most creative and honest voices in contemporary romance."
—*Romance Junkies*

JUST ONE OF THE GUYS

"Higgins provides an amiable romp
that ends with a satisfying lump in the throat."
—*Publishers Weekly*

CATCH OF THE DAY

Winner—2008 Romance Writers of America RITA® Award

"A touching story brimming with smart dialogue,
sympathetic characters, an engaging narrative and the
amusing, often self-deprecating observations of the
heroine.
It's a novel with depth and a great deal of heart."
—*RT Book Reviews,* Top Pick, 4½ stars

Dear Reader,

Hello! Thank you so much for choosing *Until There Was You*. Once again, you'll find a beautiful New England town, a heroine with a huge heart (and a huge dog, in this case) and a hero to swoon over. The story gives a slightly different take on a classic theme—the return of the bad boy. Now, we all love bad boys, don't we? I was amazed at how much fun it was to write one... that hot guy from high school with the motorcycle, the tattoo and the bad attitude. Is it any wonder that Posey, the scrawny kid who watched from the sidelines, fell for him? He was out of her league, barely noticed her...but he managed to break her heart just the same. Now he's back and seems exactly as appealing—and potentially dangerous—as he was back then.

This book contains a first for me—the hero's point of view! As the widowed father of a teenage girl, Liam lives in fear that his daughter is going to fall for a guy who's just like he was. Overprotective? Just a little! He's come back to Bellsford, New Hampshire, to be closer to family. But Liam hasn't counted on just how much his past still matters...especially to Posey, who has to figure out if Liam's any different than he ever was. I had a lot of fun examining the themes of what it means to belong in this book, to be chosen and loved, as well as how events from the past shape the present...and the future.

There are a lot of great secondary characters here, too—Jon, was a special favorite, as well as Brianna, the mouthy teenage girl Posey befriends. And I had such fun with Guten Tag! I hope you'll love *Until There Was You,* and once again, thank you so much!

Kristan

www.KristanHiggins.com

KRISTAN HIGGINS

Until There Was You

HQN™

Recycling programs
for this product may
not exist in your area.

ISBN-13: 978-0-373-20284-3

UNTIL THERE WAS YOU

Acknowledgments

Eternal thanks to Maria Carvainis for her sure-handed guidance of my career, as well as to Chelsea Gilmore, Martha Guzman and Lyndsey Hemphill for all they do for me. At HQN Books and Harlequin Enterprises, thanks to my brilliant and kindhearted editor, Keyren Gerlach, as well as to Tara Parsons, Margaret Marbury O'Neill and the rest of the Harlequin family for their tremendous enthusiasm and support.

Thanks also to...

Kim Castillo, world's best PR assistant and my favorite breakfast buddy; the wonderful, good-looking gang at CTRWA; Shaunee Cole, Karen Pinco and Kelly Morse, who once again helped me kick this bad boy off, and who made me have Liam be a motorcycle hottie instead of something girly; Jimmy Spencer, who took me out on his Harley (I'm free whenever you want to do that again, Jimmy, just saying); my dear mom, Noel Higgins, who proofreads all my manuscripts (and gave me life and raised me and all that other good stuff); Annette Willis who once again answered questions on family law; Christine Michaud, forever my consultant on all things Red Sox (may they never defeat the Yankees again so long as I draw breath); Terence Keenan, who filled in all the blanks on motorcycle parts and forced me to watch Orange County Motors; the wonderful Diana Phung, who sends me all sorts of good stuff to keep the batteries charged. And very special thanks to Dena Umberger, Lillian Lanouette and Joe Avellar, who shared their experiences on being adopted.

Biggest thanks of all to my beautiful, wonderful, brilliant kids, whom I love more than I could ever put into words, and to my husband, who is simply the best man I know. Don't know how I got so lucky with you three, but I'm very grateful I did.

And to Digger, my faithful dog, who was by my side for every book I've written to date. Thanks, old friend. Miss you.

Also available from

KRISTAN HIGGINS

and HQN Books

My One and Only
All I Ever Wanted
The Next Best Thing
Too Good to Be True
Just One of the Guys
Catch of the Day
Fools Rush In

CHAPTER ONE

EVERY WOMAN HAS A fantasy about running into the man who broke her heart. In such a fantasy, she'd be walking down the street, her well-dressed and gorgeous husband (let's say George Clooney, shall we, circa *Ocean's 11*) caressing her, perhaps nuzzling her neck because he can't help himself. She'd be wearing something fabulous, her hair would be glossy and perfect, she and Clooney would have just left the nicest restaurant in town, perhaps, or the poshest jewelry shop, because he *insisted* on buying her yet another token of his love—and then, oh, my goodness, who's that? Why it's *him,* the first man she ever loved, the one who didn't just break her young and loyal heart, but shattered it. He's not looking so good these days. No, the years have not been kind. He's gray—or, better yet, balding—and slackly overweight, his posture hunched. He looks at her, recognizing immediately that the biggest mistake of his life was dumping her. Pleasantries will be exchanged. Clooney will shake his hand, giving Adored Wife a wry look *(Him? Really?),* and as the happy couple walks away to their snazzy car, the heartbreaker of old is already forgotten. But *he* will gaze longingly after her, wondering how he ever could've been so blind.

That would've been nice. Much nicer, Posey Osterhagen acknowledged, than being dressed in the waitress uniform of Guten Tag, her parents' restaurant—dirndl, ruffled skirt and vest embroidered with dwarves (yes, dwarves), not to mention the green tights and painted red clogs. Cheeks bulging with the potato dumpling she'd just crammed into her mouth, as she was at the near-fainting part of her flea-like metabolism. The back door opened and there he was, standing right in front of her.

Liam Declan Murphy, the first man she'd ever loved, and the only man who'd ever broken her heart.

No Clooney. No jewelry. Just an empty kitchen in an aging German restaurant and a fist-size dumpling practically splitting her cheeks.

Posey's mind blipped into the blue screen of death—all data erased. Fatal error. Speaking was clearly not an option.

His eyes were still that unnerving shade of clear, glacier green. Black hair showed no signs of gray or thinning. Still tall—*obviously, Posey, people don't usually shrink in their thirties.* Still radiating his bad-boy *You want me/I ignore you* vibe. Oh…bieber. This was just not good. *Chew, Posey, chew,* her brain instructed. She obeyed with difficulty. It was a big dumpling.

Liam was dressed in jeans, T-shirt and leather jacket, pretty much the same thing he wore back in high school, if memory served. And memory seemed to be wicked clear where Liam Murphy was concerned. He'd come to Bellsford to live with an uncle after getting out of juvie (squee!—okay, okay, she'd been fifteen, it had seemed uber-hot back then) for car theft. Rode an old motorcycle (come on!) and, as legend had it, had turned quite a few girls into women (gack). But, to everyone's surprise, he'd fallen for the squeakiest-clean girl in school, just like a plotline on *Beverly Hills 90210,* Posey's favorite show back then. When Emma Tate had gone off to college in California, Liam had followed. Eventually, they'd gotten married. It had been in the paper, before Emma's parents had moved to Maine.

And here he was.

"Liam!" cried her mother. Stacia Osterhagen, six foot two of Germanic engineering, tromped into the kitchen, rattling the stacked dishware. "Posey! Look who's here! We forgot to tell you! Max! Liam's here! Liam, sweetheart, why didn't you come in the front?"

"Force of habit, I guess," he said with a slight smile at her mother.

"Good to see you, son," Max said heartily, shaking their visitor's hand.

Liam Declan Murphy.

Holy Elvis Presley.

"You remember Liam, don't you, honey?" Stacia said.

Cheeks still bulging, Posey nodded. Could she look any more ridiculous? Not that she was exactly gifted with girliness when it came to clothes—her work required sturdy stuff, so, sure, there was a lot of flannel, a lot of Carhartt. But even that would be better than her uniform (same one from high school, still regrettably roomy in the bust, as Germans didn't take small chests into account when designing clothes, apparently).

"Hey," he said with the same disinterested tone she remembered with unfortunate clarity. "How are you, Cordelia?" His tone implied he really didn't care. And *Cordelia*. That was another thing. He'd always called her by her real name, for some reason...a name Posey hated. Honestly—bad enough to have been stick-figure skinny in high school, but to bear the name Cordelia Wilhelmina Osterhagen (named for a half-blind great-aunt who'd died by falling into a well)... Obviously, she'd had more than her fair share of mocking.

"I'm good," she squeaked, finally swallowing the last of the dumpling. "Hi. How are you?"

"Fine, thanks."

"Good! Good. Um...how's Emma?"

"She died," he answered coolly.

Posey's head jerked back in shock. "What? Are you kidding?"

He gave her a glacial look. "No."

How had she missed this news? "But...when did this happen?"

"It'll be three years in October."

That explained something, at least. Two and a half years ago, in October, Posey had taken a rare vacation and spent a few weeks in North Carolina. And she'd been a latecomer to Facebook, so if there'd been chatter, she'd missed it. And she and Emma hadn't exactly run with the same people.

"I'm so sorry," she said, her face burning.

Emma Tate, *dead*? Crikey! She'd been a nice girl. A *very* nice girl and a very popular girl back in high school, when such things seemed mutually exclusive. "So, what happened?" Posey asked. Then, aware that perhaps this was none of her business, she added, "I mean, you don't have to tell me. It's... I don't have to know. It's your...private, um...thing."

"Leukemia," Liam answered.

Posey flinched. "I'm so, so sorry."

"A tragedy," Max added. "Such a sweet girl."

"He told us at Home Depot the other day," Stacia said. "You know how the fan in the upstairs bathroom has been broken for years? Well, we thought it was time to finally fix it, since Gretchen's coming home, and there we were and who did we see but this handsome boy! We were so sad to hear about Emma. So sad."

Granted, not sad enough to tell Posey, despite the fact that Stacia called her every morning at 8:15. Then again, not passing on big news was a family tradition. Stacia had told Posey about Carol Antonelli's gallbladder surgery in relentless detail, as well as how much they'd saved by driving forty miles to buy coffee at Stop & Shop instead of Hannaford's, sure. But bigger news—deaths, births, marriages, etc.—tended to fall through the cracks.

A sudden flash of memory caused a lump to come to Posey's throat—Emma at Sweetie Sue's Ice Cream Parlor, loading up a waffle cone with four scoops instead of three, a conspiratorial wink as she handed it over the counter.

"I'm really sorry," she said more quietly.

"Thanks," Liam said, still staring with that cold, disinterested gaze.

Posey looked away, torn between sympathy, guilt for not knowing about Emma, trepidation (Liam had done some damage, after all), and, yes, lust. "You guys have a kid, right?" she asked. At least she remembered that.

"Nicole. She's fifteen now."

"Wow. Fifteen. That's… Wow. Fifteen."

Liam didn't answer, but his look was loaded with that same disdain Posey so well remembered.

Once upon a time, when he was channeling Bono, Liam had worked right here in Guten Tag, a miraculous and agonizing time for Posey. The fact that the Osterhagens had given Liam a job at a time when his reputation was questionable (and fascinating) hadn't caused Liam to warm up to Posey, however. Nope. He always treated her with the same interest he might give a speck of dust.

At first, anyway.

Whatever. Mom was gabbling away. "Liam, sweetheart, you haven't changed a bit! You have to stay for a drink! You have to! Did you eat? We'll feed you. I insist. Max, you insist, too, don't you?"

"I also insist," Max said, smiling.

"Just a drink," Liam said. "I have to get back to my daughter."

Just then Otto, a longtime waiter and accordion player at Guten Tag, poked his head through the door to the dining room. "Max, Stacia, the Schmottlachs are leaving."

"Posey, make Liam at home, would you? Liam, this will just take a minute. Bruce and Shirley are our best friends. You remember them, don't you?"

Liam's mouth pulled into a reluctant smile as Stacia grabbed Max by the hand and towed him into the dining room. Said smile caused Posey's girl parts to clench in a warm, strong squeeze. *Hello!* Her stomach began flipping like an overexcited dolphin. Alone. She was *alone* with Hottie McSin, widower. Oh, crikey, that wasn't nice. She shouldn't be lusting after the poor guy. Except the words *poor guy* didn't seem to apply to Liam Murphy. She swallowed, the sound louder than a gunshot in the now-quiet kitchen.

Meanwhile, God's gift to women—because, yes, he was that good…all smoldering male beauty made all the more inaccessible by that touch of disdain—folded his arms and looked around the kitchen.

It was hard to fathom that bright, bouncy Emma Tate was gone. Posey swallowed again, her throat thick. "How's your daughter handling things?"

"Pretty well." He allowed her a brief glance.

"So, what brings you here? Just visiting?"

"No. We moved to be closer to Emma's parents."

He was *back?* Staying? "Oh. Um…that's nice. Good. I mean, it's good to be close to family. Good for children, I mean."

He didn't answer. Didn't ask what she'd been up to, if she was married, if she had kids. Of course not. Apparently he was still way too cool to care about—

"So, what have you been up to, Cordelia?"

Oops. Strike that. "Oh, I'm just filling in tonight. I own an architectural salvage company," she said, well aware of the pride that tinged her voice. He didn't respond, just gave a half nod. "What about you?"

"I'm a mechanic. I build custom motorcycles."

Of *course* he was a motorcycle mechanic. This would enable him to wear leather and smell like oil and have large throbbing machines between his thighs. At the image, Posey's legs weakened. *Down, girl.* It wouldn't do to wrestle him to the floor here in her parents' kitchen. But he'd always had that effect on her—and every other female. He was like the Death Star's tractor beam, pulling in whatever the heck it wanted. "Motorcycles. Neat-o," she managed.

Liam's glance bounced around the kitchen once more. He sighed, perhaps irked that there was no one else to talk to, then looked back at her. "You married?"

"Um, no. Nope. Not married. Not yet, I guess I should say. I, um…well, you know. Haven't met the right guy." Oh, bieber. That made her sound…unwanted. "Not yet. I mean, actually I'm seeing someone… um, and, you know, I came close once or twice, but—"

"Came close to what?" Stacia asked, banging through the kitchen doors once more.

Posey jumped. "Nothing," she muttered, tugging at her dwarf-embroidered vest.

"Cordelia was telling me about when she almost got married," Liam said. Was that derision in his voice? Probably.

"What? You almost *what?*" Stacia pressed a large hand to her ample bosom. "My own child, and I don't know this—"

"Mom, stop. It was...you know." Posey took a deep breath. "Ron. You remember."

"The one with the rash?"

Posey grimaced. "It cleared up very quickly."

"He was the one who turned gay, right? Liam, honestly. Posey just cannot find a normal man, not that she tries very hard, working out at that junkyard—"

"It's not a junkyard. It's architectural salvage." *And I am seeing a normal man, I just don't want you to keel over if I tell you who.*

"I always say, if she'd just clean up a little, some man would see what a beautiful, sweet—" Stacia broke off, a religious gleam beginning in her sky-blue eyes. Ruh-roh. Posey knew that look. It was the look of Matchmaker, one Posey had seen far too many times over the years. Ron the Gay with the Rash had been one of Stacia's better picks, actually. There'd been Carol Antonelli's nephew, who'd taken her to McDonald's on their first date and didn't even pay for her Big Mac. The restaurant-supply guy who'd turned out to have two families, one in New Hampshire, one in Delaware. And now, the look of Matchmaker with Liam.

Don't do it, Mom, Posey begged silently, hunching her shoulders to ward off the blow.

The blow came, though not the one she expected. "You'll have to come back and meet my niece, Liam," Stacia said. "Gretchen? From *The Barefoot Fraulein?* On the Cooking Network? She's my late sister's daughter. We're so proud of her! Have you ever seen her show?"

"Can't say that I have," he murmured. He glanced again at Posey, eyes dropping to her costume. Just in case she forgot that she looked like an idiot.

"Well, you'll have to come by," Stacia said. "We were just thrilled when she told us she wanted to come work here! And she's such a sweet, sweet girl." Mom paused cunningly. "Very pretty, too."

Gretchen *was* very pretty, Posey would give her that. She looked much like Stacia—tall, blonde, blue-eyed, voluptuous—German beauty at its finest. Posey, on the other hand, was adopted—five foot three (five two and a half, why lie?), a hundred and seven pounds, dark, short, difficult hair and brown eyes. As for Gretchen's sweetness... Posey stifled a snort.

"We could use a little help, to be honest," her mom continued. "Ever since that—" Stacia took a meaningful breath "—that *Italian* restaurant moved in down the street, business has been a little slow."

Business had been slow well before Inferno opened, though Posey knew her mom would never admit it. Guten Tag's food wasn't bad, if you liked old-school German cuisine (which, it must be said, most people didn't). The slogan—*We'll feed you till you're stuffed!*—didn't exactly scream gourmet dining.

Inferno, on the other hand, was only six months old and had already been reviewed by the *New York Times* (four stars). They had a slogan, too, one that appeared on the local television stations and in swanky tourist magazines—*Our life's mission: to make the best meal of your life.*

Dante Bellini, the owner, had recently earned the undying wrath of her parents when a reporter asked about other restaurants in the area. His reply was, "There's a kitschy institution down the street, but no real competition." Stacia and Max found the words more offensive than if he'd burned their house to the ground.

The restaurants were indeed very different. Guten Tag was all about fun, not food—the costumes, the music, the cries of "Zicke zacke, zicke zacke, hoi, hoi, hoi!" every time someone ordered a beer. Inferno was sophistication incarnate. Its interior was gorgeous, as Posey well knew—Dante had bought more than ten thousand dollars' worth of furnishings from Irreplaceable Artifacts, her very own business. This was still a sore spot (or a pulsating ulcer) with the elder Osterhagens. Nevertheless, Inferno boasted the fountain Posey had rescued from the old monastery in New York, marble columns from the public library in Lowell and four sculptures of Italian saints from a church in Vermont.

Yep, Dante Bellini knew how to run a business.

He was also pretty good in bed.

Of course, Posey would kill herself before telling her parents that particular nugget. Still, it made her stand up a little straighter.

"But come, come," Stacia said, taking Liam by the arm. "Our son and his partner are here. Did you ever meet Henry? You must have, even though he was in medical school back when you worked here. Posey, don't just stand there, sweetheart, come out and have a drink with us."

"I have to run," Posey said, grabbing her jacket from the hook by the door. "Mom, see you soon. Um, Liam…nice to see you again."

Liam nodded, barely looking at her.

"Posey, wait," Stacia said. "Let me get you some brisket. I don't like you eating that garbage you buy from the store. I saw those pizzas in your freezer. You shouldn't be eating that, even if you do want to fatten up a little. Liam, the girl just cannot gain an ounce! I wish I had that problem!"

Posey closed her eyes. "Bye, Mom."

She pushed open the back door into the blessed silence of a Thursday night in Bellsford, New Hampshire. It was cold outside, the wind coming off the Piscataqua River. March hadn't released its hold on New England, that was for sure. Posey shivered as she walked down the alley behind the restaurant to the street. Skirts in March…not practical. She hoisted herself into the truck, adjusted her skirt and started the engine, which took a moment to catch before coughing to life. As she drove down the street, Posey slowed in front of what had once been Kirby's Auto Repair. There was a sign in the window. *Coming Soon: Granite State Custom Motorcycles, Liam Murphy, Proprietor.*

Time for that emergency Almond Joy in her glove compartment. Posey ripped off the wrapper and practically inhaled the candy bar.

Poor Emma. Posey was truly sorry about that, and felt a tug of sympathy for the daughter, poor kid. And for Liam, too. It couldn't be easy being a single parent to a teenage girl who'd lost her mother at such an impressionable age. Not that he'd be single for long. Probably had a girlfriend already, maybe more than one, because who could resist a widower with a kid?

Liam Murphy, back in town. To stay. On the one hand, she had to admit that it was thrilling, in the same way that cliff diving might be thrilling…thrilling and often fatal.

"Try not to be an idiot this time around," she said aloud. With that, she whacked the dashboard of her truck so the iPod would play, then selected Neil Diamond's "Brother Love's Traveling Salvation Show" to jump-start a better mood.

The thing was, once upon a time, Posey had fallen for Liam Declan Murphy, and fallen hard. She'd loved him with all the fervor a teenage girl could love a boy, would've gone to the ends of the world for him. But without so much as a backward glance, he broke her heart in one stunning blow.

And he still had no idea.

CHAPTER TWO

LIAM MURPHY CLOSED the door behind him and locked the door. Then he unlocked it. Then he relocked it, just to make sure the dead bolt was solidly in place. It was. At least, he thought it was. He unlocked it, then sort of slammed the dead bolt back. Maybe that was too hard, though, maybe he'd thrown something off, so he unlocked it again, then relocked it once more. Just to be sure that being sure was really sure.

He sighed, shook his head in self-disgust. Pretty soon, this…this obsessing…it had to end.

"Nicole? I'm home," he called. There was no answer, which didn't mean that his daughter wasn't home. It could just mean she was in a Mood—and, yeah, the capital letter was definitely needed. Ah. The thumping of a bass guitar began. His daughter was home indeed, and had recently "discovered" the Ramones. At least her taste in music was improving. If Liam had had to listen to one of those prepubescent boys for another hour, he thought he might have to shove a screwdriver in his eardrums.

He went into the kitchen, turned on the water, counting to fifty-five as he soaped up. When Emma was dying—there was no reason to sugarcoat it, to say When Emma was sick or When Emma was in the hospital—when Emma was dying, the doctor had told him that thirty seconds almost always killed the germs, but forty-five would do it for sure. And so forty-five it was…until six months ago. Since then, Liam had started to worry about little things more and more. Case in point: hand washing. What if he counted too fast? What if there were a few really strong germs that could hang on for forty-five seconds? So, fifty-five it was. Nicole, watching him in this little ritual, had already told him he had OCD due to PTSD brought on by Emma's death, which was close. In truth, it was his own brush with death that seemed to trigger the OCD—the lock-checking, the germ phobia. It tended to be worse in times of stress, and as the single father of a teenage girl, Liam was pretty much stressed as long as he was awake. But since Nicole didn't know about his…brush…he let her think it was grief. Seemed safer that way.

Drying his hands on a paper towel (who knew what lurked on the dish towel?), he walked down the hall to greet his daughter.

"Hi, honey," he said, knocking before he opened the door.

"Hi, Dad!" she said, sitting up on her bed. "I didn't hear you come in." She smiled, and Liam's heart did that thing where it seemed to pull in a nearly painful way, same as it had the instant he'd first seen her, slimy and squalling, fifteen and a half years ago.

"How's my girl?" he asked.

"Not horrible," was her answer. "Want me to help with dinner?" And Liam felt such a rush of love and gratitude that his chest ached.

"Sure," he said.

When Liam found out that his girlfriend was pregnant, he'd been surprised…and surprisingly thrilled. Emma wasn't, which was understandable. She'd been a senior in college, already accepted at UCLA Law, and a baby was most definitely not on her list of things to do at that moment. Breaking up with him…that might've been on her list. But she'd said yes when he suggested marriage, especially after he promised he'd do the brunt of the childcare so she could continue with her plans for school.

A baby. At age twenty-one, Liam found himself reading books on childbirth and parenting, asking

Emma what she thought about epidurals and sleep training. And when the great day came, it seemed to Liam that his purpose in life had finally been revealed.

To the surprise of everyone—Emma, her parents, the guys at the garage where he worked, and Liam himself—he was a great dad. He got up in the middle of the night and fed the baby, walking her back and forth or taking her for drives at 3:00 a.m., since Emma had to get up early for class. He didn't flinch at changing diapers, figured out that red and white don't mix in the laundry, bought organic baby food, cut back on his hours so he only worked when Emma was home or when her parents came out to stay for a week or two. The garage where he worked made custom motorcycles for the very wealthy, and the owner liked Liam. Even part-time pay was enough to cover the bills. When Emma started work as a corporate tax attorney, with its long hours and healthy salary, Liam was the one to take Nicole to school, the one to go to the parent-teacher meetings or pick up Nicole if she felt sick.

His own childhood had been bumpy—his mother died when he was nine, and his father was in and out of jail, so Liam became well acquainted with the foster-care system. He was a crappy student—a whopping case of dyslexia undiagnosed till he was ten didn't help his attitude. Aside from a better-than-average knowledge of engines, thanks to his father, who ran a chop shop, Liam didn't have much going for him. Once, a preppy, pain-in-the-ass kid in one of the schools he'd joined mid-year called him "no one from nowhere," and Liam couldn't help thinking that it was a little bit true. That hadn't stopped him from punching the arrogant little dick in the mouth and getting a week's suspension.

Then, around eighth grade, Liam discovered the power of sex appeal. Suddenly, females of all ages loved him. No one from nowhere was suddenly prince of the city, and he tomcatted around for a while until he met Emma Tate and fell. Hard. And she loved him, too, for a while, anyway, and when she told him—grimly—that she was three weeks late, Liam discovered what destiny felt like.

Nicole—she was perfect. Moody these days, yes, and not the best at math, and she had a temper, and she thought she'd be prettier with pink streaks in her reddish-blond hair, and she'd thrown a huge hissy about the move…but she was perfect. The best thing in his life, the best thing ever.

"So, my math teacher, she, like, hates me," Nicole said as they stood in the kitchen, working on dinner. They were eating late, still adjusting to the time change from California. Nic was peeling carrots, which had been her favorite veggie since she was eight months old. "She made all these totally snide comments about me being allowed to slide last year in algebra, and I was like, lady, hello? My mother died, okay? Sorry they didn't bring out the whip and chains, but maybe in California, they actually like children."

"Did you say that?" Liam asked, nudging the chicken as it sizzled in the pan.

"Duh. No, Dad," she said, fondness softening her words. "So then we go to science, and it's exactly what I was doing last year, and I was so bored I wanted to cry." Nicole went on, detailing the shortcomings of the Bellsford school system, the cliques of her school, her fear of not fitting in—people had been nice so far, but you could never tell if they were being fake till they stabbed you in the back, right?—her dilemma over doing spring track or the school play or maybe trying lacrosse, the ugliness of mud season in New England, and the cold weather.

Her words were music, though. She was talking, and talking was good.

"One really good thing did happen today, though," she said as they sat down at the table.

"What's that?" Liam asked, taking a sip of his beer.

"I met a really cute boy."

Good? This wasn't *good*. Not at all. "What kind of boy?" he asked.

"The nice kind."

"What does that mean? What did he do that was nice?"

"He just was." She smiled, a sweet, private smile, and Liam felt sweat break out on his back.

"How? How was this niceness demonstrated, Nicole? How is someone nice just by being? There must've been something he did or said—"

"Jeez, Dad. Chill. You don't have to wig out. I'm not pregnant or anything."

He lurched to his feet. "Of course you're not pregnant! Because you're not having sex! Because you wouldn't do that. Ever. Are we clear on this?"

Nicole rolled her eyes. "Dad. Relax, okay? I was joking."

"Yeah, well, this nice boy is not nice. Trust me. I've been a boy. You have no idea how not nice we are." He sat back down.

"We might go to the movies."

"No. You're too young to date."

"Daddy," Nicole said, that sweet little-girl note in her voice that worked so well. "Don't be a jerk, okay?"

"Not dating. Too young. Eat your supper."

"Fine! I won't ever date! Like I'm not *enough* of a freak because Mom died, I'll just stay locked in this stupid apartment for the rest of my life. Would that make you happy?" She shoved her plate back, stood up and stormed off to her room.

"Nicole," he called. Her door slammed. "Don't forget you have that Spanish test tomorrow."

The Ramones began again—"I Wanna Be Sedated." They weren't the only ones.

Liam looked at his plate, sighed and pushed it away. His beer, on the other hand, was most welcome. He took a long pull, then looked at the ceiling. "Thanks, babe," he said quietly. "You had some nerve, leaving me alone with a teenage girl."

Maybe this hadn't been the right move after all. Maybe he was screwing up Nicole beyond repair, and she'd end up tattooed and pregnant and on the back of some idiot's motorcycle... Shit. Aside from the tatt, Emma had ended up just like that, and he'd been the idiot in question.

But Emma had turned out just fine—a successful lawyer, a good mother. But it was one thing to have a motorcycle-mechanic boyfriend who picked you up from your dorm and took you out for a drive along the coast, then back to his apartment for sex. It was another to marry him.

She'd tried. They both had. She'd tell him about the other people in her classes, he'd tell her about work, they'd acknowledge that their daughter was not only the most beautiful baby ever born, but also the smartest and sweetest. But as the years passed, their conversations grew shorter. They fought more. Spent less time together. Pretty typical story for two people who got married too young.

It was a bad, bad feeling, knowing the gap between you and your wife was spreading into a canyon, being helpless to breach it. He loved her; that never stopped. Hoped that things would turn around someday. Then came the call from that doctor, and though he knew it wasn't exactly sane, Liam would've cheerfully killed Elliot Kramer, because with that phone call the doctor had taken away any chance Liam and Emma might've had at working things out. Eight months later, Emma was gone for good.

Liam stood up and started clearing the untouched dinner. Despite Nicole's complaints, it felt good to be back in New England, back where there was real weather, away from the relentless perfection of San Diego. Away from the site of his marriage and those complicated memories. Bellsford was the first place he'd landed out of juvie, his great-uncle finally agreeing to let Liam come live with him. He liked this little town with its twisting alleys and odd little shops, the river on one side of town, Maine just across the bridge.

It'd been nice to see the Osterhagens today. Good people, those two. Funny how little that restaurant and the two of them had changed. Cordelia, too, didn't look a day past sixteen—still looking a little like a chick fresh out of its shell, still staring at him as if he had two heads.

But being back in the kitchen where he'd worked in high school...it brought back a lot. The whole time he was there, he'd half expected to see Emma come in, same way she had back in high school. Back when she was on her way home from whatever after-school club she'd been running at the time. Her ponytail would swing, and she'd smile at him as he scraped plates and washed pans, and that smile would make Liam forget that he was some asshole juvie who'd followed in his family's footsteps toward a life of petty crime.

He'd only been back in Bellsford a week, but already the apartment felt safe, housed in a solid old factory building that had been converted to apartments five or ten years ago, according to the Realtor. Three bedrooms, two and a half baths, living room, kitchen, den. No memories of Emma walking through the door, which was both good and bad. In his closet hung Emma's bathrobe... Sunday mornings had generally been their happiest times, when she didn't work and he made pancakes and she looked so damn sweet in that pink puffy thing....

Well. Memories and all that.

"Things'll be okay," he muttered, scrubbing a hand across his face. He was astonishingly tired. Not that he'd done much today, aside from overseeing a shipment of equipment at the shop. Hopefully, a custom bike shop could bring in as much money here in New Hampshire as it did in Southern California. One thing that always surprised his in-laws—the blue-collar idiot their daughter married always made a decent living. Not as much as their daughter, but pretty good nonetheless.

Nicole's door opened, and she stomped down the hall. "I have something to say," she said, giving him the Slitty Eyes of Death. "You're totally unfair, and if I run away, you shouldn't be surprised."

"Don't make me put a computer chip in your ear," Liam answered.

"It's not funny! I hate you."

"Well, I love you, even if you did ruin my life by turning into a teenager," he said, rubbing his eyes. "Did you study for your test?"

"Yes."

"Good." He looked at his daughter—so much like Emma, way too pretty. Why weren't there convent schools anymore? Or chastity belts? "Want some supper? I saved your plate."

She rolled her eyes with all the melodrama a teenager could muster. "Fine. I may as well become a fat pig since I can't ever go on a date."

"That's my girl," he said and, grinning, got up to heat up her dinner.

CHAPTER THREE

SHILO, DON'T BE AFRAID. It's just Al," Posey said, trying to woo her dog from underneath the statue of Arpad the Archer, patron saint of Hungary, that currently graced the front yard of Irreplaceable Artifacts. "We love UPS! Don't be scared." Shilo whined, his tail wagging, but the truth was, the dog was a coward.

"I have a cookie," Al said, kneeling down. Shilo whimpered and backed up, ramming his massive haunches against an old birdbath.

"He's already eaten three donuts," Posey said. "You have to up the ante, Al. Maybe a filet mignon."

"I'll keep that in mind," Al said, getting back into the giant brown truck. "Have a good day, Posey."

"You're such a baby," Posey told her dog. "Some watchdog you'd make. You'd hide and watch the killers hack me to pieces, wouldn't you?" With the UPS truck safely gone, Shilo gave a fond woof and licked Posey's wrist with his massive tongue.

Last year, Posey had made the mistake of going to the pound. Being adopted herself, she'd taken one look into Shilo's red-rimmed eyes and just couldn't say no. Bad enough that she'd inherited three cats with the church she'd bought, now she owned a 150-pound black-and-white Great Dane whose talents seemed to be sleeping, baying and cowering from deliverymen. He was, however, deeply devoted to Posey during his waking hours and didn't quite realize that he outweighed her by a third; he often tried to sit on her lap (and succeeded more often than not).

Now that he was safe from Big Brown, Shilo went to sniff the pair of giant concrete lions from the old library up in Maine. Though her parents often frowned over why Posey had devoted her career to things that had outlived their purpose, Posey felt just the opposite. Salvage was practically a religion to her. Someone would want these things—the barbershop pole all the way from the Bronx, the wheel from an old tugboat, the stained-glass windows from an old Victorian, the chipped gargoyle from a church in Winooski—and they'd be cherished and enjoyed once more, and Posey's job would be done.

But now it was donut time. Today was Thursday, the day when her two closest pals came over for goodies after school. Jon, her brother's longtime partner, and Kate, Posey's friend from grammar school, were both teachers at Bellsford High. Jon taught home-ec and was quite adored by the students… Kate, as phys-ed teacher, was not. Each year without fail, the seniors would dedicate the yearbook to their beloved Mr. White, something Jon enjoyed lording over the other teachers.

"Hi, guys!" Posey called, holding the door for her dog, who trotted happily inside, licking his chops. Three cream-filled pastries had apparently not been enough.

"Hi, Posey! How are you?" Elise Wooding, one of Posey's two employees, beamed at her as if it had been years since they'd seen each other, not two hours. "How was Vivian today?"

"Well, she was Vivian," Posey answered. "She didn't love my haircut. And she didn't sign anything, of course. Down East Salvage is taking her to dinner on Friday, as she told me three times. She showed me the date on her BlackBerry, just in case I was getting cocky." Though a hundred and one years old, Viv was quite current when it came to the latest tech.

Vivian Appleton was the owner of The Meadows, a glorious old Victorian home on ten acres of land. The house was stunning—a three-story Victorian with ornate fireplaces and a butler's kitchen, curved staircases and window seats. Every corner seemed to offer a treasure, whether it was an iron heating grate or a slipper tub as pretty as a calla lily. Viv didn't live there anymore, having moved to a swanky elderly housing complex in Portsmouth. For more than two years, Vivian had been dangling the rights to The Meadows in front of every salvage operation in New Hampshire, Maine and Vermont.

Vivian's heirs, four grand-nieces and -nephews, planned to tear down the beautiful old house, the caretaker's cottage and the barn and sell the land, with its orchards and stream, to a developer. It was a tragedy, Posey thought. But the heirs—or the Vultures, as Viv called them—would get more for the land than they could for the house and property, and Vivian was determined to let them do as they wished—some sense of Yankee familial duty or something. But if the house *was* going to be torn down, Posey wanted to be the one who did it. It would be like giving last rites to a much-loved friend, and she and Mac, her pathologically shy carpenter, would take the time to do it right, with care and respect, and yes, even love.

Despite being something of a diva, Viv recognized Posey's love for the place and had given her the code to the alarm system. About once a week, sometimes more, Posey went out to The Meadows, just to walk around the empty house and still-lovely grounds, check the roof in the winter, make sure the place was untouched by vandals or kids.

"She'll sign with us? Right? I just know it." Elise had the habit of making all her comments into questions, but she was a sweet girl—only six years younger than Posey, but seeming much more. "Oh, right? I forgot? Brianna's here already. With Mac?" Elise blushed from her cleavage on up—she'd had a crush on Mac since the day she started here two years ago.

Posey went to the back of the barn, where Mac, balding, stoic and solid, did restoration work on pieces that needed repair or refinishing. He was talking (a rare occurrence), his voice low, telling Brianna how to see the difference between oak and maple. Brie looked up in relief.

"There you are. You're late. I'm reporting you." Brianna folded her chubby arms across her chest and glared, then relented when Shilo trotted up to her and licked her elbow.

"Hi, Mac," Posey said. Her right-hand man nodded at her. A man of few words, Mac, but the reason Posey could run Irreplaceable. "You guys hungry? I brought donuts."

"Duh. Yes. Aren't you? Aren't you always hungry?" Brie said.

"Drop the attitude, twerp." Brianna had been her little sister through Big Brothers/Big Sisters for two years now, and despite the fact that the girl was thirteen, Posey loved her. "Mac, you want a break?"

"I'm good," he said, glancing up to the front desk with what could only be described as fear. Elise waved. Mac looked away.

"How was school today?" Posey asked Brie.

"It sucked. As usual. The teachers all think I'm dumb."

"I find that hard to believe." She reached out and touched the girl's shoulder, which Brie tolerated. Brianna came over after school at least a few days a week—the kid's home life was crap. Her mom was only twenty-nine and had an endless parade of boyfriends living with her, so Posey was more than happy to have the girl with her.

"So when does coffee hour start?" Brianna asked.

As if on cue, the barn door opened, and in came Jon and Kate, bickering amiably. Posey's two best friends were as opposite as could be—Jon was sleek, graceful and charming and made everyone around him feel like his favorite person on earth; Kate tended to view her whistle as a primary form of communication, was built like a Brahma bull and had no issues with, ah, personal boundaries.

Kate's fourteen-year-old son, James, was also there, as Kate tended to drag him wherever she went. Like Posey, James had been adopted, though at the ripe old age of seven, whereas Posey had been only hours old when Stacia and Max had taken custody. The lad seemed to be developing a crush on Brie, which Posey thought was wicked cute.

"Hey, guys," Posey said, feeling a warm flush of pride. It never failed to thrill her, having her friends drop in. Made her finally feel like a cool kid after all these years. Not that she could blame them—Irreplaceable was a great place to hang out. Shilo woofed happily at the sight of Jon, then collapsed on his back, jowls flapping to reveal his enormous teeth, just in case Jon was in the mood to rub his tummy.

"Hi, Jon, hi, Kate!" Elise sang. "How are you?"

"I'm a little yeasty," Kate answered thoughtfully. James winced.

"Elise, sweetheart, please don't put our names together," Jon said. "People will think we have eight children and hate each other. Bad enough that we work together, right, Kate? Hello, Brie, you beautiful thing."

"Hey, Mr. White," Brianna said, blushing. Most straight females had a crush on Jon, and Brie was no exception. Jon poured himself a cup of coffee and sat down at the counter, which was from a diner, and spun around on the stool.

"Oh, donuts!" Kate lunged for a cream-filled pastry. "I'm starving. James, want a bite?"

"I'm good, Mom."

"Take a bite. You'll love it." Kate waved the donut in front of her son's eyes as Shilo watched, hypnotized and drooling.

"I'm fine."

"James! A bite!"

"Okay!" James gave Posey a dark look—*see what I have to put up with?*—then took a bite of his mother's donut. "I love it. My reason for living has been revealed. Hi, Brianna." Brianna didn't deign to answer, simply looked at James until his face went from pink to nearly purple. "Okay. I'll go do homework. Oh, hey, Posey, I have a question for you."

"Shoot, kid." She chose a chocolate-covered donut and took a huge bite.

"Did you ever look for your birth parents? I have this workbook…. Did you ever do anything like this?" He pulled a book out of his backpack. *Before You Find Them.*

"No, I never did," Posey answered, glancing at Kate, whose concentration was still on the donut. She flipped through the book. "But this is cool. How's it going?"

"Well, I haven't really started yet," James said. "This is just stuff to think about. Some wicked cool horror stories in here. Some nice ones, too."

"What are the horror stories?" Brie asked.

"Um…come on, I'll show you the worst ones." He gestured toward a Victorian sofa, and after a long stare, Brie sighed and got up.

"Very smooth," Jon murmured as the two teenagers walked away.

"A few more decades, and she might like him back," Posey said, a trifle proudly.

"So, Kate, how do you feel about that?"

"What? Oh, the birth parents thing? Go for it, I say," Kate answered blithely. "If he wants to know, I'm all for it." She licked some cream off her pinky finger.

"So, like, Posey?" Elise said, dragging her eyes off Mac, who continued to work silently in the back. "I heard your cousin's coming back? The Barefoot Fraulein? Seriously? Because I'm a huge fan. She's so pretty, right?"

Posey exchanged a look with Kate and Jon. "Yeah, she's very pretty," Posey said.

"Also, a bitch," Jon said.

"Seriously?" Elise breathed. "Oh, no!"

"Oh, yeah," Kate confirmed.

"Gretchen hates Posey," Jon said.

"How could anyone hate you?" Elise looked like Jon had just bitten the head off a kitten. "No way!"

"Way," Jon said. "They're rivals."

"She's not my rival," Posey corrected. "But she always seems to be gunning for me, it's kind of true."

"I blame Gretchen's mother," Jon said.

"Well, she's dead, so that's not very nice," Posey murmured, reaching for another donut.

But it was true. Ever since Posey could remember, Gretchen had been doing her best to make Posey feel inferior. Why, Posey had no idea, because Gretchen sure seemed to have it all. Stacia and Gretchen's mother, Ruth, were identical twins. The Heidelbergs also had a German restaurant, but in New York City, which they considered vastly superior to Bellsford. Both Stacia and Ruth had had trouble getting pregnant. The same year Max and Stacia adopted Posey, Ruth and Ralphie had had Gretchen, and the comparisons began. Ruth would call Stacia, detailing Gretchen's list of many triumphs, from losing her first tooth to baking her first batch of pfeffernuesse, often remarking on Gretchen's great beauty and strong resemblance to their mother. And Gretchen *was* beautiful. Posey was not. Gretchen was tall and confident, with long blond hair, bright blue eyes, and a generous, curving figure she'd been showcasing since she'd bought her first bra at age nine.

As a kid, Gretchen had always been full of advice when the families got together—"Posey, you should let your hair grow so people can tell you're a girl. Posey, if you eat more cheese, you might get boobs." As they got older, she'd simply ignore Posey—unless the adults were watching, when she'd be saccharine-sweet and utterly fake.

Then, horribly, Aunt Ruth and Uncle Ralphie had died in a car accident. Gretchen and Posey had been seventeen, and Gretchen came to live with the Osterhagens. All through senior year, Posey had tried to be kind, trying to include Gretchen in her own meager social life, telling her she looked pretty in a certain shirt or sweater. But Gretchen had been too good for all that. She loved Stacia—her mother's twin, after all—and Max, and was pleasant toward Henry on the rare weekends he came home from medical school, but as for Posey, she had nothing but veiled insults and fake affection.

"Should I, like...hate her now?" Elise asked.

"Yes," Jon and Kate answered.

"No!" Posey said. "She's...you know. She's fine. It'll be nice for my parents to have the help. And who knows? Business might pick up a little."

"Why is she leaving her show?" Elise asked. "No offense to your parents, right? But it's kind of a step down? Was that rude to say?"

"Probably ratings," Kate said. "Up against Rachael Ray? Please." Kate was a veteran of food and cooking shows, owned literally hundreds of cookbooks and knew every celebrity chef out there. Not that she cooked—another thing Posey and she had in common.

"Not according to her," Jon said. At Posey's questioning look, he added, "She sent Henry an email last week. Oh, is that the new model you're working on?" He got up and went over to Posey's work area, where a half-constructed model of a Colonial home was underway.

"Yep," Posey answered. "That's the Austin house. Mac and I took it apart last fall, remember?"

"Right, right," Jon murmured. "We should have you come into class sometime. Well, maybe the art department should have you. This is gorgeous, Pose."

Before Posey had gotten into salvage, she'd been a model-maker for an architect. The tiny details, the precision of the work, the lovely, warm idea that she could condense something so big...it was addicting. When she opened Irreplaceable Artifacts, she'd kept it up. Now, instead of creating a replica of a building that would someday be built, she made models of buildings that would soon be demolished... her gift to the owners, and a way of preserving the past.

"James!" Kate called. "Hey, bud, can you run out to the car and see if I have any tampons?"

"Mom, no. I have boundaries. I'm fourteen. Get your own tampons."

Jon snorted. "Kate. Be kind to your boy."

"What? We're very close, that's all. Right, James?"

"Not that close."

Brianna was wheezing with laughter, and James gave her a look, then smiled.

"So, guys, guess what?" Posey said, lowering her voice. "I'm having a talk with Dante tonight."

This brought Jon back to the counter. "And what are we saying?"

"Are you gonna propose? Because that would so romantic? Oh, my gosh. Wow," Elise said.

"No, no. No proposals. Just...you know. Time to take things to the next level."

Jon and Kate exchanged a look. "Best of luck with that," her brother-in-law said.

"What? You don't like him?"

"How could I say? I've never met him, except when I ate there, and if you tell Stacia that Henry and I went, I'll murder you in your sleep. No, Posey, it's just...I think he's using you, that's all."

"For sex. He's using you for sex," Kate clarified.

Posey glanced over at the kids, who were fortunately immersed in birth-family horror stories, snorting with laughter. "Oh, I don't think so. It's just early days, that's all."

"Well, if he only calls you after 9:00 p.m. and only wants you to come to his house for a shag, has never introduced you to his friends or family, has no interest in meeting yours, I'd say Kate's spot on," Jon said, raising an eyebrow.

"We have a date tonight," Posey protested.

"What time and where?" Jon asked.

She hesitated. "Nine-thirty. His place."

"Call me after," Jon said. "I have to go. Believe it or not, home-ec teachers have papers to grade. Ciao, *bellissimas!* Oh, and Posey, just in case things don't work out with Dante, I'm teaching a singles cooking class for the adult-ed program. You're welcome, too, Kate."

When she closed up shop later that day, Posey came upon James's book about finding birth parents in the cushion of the sofa. She'd never looked for her birth family. Max and Stacia were her parents, the end. Well, that wasn't exactly true. Of course she'd wondered. Conjured the typical fantasies as a child. To say that Max and Stacia—especially Stacia—were overprotective was an understatement. Every time Posey wasn't allowed to go to the public pool with her friends ("The pool? The *pool?* That's where people get kidnapped!") or was whisked to the E.R. to rule out concussion ("But she bumped her head, Doctor! She has a lump! You think it might be a tumor?"), she'd imagine more mellow parents, parents who didn't view sauerkraut as a daily necessity for a healthy diet, parents who were—forgive her—cooler, younger, more hip.

But aside from that, no. Max and Stacia were wonderful, and she'd never been inspired to find her roots. She tucked the book in her backpack to make sure she got it back to James, then went home to get ready for her date. If it was a date. Jon and Kate had a point.

In eight weeks, she'd seen Dante six times. That seemed like dating…sort of. The truth was, Posey's record with men was a little sporadic. Ron the Gay had been pretty great, the whole "we both like boys" thing aside. You'd think a woman with a gay brother would sense a tremor in the Force, but no. One night, as they were curled up in front of CNN, Posey had admitted to wanting just one hour alone and naked with Anderson Cooper. "Who wouldn't?" Ron had murmured appreciatively. Then they'd looked at each other, realization dawning for both of them. Ron later wrote an article for *GQ* magazine: "How Anderson Cooper Helped Me Out of the Closet." He still sent Posey Christmas cards.

Then there'd been Jake—perfectly nice, a carpenter she'd hired as a subcontractor for a job in Maine. It was his suggestion that she get breast implants that ended their thing. Kind of hard to overlook that. A few first dates here and there, sometimes a second or third date, once in a great while a fourth…but no. Posey hadn't been in a real relationship for quite a while.

So Dante needed to pony up, Posey thought as she held the truck door for Shilo, who gazed at her beseechingly until she hefted him in. She wanted a real boyfriend. Even if she had a great dog and three cats. And especially—this was a little hard to admit—but especially because Liam Murphy was back in town. Having a boyfriend would just put him to rest, that was all. Make her feel a little safer.

To be honest, Dante Bellini's interest had been a surprise. He was suave and urbane—not words she'd have pinned to herself, that was for sure. Extremely good-looking in that Mediterranean way. Extremely well off, too, which certainly didn't hurt his appeal. He lived in Midnight Cove, a complex of gorgeous condos on the water. The ocean, not the river, which offered a much more working-class view. It might be a case of opposites attract, but clearly there was something there.

Yep. Time to shore up the defenses. Dante liked her. They'd slept together six times. She'd head home, put on pretty underwear and girl clothes, tell Dante how she felt, and he'd say yes. He probably wanted the same thing.

"You don't?"

"It's not that, Posey. I just don't have the time right now. The restaurant. You understand, I'm sure."

Dante smiled, his white teeth glinting like a pirate's against his swarthy skin. "But I really do enjoy spending the time with you, even though it's not enough time." He handed her a glass of wine and reached out to touch her neck.

"Um, right." The fire crackled in the fireplace, and across the cove, the lights of other houses gleamed discreetly. Posey shifted on the leather couch. She kept sliding down, and it was irritating. "It's just that we can't stay at this level forever. I mean, I'm not asking for a ring and a date, Dante. But don't you want to…move things forward a little? Do stuff together? Meet my parents?"

"God, no," he said, then seemed to realize what he'd said. "I mean, I'm sure they're nice people. It's just that they hate me."

"Well, they don't hate you per se," Posey murmured. "It's more your restaurant."

"Right. Even so."

She took a deep breath. "Okay. Look. We've been, um, together for what…a few weeks?" *Eight weeks, Dante. Six times.* "But I'd like to go out to dinner once in a while. Catch a movie. Be able to…be seen with you, Dante. I like you. You're fun. This isn't really enough for me."

"And you're fun, too," he said, smiling.

"So…it's not like I'm naming our babies, I promise," Posey said.

"I know. But Inferno needs every spare moment. This, though…this is perfect." He picked up her hand and kissed it.

"Huh," Posey said, slumping back against the couch and sliding down yet again. Dante took this as an invitation to kiss her neck. He smelled awfully good… Whatever shampoo he used, she was sure she couldn't afford it. She sighed…not in rapture, either. Dante's hand moved under her shirt. She grabbed it. "Okay, wait a sec."

He raised his head, giving her that sleepy, sexy look that had first gotten her attention as she lugged in the statue of the martyred virgin St. Agnes of Rome. "Shall we move to the bedroom?"

Men. "No, Dante. You just told me this is as good as it gets for the foreseeable future. It's not good enough for me."

"What are you saying?"

"Well…" *Time to take a stand, Posey, or be a booty call forever.* "Maybe we should put things on hold. For a while. See how we feel then."

He blinked, opened his mouth, then closed it. "Well, fine. If that's what you want."

"No, I just told you what I want. More than coming over once a week. Because that feels like a booty call, and I'd like to be more than that."

"Fine." His voice was sharp. "I'm sorry I don't have more time. I thought you, as a successful business owner, would understand that."

"I do. I just… I'm sorry. But you know, why don't we kind of reassess things in a month or so? Maybe a little time apart will…clarify things."

"Fine."

"Great." Posey folded her arms across her chest. To think she'd put on a lace bra for this. It itched.

Dante stood up and ran a hand through his hair. "I have to say, Posey, I'm a little surprised. You don't seem like the type."

"What type is that?"

"The settling-down type. I thought you were… Well, I thought you were different."

"Apparently not," she muttered.

"It's just that you seem very…untraditional."

"Because I don't wear skirts and high heels? Does that mean I don't want a normal relationship somehow?"

"Well, in some ways, yes. It sends a message." He looked her up and down. Her jaw clamped shut. Lace bra. For this. And this *was* her girly outfit. Jeans (made for a woman and everything). Flowered shirt. Flowers! On the shirt! A peachy-colored, itchy lace bra and matching panties, come on! What kind of message was that? A traditional one, that was what!

"Okay, I'll be going now," she said, standing up.

"I didn't mean to insult you," Dante said, cocking his head and giving her a sorrowful look.

"It's fine." She sighed. "So...a break? We'll talk again?" A small spark of hope flared in her chest. Maybe this was what they needed. Or what he needed—time to see how great she was.

"Sure." He leaned in and kissed her, and she let him. "Want to stay for a while?" he murmured, moving to her neck.

"No. Gotta go. Thanks, Dante."

All the way home, she alternated between mild fuming and healthy insecurity. A message, huh? Just because she wasn't built like J-Lo, just because she lacked the feminine skills that so many of her gender expressed without effort—the flirting, the hair and makeup, the softness—it didn't mean that she didn't want to settle down. Of course she did. How could she look at her parents and not want what they had, that effortless, seamless togetherness? Or Jon and Henry, together since college? Of course she wanted that.

She pulled into her driveway and went inside her home, seeing it through fresh eyes. She lived in a restored—well, a half-restored—church rich in cobwebs, creaky floors and character. Someday—about a hundred thousand dollars from now—this place would be on the tour of homes. For now, though, the roof needed to be replaced. The belfry might be a little dangerous, given that the mechanism that held the 800-pound iron bell was not only broken, but rusting, and rusting fast. Furnishings-wise, the place was a little cluttered with the things she couldn't bear to part with, things that hadn't sold at Irreplaceable. The Victorian birdcage. The statue of the elephant. The bishop's chair.

Shilo, sensing his mistress needed some love, gave a bay of joy at the sight of her, and Jellybean, the largest of her triumvirate of cats, trotted over as well, as he seemed to be half dog. "Who are my good boys?" she said as Shilo head-butted her in the stomach and Jellybean pricked her with his claws (lovingly, of course). "You hungry? Want some Stouffers? Huh? Want some delicious French bread pizza? You do? So do I, pal."

But even as she cranked the Neil Diamond ("Sweet Caroline," because, come on, what else would you play in a bad mood?), the thought came to her that maybe ending her arrangement with Dante, flimsy though it was, might not have been the smartest move. Not because it was meaningful and special (not yet, though she'd thought they had potential), but because she'd just lost even a small barrier between her heart and Liam Murphy. Since the moment she'd laid eyes on him in Guten Tag's kitchen, not an hour had passed without Liam crossing her mind.

And that was not good.

CHAPTER FOUR

"LIAM, YOU'RE SO wonderful to do this. Really, dear! I didn't know what I'd do!" Stacia Osterhagen beamed at Liam, her eyes scanning him up and down like a farmer assessing a stud bull at auction. He was almost surprised she didn't circle around him and ask him to open his mouth so she could check his teeth.

"It's no problem, Mrs. O," he said. "Happy to help. So, what seems to be the matter?"

"Something's stuck in the drain," she said. She glanced at her watch, then at the door.

"Okay, I'll take a look."

He'd been at the garage when Mrs. O had called about ten minutes before, and from the way she kept looking at her watch, the door and his ass, Liam suspected she was waiting for someone...someone for him. The niece or cousin or whatever. Older women had the tendency to either proposition him or offer up a younger relative. Nevertheless, she'd asked for help, and he hadn't forgotten how good the Osterhagens had been to him back then, so here he was. Better get to it. He knelt on the floor, opened his toolbox, took out a wrench and put a dishpan under the pipe he was about to take apart.

"A prince. That's what you are. Oh, if only we had a son who could do this. Well, Henry *could,* of course, but he's a surgeon, of course, and his hands! So special, Liam! They're insured, did you ever hear of such a thing?"

"Can't say that I have," he said, lying under the sink and loosening the pipe fitting. Whatever liquid was in the pipe gushed out into the pan. Liam took a flashlight and shone it into the pipe—something metal, something white, and some string. He poked it with a screwdriver, but it was stuck tight, the metal thing wedged in there real good. Jammed, really. Felt like a fork...maybe some raw potato...

A rush of cold air wrapped around his legs as the back door opened.

"I might have to leave early," said a rather deep feminine voice. "I have a cyst. You don't want to know where."

"You're right. I don't." That was Cordelia, if he wasn't mistaken. The offering, perhaps. He didn't look up.

"It's just below my left nipple."

Women. Was there nothing they wouldn't talk about? Honestly, every time Emma had had friends over, talk turned to gruesome tales of childbirth or periods.

Then someone kicked him in the leg; there was a thunk, a yelp, and the next thing he knew, something with a lot of sharp angles had sprawled on top of him.

Liam pulled his head from under the sink. Cordelia was half across his lap, wincing as she touched her jaw. Her knee was about two inches from making sure Nicole would stay an only child, but no real harm done. Her sweater had ridden up a few inches, giving him a glimpse of some very white skin. Pretty. Nice to see flesh that wasn't perpetually tanned, the way everyone's seemed to be in Southern California.

And nice to have a woman on his lap, regardless of how she got there. The unexpected jolt took Liam by surprise.

"Baby! Are you okay? Who's the president?" Mrs. O leaped over, the floor shuddering under her impressive weight. "Should I touch you? Is your neck broken?"

"Dang it!" Cordelia wiggled her jaw and patted her mother's outstretched hand. "I'm fine, Mom."

"No, you're not! How could you be?" The floor thudded again as she bounded away, pretty fast for an older lady.

Finally, Cordelia turned and looked to see what had tripped her. Her face froze. "Oh, hi, Liam," she muttered, jerking her sweater back down where it belonged. "What are you doing here?"

"Being trampled on by you, Cordelia," he said.

She answered with the Slitty Eyes of Death. "Maybe you shouldn't be flopped down on restaurant floors, ever think of that?" She hauled herself off the floor and touched her jaw again.

"Well, well, well, the return of biker boy," her companion said. "Heard you were back in town, hottie."

This warranted sitting up. Liam smiled. "Nice to see you again. Katie Ellington, right?"

"Kate now. And likewise," she said.

She'd been a jock during his two years at Bellsford, he remembered that. Baseball or rugby or something. As he continued to look at her, some pink crept into her cheeks. Cute. He'd always assumed she batted for the other team, but maybe not. Liam grinned. Kate's blush deepened. Cordelia glared.

"Here, honey. Do you know who I am?" Mrs. Osterhagen returned with an industrial-size bag of peas and pressed them against Cordelia's face.

"Thanks, Mom," Cordelia said.

"What month it is?"

"It's March. Still." Cordelia sighed and tilted her head so Mrs. O could palpate her spine, and Liam chuckled. "Ma, I'm sure I'm fine. I wouldn't be able to stand if my neck was broken."

"You never know," her mother said. Then, with another significant look at Liam, she added, "Your cousin, Posey? She got in this afternoon. Very disappointed you weren't there to welcome her home. But—" another meaningful look at Liam, complete with raised eyebrow "—she should be here any minute. Stay. You can see her. I know you've missed her."

Liam picked up his wrench once more. Women would keep talking no matter if you stuffed a sock in their mouths, so if he waited for the conversation to end, he'd be here all night. Besides, Kate Ellington was clearly thinking dirty thoughts about him, because her eyes were fixed on his groin. She licked her lips. Yep. Time to go back to the clog. He half listened as he wedged the screwdriver against the clog and wiggled. Man. Getting a fork *and* a knife *and* half a potato down a drain took some serious doing. Mrs. O had worked hard tonight.

"Well, I'd love to hang out, Mom, but I didn't realize Gretchen was coming tonight, and Kate and I have plans. Right, Kate?" she said.

"What's that?" Kate said.

"Our thing? Tonight?"

"Uh-huh."

"Well, your brother's in the operating room, so he can't come, either. Liam, our son is a doctor. An orthopedic surgeon, just in case you break anything, dear." Clearly, the son's profession could not be stated often enough.

"Good to know," Liam said. There. A chunk of potato fell out, nearly hitting him in the eye.

"Why is he here, Mom?" Cordelia whispered, the words easy to catch.

"He's fixing the sink," Mrs. O replied.

"He's a mechanic, Mom."

"So?" Stacia hissed. "He's here, Gretchen's single."

Liam sighed. There. He got the knife free, then worked out the fork. Messy job, but not as bad as a carburetor, that was for sure.

Just then the back door opened, and Liam glanced up again. Ah. The niece. What was her television show? "The Naked Fraulein" or something? Naked would be A-okay. Wow. The woman. Was built.

Kim Kardashian curves, long blond hair, blue eyes, ultra-white teeth, the same kind of perfection you saw in hordes in San Diego…but nicely done, by nature, it seemed, not a plastic surgeon.

"Posey!" she cried, beaming a thousand-watter, throwing her arms around Cordelia, her cleavage practically swallowing the smaller woman.

"Gretchen!" Cordelia echoed back, her voice muffled.

"Oh, it's so good to see you! There's nothing like *Verwandter!*"

"Sorry, what does that mean?" Cordelia asked, pulling back. "No one in our family's spoken German since World War II."

"Oh, you! It means *family*. Just look at you!" She pulled a face. "Have you lost weight?"

"No, I haven't," Cordelia returned. "Have you gained any?"

Ah. A cat fight had to be looming. He'd put his money on Cordelia—scrappy vs. soft. Still, better to get while the getting was good. He finished tightening the washer around the pipe and stood up. The niece's eyes slid to him…slowly. "Hello there," she said, her voice dropping. "I'm Gretchen Heidelberg."

"Hi. Liam Murphy." He turned on the water and started washing his hands, counting automatically. The woman's too-long-to-be-real eyelashes fluttered. "Do I know you?" she asked.

"I used to work here. A long time ago."

"We must've met, then," she murmured.

"Maybe," he said, drying his hands.

"Of course, I'm pretty familiar with this kitchen myself," she said, giving a slight wriggle, in case he missed the mighty rack. "I filmed my audition tape here."

Danger, my son, Liam told himself. *Maneater in the vicinity.* "Cool. You're all set here, Mrs. O. Just a chunk of potato stuck in there and a few pieces of silverware."

"I'm the Barefoot Fraulein," the cousin went on. "Thursdays at five on the Cooking Network? Have you ever seen it?"

"Can't say that I have," he said, smiling to be polite. If he ignored her completely, she'd take it as a challenge, and God protect him from women who saw him as a challenge.

"Oh! Liam! You're so clever! And so wonderful to help," Stacia said. She glanced between Cordelia and Gretchen. "You girls should stay! You should all stay! I have some beautiful apple kuchen! Liam! Stay! Talk!"

"I'll take a rain check on the cake, Mrs. O. My daughter's home alone." He turned to the cousin. "Nice meeting you. See you girls around," he said to Cordelia and Kate, punching Kate lightly on the shoulder.

Then he got out of there, before Mrs. O tried to marry him off.

"WHO *was* THAT?" Gretchen said, actually licking her lips. Posey rolled her eyes. Gret should just smear him with sour cream and lick him off. It'd be more subtle.

"That's Liam," Stacia said. "He's a widower. More than two years. I think enough time has passed, don't you?"

"He touched me," Kate said, her voice a little dazed.

"A widower, huh? Nice," Gretchen said. She tilted herself back a little so that her cleavage heaved itself upward, the kind of trick Posey couldn't have done without a couple of double-D implants and a gun to the back of her head.

"Gret, Mom, sorry we can't stay, but Kate and I have plans," she said. "Kate? Our plans?"

"Posey! What? We've hardly had time to catch up!" Gretchen fake protested.

"Well, we're having dinner at my parents' house on Sunday," Posey said.

Gret pouted. "Don't you want to hear about what the producers of *Top Chef* told me last week? I shouldn't say anything, but I think they're scoping me out as the new host of… Oops. Better not say anything till the contract's signed."

"I thought you were back to help Mom and Dad," Posey said.

"Mmm-hmm. For a while, anyway." She flashed another smile, practically blinding Posey with her glow-in-the-dark white teeth.

"Hi." Kate stepped forward. "I'm Kate, Posey's friend. We've met before, back in high school. I'm a big fan."

Posey choked, and Kate gave her a guilty look.

"Oh, yes, of course! And *thank* you! You're too nice!" Gretchen cooed.

"Kate?" Posey said. "The time?"

"Where are you two going?" Gretchen asked.

"Um…a class," Posey said.

"A singles thing," Kate added, and Posey closed her eyes. Her friend was pathologically honest.

"A singles thing?" Stacia asked, her mouth falling open in dismay. "Why not meet someone the old-fashioned way?"

"On a bender? Or in jail?" Posey asked, earning a glare from her mom.

"I'm just going to keep Posey company," Kate stated. She picked up a piece of raw onion and ate it. "I'm not really looking."

"A singles *thing*? What kind?" Gretchen asked. "I have to admit, I'm intrigued. I've never done anything like that. Then again, I meet a *lot* of people." She smiled. "Well. You two have fun. Good luck meeting Mr. Right! Do they do background checks at these things? You have to wonder who signs up. Oh, my gosh, that sounded so snooty! I didn't mean *you*, Posey."

"You should come, Gret," Posey said pointedly. "You're not seeing anyone these days, are you?"

"As a matter of fact," Gretchen said, smiling coyly, "I don't want to name names, but I think we all know a certain blond Brit with a potty mouth, a chain of restaurants and a TV show…but I better not say any more, because he's actually quite shy. And sweet! You wouldn't believe it."

"You're dating Gordon *Ramsay*?" Kate barked.

"You didn't hear that from me," Gretchen said.

"Isn't he married?" Posey asked.

"What about Emeril?" Kate said. "Do you know him? Is he short? He seems short."

"*Know* him? He's my mentor," Gretchen said. "Not as short as you might think. He has a certain earthy charm, don't you think?"

"Yes!" Kate exclaimed. "I do! When he says 'Bam,' I swear, my knees go weak."

Posey grabbed Kate by the arm. "See you later," she said. "Bye, Mom. Bye, Gret. Tell Gordon we said hello." Dragging Kate behind her, she pushed open the back door. "You're a big fan now? I thought you were my friend!"

"Well, you know how it is," Kate stammered. "You meet a celebrity, you become an ass. I mean, I haven't seen her since she lived with you guys in high school, you know? But I've watched her since that show started. I got caught up in the moment. Sue me."

"I should beat you, that's what I should do."

"As if," Kate said, slapping Posey on the back so hard she staggered. "Come on, now. On to meet your future husband. Though if you could find a way to dry-hump Liam's leg, I'll bet it'd be the best sex you've had in years."

An hour later, Liam's leg was looking better and better. It had looked pretty good in the restaurant, but here in the basement hallway of Christ Lutheran Church, the leg was taking on legendary appeal.

Note to self, Posey thought. *Avoid singles events in church basements.* The AA meeting was just about to wrap up (though the Serenity Prayer could be applied to dating: God grant me the courage to date the men who aren't idiots, the serenity to accept the fact that many men *are* idiots, and the wisdom to know the difference).

Kate was busy texting her son, laughing softly. Despite their slightly odd relationship, the two were really close, and Posey couldn't help the flash of envy she felt. Imagine, being the mother of such a good kid as James. Having him respond to your texts and acknowledge you in public. Posey was James's godmother and so got a little trickle-down of his wonderfulness, but still. She was thirty-three years old. Her boyfriend—for lack of a better word—didn't want to take things to the next level, and at best, their relationship was on hold. More likely, it was over.

There were numerous murmurs of denial and explanation as the singletons waited for the alcoholics to finish up. *I've never done anything like this…. My sister dragged me here…. It's not that I don't meet people on my own, I'm actually researching a book…. Match.com kicked me off for violating their no-stalking rule….* That last one had come from the only cute guy here, Kevin Krepsinski, an old classmate who'd recently gotten out of jail for bank fraud. "Hey, Posey," he said.

"Kevin. Nice to be out?"

"You bet! You still single?"

"Mmm-hmm."

Kevin glanced at her chest, then started talking to the woman next to him, a middle-aged woman whose bosom could shelter a family of four and their Bernese mountain dog. Posey sighed. There was Emily Rudeker, who played on Stubby's Hardware's softball team; she nodded hello to Posey and Kate (Stubby's was Guten Tag's arch rival, having beaten them every game last season, thanks in large part to Posey's complete inability to hit the ball). There was Reverend Jerry—this was his church, though, yes, he was single. He smiled broadly at Posey, and she smiled back, unsure if that was a *Want to date me?* smile or just *How's your soul these days?*

The appeal of online dating was becoming more and more attractive by the nanosecond. At least you could do that in your PJs. At least you could screen pictures and not end up standing next to a man roughly forty years your senior who smelled like fish. The truth was, Posey had tried to register on a dating website the night Dante dumped her, but lost patience after question number eighty-two.

She didn't *feel* desperate…well, a little. Her birthday was in May. She'd be thirty-four, and that was mid-thirties, which sounded much more advanced. As in, *Sorry, it's advanced. And terminal.* And it was, because after mid-thirties came *late* thirties, then forties, then death.

"If you crack those knuckles one more time, I'm slapping you." Kate sent her a murderous glare.

Posey put her hands in her pockets. "Sorry."

The woman on Posey's other side sighed loudly. "This doesn't look too promising," she said. "And I could be home right now, watching *Valentine's Day* and fantasizing about Taylor Lautner." She was around fifty, plump, and encased in a low-cut blouse that sealed her torso in a sausagelike casing. "I know, I know," the woman continued, not looking at either Posey or Kate. "He's still a child. But come on. I don't understand that Bella, do you? I'd like to slap her."

"Preach it, sister," another woman agreed, nodding sagely.

"Oh, finally! It's starting. Thank God, my bunions are killing me." As the AA members left (a much more cheerful lot than the singletons, Posey couldn't help noticing), the Taylor Lautner fan looked down at her cleavage, frowned, adjusted her left breast, then glanced at Posey. "Good luck."

They trudged in. One wall showed a mural of rainbows, flowers, white lambs and the head of John the Baptist on a platter, the words *Prepare Ye the Way of the Lord!* in a balloon coming from his slackly opened mouth.

"Romantic," Posey murmured, suppressing a laugh.

Small tables had been set up with cutting boards and knives and a variety of vegetables and herbs at each one. Jon clapped his hands to get everyone's attention. "Okay, people! Thank you so much for coming! This is Italian Cooking for Singles, and my name is Jon. I'm so happy to see you all here!" He beamed, and Posey watched as several women and one man fell in love. "The rest of our classes will be at the Bellsford Community Center—tonight's the only night we have to look at poor J the B here. Not appetizing, am I right?"

Jon went on to detail the class. Tonight would be basic prep, slicing and dicing, how to sweat garlic to preserve the flavor, what kinds of tomatoes to use for different purposes, why fresh herbs were the core of any great Italian dish, when to tell if pasta is ready. "I'll tell you, gang," he said confidentially, "overcooked pasta is a great American tragedy. Now! We'll partner up for each stage, boy-girl, boy-girl, and rather than do the boring old questions—because we've all been there, done that—let's be creative!

Not 'What do you do for a living,' but rather, 'Which tree are you most like?' or 'If you got a new puppy, what would you name it?' Be imaginative! Have fun! You never know…tonight you might meet your future spouse!"

"I'm looking for some maples, possibly a dogwood," Posey said.

"I heard that, Posey." Jon grinned at her. "Guys, Posey is my sister-in-law, so everyone has to be nice to her, or I'll poison you. Okay? Posey, let's put you with…Wayne, is it?" He waved to the fishy older man, then dropped his voice to a whisper. "This is just to get you started. I have my eye on a cute guy for you, but I don't want anyone to think I'm playing favorites, which I totally am." He smiled brilliantly. "Wayne, this is Posey! You kids have fun. Okay, everyone, start slicing the garlic. I'm not a believer in crushing, I want you to peel, then slice, and I want wafer-thin, I want translucence, I want you to inhale the smell of the greatest food ever invented. Cooking is all about love, after all, and who doesn't love garlic!"

"Is he gay?" Wayne asked.

"Yes," Posey answered. "Hi. I'm Posey."

"Hi," he said. "I'd like to be honest here. I'm looking for a wife, let's cut right to the chase, and, yes, I'd like someone younger. I'm tired of hearing about knee replacements and hot flashes. How old are you?"

"Oh. Um, I'm thirty-three," Posey said. "But I'm not—"

"I have to say, you're not *quite* as built as I like my women to be, but I could overlook that. I like long walks on the beach, sunsets and a highball or two at the end of the day. And sex, of course. The little blue pill changed my life, you know what I'm saying? My cardiologist says I should be careful, but he's also the one who wants me on a low-salt diet. But please. Why eat if you can't have salt? How about you? Do you like sex?"

Posey tilted her head. "I'll get to work on the garlic, then."

"Is that a no?"

She narrowed her eyes. "If you were a tree, what tree would you be?" she said.

"I don't know. Kind of a dumb question, isn't it? What do you think, want to go out sometime?" Wayne looked at her and smiled.

At the table behind her, she could hear Kate detailing her needs. "I get pretty moody around the tenth of each month. We eat dinner around five—I'm cranky when I'm hungry. Most nights, I'm in bed by nine. I don't like shellfish. I'm not allergic, I just don't like it."

"Okay!" Jon's voice rang out. "Your garlic is looking beautiful, people! Time for the gentlemen to move to the tables to their left."

"Nice meeting you, Wayne," Posey said.

Jon looked over at her and widened his eyes dramatically. Ah. A *very* handsome man was approaching her. She'd missed him in the lineup outside; in fact, quite a few new people seemed to have drifted in. She took a quick scan—nope. Liam was not among them. Not that she noticed. Or cared. Oh, bieber. Here she went again.

"Hi, I'm Gus. Please tell me you're not on Team Jacob," the cute guy said, grinning.

"I'm so over him," Posey said, smiling back. "Hi, I'm Posey. If you could name a pony, what would you call it?"

"Boy or girl?"

"Girl."

"I'd call her Misty of Chincoteague."

"A classic." Posey smiled. "You get a point for that." So far, so good. Jon called out instructions on how best to slice plum tomatoes, and she and Gus got to work.

"I'm not a huge fan of these singles things, but who is, right?" he said, glancing down at her. "And you're adorable. I'll bet you've never been to one of these in your life."

Well, bless his heart! He was *cute*. "This is my first time," she acknowledged.

"What do you do for work, Posey?" he asked.

"I own an architectural salvage operation."

"Cool!" he said. "I love old things."

The night was getting better and better. He crossed his arms. Nice arms, she noted. Nice everything, actually. A little stir of attraction tickled her stomach. She sliced her plum tomatoes obediently as Jon waxed rhapsodic about sauce. "And what do you do, Gus?"

"I'm an actor."

"Really!"

"That's right." He grinned proudly.

"Full time?"

"Full time."

"Wow." Posey couldn't say that she met a lot of actors…a few community theater buffs here and there, but paid actors? "So, you get enough work up here? I mean, we're hardly New York or L.A."

"Actually, yes." He smiled and sliced, rather adept with a knife. "I get plenty of work. I've made a pretty good living at this for years now."

Should she recognize him? Was he someone famous? "Have you been in anything I might've seen?" she asked.

"Maybe," he said. "What do you like to watch?"

Now was probably not the time to mention that last night, she'd watched *Phantom of the Opera* for the ninth time…might make her seem a little on the fetishist side. "Um…I like just about everything."

"Have you ever seen *Heat Rising?*" he asked.

She thought for a minute. "I don't think so. What was that, an action flick?"

He winked. "It sure was."

"Is that the one where the submarine is stolen by the pirates?"

Gus smiled. "Getting colder. It was…" He paused dramatically. "An adult entertainment film."

Posey blinked. "Say again?"

He lowered his voice to a whisper and gave her a very adorable grin. "I'm a porn star."

She gave a hearty laugh. "Yeah. Me, too. *Posey Does Portsmouth*. Have you seen it?"

He stood up straighter, and the smile left his face. "Posey, I act in adult films. That's my job."

Holy Elvis Presley. He was serious. "I thought… I didn't think you were…" She glanced at Jon, but he was helping the Taylor Lautner fan, who was using her knife like a hatchet. "So. Wow. That's… interesting."

"It is, isn't it? And it's not nearly as sleazy as it sounds," Gus went on. "I mean, do I get more than my share of tail? Sure. But I'm looking to really connect, know what I mean? Fall in love. *Make* love. Which is so different from acting, where some know-nothing director is telling me what to do. And it can be hard, you know? Some of the scripts we get are absolute crap. There's no story, you know? I mean, what are these characters looking for, right? Other than a good lay?"

Posey nodded. Tried to picture bringing this guy home to her parents' house, where pictures of Pope Benedict, son of the Fatherland, hung in three of the six rooms. *He's a porn star, Ma. A porn star.* Nope. Wasn't gonna happen.

"I should probably be honest here," Posey said, trying to take a note from Wayne. "I…I think your job would probably rule you out in terms of dating. I'm sorry."

"Who asked you, huh?" he snapped. "Man! You're so prejudiced! So I screw people for a living! So do lawyers! Would you go out with a lawyer?"

"Um…probably," Posey said.

Gus tossed down his knife and folded his arms in full sulk. Her brother-in-law gave her a questioning look, then clapped his hands once more. "Gentlemen, take a stroll to your left, won't you?"

"Holy crap! Posey Osterhagen, right? Shit! Long time no see!"

Posey felt every muscle in her body stiffen. "Rick. Yep, it's been a while."

"What are you doing here?"

"Same thing you are, Rick. Why don't we just skip each other? No need to waste time, right?"

"Smell the basil, gang," Jon was crooning. "Isn't that glorious? Now you know why you paid so much to take this class. This basil was flown in from Cyprus, okay? Heaven!"

"I don't want to skip," Rick said. "Dude, relax, okay? It's just a cooking class."

True enough. But by all that was holy, she didn't want to spend a nanosecond with Rick Balin.

Rick was a native of Bellsford, too, and like Posey, he'd moved back after college. But they hadn't spoken since high school, though of course she'd seen him here and there, at the bank or a town meeting. Rick "managed" one of his parents' marinas, which, according to the gossip at Rosebud's Bar and Grille, meant that he came into the office, downloaded porn (hey, maybe he'd recognize Gus), then left around three to start cocktail hour.

"So, how are you?" Risk asked. "It's been a while, right?"

She gave a tight nod. The only saving grace was how horrible he looked, even worse up close. The years had taken a toll—the years, and several thousand bottles of beer, she guessed, based on his large belly and florid face. Even so, Rick Balin still oozed that rich-boy smugness (that, and alcohol fumes) as he lackadaisically chopped basil.

For a second, it was as if they were back in high school and Rick was leaning against her locker, blocking her from opening it. Back then, Rick Balin had lived the cliché of trust fund brat: he was beautiful, he was spoiled and he was cruel.

He'd also been her prom date.

"So, you're still single, Posey?" Rick asked.

"Mmm-hmm," she answered.

"Me, too. Divorced. Twice, if you can believe it."

"Oh, I can."

"So, maybe we can hook up sometime."

"No, thanks."

He shrugged and gave her a once-over. "Still scrawny," he said. His eyes, which Posey had once thought beautiful, settled on her breasts. "Then again, anything more than a mouthful's a waste."

She flinched, her arm hitting his, and suddenly Rick was screaming. "What the hell! What the hell!" and blood was pooling on the cutting board, totally ruining Jon's beautiful basil, because Rick had just sliced into the tip of his little finger.

Which, though she probably shouldn't, Posey found deeply satisfying.

Jon leaped over with a towel, yanked Rick's arm up.

"She cut me! She did that on purpose!"

"Oh, grow a pair, Rick," she said. "You cut yourself. Maybe you shouldn't drink when using sharp instruments."

"Did you hear that? She's so mean!" Rick said.

"It's a just a cut," Jon said.

"Dude! I'm gushing blood! I need an ambulance!"

Jon sighed. "Fine. Good thing you all signed that waiver, huh?"

Someone called 911, and Rick was led out of the room. As he left, he turned back to glare at her. "Whoops," she mouthed.

Granted, it hadn't been planned. But it was wonderful nonetheless.

"So that was fun," Kate declared as they drove home. "Did you have fun? Find anyone to marry?"

"The porn star was kind of cute, but then I remembered my mother's angina, so no."

"You okay about seeing Rick?" Kate asked, glancing over. She reached out and patted Posey's knee. "Awesome that you sliced off his finger." The boo-boo had already taken on legendary proportions.

"I actually didn't. It was the divine hand of fate, that's all. He was half-drunk."

"He stood you up at the prom," Kate said.

"Yeah, I remember."

It was true. But though Rick had indeed dumped her at the prom, it was Liam Murphy who'd done the real damage.

CHAPTER FIVE

THE FIRST TIME Posey laid eyes on Liam Murphy, her life changed.

Until high school, Posey's childhood had been great—a big brother, Guten Tag as a second home, parents who constantly assured her of her specialness, her beauty ("Cuter than a bug's ear!" her dad liked to exclaim), her talents (bricklaying…she'd done the entire patio, just for fun). Sure, her parents laid it on a bit thick—after all, Henry had already delivered the goods one pictures when thinking adoption: Asian, IQ of 164, gifted at violin. Posey's greatest public moment had come when she was cast in her fourth grade's production of *Farmer Smith's Bunny*, in which she played a nonspeaking turnip. But she knew she was loved.

So, yes, despite Stacia's conviction that Posey was teetering on the edge of death, disaster or kidnapping at all times, life was good, and Posey felt like a pretty normal, happy person, despite her friends' fascination with her adoption. It was only when Ruth, Ralphie and Gretchen came to visit that the little wounds of insecurity were cut open. Her aunt and uncle showed Gretchen off like a prized dog at Westminster. "Isn't she the image of Oma? Look at those eyes, like the sky, Stacia! Have you tasted this torte? Amazing!" There was no getting around it—Gretchen was everything good the family genetics had ever produced.

Gretchen was also full of information—older by two months, she seemed to feel it was her job to fill in the blanks for Posey. Gret told her how you got pregnant (French kissing), how babies came out of their mothers (pooped out), where Posey's real name came from (Great-Aunt Cordelia, who only had one eye and fell in a well and died, but Posey shouldn't bring that up, because it would make their mothers cry).

Gretchen also told Posey the reason she'd been adopted—Stacia had a baby girl who had died, and Posey was the replacement.

Henry had confirmed that one. In his factual way, he told her their mom had been pregnant when he was in kindergarten, then went to the hospital, and no baby ever came home. That was all he knew.

But all in all, childhood had been A-okay. Posey had friends, was allowed to run cross-country in middle school, deemed the least dangerous sport by her parents. Being a good six or eight inches shorter than most of the other girls, she never won, but it was fun nonetheless. Her grades were solid, her brother was tolerant and helped her with homework. She was invited to birthday parties and had friends over.

And then came high school.

Somehow, everything changed the summer after eighth grade. Girls she'd been friends with were now obsessed with boys or their own beauty, their long hair, their thrilling boobies. Posey was left out, still skinny as a toothpick, uncurvy, undeveloped, uninterested in whether Brandon really had checked out Emily at recess. The boys who'd once played kickball with Posey now made rude comments about her flat chest. When her freshman class read The Diary of Anne Frank, there were giggles and whispers. Posey found energy bars and candy in front of her locker for weeks. Just before the freshman chorus concert, when all fifty kids were waiting to file onto stage, Kyle Stubbins asked her if she had a tapeworm. It was stunning to her…she'd gone to Kyle's birthday party in fourth grade, gave him a Magic 8

Ball, which he'd really liked. But high school was a cold, alien world, one where old friendships didn't seem to matter.

So Posey took the tried and true route of teenage survival: invisibility. She was friends with Kate, but they didn't have many classes together. Posey didn't raise her hand too much, didn't try to talk to the popular kids, just floated along at the fringes, ignored the occasional insult and chose extracurricular activities that were underpopulated: the French Club, woodworking. It worked; if she wasn't noticed, at least she wasn't tormented.

Then, in the springtime of her freshman year, *he* came to town.

Posey was standing in the hall, waiting for the popular kids to get out of the way so she could get her lunchbox out of her locker. This simple act was a painful daily event, as all the cool kids got hot lunch and would *die* before bringing in homemade lunches. Worse, Posey's locker was next to the locker of Jessica Blair, a junior and reigning queen of the evil popular crowd. Jessica was going with Rick Balin, tanned, blond, and beautiful, star tight end of the football team, and their minions swarmed around them.

Posey waited, hugging her books to her chest. "Excuse me," she said, trying to ease past Jamie High-gate. He didn't move, so she wriggled past. Rick was leaning on her locker door and (of course) didn't notice her. "Excuse me," she said again. "Sorry, I need to get in here." Rick finally moved, though he didn't look at her. And great. Now Mitchell Oberlin was in the way. Despite having had four cheese blintzes for breakfast, Posey was lightheaded with hunger. "Excuse me," she said once more, managing to open her locker door an inch, just enough to glimpse her salvation in the form of a giant blue lunchbox. "Excuse me. Sorry. Can I—"

And then…and then *he* came down the hall, black hair thick and rumpled, flannel shirt open over a T-shirt with mysterious logo, faded blue jeans. Scuffed black leather jacket. He was unshaven (unshaven!), and his motorcycle helmet (motorcycle!) indicated his form of transportation. The principal was with him, lecturing him about behavior and second chances, and from the look in his eye, this guy could care less. The crowd around Jessica and Rick fell silent at the spectacle of this…this *god*. His eyes cut around the hallway, assessing and unimpressed.

For one second, the clear green gaze landed on Posey, and all other sounds were instantly blanked out except the thudding of her heart. Her cheeks tightened with a blush. Knees tingled, mouth went dry. Who *was* that?

For the next few weeks, Posey found out all she could about this new deity. Liam Declan Murphy… sigh! He was just out of juvie (juvie!) for stealing cars. Every day, he arrived on a battered Triumph motorcycle, which Posey learned was uber-cool, way more so than a newer, shinier make. According to the rumors that flew thick and fast, he played guitar (guitar!) in a band in some sleazy bar (squee!) across the river in Kittery. He lived with an uncle over by the quarry. Parents were either dead, in jail or witness protection.

Each bit of information was utterly thrilling. Suddenly, the world had more meaning, more layers, more color. He was a junior, she was a frosh, so their paths didn't exactly cross, but she ogled him from across the parking lot, made a point of going from Latin to Algebra via the second-floor hallway, despite the fact that both her classes were on the first floor. But even the small possibility of glimpsing him—unkempt, beautiful, aloof—was more than enough justification.

And then came that miraculous day when she tore into the kitchen of Guten Tag for her after-school strudel fix, and *he* was there. Him! Liam Declan Murphy! Was there! In her parents' kitchen! She could *smell* him…oil and soap and just the slightest hint of something warm and spicy, like pumpkin pie.

Posey managed to close her mouth, abruptly aware that it was hanging open. Her backpack slipped from her limp fingers, alerting her mother to her arrival.

"Oh, hi, sweetheart! Liam, this is our daughter, Cordelia," Mom said. "But everyone calls her Posey."

"Niih," Posey breathed. This was *amazing!* God *so* loved her!

"Hey," he said.

"Liam will be working here in the kitchen," her father said. "Washing dishes, cleaning up."

"I… That's… Hi," Posey said. Working *here?* Unbelievable! They'd become friends, she could see it immediately. They'd hang out, Liam would grin and talk about those dumb popular kids. They'd become BFFs…then, yes, she could see it so clearly, they'd fall in love. High school would be a dream of happiness. Prom queen, okay? No more invisibility, no more slinking through the halls. He'd wait for her to graduate, then they'd head off for the same college. Get married, have a house on the water, make out every single night. Oh, Elvis Presley, they'd *sleep* in the same *bed!*

Every day from then on, Posey tried to get his attention, to make him see what a great friend she could be. But Liam was always busy, always offering to do something else once a task was done. "Mr. Osterhagen, you want me to break down those boxes in the back?" he'd ask, and her dad would thank him for being so diligent. Other than grunting hello, Liam really didn't speak to her. He was polite and respectful to her parents, though he was rough around the edges, but whatever affection he may have had for Max and Stacia didn't transfer over to her. It wasn't that he was rude; it was more that he didn't seem to think there was any reason for them to talk. At school, he might acknowledge her with a nod (which she'd relive over and over, admitting that yes, she was pathetic, but he *nodded* and it was *thrilling*).

Posey wasn't the only one obsessed with Liam, that was clear. It was his attitude. And his looks. Liam was gorgeous. He was aloof. He had hidden depths and a tragic and secret past. Everyone wanted to be him or do him. According to the girls' room gossip, which Posey both lived for and dreaded, Liam was *such* a good kisser. Yes, Amanda Peters *was* planning to meet him under the bleachers after school—who wouldn't? And everyone knew that he'd already done Taylor Bennington, but what guy hadn't, right?

However many girls Liam did or didn't do, he didn't talk about it. He might give a slow smile or a smoky look—the meaning of the term "bedroom eyes" became abundantly clear. But he didn't brag about his conquests (not that she could tell) or his motorcycle, didn't talk about his misdeeds. He just didn't seem to care, and that was the most exciting thing of all.

But Posey knew a little something about being on the outside looking in, and there were times when she swore she saw the same yearning in Liam's expression, that little flash of vulnerability. He may have been admired, but he didn't belong.

Previously, Rick Balin had been the alpha dog of Bellsford High. His family had lived in town forever; they'd owned mills, then boatyards, and Rick was the type of kid who got a red Mercedes convertible for his sixteenth birthday, crashed it before the week was up, and got a silver Mercedes as reward. He was blond, he was solid, he played football, he was careless and smug and it worked. Only at Bellsford after he'd flunked out of Choate, Andover, and St. Paul's, Rick was widely regarded as a catch, and Jessica Blair daily trumpeted her status as his girlfriend.

But from Liam's first day forth, the order changed. Liam was the lone wolf in the pack's territory, and rather than challenge Liam, Posey watched as Rick and the lesser dogs began to mimic him. If Liam's jeans had holes in the knees, the next day Rick's would, too, though Rick probably ordered the maid to age and rip his own. At first, Liam ate his lunch alone in the courtyard, rather than in the cafeteria; Rick and his followers started eating outside, too. Eventually, the pack eased around Liam, trying to impress, to assimilate him. Liam tolerated their presence, but Posey could tell it was tolerance only (well…that's how it looked). He let them hang out, but he didn't become one of them, and in some ways, he seemed more alone than ever.

Sure, he might (he did) sleep with a few (more than a few) girls here and there—hard to avoid, as they practically hurled themselves at his groin, but he hadn't truly connected with anyone. Yet. Maybe once she finally *blossomed,* as her mother put it, he'd notice Posey. It was what she prayed for nightly, heaven knew.

Then one day after school, as Posey was walking to the restaurant, she spied Liam out by the trash cans in the alley. He was kneeling down, holding something in his hand. Posey froze, drinking in the sight of him—the torn jeans, the faded black T-shirt, the way the wind ruffled his hair. Then a tiny, striped cat came out from behind the trash can, warily, slowly. It sniffed the air, then leaned forward, closer. Liam said something too quietly for Posey to hear. The cat sniffed again, took another step closer…then took the offering in his mouth and scampered back to safety. Liam smiled, stood up, and saw Posey.

"Hey," he said.

"Hi." Her face heated in a rush.

"Don't tell your parents, okay? I probably shouldn't be feeding him, but…" Liam shrugged.

"I won't tell anybody."

"Thanks." He started back into the restaurant.

"Is he tame? Do you think he's lost?" she blurted, terrified this would be their last conversation.

He turned around. "I think he's a stray. It took two weeks to get him to come to me." The sound of his voice—the fact that he was *speaking* to her—was breathtakingly amazing.

"Does he have a name? The cat? Did you name him?" Posey babbled, unwilling to let him go. The intimacy of the moment, the hidden *depths* of this mysterious alpha male, oh, it was so romantic! He was *feeding* a starving *cat!* Him! The motorcycle guy who had girls crawling over him!

Liam paused. "I've been calling him Joe," he admitted with a crooked grin, and Posey almost died.

"That's a good name," she managed.

Liam's smile grew. "See you, Cordelia." With that, he went inside.

The simmering lust, the raging interest exploded into love. Who wouldn't fall in love with a man who took the time to feed a homeless kitty? She held that image against her heart like a secret jewel. Only she knew about it, she was sure. Those girls Liam might've slept with, girls who left their panties in his locker or wrote things about him on the bathroom walls…they didn't know what Posey knew—Liam Declan Murphy was not just the hottest thing ever to grace Bellsford High…he was a softy, too.

It took a week or two of screwing up her courage, but Posey finally spoke to Liam in school. After World History, she ran up the stairs, then galloped to room 224, where Liam would be going from Physics to English. She slowed down, not wanting him to see that she was out of breath, and glanced at her chest to make sure the tissues she'd stuffed in her bra hadn't shifted.

Liam was smiling that half grin at some girl who was telling him he really should hang out with her sometime. Tramp. Posey pretended not to notice them, then, when she was just a couple of feet away, looked up. "Oh, hey, Liam."

"Hi," he said, a little cautiously. They didn't speak in school (or ever, really, except for that one time in the alley).

"How's Joe?" she asked.

He paused. "Joe's fine." Then he grinned, and Posey's knees weakened so fast that she wobbled.

"So, anyway, you could definitely come over," the slutty girl said. "You won't be sorry."

"Is that right," Liam murmured, turning his attention back to her. Posey didn't mind. She and Liam had a secret. Later that day, when she came to the restaurant, she slipped into the closet where Liam's coat was and tucked a can of tuna into his pocket. No note. Let him wonder. Let him think about her the way she thought and thought and thought about him. Later that week, this time after Liam's Spanish class, he spoke to her. "Hey. Joe says thanks." And he smiled at her as he walked past and for a second, Posey was literally blinded with love.

"Do you, like…*know* him?" asked Melissa Shields, one of Posey's classmates.

"Sure," Posey said casually.

Timing it carefully so she didn't seem too eager (though if she'd put as much time into her algebra class as she did into tuna cans, she would've had an A+), Posey once again left a gift for Joe in the pocket of Liam's worn black leather jacket. For one blissful moment, she held the coat to her face, breathing in the smell—leather and soap and cloves—before sneaking back into the restaurant. Then, just before lunch on Thursday, Liam acknowledged her once more as he was going into the courtyard. "Joe's getting spoiled." He raised an eyebrow as if saying *You. You're so dang cute.*

"Where is all our tuna going?" Stacia wondered aloud, but Posey just smiled. Counted the days until she could plant another can. Despite the fact that there was fish involved, it all seemed incredibly clandestine and romantic. She could almost imagine them rehashing it someday in front of a roaring fire in a cabin on a mountain somewhere. Liam would gaze into her eyes and say, "Remember when you used to sneak me food to give to Joe? That's when I first fell in love with you." Then Joe, whom they would've adopted, would climb into her lap, purring noisily, and they'd laugh. And then kiss. Maybe even French kiss. Just the thought of it made her flushed and squishy.

But one day, as she was sitting at the table in the restaurant kitchen, Liam came over, holding the latest can of tuna she'd slipped into his coat pocket an hour ago. "Looks like Joe's moved on," he said. He set the can down.

"Moved on? Where?"

"Someone adopted him," Liam said.

"What?" she yelped. "Who?"

"I don't know. Some lady was out there, trying to get him to come out from behind the Dumpster. She asked if he belonged to anyone, and I said no, and she took him."

"But…but who was she? We don't even know her! She can't just…take him." Her voice thickened with tears.

Liam gave her an odd look. "I'm sure he's fine." Then he turned and walked away, his shift over. And though Posey tried and tried, wracking her brain in bed at night, she couldn't think of anything else to say that would reestablish that bond, that secret, lovely feeling. What about Joe? Was he happy? Was the woman nice? Did Liam miss his little pal? He didn't seem to be particularly suffering, surrounded as ever by a throng of admirers, male and female alike.

Summer came; Liam took another job at a garage, and Posey saw him less—and counted the days till school started once more. The first day of Posey's sophomore year, however, was also the day that Emma Tate returned to New Hampshire.

Emma hadn't been in school the past year; her dad, a politician, had made friends with the right demigod in Washington, and the Tates had been living in London. That was the kind of luck Emma had…a year in London.

She and Liam first saw each other in the courtyard at lunch, and when Liam's eyes locked on Emma's, Posey, who was watching from three tables away, felt her cheeks warm as if *she* were the one Liam Murphy was looking at. Except, of course, she wasn't. Even so, her insides turned to gooey caramel as Liam stared at Emma as if she were the only other person on earth.

Even before that moment, just about every female in high school would have liked to have been Emma, Posey most definitely included. Emma Tate had long blond hair. Was five foot seven…tall, but not too tall…blue, blue eyes. Boobs. She knew how to dress, not like a mannequin from Abercrombie, but with true style. And she was *nice*. Her family went to St. Martin's, just like the Osterhagens, and she always said hello, warmly, too. She'd had a boyfriend at Lawrence Academy, but they'd broken up when the Tates went abroad.

Of course, Liam—that bad-boy god—would fall for someone like Emma, the squeaky-clean and uber-nice princess. Posey knew that. She'd been studying Liam for months now and already felt like she knew him better than anyone. Still, her heart collapsed as Liam walked across the courtyard, straight to Emma, who looked right into his gorgeous, perfect, *unshaven* face and smiled, and that was that.

Once in a while, Emma would drop by the restaurant. Those times were the worst, when Posey, sitting on her stool doing homework and secretly watching Liam, would have to witness the secret side of the man she loved, the side she'd *known* was lurking under his tough, guarded exterior. Liam would smile… right there, Posey's heart would lose another healthy chunk. With Emma, he'd talk…the rumble of his voice, already a man's voice, deep and steady, causing her stomach to tighten with lust. And then—oh, the pain of it—then he'd give Emma a quick kiss goodbye, so natural and so…so…so perfect that Posey, inevitably eating something as she did her homework, would stop mid-chew, pen frozen above the paper, unable to tear her eyes off the two of them.

Emma was far too nice. "Hey, Posey, how's it going?" she'd say. "Do you have Mr. Rivers for math? Oh, my God, he was the worst!" One time… Oh, the horror, the horror. "Posey, Liam and I are going to the movies. Want to come along?"

Sure, right after I jump off Memorial Bridge, Posey thought. "Oh, thanks, but I have plans," she chirruped. Right. Plans to do what? Lie on her bed and fantasize about Liam? Wonder what it would be like to be kissed? Still, she knew better than to tag along like some unwanted orphan.

As for other boys, nah. By the time she was sixteen, Posey's bra size was a roomy 32A. Pants a size 12, boys' slim. Her weight concerned her mom, who was six feet tall and weighed more than two hundred pounds, and so Posey was dragged to the pediatrician, who concurred.

"Well," he announced, glancing at her paperwork, "your thyroid and blood work are normal, but I'm a little concerned."

"I eat everything that's not nailed down," Posey protested. At his sharp look, she added, "And I don't barf it up. I just have a fast metabolism."

"She's like a hummingbird, our little girl," Stacia agreed fondly.

"Right," he agreed. "But if you got sick, you don't have anything in reserve. Two days of stomach flu, and we'd have to admit you to the hospital. And down the road, it can contribute to fertility problems."

"Oh, no!" Stacia exclaimed, clutching Posey's hand.

"Are your periods regular?"

Posey blushed. "Yes. Sort of. For the most part."

"Will she be infertile, Doctor?" Stacia asked in a whisper.

"I can always adopt," Posey said, her voice sharp. Stacia squeezed her hand again.

"It's too early to talk about that," the doctor said. "But let's try to pack on a few pounds, okay? And listen. Most girls would love to have this problem. You'll never be fat, look at it that way."

"Well, I'd like to have boobs," Posey grumbled. "Got anything for that?"

"It's mostly hereditary," the doctor said amiably. Great. Apparently, Posey's birth mother was a stick insect. *Gretchen* was already a C-cup, something Aunt Ruth had called to announce that very morning. "But a little fattening up will help, too."

Which is why Posey started going to Sweetie Sue's Ice Cream Parlor every day after school. Sweetie Sue's, where Emma Tate worked.

"Hi, Posey!" she said, looking irritatingly adorable in her pink uniform. "Good thing you came in, I was just about to fall asleep, it's so dead in here." She smiled. "What can I get you?"

Seeing Shiny Emma just reinforced all that was wrong with her. Posey swallowed, for once not hungry. "Can I have a hot-fudge sundae? Coconut ice cream, extra whipped cream, extra nuts."

"You bet." Emma scooped up the ice cream, drizzled the hot fudge, seemed to spray on the whipped cream for three full minutes. "Here you go," she said, smiling as she handed it over. "I sure wish I could eat like you."

Suddenly, Posey's eyes were wet. "No, you don't," she whispered.

"Posey? You okay?" Emma's pretty face creased in concern.

"I have to eat six times a day or I get lightheaded," Posey blurted. "I eat more than my father, but I can't keep any weight on, I don't have any boobs, and the doctor just told me I might have trouble getting pregnant someday. This isn't fun, you know."

Emma's hand went over her mouth. "Oh, Posey, I didn't mean… I'm really sorry, I am."

It was Emma's niceness that did Posey in. To her horror, she started to cry in earnest, the words tumbling out. "It's just…I can't even wear girl clothes. Do you know where I shop? In the junior boys' section, ages 8 to 12. Not one guy has ever checked me out, let alone *asked* me out."

Emma came around the counter and put her arm around Posey's shoulders. She guided her to a table, pulled some paper napkins from the dispenser and handed them to Posey.

"The stupid doctor told me I have to gain weight," Posey said, her voice wobbly. "All I do is eat, and I just burn it all off, and I hate the way I look."

"But why?" Emma said. "You're so cute, Posey! You are!"

"Right. Which is why my nickname is Anne Frank."

"No! Who calls you that?"

"The mean girls." Posey cut her a look. "You know."

"Yeah, I do," Emma said grimly. She sighed. "So your doctor said you have to eat ice cream? I'm sorry, but that's hardly cancer, okay?"

Posey couldn't help a smile. "I know. As prescriptions go, it's pretty good."

"Exactly. So listen. Come here every day, and I'll help you, okay?"

And so began a sort of friendship. Not that they hung out. The two-year age difference was significant, at least in high school, and Emma was one of the popular kids. She was going to Pepperdine in the fall, she had friends, cheerleading, student council. And Liam, of course. Emma seemed so much older, so much more…together. But at school, Emma did something rather stunning—she acknowledged Posey. Said hi sometimes, or waved in the halls, causing Kate to ask if Posey was blackmailing Emma.

About six weeks after she started the Campaign for Boobs, as she thought of it, Posey was power-eating a Snickers ice-cream sundae with caramel sauce and Reese's Pieces when Emma asked, very casually, "Posey, has anyone asked you to the prom yet?"

Posey snorted, having become quite comfortable with Emma. "No. And no one will."

"Well, if someone did ask, would you be interested?"

"Sure. I'd also be interested in taming a unicorn," Posey answered, flicking through a magazine. "Also, I always thought it'd be cool to talk to undersea animals, like Aquaman."

"Listen," Emma said, ignoring the sarcasm. "Rick Balin just broke up with Jessica, who had it coming, let me tell you. He said he'll go to the prom solo, but I thought you and he would make a cute couple." She wiped her hands on the dishcloth. "So what do you think?"

Rick Balin? Blond, rich, good-looking Rick Balin? Second to Liam, Rick was…well. It was silly even to discuss. "That would never happen," Posey said.

"I think it would!" Emma bounced over to her and sat down, golden ponytail swinging. "You're wicked cute, even if you don't know it. And you've gained a few pounds, haven't you?"

"Four," Posey answered. The ice cream had definitely been helping, as well as the three scrambled eggs with cheese she ate right before bedtime.

"And if we got you one of those demi push-up bras from Victoria's Secret, you'd have a nice little package there. I totally bet he'd ask you! Especially if I give him a nudge!"

How could Posey resist? It wasn't lost on her that if pigs did fly and Rick asked her out, she might be hanging out with Liam a little more. And just being near him, outside of the restaurant…that would be worth quite a bit indeed. Not that she wanted to break him up from Emma or anything. Just the chance to get him to remember how they'd bonded over Joe…to be able to tell him something funny and get him to laugh, just to be—perhaps—his friend…that would be enough. More than enough. That would be *wonderful*.

A week and a half later, and one pound later, and one thirty-five-dollar push-up bra later as well, Rick Balin approached Posey at her locker. "Posey, hey."

"Hi, Rick," Posey said, as if she'd ever said anything other than "excuse me" to him.

"So, Emma said you might be free for the prom," Rick said, his famously soulful brown eyes scanning her up and down, pausing on her chest. That bra was worth every cent.

"Um, yeah. I'm free," Posey said casually, her cheeks scalding. But Emma had coached her on strategy, and she knew to play it light.

"So, you wanna go with me?" Rick asked, grinning.

She shrugged, though her hands were shaking. "Sure." She glanced at him, gave him a little smile, then looked back into her locker.

"Great. I'll call you with details. Ciao."

"Ciao."

Rick sauntered off. Posey fought off the urge to faint.

Emma was smug with pride. Gave dress advice, discussed hair styles. Kate was a little grouchy, but Posey reveled in the glamour of prom, of Emma's friendship, of possibly changing her status in Liam's eyes.

On Saturday afternoon of the sacred event, Posey had her hair done at Curl Up and Dye, the best salon in town. Her short hair was highlighted, trimmed and blown dry so that finally it seemed to have some semblance of style. Then she dropped by the restaurant to meet her mom so they could go home together, do makeup and put on her beautiful shimmering green dress, take a thousand or so pictures. This night was a coup for Stacia, too. Gretchen, also a sophomore, *hadn't* been asked to the prom, something Ruth tried very hard to pretend didn't matter.

Posey went in the front door of the restaurant for a change, rather hoping to make a grand entrance, delight her father and possibly dazzle Liam into seeing her as a *woman*. It was still early, only three, so most of the staff wouldn't be there yet. As she approached the doors that separated the dining room and kitchen, Posey paused at the sound of some voices. Liam's. And Rick's (she could identify his because he'd called her—twice!—and also from all the times he'd blocked her locker). There were other voices, too, an explosion of male laughter. Posey peeked through the crack in the door.

There they were. The popular boys, who occasionally swung by when Liam was working. No sign of an adult, which made sense, since it was early. Liam often opened the restaurant for her folks, which Posey thought showed how trustworthy and wonderful he was.

Suddenly shy at the thought of encountering them en masse (they were seniors, after all), Posey stepped back a little. But she could hear them.

"Dude," one of them—Luke Mayhew?—said. "You're killing me by still being with Emma. God, she's beautiful! Give someone else a chance, right? I mean, come on! Just the way she walks down the hall, you can tell—"

"Shut up," Liam growled, and Posey felt a flush of pride. Liam Murphy, defending his woman. He had class, juvie or no juvie. Someone else said something—the water was running and she couldn't quite hear. Then Rick, or possibly Luke, said something, but it was lost too, and the guys all hooted and hollered.

The water shut off.

"Here's what I want to know," Liam said, and Posey couldn't resist another peek. He was unloading the dishwasher, stacking the plates just the way Stacia liked, and the other guys were grouped around him. "Rick, my man, Posey Osterhagen? I mean, I know I work for her parents, but were you that desperate? She's nothing but a bag of bones. Built like a ten-year-old boy."

Their roar of laughter drowned out the little squeak that escaped Posey's mouth. Her hands flew up to cover any more noise, and silently, so carefully, she backed away from the door, her legs watery with shock, heart twisting and convulsing. When she was far enough from the door—from them—she turned and tiptoed to the front door of the restaurant as fast as she could, colliding right into her mother.

"There you are, sweetie! I went to the salon to get you! Did you forget? Or were we supposed to meet here? Oh, look at your hair! It's so beautiful!"

Mom didn't notice that Posey was quiet...or she did and assumed it was nerves. A floating feeling settled over Posey as they drove home. She went through the motions—makeup, dress, jewelry—and smiled as her father took pictures. Henry was home for a rare weekend, and he looked up from his textbooks, acknowledged that his little sister was growing up and smiled, which was lavish praise for him.

When the doorbell rang, she was somewhat shocked to see that Rick had actually shown up. And he was nice. Polite, attractive, looking somehow younger in a tux than he did at school. He shook hands, posed for a few pictures. There was no limo; Rick had driven his latest Mercedes, and Max asked the usual fatherly questions and issued warnings against drinking and driving.

Posey barely heard. "Bye!" she called as her mother dabbed her eyes. Rick held the car door for her. Got in the driver's seat. *Maybe this won't be so terrible,* Posey thought. *Maybe Rick really likes me, no matter what Liam said.* At the thought of his name, pain speared her heart. It was still so shocking that Liam—her Liam—thought of her that way. So vicious, those words, that she flinched at the thought of them.

She swallowed and looked at Rick, biting her lip. Maybe he, too, had hidden depths, and she could fall for him, instead of...the other one. Rick's pretty brown eyes were on the road, his blond hair ruffling in the breeze.

"You look really nice, by the way," she said.

He didn't answer.

"Are you excited?" she asked.

Rick still didn't answer. Didn't look at her, either. *Stupid question, Posey!* her brain hissed.

Years later—heck, hours later—Posey would berate herself for not standing up for herself. She should've said, "Hey, idiot, I'm talking to you." Surely her older self would have. But at barely sixteen, having no experience with boy-girl stuff whatsoever, terrified at the thought of offending one of the cool kids, she just…pretended. Pretended it was okay that her date drove in silence, even as her stomach ached and her hands went clammy. Pretended not to notice when he didn't open the door for her when they pulled up at Whitfield Mansion, didn't wait for her, didn't even look back.

Don't go in, her brain warned. But what else could she do? He drove. She was here. People were swarming inside. Maybe he just wanted to find his friends. Maybe he'd be nicer once they were, um, settled.

She went in, knees twanging with nervousness.

The place was mobbed. Whitfield Mansion was utterly gorgeous, high ceilings, black-and-white tiled floors, chandeliers and French doors. Posey looked around. It seemed like her trick of being invisible had worked brilliantly, because no one acknowledged her, no matter how nice Emma had been in the past month. Still, Posey fake-smiled at no one in particular, praying to see a familiar face, a friend. Rick was nowhere to be seen, and her heart raced with humiliation and fear. The smell of too much perfume and hairspray was making her sick, and, dang it, she hadn't eaten since lunch, which meant there was a very good chance she'd faint. But who could eat with Liam's words echoing in her heart?

And suddenly, there was Liam, right there in the huge foyer. Not in a tux…in a black suit with a black shirt, looking like he should be at the Oscars instead of a prom. His eyes met hers, and he gave a little chin jerk in recognition. He even smiled…a little smile, his mouth pulling up on one side, and that was when Posey really thought she might faint, because what the *hell?* He smiled at her after saying those horrible things? Her throat tightened, eyes stung with hot and angry tears.

"Hey! Posey, oh, wow, you look *so* pretty!" It was Emma. "Are you at our table? I asked Rick, but he didn't know, I mean, I thought all of us would be together, right? Oh, hang on, there's Lily. Can you believe Luke wore a maroon tuxedo? She's ready to kill him. Be right back! Stay here, don't move a muscle."

Posey had no intention of staying put. *Just stick to the walls and pretend you're happy,* advised the wiser part of her brain. *Just hang in there. Don't lose it.* She made her way into the banquet room, which was mobbed as well, candles flickering on the tables, the smell of hothouse flowers gumming up her throat. She didn't see Rick—she hated Rick. But, heck, if he'd showed up at her arm with a soda and a smile, she'd forgive him in a heartbeat. Maybe there was an explanation. There had to be. Because if there wasn't, Posey had no idea what she was supposed to do.

"What are *you* doing here?" came a voice, and Posey's heart took a header. It was Jessica Blair, whose locker was next to hers, who'd dated Rick for almost a year. Her hair was piled on her head like Nefertiti's, and she wore a dress that showed off three-quarters of her significant breasts. "This is *senior prom,* okay? Not for underclassmen."

"I—" Posey cleared her throat. "Um, I'm here with someone," she said.

"Really?" Jessica said. "Someone, who?"

Posey's legs started shaking. "Rick. Rick Balin." Her voice was barely audible to her own ears.

"You're here with Rick Balin," Jessica repeated, as if for clarification. Two of her cheerleading friends had joined her, and all of them glared at Posey. "You sure?"

"Yes," Posey whispered, looking at the floor.

"Then why was his tongue in my mouth, like, five seconds ago?" Jessica said. Her minions snickered, and then Rick came up, glanced dismissively at Posey, and slung his arm around Jessica, his fingers caressing the top of her exposed breast. "Babe. You ready?"

"So ready," Jessica said, and with that, she turned and kissed Rick, an open-mouthed, sloppy kiss that seemed to last forever. When she finally tore her lips off of Rick's, she gave Posey a demeaning once-over. "Padded bra, Anne Frank?" she asked, and her evil handmaidens howled with laughter.

Posey abandoned any thoughts of clinging to her dignity. Instead, she fled for the bathroom. Thank the Lord, it was empty. She ran to the stall furthest from the door, snapped the lock and clenched her arms over her stomach, her breath jerking in and out in sharp little gasps. What was she going to do? How could she get out of here? Her parents would be devastated.

The bathroom door opened. "Posey?"

It was Emma, stupid, well-meaning, oblivious Emma, her voice soft with concern and sympathy. "Posey? Are you okay?"

For a second, Posey hated her. Then she stood up straight, took a deep breath, and opened the stall door. "Oh, Emma, I'm so sorry, but I have to go home. I have a wicked bad migraine. I feel horrible. I was hoping it'd get better, but it's not."

It was, perhaps, the first time she'd ever lied.

Emma wrung her hands. "Um…Posey, I just saw Rick—"

"I know," Posey said. "I feel rotten standing him up at the prom, but guess what? I think he and Jessica might be getting back together, don't you? To be honest, I kind of hope so, because you were so sweet to go to all this trouble, but I'm not gonna be able to stay, this headache, wow, it's really bad, and I don't want to leave Rick in the lurch, but the thing is, Emma, he's not really my type anyway. You know?"

Her voice was tight and fast, and her words didn't fool Emma.

"He's an idiot," she whispered.

He's just following your boyfriend's lead, Posey thought viciously, and again, the wave of shock and heartache threatened to crash. "I have to go, Emma," she said, her voice shaking but acceptable. "My ride should be here any sec. I'm really sorry. Thanks for everything. You have fun, okay?"

"You want me to walk you out?" Emma asked.

"No! No. Just…go have fun. Bet you'll be prom queen." Posey forced a smile. "Bye! See you soon."

After a little more hand-wringing, Emma finally left, and Posey sagged with the effort of lying. Stupid, naive, perfect Emma Tate. No one would stand *her* up at the prom, you could bet on that. Liam Murphy *loved* her; he'd kill the guy who hurt her feelings, who drove her into the bathroom to hide. The hypocrite.

The door opened again, and without thinking, Posey dashed into the stall once more, sat on the toilet and pulled up her feet, wrapping her arms around her legs so her dress wouldn't show.

"Did you hear about Rick and Jessica?" one of them said. Of course.

"What? Are they back together?" the other asked.

"Totally. But Rick brought—get this—Posey Osterhagen as his date."

"Who's that?"

"You know. Everyone calls her Anne Frank? Kinda weird-looking, looks like she's in fifth grade. Her parents own that grubby German restaurant?"

"Are you kidding? Her? Why?"

"No clue. Hey, do you have any hairspray? I love your earrings, by the way."

It was the comment about Guten Tag that started the tears. Her parents' restaurant was *not* grubby. It was immaculate. Did those twits know how hard it was to clean that place? Did they have any clue how many hours Stacia put into the restaurant, because of course a cleaning service wasn't enough, and the Osterhagens themselves polished those steins, scoured the bathrooms, dusted the Hummel figurines and the broken antler on the mounted moose head she'd named Glubby when she was three?

Well, she wasn't about to give the mean girls—or Rick—or Liam—the satisfaction of seeing her picked up in front of the Whitfield Mansion. The bathrooms were directly across from the kitchen, and she slipped in through the doors, ignoring the looks from the staff, and simply walked out the back.

It was raining. It might've been May, but the temperature was in the low fifties, and before long, her teeth started to chatter. The mansion's long driveway was bordered by woods thick with dripping pines. Dreading the idea that people coming to the prom would see her, soaked, dress ruined, hair and makeup a joke, Posey chose the woods. Her shoes—her first pair of heels—sank into the muddy ground, and she twisted her ankle more than once. The now-sodden gown flopped around her legs like a dying bird, making her skin raw. How much had her parents spent on this night? Four hundred dollars, maybe, for her gown and shoes and special-order bra, her hair, the necklace and bracelet her dad had given her just last night? They'd been so proud, so excited...and now look.

A car turned into the mansion driveway, and without further thought, Posey leaped behind a tree and crouched down, hating herself for doing it, unable not to. Hiding in the woods in a ruined prom dress, all because Rick Balin had dumped her.

And Rick, she knew with absolute certainty, would never have done that without Liam Murphy first planting the idea.

Nothing but a bag of bones. Built like a ten-year-old boy.

There was a 7-11 on the main road, about a mile from Whitfield Mansion's entrance. By the time she reached the store, she was shuddering with cold. She fished a quarter out of her purse and deposited it in the pay phone outside and called her brother.

"Henry?" she whispered when he answered. "Don't tell Mom and Dad, but I need you to come get me. And can you bring me some dry clothes?" Then she started to cry in earnest.

She hid in the potato chip section, dripping onto the floor, until Henry came. Then she changed in the 7-11 bathroom, and her brother took her out to a diner two towns over, and she sobbed out the whole story over a hamburger club with extra fries, from her love for Liam to the comment about Guten Tag's cleanliness. For once, Henry's lack of conversational skills was a blessing.

"I'm sorry, Posey," was all he said. But he reminded the waitress that she'd need extra mayo on the side and didn't protest when she told him they needed to stay out till past eleven, knowing that Max and Stacia wouldn't be able to stay awake that long no matter what.

"You can't tell Mom and Dad, okay?" Posey asked as they pulled in front of their house. Their parents' windows were dark.

"Okay," he said. Then he hugged her—such a rare event—and waited till she was showered and in bed before going to bed himself, just in case she needed anything. The next morning, she told her parents she'd had a great time, but ended up with a headache, and called Henry to come get her just before the end of the night. They bought it.

Emma called that same day. "I told everyone I was really disappointed you'd gotten sick," she said, her voice horribly kind. "I told them what a great friend you've been, and it was just crappy luck that you got one of your migraines. But also that you were totally cool about Rick and Jess. You were only in it for the dress anyway, right?"

Posey understood. Emma was using her popularity as a shield, and if anyone was going to make fun of Posey, they'd suffer her disapproval. Not that anyone would really believe the story. But back at school, no one openly made fun of Posey, and though she'd been dreading hearing echoes of Liam's words, she wasn't subjected to them again. She stopped going to Sweetie Sue's for ice cream, because she just didn't want to see the pity in Emma's eyes.

She didn't see Liam until five days after the prom, at the restaurant, where for the first time ever, he initiated conversation. "Heard you got sick at the prom."

Why would he talk to her *now?* "Yeah."

"You okay now?"

"I'm fine." Her voice was calm and cool.

Then she packed her books, told her parents she'd see them at home. For the last month of her sophomore year, she told her mom she was better able to do her homework back at the house. She found herself studying harder, raising her hand more often, walking through the halls with an edge she hadn't had before. She barely saw Liam, and that August, he left for California.

That moment when she'd crouched behind the tree…it did something to her, something that made her grow up and toughen up. But one question throbbed in her brain for a long, long time. Why? Why would Liam say something so hateful? How could he—who had tamed a stray and starving cat—be so cruel to a girl who had only ever wanted to be his friend?

CHAPTER SIX

"A LOT OF US REMEMBER Liam from way back, of course." The president of the chamber of commerce stretched her lips in a smile so insincere that Liam actually winced. Maya Chu. Yep. He'd slept with her—or came close, he couldn't quite remember—back in the day. "So we're thrilled—thrilled, I tell you—that he's back. Yeah. Super to have a new business in this building. So, best of luck and all that, Liam. Here's to the success of Granite Motorcycle Garage or whatever."

Grand openings were just not his thing in general, but being introduced by a woman who clearly wanted to stick a pin in his eye—or some other soft part—kind of put a damper on things. But the garage looked great—all the machinery set up and gleaming, a few cool bike designs, matted and framed, hanging on the wall. In the far bay was the big Chevy truck and trailer he used to pick up and deliver bikes, his logo stenciled on the side. And there, right in the middle of the garage, currently being fawned over by a dozen or so people, were two custom bikes he'd built in California and his own special-edition Triumph.

But Nicole was supposed to have come right after school, and she wasn't here. And wasn't answering her phone. As he shook hands and accepted congratulations, he mentally reviewed her schedule. Lacrosse practice on Monday and Tuesday, debate team on Thursday…nothing on Friday. So where was she?

"Hi, I'm Bruce. Bruce Schmottlach. I met you at Guten Tag the other night, remember? I also taught band at the high school, though I don't think I had you. You played guitar, right?"

"Right," Liam said, surprised. "Thanks for coming."

"So, I was out for a run the other day," Bruce said, "maybe six, seven miles out of town on Cemetery Road, and some future organ donor flew past me on a Harley, must've been doing over a hundred miles an hour, no helmet. That wasn't you, was it?"

"No," Liam answered, glancing again at his phone. Still no return call or text from Nicole. "I wear a helmet. And I don't ride a Harley." Or any bike, since the accident.

"Okay. Well, whoever it was, he'll be dead soon, and the world will be a little safer. Oops, my wife is giving me the sign. Nice seeing you, son."

"Same here, sir."

The man wasn't the only one with an elephant-like memory. In the weeks since he'd been back, he'd heard from seven women who remembered him from high school and wanted to take him out for a drink for old times' sake. He'd run into at least that many women who seemed to want to knee him in the balls, including Maya Chu, who kept shooting him the Slitty Eyes of Death.

Just about every business owner in the downtown had come to his grand opening. The Osterhagens, the woman from the yarn shop (how she paid her rent was a mystery to Liam. Yarn? How much yarn would you have to sell to make a living?), Rose, the owner of Rosebud's, the local bar, who'd made a pass at him last week…the guy from the bookstore.

"Is this your bike?" asked a woman about his age. Redhead, short hair, gorgeous. And not interested in him, if his gaydar was working properly. He felt his shoulders relax a little.

"That's my bike," he answered. "A 2009 T100 50th Anniversary Bonneville Triumph. All the glamour of old, all the comfort of today."

"Pretty gorgeous," she said. "Lola! We should get a bike, don't you think? I'm Kelsey, this is my partner, Lola, and we run the bakery down the street."

"Great bagels," he said.

"Thanks. Lola, doesn't this place make you want a bike? We've been talking about it for a while. You could make us matching rides, couldn't you?"

"I sure could," Liam said, smiling. See? Not every woman hated him or wanted to do him. He should find more lesbians to hang out with.

"Let's do it," Lola said. "You're right, babe. Life is short."

"Shorter if you ride a motorcycle," someone said. Ah. Mrs. Osterhagen. "But Liam, you'll be careful, right? You don't want to die in some horrible accident and leave that beautiful girl of yours an orphan. Poor thing's suffered enough."

Liam found his shirt was suddenly clammy, and his heart was squeezing in painfully slow, crushing beats. "Speaking of my daughter, I have to, uh, check in. Back in a flash."

He ran into his office and called her cell. Voice mail, damn it. "Nicole, this is your father. Where are you, honey? It's the grand opening, I was hoping you'd be here. Call me." Then he called their home phone and left the same message.

He took a deep breath. He'd give this opening about ten more minutes; then he had to find his daughter. The second he left his office, a woman pounced. "Hi, Liam. Long time no see."

Oh, shit. Another one. "Hey. How are you?" he said, wracking his brain for a name, a memory. Nada. Maybe because he'd lived in so many places, maybe because he'd been away for almost twenty years, but hell, he just didn't have the same recall as Bellsford residents seemed to.

"So, I couldn't help thinking about that time in Mr. Bowie's history class, you know?"

"Um…yeah. Sure." Nope, still nothing. But obviously he'd gone to school with this woman, even if she looked fifty—three chins, lank hair, those weird square glasses that made women look like they wanted to kick something.

"So, maybe we could grab a beer sometime, catch up? I'm divorced. No kids."

"That's really nice of you, but my daughter needs a lot of…you know…time. And attention."

"Sorry about Emma, by the way." She lifted her skinny eyebrows—*We're both single, get it?* Sorry, his ass. For all her popularity in high school, women didn't seem to miss Emma all that much. Well. Cordelia Osterhagen had gotten all teary-eyed. That had been…sincere.

"So, how about it, Liam? I still have that tattoo you-know-where."

Eesh. "I have to run. Nice seeing you," he said. He went out into the garage and cleared his throat loudly. "Okay, guys, thanks for coming and checking out the place. Um…we're available for motorcycle repair, customizing your existing bike or building you something from scratch. Great seeing everyone. I'm sure we'll run into each other around town. Thanks again."

"Oh, and Liam, if you don't mind…" Max Osterhagen stood on a crate. "Tonight, folks, as you might know, Guten Tag is welcoming back our wonderful niece, Gretchen Heidelberg, also known as the Barefoot Fraulein from TV! So please come by, open bar, lots of great food, and stay till you're stuffed! And meet our famous and beautiful niece!"

At the mention of "open bar," the garage began to empty. Finally.

One more call. But his daughter, his baby, his precious angel, the one thing he'd done right in his entire life, still wasn't answering. "Nicole, it's me," he said trying to sound calm and authoritative and not in full-blown panic. "I'm on my way home. Call me if you get this. Be there in a sec."

Maybe she was texting the nice boy. Or listening to music, so she didn't hear either the landline or her cell, which was usually glued to her hands. Or she was in the shower. Or being held at gunpoint. Or lying in the trunk of a Buick, wrists and ankles wrapped in duct tape, about to be tossed in the river, wondering why, oh, why her dad hadn't charged to her rescue, as fathers were supposed to.

He left the garage at a run, waving to a few people as he dodged down the brick sidewalks. Past the bakery with the biker-chick owners, past the head shop, past the Italian restaurant that always smelled so good. Down the little alley, onto Court Street. It was 1.7 miles from the garage, which was the last business in the downtown section of Bellsford, to home. The sweat that plastered Liam's shirt to his back had less to do with the fact that he was running and much more with the fact that he was…yes, it was certain now…freaking out. The rational part of his brain knew his worst fears had very slim odds of being realized. He was freaking out nonetheless. The sound of his footsteps on the pavement counted out the seconds till he could be sure Nicole was safe.

When Emma had died, it had been awful, of course. Eight months from diagnosis to death, eight months to try to prepare their child for heartbreak. The shock of grief is perhaps the worst part, that stunning realization that your time with this person is simply up. No arguing, no bargaining, no maybe tomorrows. Over.

But he and Nicole had done okay, so long as "okay" was a relative term. They'd gone for some grief counseling; she'd joined a group made up of kids who'd lost a parent, and he'd joined something similar for spouses. Life didn't change so much as shrink. It had been awful…but also manageable. Were there times when Nicole had sobbed in his arms, inconsolable? Of course. Nights when Liam had sat at the kitchen table with a glass of whiskey, unable to set foot in their bedroom? Yep. But there were other times when Nic had come home from school and giggled over her math teacher's polyester shirt. Nights when Liam had gone to bed and fallen right asleep.

His main focus had been Nicole, getting her through the worst parts, being father and mother both, adjusting to the fact that no one would spell him, no one would ease the crushing responsibility of raising a child, no one else would love Nicole as much as he did. It was brutal. But he was getting through it.

Until the accident. Then everything got messed up somehow. And Nicole, who didn't even know there'd *been* an accident, was starting to sense weakness, and when a kid senses weakness, and that kid is fifteen years old, and way too beautiful and completely unaware of just how filthy were the thoughts of men, and when she wanted some freedom and some space…well…things weren't so *manageable* anymore.

There. The apartment building was just ahead. Liam sprinted the last block and burst into the foyer, then, because the elevator gave him some major *agita* lately, bolted up the stairs. One flight…two… three…shit, he was getting old, this was taking forever, his legs felt like lead… What if he had a heart attack right here on the landing…four…and Nicole found his dead body…five.

Liam burst into the small hallway that separated the apartments and dug in his pocket for the key.

"Liam? Is that you?" A small gray head peeked out from underneath the security chain on 5B.

"Hi, Mrs. Antonelli, can't talk now."

"Well, I saw you running all the way down the street! Look at you! Is everything all right?"

"Everything's fine. Just a little late, that's all." He flashed her a smile and went in. "Nicole? Nic? You around, hon?"

No answer.

He ran down the hall to her room. "Nicole?" Shoved the door open.

"Dad! Could you, like, knock? Don't I get some privacy around here?"

There she was, his baby. Earbuds in, eating popcorn, lying on her bed and looking at a magazine, not in the trunk of some car, not duct-taped, not at the bottom of a river.

"I called you." He was panting, sounding, yeah, like he might drop dead any second.

"Oh. Guess I didn't hear."

"Nicole, you have to answer the phone if I call!" he barked.

"Dad, I said I was sorry!"

"No, you didn't!"

"I'm *sorry*." She finally looked up. "You okay?" Her face creased in a frown. "Daddy, you're all sweaty."

"I'm fine."

"You're a whack job," she said, returning her attention to the magazine. "What, did you think there'd been, like, a break-in?"

"No," Liam said, still panting like a dying racehorse. "Nope, just felt like running. Exercise. Stay healthy. You know. But I was glad to see you locked the door. Good girl. Don't ever forget that."

"Whatever."

"No, not *whatever,* Nicole. You always lock the door. The dead bolt and the doorknob lock and the safety chain."

"*Okay,* Dad. I will lock the door against the alien hordes, I swear to God." She gave him an ironic smile, looking so much like Emma that it made his chest ache even more.

"So, I thought you were coming today, Nic."

"Coming to what?" She flipped the page and cooed over an outfit.

"Nicole, today was the opening of the garage. It would've been nice if you'd been there."

His daughter frowned. "I thought it was on the twenty-first."

"No. It was today. The twelfth."

She heaved herself off the bed and went to the kitchen, where the calendar of their daily events hung in the pantry closet. "Look, Dad. Right here, your handwriting, the twenty-first." She gave him a fond smile. "You messed up, Captain Dyslexia."

Liam stared at the calendar. She was right.

"Sorry I missed it, Daddy."

"That's why I called you. A lot."

She pulled her phone from her jacket, which hung over the back of a kitchen chair, no matter how many times he'd told her to hang it up properly. "Oh. Wow. Eleven times. That's really neurotic." Another tolerant smile.

"Nicole, it's not funny. You really have to answer the phone. I was worried."

"Dad. Please. I'm almost sixteen."

"Exactly." Liam went to the sink and washed his hands—fifty-five seconds—and then splashed water on his face.

"So," Nicole said. "I have that party tonight at the Graftons', remember? And I'm sleeping over?"

Liam exhaled slowly and tossed the paper towels in the trash. "Right. Except we need to rethink that."

Nicole's tolerant mood evaporated instantly. Her hands went to her hips, and her chin jutted out, just as it had when she was three. "Dad, you told me last week I could go! You said! You promised!"

"I didn't promise. I said yes, but it was conditional."

"No! It wasn't!"

"Look," he said carefully. "I don't really know the Graftons—"

"Mrs. Grafton called you! Twice! You met her at the band concert!"

"Right, but what do I know about her really? And this party… Are there guns in the house? Dogs that bite? Alcohol?"

"No, no, and yes. No guns. A cockapoo puppy, so I don't think anyone's going to get, like, mauled. And yes, they have alcohol, Dad, the parents are allowed to drink, but it's not like they're going to serve us martinis, okay?"

Liam sighed and looked at the ceiling. "Something's come up. The Osterhagens are having a party tonight at the restaurant, and they want us both to come. They like you." It was true. Liam had taken Nicole to Guten Tag for dinner last week, and both Osterhagens had fussed over her. Him, too, which had been kind of nice.

"Of course they like me," Nicole said. "I'm adorable. And they're really nice and stuff, but I'm not coming. I'm going to Alexa's party, and I'm sleeping over. You gave me permission, I've been an angel all week, so you can't ground me, I got an A on my physics test—"

"You did? Good girl."

"And Alexa is my first new friend, and I'm going. And that's all she wrote, Dad."

It was one of Emma's sayings. She used to slap down the lid of her laptop and say just that.

"You'll call me every fifteen minutes," Liam said.

"No, Dad. I won't. But I'll call you once, okay?"

"Every half hour. Text or call. It's reasonable."

"It's *insane*. I'll text you twice and call you once. And I'll call you before ten tomorrow morning and let you know when I'm coming home."

"You'll text me four times and call me four times."

"Three texts, two calls. That's my final offer. Otherwise, I may lose this cell phone."

Liam grinned and kissed his daughter's head. "You lose that cell phone, and I'll have the police at the Graftons' house so fast you won't know what hit you."

"That'd be funny, except it's so tragically true." She smiled up at him. "So I can go, right?"

"Yeah. If you want your old man to go off to a party all by himself and have no one to talk to, you can go."

Nicole opened the fridge and took out an apple. "You won't be going alone. Mrs. Antonelli's going, too. I told her you'd take her."

"Wow. Thanks. She's definitely my type. Some people think the over-eighty crowd is past their prime, but not me."

"Dad, gross, okay?" She took a bite of her apple and gave him a critical scan. Time was, she used to come running to meet him, jump into his arms and want to do nothing more than snuggle against his shoulder. He reached out now, touched a strand of her pretty hair. She gave him a distracted smile, then tucked the strand behind her ear.

"Is the cute boy going to the party?" Liam asked, bracing for the answer.

Nicole shrugged, but her cheeks turned pink. "He was invited."

"And does he have a name?"

"Tanner. Tanner Talcott."

What a *stupid* name. A pretty-boy name, a boy-band name, the name of a boy who knew how to get a girl to do things that would give her father cardiac arrest. "Tanner Talcott. Well, listen, sweetheart. Boys only want one thing, of course, and guess what that means for you? Heartbreak. Pregnancy. Chlamydia, herpes, syphilis, crabs."

"That's beautiful, Dad. You should set it to music."

"I was a teenage boy once," he said. "One thing. Sex."

"Again. So gross."

"No drinking. No smoking. No drugs. No sex."

Nicole repeated the phrase, rap-style.

Liam sighed. "Yeah, okay, honey, but if you have any problem—any—you call me, okay? Your dear old dad will always come rescue you."

She smiled. "I know." Her phone chimed. "Oh! They're here!" She ran down the hall and returned with her overnight bag, already packed, and her Cookie Monster stuffed animal, which she slid into a side pocket. She'd slept with Cookie Monster since birth. Good. How much trouble could a girl get into with Cookie watching?

"Don't obsess, okay, and try to get a life, Dad. Have fun at the party. Talk to people. Smile." She kissed him on the cheek. "And take a shower. You smell like a locker room."

Liam walked his daughter down, waved to the Graftons—Bill was a police officer, Leah was an E.R. nurse, so how bad could it get? Then again, George Tate had been a congressman, Louise Tate a gynecologist, and he'd managed to do all sorts of things with their daughter.

Shit.

Banging his head gently against the wall, Liam wondered, not for the first time and most definitely not for the last, just how the hell he was going to survive his daughter's adolescence.

"Is that what you're wearing? To a party? In my day, we'd have at least dressed up."

Posey sighed. "Well, this is dressed up for me, Vivian. But thanks."

The ancient lady peered through her glasses as if examining human remains, then frowned even more and picked up her iPhone, her arthritic old thumbs tapping out a message. "Why don't people dress for parties anymore?" Viv muttered. "And…there. Posted on my wall. Is that how you're wearing your hair, Posey? It doesn't suit you."

Self-consciously, Posey reached up and tried to smoosh down the back cowlick, the one that defied even the strongest goo out there. So much for delighting Vivian with her girliness tonight. "Anyway, Viv, I swung by the estate today."

The old lady's face softened. "Did you? How does it look?"

Posey smiled. On this, at least, she and Vivian agreed. Viv's former home was magnificent. "So beautiful. The apple trees are just budding out, and the sun was streaming through the stained-glass in the foyer."

"You went in the morning, then?" Viv asked wistfully.

"Mmm-hmm."

"That was my favorite time of day. Just about ten o'clock, the house so quiet, the birds singing. I'd write letters at the little desk in the rose parlor.…" Her creaky voice trailed off.

Posey took Vivian's hand in her own. "Why don't you let me take you out there, Vivian? Might do your soul some good."

Viv straightened up indignantly, removing her hand. "My soul is none of your concern."

"True enough," Posey said. "But I'd love to take you just the same."

Vivian gave her a cool look. "You'll be late for your party if you don't leave now," she said. "And you may well want to go home to change into a proper dress first."

"This is as good as it gets," Posey said. "But you're right. Can't put it off any longer."

"This is the welcome home party for your sister?" Viv asked.

"Cousin. But yes. You sure you don't want to come? Everyone would be wicked glad to see you."

"And by everyone, do you mean that chatterbox you employ and the silent man who's afraid of her?"

"Mmm-hmm."

"Thank you, no. I have bridge tonight."

"Roger that. Wish I did, too." Posey stood up and straightened out her frock. Vivian was probably right…the dress was a little goofy, blue with pink flowers and silly little strings that tied on her shoulders. Plus, it had that smooshy gathered fabric over the chest, and it itched. But it wasn't easy to find something in her size…especially at the last moment. Stacia had specifically requested that she wear a dress, and so here she was. Itchy and feeling less than beautiful. "Knock 'em dead," she said, kissing Vivian's soft and withered cheek.

"We're all over ninety," Vivian said. "There's a high probability of death on any night. If you come back on Monday, I may be ready to sign the salvage rights to you. We'll see."

"I come by every Monday," Posey said. "You don't have to bribe me."

"Don't I?"

"You don't. See you Monday."

As she struggled into her truck, Posey sighed. Tonight was the official start of the Barefoot Fraulein taking over as head chef of Guten Tag.

Hard to believe Gret was back. Posey was positive there was a story here—the Barefoot Fraulein living in Posey's old room? When Posey had asked her plans at dinner last week, Gretchen had been vague. "It's so good to be back," she said, squeezing Stacia's hand. "Why rush me off, right, Auntie?" And Stacia, of course, had clucked her assent as Max nodded.

Posey acknowledged that it would've been nice to have had a date for this. The night would've felt a lot different if she'd had Dante on her arm, giving her those dark Mediterranean looks he did so well. But she hadn't had so much as a text since The Talk.

Dang it. She pulled into a parking space and headed toward Guten Tag, catching a glimpse of herself in the windows. She didn't have girly shoes—well, she had one pair, but the heels were almost fatally high. The boots had looked cute enough at home, but you know, maybe they weren't working. Steel-toed engineer boots and sundresses…then again, maybe she'd start a trend. It had a certain carefree appeal, right? Maybe? No? She checked her reflection again. It was a no. Ah, well. Too late now.

Guten Tag was mobbed, which was weird enough. A giant banner hung across the front—*Guten Tag says Wilkommen to the Barefoot Fraulein, Gretchen Heidelberg!* And there was a life-size cutout of Gretchen herself, dressed in traditional German clothing, boobs pushed up almost to her chin.

"Wow," Posey said as her brother and Jon approached.

"That bra must be made of steel," Jon said. "That, or they Photoshopped out the two dwarves standing under there, hefting those puppies up."

Posey laughed. "Having fun, boys?"

"Your brother's hoping for an amputation to get him out of this."

"I'm actually hoping for a reattachment," Henry said, perfectly serious. "I've done three amputations this week alone."

"We have friends here from Boston," Jon said. "Come! Meet! And, oh, sweetheart, those boots? Why didn't we call me?"

Jon and Henry's friends seemed to be having a jolly time. Posey chatted a few minutes, then announced the need for a beverage.

"Posey," Jon added. "We're planning to ditch in about an hour and head to Portsmouth for dinner. Want to come?"

Posey grimaced. "Yes. But I can't. I'm the daughter."

"You can do it! If Henry can…"

"Well, you know, Henry's the son. He can do whatever he wants."

Jon sighed. "Sad, but true. Oh, the curse of the double standard! You sure? You can sneak out. Gretchen won't notice."

"No, but Mom and Dad would. That's okay. It's fine. You guys have fun." She patted his arm and headed for the bar, only to bump right into the Barefoot Fraulein herself.

"Posey! I'm so glad you're here!" Gretchen pounced and, holy Elvis, could she show more boob? More leg? She wore a silky cream-colored scrap of fabric that clung to her curves, most notably the junk in her trunk. "You look so cute!" Gretchen pinched her cheek, and Posey twisted away.

"Gretchen. Don't you look…pretty."

"You're so sweet! Let me introduce someone. Posey, this is Dante Bellini. Dante, this is my little cousin, Posey Osterhagen."

"We've met, Gretchen," Posey said, her stomach flipping. Dante? In Guten Tag without turning into a pillar of salt?

"Good to see you, Posey." He smiled, and a little flare of hope fired in her chest. Had he come because he knew she'd be here?

"Of *course* you know each other! I keep forgetting how small a town Bellsford is. I guess I'm still used to New York. Oh, I'm sorry, the reporter from Channel 2 is waving. You two chat, get something to eat, have some tapas. *Essen und geniessen!* Or, as you might say, Dante, *mangia!*" She flashed her painfully white teeth and wove through the crowd, leaving Posey and Dante in a cloud of her musky perfume.

Tapas? Since when did German restaurants have tapas?

"How are you?" Dante asked.

"I'm good." She smiled. "How've you been, Dante?"

"Great. I have to say, I didn't realize you knew her." Dante's eyes drifted over to Gretchen, who had seemed to have surgically attached herself to the reporter from Channel 2, laughing and tossing her hair and posing for pictures. "She's quite a force to be reckoned with."

"Um…yeah." That dark Mediterranean look was still on Gretchen…her boobs, specifically. Posey crossed her arms over her chest, which made things itchier, then unfolded them. "I'm a little surprised to see you here, Dante."

He had the grace to look sheepish. "Well, Gretchen invited me. Said there's plenty of room for two gourmet restaurants on the same block, no reason to be enemies." He took a sip of his drink. "I had no idea you were related."

"Yeah, well, I guess you and I didn't do too much talking," Posey said, a trifle sharply.

Dante didn't bat an eyelash. "You two close?" he asked.

"I guess so. She's my only cousin."

Finally, he turned his full attention back to her and gave her a long look, then a smile. "It's good to see you."

Much better. "You, too," she said, feeling the same pull of attraction she'd felt two months ago. Maybe this break was just the thing to get them to move to a real relationship, after all.

"Posey!" Mrs. Schmottlach swooped in and gave Posey a big smooch on the cheek. "You look beautiful!"

"Hi, Mrs. S. Thanks, same to you."

"Isn't this so exciting for your parents?" she said. "That Gretchen is a wonder. So pretty, and *so* talented. Oh, honestly, there's Bruce. The man can't be alone for more than ten seconds without wondering if I've left him for another man. Bye, sweetie! I love you in a dress!"

Posey turned back to Dante. He was gone. Dang it.

Standing on tiptoe, she could just glimpse Henry, Jon and their friends in a corner, schmoozing and laughing (well, Henry was checking his phone, hoping for a reattachment).

Time for that drink. Posey slipped and slid through the crowd, saying hello here and there, getting a kiss or hug from her parents' friends, until she made it to the bar, where Otto was on duty. "Hey, there, look at you, in a dress and everything!" he said.

"It happens," she answered. "How about a whiskey sour, Otto?"

"Coming up!" A minute later, he handed her the drink.

"Thanks, pal." She slid a ten into his tip jar and sat back to look around. There were a number of waiters she didn't recognize—college kids, probably—who looked out of place in black jeans and white T-shirts when the regular staff wore the traditional German costumes.

Suddenly, her dad's voice boomed out. "Zicke zacke, zicke zacke!"

"Hoi, hoi, hoi!" Posey chorused along with the rest of the crowd.

"Folks, it's so wonderful to have you here! Thank you for coming! Without further ado, the Barefoot Fraulein, Gretchen Heidelberg!"

Posey clapped dutifully as her cousin, feigning modesty, slipped her arm around Max. "Uncle Max, Aunt Stacia, thank you so, so much! It's such a thrill to be here, back with my family, taking over Guten Tag. And you all have been so warm and wonderful in welcoming me, thank you all so much!" She flashed her teeth again and wiped a tear (or pretended to wipe a tear). "Guten Tag will be undergoing some changes, a new look, and maybe even a new name! But you'll always have the same wonderful time you've always had here. So zicke zacke, zicke zacke!"

"Hoi, hoi, hoi!"

A new look? A new name? Since when? Posey closed her mouth, then took a slug of her drink. Granted, the restaurant could use a little…updating, maybe. But Stacia and Max loved it, didn't they? And to Posey, it was as much home as her parents' house.

Another hipster waiter walked past with a tray of something. Posey snagged an appetizer and popped it into her mouth. Flaky dough, cheesy, some meat inside. Fantastic, if minuscule. Before she could grab another one, the waiter was gone.

The reporter from Channel 2 was gesturing for Max, Stacia and Gretchen to stand together. Posey couldn't hear what the question was, but Gretchen, standing in the middle, did most of the talking.

Huh. Her drink was empty. Time for another, that was clear. She waved to Otto and held up her empty glass. She was already a little dizzy, but in a pleasant way. And pleasant was called for. She caught a glimpse of Glubby, the moose with the broken antler. Would Glubby make the cut in the new look? If not, he'd always have a home in her church. She would not leave Glubby, that was for sure. Glubby was her friend. Glubby and his broken antler were more than welcome at her house.

People who weigh a hundred and seven pounds should not have two drinks on an empty stomach, a voice in her head warned. True enough. She would kill to scratch her boobs right now. Probably not advisable in public, though. Oh, to be home with Shilo right now, searching Google for pictures of James Franco. It would sure beat this.

"Thanks, pal," she said as Otto handed her the whiskey sour. There was another waiter with another batch of tiny appetizers. Could she take the whole plate? She was starving. She managed to snag one—more flaky stuff—and popped it in her mouth. The room spun just a little. Kinda fun.

"Hey," came a voice. Posey looked, then closed her eyes. Liam Murphy. Black high-tops, black pants, black shirt, black hair, looking like a really hip Lucifer. *Hey, there. Feel like a sin or two?*

"Yes," she said. A flake of pastry fluttered out of her mouth. Great. Smokin' Hot Lucifer and the Simple Farm Girl.

"Nice dress," Liam said, giving her a disdainful scan.

"Bite me," Posey said.

His eyebrows rose in surprise. "Sorry?" he asked.

Oops. Maybe he wasn't disdainful. Maybe she was channeling or projecting or whatever that word was. "Nothing. How are you, Liam?" He didn't answer, engrossed in his phone. Ass.

The last appetizer (tapas…please) had something spicy in it. Posey's lips stung, so she took another sip of whiskey sour. It didn't work; her lips still stung. She licked them. Liam glanced up, as if sensing tongue, then went back to his phone, dismissing her. Which he was good at, it must be acknowledged. A true gift.

Posey looked around. Mom and Dad, perpetually welded together at any social event, were schmoozing off by the kitchen; she could hear Dad's booming laugh. Did they really want to change Guten Tag? In her entire life, it had never been discussed. And you know, maybe they could've asked her opinion. Asked for some help, being that she had the furnishings to redecorate ten restaurants in Irreplaceable's barn.

There must've been a hundred people here—she recognized the mayor and mean Maya from the chamber of commerce who never remembered her name. Kelsey and Lola from the pastry shop waved; Posey probably stopped there enough to fund a mortgage payment. Sure, she knew everyone. But she was still alone. And being alone at a party, even a party hosted by your parents…well, it sucked. Kate and James had a standing movie date on Friday nights, carved in stone, though how much longer the kid would put up with that, Posey didn't know.

She glanced at Liam, who was still checking his stupid phone.

"How are you, Cordelia?" he asked without looking up. And did he have to use that name? Huh?

"I have leprosy," she said.

"Cool," he murmured, his thumbs texting away. Posey rolled her eyes. Whee! The room spun.

"So, how do they treat leprosy these days?" Liam said, sliding his phone into his pocket, and Posey choked a little on her drink. Okay, first of all, apparently he had been listening. And second of all, hot *diggety,* he was gorgeous. Eyes so green and clear, just the hint of a smile on his face, like he was just a sin begging for a taker. Posey forced herself to look away, her face practically crackling with heat. Bieber! The man. Was. Edible.

His hands were in his pockets, and he seemed to have no inclination to leave. "Is your daughter here?" she asked.

Liam shook his head. "She's at a sleepover. Teenagers, you know."

Wow. Two whole sentences. Well, one sentence and a fragment. Still, it dawned on her that this could be classified as a real live conversation, which in turn made her mind go completely blank. If—just if—she wanted to charm Liam (not that she'd be dumb enough to try, mind you), but if she wanted to make him see that she was someone worth knowing and perhaps regret that he'd ever said anything mean about her, thus altering the course of her life (sort of)—now was the time.

"So," she offered. Not exactly brilliant repartee. "How's business?"

"We opened today."

"Oh." Wow. They were on a roll now. *Think of something to say, idiot,* her brain commanded. Otherwise, it was devoid of conversation ideas. She sighed and took another slug of her drink.

"Liam! My man! Dude, how you been?"

Ah, bieber. It was Rick. Rick Balin, world's worst prom date, New Hampshire's biggest beer belly. His little finger was still bandaged. Weenie.

Liam took the offered hand. "Hey," he said.

"Dude, I heard you were back in town! So cool. And that motorcycle place? Awesome. Meant to come by today, couldn't. I've been thinking about getting a chopper myself. Gotta have a sweet ride, know what I mean? Of course you do. What are you riding these days? Dude, we have to hang out. Wanna grab a beer sometime? Catch up?"

Liam's expression was totally cool...and totally blank. Well, well, well, Posey thought, leaning against the bar with a very slight wobble, Batman didn't remember Robin. Robin had, of course, gained about seventy pounds, lost half his hair, but still. Kinda funny.

"Man, we had some fun in those days, didn't we? God, I miss high school," Rick said, sighing. "Dude, Grey Goose martini, make it dry," he said to Otto. "I love my Grey Goose," he added to Liam. He had yet to acknowledge Posey, which was A-okay by her. "Sure, it costs more, but who cares? Gotta have the best. Right?"

Liam gave Posey a level look and smiled. Eyes crinkling, gorgeous, smokin' hot. He looked right into her eyes, like she was the only other person in this entire restaurant, and Rick the Idiot Balin was their own private joke.

Holy Elvis. She was halfway to Planet Orgasm. Imagine if they bumped heads or something. She took a quick gulp of her drink and looked away.

Hello? Been here, done that regarding Hottie McSin here, a faint little voice said from far, far away. But that smile...and those eyes...

"Hello, hello! Posey, why are you hiding over here? Come out and mingle! Auntie and Max are looking for you!" Gretchen appeared, grabbed Posey by the arm and heaved her away from Liam. "Hi, there. We met a couple weeks ago. I'm Gretchen Heidelberg? The Barefoot Fraulein?"

"I remember," Liam said, turning that smile to Gretchen, and whatever champagne bubbles were just dancing merrily through Posey's veins went abruptly flat.

"Holy crap!" Rick brayed. "You're even more beautiful than on TV!"

Posey turned to the bar to give Otto her glass—she knew better than to have another, that was for sure. When she turned back around, she was presented with Dante's back, because the two men had flanked Gretchen. Because apparently it was the law that if you were male, you had to worship the Barefoot Fraulein.

Posey tripped off to find her parents. Good thing she hadn't remembered to wear girly shoes, because it was getting dizzy in here. There they were, Stacia and Max, holding hands. So cute, her parents, and resembling each other more and more these days. They were roughly the same height—six-two—both with the fading blond hair and the strong-boned features of Bavaria. Soon, Posey mused, they'd just sort of grow into each other like two trees.

"Hey, you two trees," she said, smiling.

"Baby! There you are!" Stacia broke free from Max to give Posey a kiss. "Are you having fun? Oh, you're flushed. Do you have a fever?" She pressed a hand to Posey's forehead, the human thermometer. "Ninety-eight point four. Hmm."

"I had a drink," Posey explained.

"Are you enjoying the party, Turnip?" Max asked.

She looked up at them, her doting parents. They seemed so happy. And if Gretchen taking over made them happy—even if that meant Glubby had to come home with her—she wasn't going to say a word. "You bet. So much fun. So, a new look, huh?"

"We should go talk to the mayor," Max said. "Come with us, sweetie. The newspaper wants a picture."

"You know what? I'm gonna pass," she said, enunciating carefully. "I have to find some more of those green thingies. They were great. Have fun! See you later!" Posey kissed her parents, almost but not quite losing her balance. She watched as they schmoozed and laughed, but when Gretchen joined them for the photo op, Posey decided it was time to become invisible again.

CHAPTER SEVEN

"DID I TELL YOU I'M on a new hormone replacement?" Mrs. Antonelli asked.

Liam choked on his beer. "Uh...no. No, you didn't."

"It works *much* better," she said.

"I—I'm glad," he said, not daring to look at her. Did she go around telling everyone this kind of thing? Was this some kind of geriatric pass? Would this party ever end? Liam glanced at his watch.

"What time is it, dear?" Mrs. Antonelli asked.

"Almost nine," he answered.

"Oh! I have to go. I have to take my blood-pressure medicine at nine-thirty. And that estrogen. Don't want to be late with that, if you know what I mean."

He didn't. But he had come with the old lady, so taking her home was his duty. Hopefully, he wouldn't be fending off any Bengay-scented passes in the elevator. Meanwhile, a woman was giving him the eye, doing the hair toss and sidelong look. Why not just whip her bra off and toss it to him, huh? The message was received. Just not wanted.

His phone buzzed. *Nicole,* the screen read. Good girl, right on time for her check-in. "I have to take this, Mrs. A," he said, taking the phone out of his pocket. "It's my daughter."

"Oh, that's fine, sweetheart. I've got a ride with Lenore. She's coming up to watch *CSI: Miami.* It's our tradition. See you at home!"

God bless you, Lenore. "Hi, honey," he said into the phone.

"Hi, Dad! Are you having fun?"

"Oh, yeah. You?"

"It's really great. We're about to watch *Drag Me to Hell,* so I have to make this short."

"Nic, you know you don't like scary movies," he said.

"When I was, like, *nine,* Dad. I'm fine. So, I'll call you later?"

He sighed. "That would be great. Thanks, honey."

"Love you."

"I love you, too, Nicole."

She hung up before he'd finished saying it. Well, Liam guessed if Mrs. Antonelli could go, so could he. Maybe watch the Sox, despite their wretched start this year. Pay some bills. Check the locks. All that fun stuff.

He said his goodbyes to the Osterhagens and managed to avoid the red-faced fat guy who'd cornered him earlier. Someone from high school, obviously.

Those weren't years he was particularly proud of. Then again, those years had brought him to Emma, so there was that. But before her, yeah, he'd been a shit. A few people remembered him fondly—the Osterhagens, of course, and the librarian who'd helped him stumble through Shakespeare. Marty, who'd let Liam work at his garage, had come by the other day and schmoozed about engines. Liam had even run into one of the bouncers from the bar in Kittery where he'd played a couple times, trying to pick up a little extra money before the Osterhagens hired him.

But then there were the people who weren't so glad to see him. The girls-turned-women like Maya who, though more than willing enough back then, now seemed to hold a grudge. In the supermarket the other day, some guy shot him a dark glance and muttered "Dick." No clue why, other than the suspicion that it had something to do with a female. Twenty years ago. Grudges seemed to be an art form around here.

But Bellsford was a pretty town, too, unlike anything in Southern California, Liam thought as he stepped out of the overheated restaurant into the cool night air. The downtown was crammed with little shops and restaurants, and antique iron lampposts lit the brick sidewalks. On one corner was the huge old granite bank, and across the street, the big brick church with a white steeple spearing up into the dark sky. Not the boonies, not the city, and just perfect for Nicole, he hoped.

The Tates were certainly glad to have them back. Well, glad to have Nicole back, the only child of their only child. If they had never warmed up to Liam, at least they appreciated the fact that he'd given them easier access to their granddaughter. Said access might bite him in the ass, granted; they were already asking if she could spend every weekend with them up in Ogunquit, where they'd moved when Emma was in college.

Liam crossed Boyden Street, then paused. Up ahead was a woman in a sleeveless dress and engineer boots. Cordelia Osterhagen, weaving more than walking.

He caught up to her easily. "Hey, Cordelia."

"Oh. It's you. Hi, you."

Liam smiled. "Tipsy?"

"Hmm? No, not really. Just figured I'd walk home."

"Can I walk with you?"

"You bet, God's Gift."

Wow. She was wasted.

"Do you have a car, Liam Murphy?"

"Yep. At home. You want a ride? I live down by the bridge."

"I'm walking home," she said, a little slurry. "But thanks."

Liam couldn't help a smile. Kinda fun to see little Miss Osterhagen drunk. "Where do you live?" he asked, steering her away from the fire hydrant she was about to crash into. Her arm was cold, so Liam took off his jacket and offered it to her, but she'd already wobbled over to a shop window.

"That's pretty. Don't you think?" she said, gesturing vaguely within.

He draped the jacket over her shoulders. "Very pretty. Where do you live, Cordelia?"

"I live on South Church Road. In the old church? That's why it's called South Church Road." She put her hand over her mouth and grimaced. "I think I may have overindulged, Liam Murphy."

"Gotta puke?"

"Not just yet." She took a deep breath, then looked at him. "So, how is it, biker boy? Being back, I mean. I bet a lot of people are happy to see you and a lot of people aren't."

Huh. Drunk or not, she seemed a little psychic. "That's about right. Which one are you?"

"The former. Or the latter. I always confuse those." She wove a little dangerously, and he took her arm again.

"How far is your house from here?"

"Eleven miles."

Liam blinked. "I'm driving you home, Cordelia."

"That might be a good idea. Thanks, God's Gift." Another big wobble.

"You are really drunk. How many did you have?" She couldn't weigh much.

"Two whiskey sours," she said. "But I didn't eat much. Thassa problem. The food was so small, you know? I don't like small food."

There was his building, the lights warm and welcoming. Drat. His car keys were on the kitchen counter. Liam steered her into the foyer, which was empty. "I have to run upstairs for the keys, okay? Want to wait here?" Then again, what if she wandered out? "Actually, come on up."

"Cool. I can see the Batcave."

Liam laughed. "Here we go. Into the elevator." Even if he'd rather take the stairs, he couldn't make her go up five flights of stairs when walking was already a challenge.

"This is a wicked nice elevator," she said. "I think I'll just lie down for a sec." Her legs folded underneath her.

"No, no. Up you go. Come on," he said, hauling her up by her arms. She was like limp spaghetti. "Cordelia. Come on."

"I don't feel so good," she muttered.

"Do not throw up on me," he warned, slipping an arm around her.

"Why, pretty boy? You too good for that?"

"Two drinks, huh? I'll have to remember that." The bell dinged for the fifth floor, and as she didn't seem capable of getting out of the elevator under her own power, he half dragged her into the hall, then sort of propped her up against the wall. She started to slide down, so he leaned into her, pinning her there as he pulled out his keys. With luck, Mrs. Antonelli was engrossed in her TV show…at least she wasn't peering through the door, offering suggestions. Liam managed to get the key in, then turned it and pushed the door open.

He glanced at her face—her eyes were still closed. Long eyelashes, kind of wispy. She smelled nice, like oranges. She also may have been asleep. The thought of driving her home and leaving her alone… maybe it wasn't such a good idea.

"Cordelia?"

"Mmm-hmm?" she said, not opening her eyes.

"Want to stay here tonight? I have a guest room."

She opened one eye. "I don't think your kid should see me sleeping over," she whispered. "But it would be great if you could get me home."

It was kind of thoughtful of her, he had to admit, worrying about Nicole. "My daughter's at a friend's house."

"Oh. Okay, then." She took a wobbly step, bumped into the door frame. Screw it. He picked her up—he was right, she didn't weigh much—and carried her inside.

"Nice place," she murmured, though her eyes were still closed. Liam grinned, tried not to hit her head on the wall and carried her down the hall to the guest room door. The bed looked like an ad in a magazine, all those dopey little pillows that served no purpose he could see. Nicole had made it up during one of her domestic moments, wanting to make the room look less lonely, she'd said. Emma had always been unable to let a bed go unmade, too, even at hotels. Funny, the things you inherited.

Liam deposited Cordelia on the bed. "Comfy," she mumbled, lying back. One of the little pillows fell over her face, and, without opening her eyes, she grabbed it and flung it off.

"Glad you like it." He unlaced Cordelia's boots and pulled them off. Ugly brutes, those. Emma would've killed herself before wearing man-style work boots. Or wool socks, which Liam also removed.

"You need anything?" he asked. She didn't answer. Might have been sleeping already. Liam stood there a second or two. Should he put her under the covers? He hesitated, then just folded the bedspread over her and looked around. Back in his youth, he'd been something of an expert at putting drunks to bed, but it had been a while. He put the trashcan next to the bed in case she needed to puke. Went to the kitchen, got a glass of water and a couple aspirin and put them on the night table, then glanced around to see if there was anything else she might need.

This room hadn't been used yet; he and Nicole hadn't had any guests, though Cammie, her closest friend from San Diego, might come out this summer. And someday, much sooner than he wanted to acknowledge, his daughter would go off to college, and he'd be stuck with two empty bedrooms instead of just one. Then again, maybe she'd come back to visit and bring some friends, and the apartment would be full and happy.

Cordelia gave a little snort, then murmured something.

She was kind of cute in an elflike way, with that stick-up hair and little chin, those long wispy eyelashes. And that mouth. Not an ounce of fat on her, not much in the way of a rack, either. Nice legs, cute feet. His eyes wandered back to her mouth. That was a nice mouth. All the rest of her was lean and spare, but her lips were lush and full and pretty damn tempting.

Cordelia used to have quite a crush on him back in the day, he remembered. She'd follow him around like a little duckling who'd imprinted on the wrong thing. Given that the Osterhagens had been good to him, he kept his distance. Wouldn't be cool to let their kid fall for some punk fresh out of juvie. So he ignored her many attempts at conversation until her initial crush cooled.

Suddenly the red-faced guy clicked. Had he dated Cordelia? Liam had some flash of memory of that guy…Rob? No, Rick. Rick and Cordelia together…or maybe not. Maybe he was thinking of someone else. Those days were kind of a blur.… Bellsford was the eleventh place he'd lived in seventeen years, and he'd learned not to get real attached, which had worked just fine. Until Emma, that was.

His charge gave another snort and turned on her side.

"'Night, Cordelia," he said and closed the door gently behind him.

POSEY'S FIRST THOUGHT on waking was not optimistic. No. It was that the sunlight hated her, and really, God was quite cruel in sending this blindingly painful day, and why did her mouth taste like a landfill for poopy diapers?

She clamped a pillow over her head and groped for the comfort of Shilo. Empty. And hang on a sec… this pillow…it was foam. And her pillows were not. Hers were down. She cracked open an eye. These sheets were blue.

Her sheets were yellow.

Posey bolted upright, pain kicking her head like an angry mule. Where was she? Holy Elvis Presley, where was she? The room was nowhere she'd ever been. Ever.

In a panic, she looked around, wincing. Oh, man, the party. Otto passing over drinks like they were M&Ms, those tiny appetizers, Gretchen taking over Guten Tag. So, what happened after that? She must've gone home with someone. She'd picked someone up. Or been picked up. This was something she'd never, ever done before.

But that dress on the floor…that was hers. Boots…hers. Panties…oh, man! They were hers, too… Which meant…

Posey lifted the covers and glanced down.

She was naked.

Oh, *bieber*. Who? How? What?

Just then, a soft knock came on the door. She opened her mouth to say something, but only a squeak came out.

The door cracked. And Liam Declan Murphy looked in.

Posey yanked the covers to her chin, thoughts sloshing around like toxic waste in her sore brain. Liam? Liam Murphy? Oh, no. Oh, man. She was officially a slut. A slut! And for nothing… She'd slept with *him*, and she didn't even remember. What a waste of her first slutty night ever!

And Liam. Did he actually take her home and…do things to her? Had he also been, um…impaired? A memory floated to the surface—Liam had carried her somewhere! Horrifying! Thrilling, too, but mostly horrifying.

"Hey," he said, and there was a very appealing half grin on his face. His unshaven face. His gorgeous, unshaven, smiling face.

"Hi," she whispered, drawing up her knees to her chin, trying to disappear. Yes. Disappearing—or melting—or spontaneous combustion, any of those would be most welcome right about now.

He glanced at her clothes for a long moment, then at her face, which was on fire. "How are you feeling this morning?" he said, and his voice was just a purr, oh, bieber, bieber, bieber!

"Um…you know," she managed to squeak.

He sat on the edge of the bed. And she was naked. Her spine was already digging into the headboard. Unless she tunneled through the wall, she couldn't get any farther away. And how bad was her breath at this moment? Because it felt like she'd swallowed a decomposing dragon.

"Want some coffee?" he asked.

"No. Thanks. No, thanks, I mean."

"So…" Liam said, and, lordy, he smelled good. He must've showered, because his hair was damp, and even though she really didn't approve of people getting drunk and sleeping with men they didn't really know that well or even like that much, Posey's lady parts seemed to stretch like a waking cat. Hello! Liam Murphy is sitting inches from your naked body. Do something. Now.

"Um…Liam," Posey began, gripping the covers to her chin.

"Yeah?" he said.

Her grip on the sheets turned into a clench. "Liam, about last night…"

"What about it?"

Posey closed her eyes. Opened them. There were her clothes, still on the floor. And here was her hungover self, still naked and in Liam Murphy's bed. Sherlock Holmes would say that, yes, she'd definitely done the wild thing with God's Gift, and while that act was one she'd imagined, oh, six thousand and fifty-seven times, it wasn't exactly making her happy now. Wouldn't she remember…something? Because there was nothing in the old memory banks. Not one thing. Not even a kiss.

"Did we…um…you know?"

"Did we what?"

That half smile on his face was making thought difficult. "Um…did we…" Make love didn't sound right. Fool around? Have intercourse? Make out? Make babies? Oh, man, what if she was pregnant at this very moment? "Did we do anything last night? Anything, um…adult?"

"You don't remember?"

"No, Liam, I don't. Can you just… Did we do it or not?"

He gave her a long, steamy look, dropped his gaze to her mouth—oh, mommy—and back to her eyes. Then he grinned. "No."

"No?"

"Please. Are you kidding? Absolutely not."

Well, okay, he didn't have to say it like that. Would a tinge of regret be too much to ask for? A little wistfulness? Huh? Hmm? Would that be so hard? "So, how did my clothes get over there?" she asked.

He took a sip of coffee and cocked an eyebrow. "I don't know. I sure as hell didn't undress you."

Again with the insults. "Okay, you know, Liam, do you have to be so…" Her voice trailed off.

"So what?"

"So…emphatic."

He laughed, the sound scraping her most pleasantly. "I was gonna give you a ride home, but you were pretty, uh, limp, so I just figured you could sleep it off here." He paused. "Rather than in the elevator, like you wanted."

Bieber. That was right. Well, it was a nice elevator, if memory served.

"Are you mad that I didn't take advantage of the situation?" he asked.

"No! Jeesh! Your ego, Liam. Wow."

He smiled; she blushed.

Memories, none of them particularly flattering, flooded back. Winding through the streets of Bellsford. Liam taking off her socks. And oh, yes, the damn itchy dress. She'd just pulled it off at some point; there was a faint recollection of the blessedly cool and un-itchy sheets. As for the panties…best not to think about panties on the floor when Hottie McSin was sitting next to her, smelling the way he did.

"Want some breakfast?" he asked.

"No, thanks. Um…my dog. Is home. Alone. With the cats. So I'm gonna run."

"Okay."

"Is your daughter here? I can sneak out the back," she said, feeling her cheeks heat up again. Imagine having to face a teenager after her father carried your drunken self down the hallway…

"She's at a friend's house," Liam answered.

Right, right, she had a vague memory of him saying something about that. "Good. Great. Okay."

"I'll let you get dressed, then." He stood up and left the room, and Posey couldn't help feeling a little… disappointed. That being said, she also wasn't about to leap out of bed naked, just in case he popped back in with a question. She grabbed her clothes and got dressed under the covers. Her panties. Liam Murphy had seen her panties, for God's sake! At least they were fairly new and not hideous. Crikey. Almost violently, she tugged the dress over her head. Still itchy.

She dashed into the bathroom, rinsed out her mouth and splashed water on her face. Man. Why not just wear a sign that said Can't Hold My Liquor? Smears of mascara made her look rather like the poster child for Les Miserables, except not as adorable and far more dissolute. Her hair, never well-behaved on the best days, was completely flat on the left side, standing up straight on the right. Gorgeous. She ran her damp hands through it, knowing it was futile, took a deep breath and went down the hall.

"Thanks for watching out for me last night," she said, barely glancing at Liam. Still, she could see enough… He was lounging against the counter like he was posing for a shoot in a GQ magazine. Too beautiful to look at directly. "See you around."

"Bye, Cordelia," he said, smiling, and with that, she fled. Once in the hall, she opted for the stairs rather than the elevator. With her luck, she'd run into someone she knew, and even though it wasn't true, she knew what this all looked like. The walk of shame. Like she'd gone home with Liam and done all sorts of delightful and naughty things until the break of day.

Which, of course, was just wishful thinking.

CHAPTER EIGHT

"COME ON, TURNIP! You can do it!" Max's video camera, a prehistoric relic from the '90s, went up, as it had every single time Posey had come up to bat in the four years she'd been playing on the town softball league. There were roughly ten games a season, and on average, Posey was up to bat four times. That meant Max had roughly a hundred and sixty movies of his daughter striking out.

Baseball was something of a religion in New Hampshire, as Fenway Park was only an hour south. Alas, it just wasn't Posey's sport. Not that she'd gotten to try many, due to Stacia's rules about body contact and danger. But a few years ago, Jon, who was one of those irritating people who was good at everything from flower arrangements to sports, convinced her to join Guten Tag's team. He played shortstop—the hottest position for the hottest guy, as he liked to say. Posey was the catcher, and not a bad one at that; she threw out a fair number of runners attempting to steal second. But when it came to the bat...not so much.

And she always struck out. Never popped up, never grounded out. Nope, she went down swinging, which had a certain élan to it. She'd been hit three times, which had been thrilling, since it got her on base, even if it did leave a bruise. But she'd never scored a run, never driven in a run, never hit so much as a foul ball. It was something of a town legend.

Now, in the bottom of the second, she was up, facing José Rivera, the pitcher for Stubby's Hardware and rumored to be third cousins with half of Major League Baseball.

Brianna and James were here tonight—Kate was first baseman for Guten Tag, an excellent one at that. Both kids were a little on the fringe of high school, and Posey was glad they were hanging out more, even if Brie pretended not to like James. Shilo was there, too, lying on his back in front of the kids, waiting for them to notice his giant belly, always ready for a scratch. When they failed to comply, he let out the occasional groan until finally, James rubbed the dog's cow-like belly with his foot, earning Shilo's croon of approval.

Posey stepped into the batter's box. Her teammates all stood up and started clapping, their way of supporting the cause.

"Eye on the ball, Posey!" called Reverend Jerry. At the sound of his owner's name, Shilo sat up and woofed.

"Swing away, Merrill!" This in unison from Jon and Kate, both fans of the movie *Signs*.

"History about to happen, Posey, hon!" Bruce Schmottlach, their oldest player at seventy-eight, had a batting average of .402. But he was a bit of a freak of nature in general.

Posey took a deep breath, dug her cleats into the earth and waited. She could do it. Even a foul ball would be a triumph. José let fly and she swung with all her might. Strike one. She'd been a little late, that was all. She'd swing earlier this time. She did. Strike two.

"Hang in there, honey!" Stacia called. One more pitch. She swung. "Strike three!" called the ump, and that was that.

"That was pathetic," Brianna called. "Points for trying, though!"

"You'll get it next time, honey!" Stacia called.

"Thanks, Mom." Posey trotted back to the dugout, got on her catcher's gear, and went back to home plate.

As the batter for Stubby's came up, her face blazed with heat.

It was Liam. She hadn't seen him since the Night of Drunken Sloppiness.

"Hey," he said.

"Hi," she answered, grateful for her face mask. "Didn't know you were playing."

"Mike Owens asked me to join. Hi. Liam Murphy." He shook hands with Lou, the home plate umpire.

"Nice to meet you," Lou said. "Whenever you're ready."

Being catcher meant that Posey was eye level with Liam's groin. Granted, she was squatting and garbed in padding, but the whole thing felt very sexual nonetheless. Then again, she guessed that she could watch Liam get an appendectomy and find it hot. Which was just pathetic.

"How good are you, Liam?" she asked as Liam took a practice swing. Oh, crap, that sounded really dirty. "At baseball, I mean?"

"Not bad."

"Go, Liam! Knock it out of the park!" The women on Stubby's were all leaning out of the dugout, and was it her imagination or was there more cleavage than usual being shown tonight?

Reverend Jerry, who was pitching for Guten Tag tonight and imagined himself quite a talent, glared down from the pitcher's mound. "Prepare to feel the power of God's wrath," he said and fired off a pitch. Liam swung, and kablammy, it was gone.

"Not bad indeed," Posey said. Liam grinned and set off around the bases.

He clobbered a triple in the fourth and a double in the eighth, driving in six runs altogether, and Stubby's won, as they usually did. Liam's teammates—especially the women—swarmed around him, and there was much patting of his back and stroking of his arms, much hair tossing and laughing.

"Gotta run. James and I have a yoga class," Kate said, trading her cleats for Nikes. "Want me to bring Brianna home? It's on the way."

"Brie?" Posey asked. "What do you think?"

Brianna gave James a long, contemptuous look, then smiled. "Sure." James flushed. Posey gave Brianna a hug, reminded her of their movie date on Sunday (another *Twilight,* but at least there'd be popcorn), and slung her bag over her shoulder, then stowed Shilo in the truck with a promise of a Whopper on the way home.

"I feel like we never see each other anymore," Jon said as they walked over to Rosebud's to buy Stubby's a round.

"We had lunch together yesterday," she said.

"True, true. How's business? You get Vivian to sign yet?"

"Business is good," she said. A young couple with uncommonly good taste had come this morning and bought four stained-glass windows, a carved mantel for their fireplace, and a concrete lion, which she and Mac would deliver tomorrow on the flatbed. "But no, Viv hasn't signed."

"A shame to have that place torn down."

"Tell me about it. Is my brother meeting us here?" Posey opened the door to the bar, and the noise of the crowd and the spicy smell of buffalo wings enveloped them in a warm embrace.

"He sure is. There he is now, fighting off Rose." Rose had tried to turn Henry straight in high school, and Henry was perversely fond of her, smiling as she flirted outrageously. Gretchen was there, too.

"Does that woman ever work?" Jon asked. "I thought she'd be at the restaurant, barefooting away."

"Seems like Willem still does most of the cooking as far as I can tell," Posey said.

"She's revamping the menu. Experimenting," Stacia announced, materializing with Max and the Schmottlachs. Posey's parents looked around disapprovingly—they didn't like going to other restaurants, even Rosebud's, which was more of a bar. "Oh, there's Henry! Henry! Over here, honey! We haven't seen you in weeks!"

"We were there on Sunday," Jon muttered, and Posey smiled. Time-telling was a subjective skill where her family was concerned.

Liam stood in a cluster of people, including Taylor Bennington, one of his flings back in the day. Posey'd bet he remembered Taylor, who'd once stuffed a thong into Liam's pocket in the hallway. And Taylor was still beautiful.

"Hello, all!" Gretchen came over to their table and set down her plate, leaning over to reveal an acre of boobage. Jon held up a napkin to shield himself from the view. "How are we tonight? Does anyone want some of this artichoke dip? Oh, hi, Posey, I didn't see you there. Heard your streak's still not broken. Too bad. Maybe if you weighed a little more?"

What does a person say to that? *Bite me?* "Does everyone want their usual?" she asked, standing up.

"I'll have a glass of pinot noir, but only if it's from Willamette Valley. The California pinots this year? Why bother, right, Henry?"

Indulging in an eye roll, Posey went up to the bar. "Four Heinekens for them, one seltzer for me. And a California pinot noir for my cousin."

"Coming up," Rose said. She gave Posey her seltzer first. "That brother of yours gets cuter every year," she added with a grin, turning away to fill the rest of the order.

Liam appeared next to her, having apparently hacked through the crowd of women vying for his attention. "So, I hear you've never hit a ball," he said.

"I've broken many, though. Just saying."

"I bet." He looked at her glass. "Nonalcoholic, I hope."

Was he *flirting* with her? No. That would be… No. Still, the very thought paralyzed her brain.

"Liam! Hi! It's so good to see you!" Of course. Gretchen materialized beside Posey, pushing her out of the way with her curvy hips, and wrapped her arms around Liam like he'd just returned from Afghanistan. "Join us! Stacia has commanded it, and you know how she is. Not someone to disobey, right?" She smiled up at Liam, and Liam smiled right back. "Come on, now, I don't want my aunt getting mad at me. Posey will be right with us, right, hon?" She leaned in a little closer to Posey. "You might want to freshen up first, though," she whispered, loudly enough for Liam to hear. "You're a little ripe."

Gretchen towed Liam over to the Osterhagen table, chattering and laughing away. They sat next to each other, too. And, for crying out loud! Now Gretchen was feeding Liam a bite of whatever she was eating. Just…gross. Both of them.

It was just as well. Lusting after Liam Murphy had been fruitless—indeed, damaging—back in high school. No point in repeating past mistakes. Almost against her will, Posey went to the loo to freshen up—Gretchen might have a point—and stopped at the bar to bring their drinks back to the table. When she got there, Liam was gone.

Yep. Just as well.

MEN SHOULD NOT have to buy tampons, Liam thought darkly. Especially not when there were fifty-seven different kinds, and God forbid he came home with the wrong one. Should've stayed at Rosebud's and been sociable, but no, he'd made the mistake of going home only to find his baby girl in the throes of PMS the likes of which the world had never seen. So here he was, at Hannaford's.

He double-checked the list, which Nicole had written in big, block letters as if she thought he was an idiot (which, given her current state of hormones, she did), and tossed it into the cart. One more item to find. He scanned the shelves, muttering the product name over and over. It wasn't here. Scanned again. Nope. Not here. They must not have it.

Liam pulled out his phone and hit Home, dreading his daughter's voice.

"I can't find the last thing on the list, sweetie," he began.

"Dad!" Baby Girl stretched the once-loved word into three syllables of shrill torture. "Come *on!* I *need* it! I'm dying here! You don't understand! You're a guy!"

And thank God for that. "Okay, well, I have the first three…." And that was another thing. Three types of feminine protection? Pads, panty liners, tampons… It was bad enough to have to shop for this stuff, but to have to stand there, painstakingly reading every frigging box. *Pearl. Sport. Super Pearl. Super Sport. Super Fresh. Sport Lite.* If you were dyslexic, *sport* and *super* looked a lot alike, the letters sliding around as if they wanted him to screw up and bring back the wrong kind, at which point Nicole's head would turn 360 degrees and she'd start puking pea soup or whatever.

Bad enough that his daughter wasn't four years old anymore, a time Liam always thought of as kinda perfect…old enough to walk and feed herself and go to the bathroom alone, young enough to still worship him. Alas, the time machine was out of service, and Nicole was home with a hot-water bottle clutched to her abdomen and a box of tissues next to her on the couch.

"Make sure you get the right kind," his princess now ordered. "*Don't* come back here with Stayfree when I specifically asked for Kotex, Dad. There's, like, a huge difference, and I'm already miserable enough, okay?"

"No, no, we don't want you more miserable," Liam said. "I have the first three things, but I can't find the…" He lowered his voice and glanced around. No one else in the aisle… "The Midol. Maybe they just don't carry it. Maybe something else will work?" Like a horse tranquilizer?

"No, Dad! It's *there!* Okay? Please just find it! Jeesh!"

"Honey, I've been looking for ten— Hello? Nicole?"

Great. She'd hung up.

Two and a half more years, and his angel would be off to college. Hard to imagine he'd miss her, sometimes. But the thought caused his chest to tighten abruptly. Super. Wouldn't that be dignified, a heart attack in the tampon aisle, paramedics swarming, the police being dispatched to his apartment to tell Nicole the bad news, her face crumpling. His baby, an orphan, left to the Tates, who would do their best to erase her memories of him—

Liam's heart revved in panic, and sweat broke out on his forehead. "Settle down, settle down," he muttered.

"Got your period?" a voice asked, and Liam jumped, guilty as a shoplifter. Cordelia Osterhagen for the second time in a day. He took an unsteady breath, then looked over at her. She was still in her baseball uniform—Guten Tag T-shirt, baseball pants and cleats. There was a ketchup stain on her left breast, and the sight of her was oddly reassuring.

"You following me?" he asked.

"Yep. And everyone knows you like to browse the tampon aisle."

He glanced in her basket. Tapioca pudding, at least four pints of Ben & Jerry's, whipped cream, a block of cheddar, a Pepperidge Farm coconut cake, two frozen pizzas and a carton of Egg…Blisters? No, Egg Beaters. "Watching our cholesterol?"

Her eyes narrowed. "The Egg Beaters are for my dog. Who bites on command, by the way. What can't you find?"

He looked back at the wall of…stuff. "Midol. Extra Strength. For that special time when you feel like ripping out your father's throat and drinking his blood."

Posey grinned. "Wrong aisle, pal," she said. "It's in with the Motrin and cold and flu stuff."

Ah. Why not put the period medicine twelve rows away from the other period stuff? Clearly a woman was in charge of this store. "Thanks."

"Sure." She started off.

"Hey, is it my imagination, or is your mother trying to fix me up with your cousin?" he asked, not quite wanting her to go.

Her face turned pink, but she just shrugged and pursed those gorgeous lips of hers. "No clue."

"Think she likes me?"

"Of course she does, Liam. It's the law, isn't it? Women must fall at your feet."

He grinned. "You don't seem to do that. Not when you're sober, anyway."

Her blush deepened. "Don't worry, biker boy," she said coolly. "You're not my type."

"No? You sure about that?" He raised an eyebrow and grinned, and her face went from bright pink to Harley-Davidson's Fire Engine Red.

"Very." She pushed her cart past him. "But you know, if you're looking for love, there's always the mirror."

She was mad. "Hey, Cordelia. Sorry. Force of habit."

"Whatever. Hope your daughter feels better. Bring her something chocolate."

She didn't look back, and Liam had to admit, it wasn't his usual effect on women. Even women who hated him softened if he gave them a little dose of charm. Sounded cocky, but it was true. Hadn't Maya Chu just been flirting with him at Rosebud's? Liam had been fielding passes since he was fourteen years old. Marriage had slowed that down from a river to a stream, but now that he was a widower, women had been swarming like a cloud of mosquitoes. One woman, someone from the PTA, had slipped her phone number into his pocket at Emma's *wake,* and six months later he'd been averaging four or five phone calls a day from a horde of concerned single women (and three married chicks as well) who wanted to let him know they were available if he wanted to talk, have dinner or get laid.

So even if Cordelia Osterhagen blushed when he was around, she was certainly one of the more subtle females he'd come across. The cousin, Greta or whoever, feeding him by hand...that was more what he was used to.

He went to the medicine aisle and found Nicole's Midol, said a quick prayer that it would work, and swung by the chocolate aisle, adding a mega-size bar of Lindt milk chocolate. Couldn't hurt.

At the checkout, there was Cordelia again. She didn't look over at him.

"So, you have a salvage yard," he said, holding the first box of girl stuff under the scanner.

"Yup."

"You think you might have something Nicole would like for her room?"

She glanced over. "What did you have in mind?"

Liam shrugged. "I don't know. Her room back home... Well, Emma had painted it with clouds and all, and Nic was saying the other day how bare it looks here. I didn't really have anything in mind. Not really good at that stuff."

"What does she like?"

Excellent question. Aside from Cookie Monster, he had no idea anymore. At Christmas, he'd bought her a Hello Kitty calendar, which earned him a lecture on how she wasn't a baby anymore. Last week, she'd come home from the store with a pair of pajamas imprinted with Hello Kitty. "I don't know. I just thought something a little different. Never mind. It's fine."

"I'll look around," Cordelia said. "I might have something."

"Thanks."

They finished scanning about the same time. Apparently, they were parked near each other, too; Liam's dark blue Honda next to a battered red pickup.

As he approached, a pony-size black-and-white head appeared in the window of Cordelia's truck. The dog, the biggest he'd ever seen, yawned then sniffed the air, maybe sensing his Egg Beaters were close by.

"That's some dog," Liam said.

"Shilo. He's a Great Dane."

"Can I pet him?"

"Do you mind if he rips your arm off?"

Liam blinked. "He bites?"

She smiled, just a little flash. "No. Go ahead."

The only dog Liam had ever owned was way back when they still lived in Pennsylvania, when Liam was about five—a pit bull his father had trained to attack and which spent its life chained to a stake in the front yard. His dad had called the dog Idiot. Liam had been bitten twice by the dog, but it had still been his job to feed him, tiptoeing up to the dog, who'd always growled, even though supper was approaching.

A little warily, Liam held up his hand for the Great Dane to sniff. Shilo licked his hand once, then closed his eyes, and Liam smiled, then smoothed his hand over the dog's warm, bony head. Clearly not in the same class as Idiot, though probably five times as big. The thing took up almost the entire front seat of the truck.

"He must outweigh you by forty pounds," he commented. "How'd you train him?"

"I don't know. The usual way, I guess."

Maybe Nicole would like a dog. "Where'd you get him?"

"The pound. See you around, Liam." With that, Cordelia got into the truck and floored it, tires screeching a little, as if she couldn't wait to be away from him.

Not his usual effect at all. But fifteen minutes later, when Nicole had snatched the chocolate from him and kissed his cheek, telling him he was the best, Liam couldn't help feeling grateful to that scratchy little Cordelia Osterhagen.

CHAPTER NINE

"OH!" KATE GRUNTED as she sat down behind her desk. "My side is killing me. I'm ovulating, I think. That sucker must be huge."

"Must we discuss?" Jon asked.

"Man up, weenie boy," Kate said.

"You man up, Venus Williams," Jon replied. "I'm a gay home-ec teacher. I never have to man up. I never *will* man up. As God is my witness, I'll never man up again."

Posey had finished a quote on taking down a barn in Chelmsford and dropped by the school to pick up Brianna for their afternoon together. Knowing both Kate and Jon had a late lunch, she'd crashed and was now happily eating half of Jon's chicken salad sandwich (with grapes and walnuts on a croissant, plus oatmeal cookies for dessert). They ate in Kate's office, just off the locker rooms, despite Jon's complaints of the faint smell of sweat.

Kate leaned back in her chair, her head touching the poster of Mia Hamm's moment of sports-bra glory. "So, James and I are thinking of taking a trip to Sedona this summer. Pilates, spa, deep meditation, the whole thing."

"What every teenage boy dreams of," Jon said. "Why not Outward Bound or a summer at sea?"

"What do you know about Outward Bound? Weren't we just discussing what a sissy you were, Jon?" The bell rang. "Oops, time to go," Kate said. She lurched upright in her chair. "Walk with me, you two. I have bus duty. Oh, and hey, Posey, we're short on prom chaperones this year. You in?"

"No," Posey said. "Though I loved the way you slipped that in. Nice work."

"You should come!" Jon declared. "We can go together, because you know your brother would rather chew off his own arm, then reattach it."

"At last, Henry and I have something in common," Posey said. "No thanks, guys."

"Oh, come on. It'll be fun," Kate said.

"Gee, I wish I could, but I'll be busy hacking my wrists that night."

"It's not *that* bad," Kate said, locking her office door behind them.

"It's so much fun!" Jon said. "I'm the most popular boy there. If I were eligible for prom king, I'd win every year."

As if on cue, a pretty girl bounced over to them. "Mr. White, I totally wish you were straight. I have *such* a crush on you."

"Take a number, sweetheart," Jon said kindly. "Did you plan out your quilt design yet? It's due on Tuesday."

"Well, I need chaperones," Kate continued. "So far I only have Jack Whalen signed up, and only because I'm blackmailing him."

"What did he do?" Posey asked.

"He subscribes to *Cat Fancy* magazine," Kate answered. "Imagine trying to be an authority figure when your students know you read *Cat Fancy.*"

"I read *Cat Fancy,*" Jon said.

"Of course you do." Kate pushed open the door into the main wing of the school. The hallway was packed, lockers slamming, kids making out, insulting each other, giggling shrilly to show how fun and popular they were, or slinking along the wall, trying to be invisible.

Posey glanced down the hall, her eyes stopping on what looked like a golden couple—the girl was pretty and blonde, her face pink with pleasure as she smiled up at a good-looking boy, who was leaning against her locker. Had to be Nicole Murphy. She was the image of her mom.

A lump came to Posey's throat. It was so strange to think of Emma Tate, that lovely, generous girl, as an adult, a mother, a wife. To picture her sick and weak…dying…when the last time Posey had seen her, she'd been perfect. In perfect health, perfect happiness, a perfect future spreading out in front of her. All that, gone, and her little girl left alone.

"That's Nicole Murphy," Kate confirmed. "Let me introduce you. It'll be nice for her to meet someone who knew her mom." Kate towed Posey over, leaving Jon behind to field another admirer. "Ms. Murphy! Hey, Mr. Talcott, how you doing?" Kate's gym-teacher voice could be heard quite clearly. "Nicole, this is Posey Osterhagen. She was a friend of your mom's."

"Oh, hi," the girl said, her smile slipping a little.

"Hi," Posey answered, swallowing against the lump. "We weren't really friends… Well, we sort of were. She was two years ahead of me. She was…she was really nice."

"Thanks," Nicole said, her voice quiet. "I have some of her teachers, and everyone always says that."

"You look a lot like her," Posey added. "She was beautiful."

The girl smiled.

"Mr. Harris! Do you *mind?*" Kate bellowed. "Excuse me, kids. Gotta run. See you later, Posey." Kate went off to quell whatever trouble was brewing.

The boy was staring at Nicole, eyes glassy with adoration. The girl gave Posey an awkward smile. Her exit cue. "Well, nice meeting you," Posey said, then turned to leave and bounced right off a man's chest. Liam Murphy's chest, to be specific.

Oh, Elvis. He smelled *so* good…soap and that sharp smell of a garage, oil and metal, and beneath that, the smell of cloves, that pumpkin-pie smell. His hair was rumpled, and either he hadn't shaved this morning or he was one of those guys who could grow a beard in a few hours. Lust tightened her insides, and the smarter part of her brain clucked in warning. She took a step away and shoved her hands into her jeans pockets.

"Nic, I've been waiting for ten minutes," Liam rumbled.

"Sorry, Dad. Ms. Ellington introduced me to an old friend of Mommy's."

Mommy. Poor thing.

Liam seemed to notice Posey for the first time. "Oh. Hey." Prince Charming this guy was not.

"Hi."

He turned his attention back to the kids. "Who are you?" he demanded, looking rather fierce.

"Daddy, this is Tanner Talcott." Nicole moved a little closer to the boy, who stuck out his hand.

"Nice to meet you, Mr. Murphy. Nicole's told me a lot about you."

Liam stared at the hand for a long, withering moment, then looked back at the boy. "Let's get this straight, pal," he said in a dangerous voice. "I know what you're like. I know what you're thinking. I know you, kid. I *was* you. I know what you have in your pants, and it's gonna stay there."

"Dad, chill!" Nicole's face was fiery red. "OMG, Tanner, see? I told you."

Liam ignored his daughter. "You can hold her hand. Maybe, after a year or so, a kiss on the cheek. Are we clear?"

Wow. This was more fun than Posey had expected. She bit her lip to keep from smiling.

The two teenagers stared at Liam, then looked at each other. "See?" Nicole said. "Psychotic."

"That's right, honey," Liam said, putting his arm around her. "She's my only child, Tanner Talcott. My princess. My angel. Got it?"

"Totally, Mr. Murphy. So, Nicole, you wanna go to the movies sometime?"

"I'd love to. Text me."

"No, don't text her. Call me and ask my permission first. But I'll save you some time. The answer is no."

"Text me," Nicole repeated in a grittier tone.

"Nice meeting you both," Tanner said, nodding at Posey. At least someone was aware that she was still standing there. He hefted his backpack onto his shoulder, grinned at Nicole, then shambled down the hall.

"What a nice boy," Posey said. Nicole beamed.

"Shut it, Cordelia," Liam said.

"Really cute, too," Posey added. "So, Liam, remember that thing you asked about?"

"No." His eyes were stony.

"In the supermarket? Last week?"

"Oh. Right."

"Are you guys gonna be around? I can bring it by later today."

"What is it?" Nicole asked, looking up at her father.

His face softened. Then he glanced at Posey—of course, he didn't know what it was. "It's…it's something for your room," he said awkwardly.

"Really? Cool! Can you bring it over, Posey?"

"That would be Ms. Osterhagen to you," Liam grumbled.

"You can call me Posey. Does five o'clock work? I have something to do first."

"Cool. Do you know where we live?" Nicole asked.

Yes, I was sleeping it off in your guest room not that long ago, intoxicated and buck naked. Posey glanced at Liam, hoping she wasn't blushing. "Yup. See you later." With that, she went off to find Brianna.

LIAM'S AFTERNOON was not going well.

First of all, Rick Balin had come by his shop. Again. He said he wanted a custom bike, but it seemed to Liam that he really wanted to relive his high-school years, one of those sad types who'd peaked at seventeen. Liam himself barely remembered high school outside of Emma. He suspected Rick had a drinking problem, as well as a heart attack lurking in the near future. Instead of making a decision on the three designs Liam had drawn up, Rick had spent an hour and a half reminiscing about the good old days, telling stories about people Liam barely remembered…Jessica something, Mitch something else. By the time he left, Liam had a pounding headache.

Then the Tates had called. Fourth time in two days, checking to see if Nicole was free for Easter break, because they'd like to take her to Paris. Paris! As if he'd let his only child fly across the Atlantic without him. The Tates had also asked if Nicole could stay overnight on Wednesday, which sounded harmless enough. But Liam knew from experience that if you gave the Tates an inch, they'd take not just a mile, but the Eastern Seaboard, too. This Wednesday would become every Wednesday. Louise would say, "But I thought you didn't mind—it's our tradition, after all." And Louise could make a tradition in about thirty seconds, oh yeah. The Tates had come out for Christmas the year Nicole had been born, and it was tolerable enough. Liam just hadn't realized it meant they'd be there for *every* holiday—Thanksgiving, Easter, Memorial Day, the Fourth of July, Labor Day, Halloween, Rosh Hashanah (no, they weren't Jewish, but why pass up a chance, right?).

Liam had wanted Nicole to be closer to her grandparents. But he hadn't realized that closer would never be close enough. His explanation that Wednesday wasn't going to work had been met with an injured silence, a goodbye that was just tremulous enough to let Liam know that Louise was deeply wounded. And no one could do wounded like Louise.

And then there was That Boy. Tanner. Just thinking the name set Liam's teeth on edge. That Boy had touched Nicole's shoulder. Not cool. Not cool at all. They'd argued about it all the way home.

"Dad, you can't just lock me in a convent!" Nicole had whined.

"Watch me," he said.

"I'm almost sixteen! I should get to have a boyfriend!"

"Says who?"

"Dad!" There it was, that three-syllable screech. "I'm like a freak or something!"

"So what? At least you're not pregnant."

"You're, like, ridiculous." She stared out the window. "I *am* going to the movies, you know. You can't lock me up."

No, he couldn't. Or, rather, locking up didn't tend to work, as Liam well knew, since George Tate had threatened the same thing to Emma, and it had only given her more motivation to sneak out of the house and meet Liam and do all sorts of things that he didn't want his daughter doing. Hypocritical? Absolutely. The essence of parenthood.

So now Nicole was sulking in her room, Bruce Springsteen blaring—another new artist she'd found. The Tates had called twice more since their earlier conversation and had emailed him an itemized list of why they should be able to take Nicole to France.

So now Liam sat at the kitchen table, dismantling a carburetor from a Harley, his movements a little too sharp to really do anything effective.

His doorbell buzzed. Super. Carol Antonelli probably wanted to discuss her hysterectomy. She'd offered to show him her scar on Monday, and Liam was giving serious thought to moving.

He stalked down the hall and jerked open the door. It wasn't Carol. It was Cordelia Osterhagen, holding a large packing crate. He'd completely forgotten she was coming by. And there was Carol in her doorway, talking through the four inches allowed by her security chain, as if worried that Cordelia was about to kick in the door and set fire to the place. As if she could. For a second, Liam remembered how light she'd been when he carried her. The way her hair had brushed against his chin. That mouth of hers, looking so soft and—

"Liam!" Carol said. "Posey here has a package for you!"

"It's true," Cordelia said. "Though it's actually for Nicole."

"A sweet girl!" Carol sang. "Lovely! Such nice manners!"

"I just met her, but she seems great." Cordelia turned to him and cocked an eyebrow. "Well, this is heavy. Liam. You gonna stand there like a fern, or can I bring it in?"

Great. More attitude. Just what he didn't need. Liam opened the door and stood back.

"Posey, did I tell you I'm having dinner at the restaurant with your mother?" Carol said. "That Gretchen! Such a gift! Of course, I love Italian food, don't get me wrong, I married Mario Antonelli, for heaven's sake, but what Gretchen does with sour cream should be against the law! I used to watch her show every day."

"You and dozens of others," Cordelia muttered. Then, in a louder voice, "Have fun, Mrs. A. Tell my mom I said hi."

She brushed past Liam, then set the box down. Cordelia wore a flannel shirt and brown Carhartt carpenter pants and looked more like Norm Abrams from *This Old House* than an actual female. Those boots could do serious damage. She might dress like a man, but there was that nice smell again. Oranges. He couldn't imagine her using perfume. Maybe it was her shampoo or soap.

An unbidden image of Cordelia in the shower, water and suds streaming over her wet skin, leaped to mind.

She cleared her throat, and Liam, abruptly aware that he was staring at her, shifted his gaze. Okay, that was…odd. Sex thoughts about Cordelia Osterhagen. Well, chalk it up to garden variety horniness and a long drought, and think about something else.

He looked past her. The door wasn't locked.

Now, intellectually, Liam knew that there weren't exactly roaming gangs of burglars wandering the streets of Bellsford, and he also knew that the Tates tended to kick the old stress level into the red zone, which tended to bring on flares of OCD, and he knew that just because the door wasn't locked didn't mean that some knife-wielding maniac was about to burst in, but the fucking door wasn't locked. And as much as he really, really would love to not obsess over that, he wasn't succeeding. Might as well get it over with and lock the damn door, because all he could think about, other than Nicole dying in a fiery

Air France crash, was the fact that the door was unlocked, and Cordelia Osterhagen was staring at him warily, and he might as well just lock the damn thing and turn to nicer thoughts. Like Cordelia in the shower.

He reached behind her, and she jumped back a step, as if afraid he was going to hit her. Or grab her. "I'm just locking the door," he said, the words a little sharp.

"Oh."

He turned the lock, listening for the satisfying thunk of the dead bolt in the hasp. Then he unlocked it. Locked it again. Unlocked it. Locked it. Taking a deep breath, he closed his eyes for a second, then glanced at Cordelia, who was looking at him steadily. Once more couldn't hurt. Unlock. Lock. Done.

"Problem?" she asked.

"No," he said. He folded his arms over his chest, vaguely aware that he was being a prick and had barely spoken to her. "Thank you for bringing this over. Whatever it is."

"Do you want to see it? It's—"

"No, that's fine. Just…her bedroom's down the hall on the right." He went to pick up the box, but she grabbed it at the same time.

"It's fragile," she said.

"I thought you said it was heavy."

"It is. Heavy and fragile." She scowled at him, looking like a little kid. Fine. She wanted to carry it, no big deal.

Liam led her down the hall and stopped in front of Nicole's door. He knocked. "Nic? Cordelia's here with your thing."

Nicole's door opened. "Hi!" she said. "Thank you so much for bringing this! But I thought your name was Posey."

"My real name is Cordelia, but everyone calls me Posey. Except lunkhead here."

Nicole laughed, the sound making Liam's heart squeeze. "Come on in. I can't wait to see what it is!"

Cordelia put the package on the bed, then reached into her pocket and withdrew a Leatherman, a very helpful tool that Liam had never before seen on a woman. She sliced the tape, then stood back to let Nicole open the box. Nic pulled back the cardboard flaps, pushed aside some tissue paper. "Oh, cool!" she exclaimed.

"Here, let me get it out for you," Cordelia said.

She pulled the rather large object out of the packaging. Liam recognized it immediately, the memory slamming him in the chest like a fist.

It was a large white clock encircled with a ring of pink neon. Painted on the wooden backing were the words *Time for Ice Cream!*

"I love it! It's so retro," Nicole exclaimed.

Cordelia glanced at Liam, who was staring at the clock. "It's from Sweetie Sue's," she said.

He didn't answer. Memories of Emma, grinning up at him in her pink uniform as she packed a scoop of ice cream into a cone, the chill of the white metal chairs where he'd sit, waiting for her shift to end.

"What's Sweetie Sue's?" Nicole asked.

Liam swallowed.

"It was an ice cream parlor here in town," Cordelia said after a beat. "Your mom worked there in high school."

"Really?" Nicole asked.

Liam distantly heard Cordelia's voice as she explained where Sweetie Sue's had been, the other things she'd salvaged from the store before it was torn down. An old freezer. The milkshake machine.

"I'm gonna put it right over my bed," Nicole announced. "It's so neat that Mommy saw this clock every day, too." She touched it gently, almost reverently. "Dad? Can we put it up?"

Liam cleared his throat. "Sure. I'll go get some tools. We can do it right now."

Nicole hopped over and threw her arms around him for a brief hug. "It's a great present," she said. "I love it, Daddy."

"Thank Cordelia. She picked it out."

Cordelia was looking at him, chewing on her bottom lip, hands in her pockets, her eyebrows drawn together.

"Well, thanks, both of you," Nicole said, going back to gaze at the clock.

"I'll get my tools. Be right back."

Leaving the two females in the bedroom, Liam headed to the kitchen closet, where he kept his toolbox. But he just stood there for a moment, the memories of Emma pulling at him like quicksand. God, he had loved her back then. The idea that a girl like that would choose a guy like him…it was staggering.

"Liam?"

Cordelia again. "Hey," he said, reaching for the toolbox.

"I'm sorry."

He glanced at her. Her hands were jammed in the front pockets of her jeans. "What for?"

"The clock. It… I should've given you some warning. I just… I didn't…"

"Well, you asked me if I wanted to see it, and I said no." He paused. "It's great, Cordelia. It's perfect."

Her eyes widened a little. "It is?"

"Yeah. Thank you."

"You're welcome."

He yanked the toolbox from where it was wedged on the bottom shelf. "How much do I owe you?"

"Nothing. It's a gift."

"Yes. A gift for my daughter, which I'll pay for. How much, Cordelia?"

Her eyes narrowed. "Nothing."

"I can afford to pay for a gift for my own child, Cordelia."

"Well, too bad, biker boy," she snapped. "Your wife was always nice to me, and I was sorry—I was always sorry she and I didn't stay in touch," she finished, and he suspected she was about to say something else. "The clock's not worth a heck of a lot, anyway." Her gaze wandered to the refrigerator, which was covered with photos. Nicole had taken a picture of their fridge in San Diego, then recreated the exact order when they moved in here. Mostly photos of Nic herself…dressed as a pumpkin for Halloween when she was four, riding her bike, missing her front teeth. But a few of him and Emma, too.

"Anyway. Sorry if it brought stuff up," Cordelia said in a gentler voice.

"It's okay. It really is perfect." He looked at her for a long minute. Her blush began underneath the flannel and crept up her neck, into her jaw and cheeks. She looked away, and Liam's mood suddenly lightened. Cordelia was a woman, a straight woman (he thought, anyway), and it was nice to see she wasn't immune to him. Made things feel more even somehow.

"Dad! Can you hang up my clock or what?" Nic called from down the hall.

"Coming, Master," he said. He grinned at Cordelia. "Stay here a sec. I want to ask you something. But duty calls."

Alone in Liam Murphy's kitchen.

Posey supposed she'd have to stop thinking of him as Liam Murphy, just trim it down to Liam, but still. He had that celebrity feel. Too hot for regular life.

As if on cue, Posey's phone buzzed. She pulled it out—a text from Jon. *Holy Justin Bieber, did I hear u say ur going 2 Nicole Murphy's? The father is totally hot. 2 young 4 me?*

I'm standing in his kitchen, Posey texted back. *Will try to steal you something.*

How about a lock of hair?

Posey grinned. *I was thinking of a sock. Gotta go. xox*

From down the hall came the sound of a drill. *Drill me, Liam.* Posey rolled her eyes at herself. Some hammering. *Nail me, pal.* "Okay, down, you ho," she muttered, wandering to the fridge for a better look at the photos there. Nicole had been a wicked cute baby. No surprise there, not with her DNA. There was a nice shot of Emma and Nicole, when Nicole was about ten. Posey's throat tightened again. So hard to believe the gorgeous woman with the bright smile was just gone.

Well. Here was another picture—Liam in scrubs, holding a tiny pink package. Now that was the money shot, wasn't it? Dopey dad-love shone in his face as he gazed at his red-faced daughter. He looked so *young*. So happy, too, and so sure. How was it that Liam Murphy had found the way to make a family at age...what? Twenty, twenty-one? Posey had grown up in the stable, unwavering embrace of Max and Stacia and had never even come close to marriage, let alone a family. Liam and Emma had met as teenagers and made something special. Those pictures didn't lie. Posey was scanning websites for a spouse as if ordering a coat from L.L. Bean. Liam and Emma had made a family before they were old enough to buy a six-pack.

"Hey, Posey, come see it!" Nicole called, and obediently Posey trotted down the hall.

"It looks great," she said.

"I love it." Nicole gave her a look. "So, Posey, if you knew my mom, did you also know my father back then?"

Posey glanced at Liam, who narrowed his eyes slightly in warning. "I sure did," she said, feeling the start of a smile warm her chest.

"What was he like?" Nicole asked.

"What was he like? Or what did he *think* he was like?" Posey asked, her grin spreading.

"Watch it," Liam muttered.

"Both! Why? Was he a jerk?" Nicole asked, clapping her hands in delight.

"It was like having Heath Ledger wander the halls of our little high school, Nicole," Posey said. "Leather jacket, ripped jeans, crappy grades, the whole cliché."

"Not all my grades were bad," he countered.

"Girls wanted to, uh, date him, men wanted to be him. He was *so* intense," Posey said, getting a laugh from Nicole.

"Dad! You always make it sound like you were perfect!"

"Oh, he was." Posey sighed dramatically. "Perfectly dreamy."

"Ew!" Nicole squealed.

"Okay, I'm gonna start supper," Liam said.

"Which is my cue to go," Posey said.

"Oh, can you stay for a minute?" Nicole asked. In the doorway, Liam paused. "I want to ask Posey about Mom," she added.

"Sure," he said and then was gone down the hall.

Odd, to picture Liam Murphy cooking dinner. Setting the table, making sure his kid had green veggies and stuff like that.

"Can you, like...I don't know, just tell me a little bit about my mom?" Nicole asked, sitting on her bed. Her expression was eager.

Posey took a seat in the desk chair. "Sure," she said. "Um, I went to Sweetie Sue's a lot." Nicole grinned, and Posey smiled back. "She always gave me an extra scoop for free."

"She was great about dessert," the girl said, her eyes getting a little wet. "Way more mellow than Dad. What else?"

"Well, we went to the same church, so I saw her there sometimes," Posey said. "Your dad worked at my parents' restaurant, so she'd drop by once in a while. She was always really friendly. Chatty. She was just...nice. Genuine, you know? She wanted everyone to be happy. Her nickname was Little Miss Sunshine."

"Really? Like how? What did she do?"

Posey paused. "Well, she was always organizing food drives and recycling programs at school. Stuff like that. And she...gave me advice about clothes and stuff."

"She had amazing clothes," Nicole said wistfully. She looked at Posey again. "Anything else? Sorry if I'm, like, pumping you for details. I just..." The girl cleared her throat. "I love hearing about her when she was my age."

Posey nodded. "Sure. Well, she...sort of arranged for me to go to the prom," she said carefully.

"Really? She fixed you up?" Posey nodded. "Did you guys go with her and Daddy?"

"No. They, uh, they were with different people. You know how it is."

"No, I don't," Nicole said with a huff. "I probably never will, either. Dad's, like, psycho about my social life. Mom would've been much cooler. She totally would let me date by now."

Posey had to smile at that—the bad boy now a stodgy old dad, clattering around making dinner.

"He needs to get a life so he won't be, like, obsessed with mine," Nicole added. "Do you know anyone he could date? Maybe that hot chick at your restaurant?"

Posey's smile felt stiff. "Uh...maybe. I—" She winced. "I could check."

"Hey," Nicole said, "do you want to stay for supper? Dad! Can Posey stay for supper?"

"Stop bellowing down the hall!" Liam bellowed from down the hall. There was a pause. "Sure. If she wants." Such a halfhearted offer that Posey rolled her eyes.

"Do you?" Nicole asked. "You can tell me more stories, okay? About Mom *and* Dad. I can't believe Dad was such a jerk!"

"Oh, um...he wasn't a jerk." Crap. "He was just...you know."

"Just what, Cordelia?"

There he was, the King of Testosterone himself. "Just a little full of himself, that's all."

Again with the narrowed gaze...kind of hot, really. Nicole giggled.

"But once he met your mom, it was true love and all that good stuff," Posey added.

"Are you staying?" Liam asked—not very nicely, she thought.

"Sorry. I have plans." *Plans with my dog, that is,* she thought, getting up from the chair. *A dog who has better manners than you.* "Maybe another time."

"Bye, Posey! Thank you so much for the clock! I love it." The girl bounced off her bed and hugged her.

"See you around," Posey said, patting Nicole on the shoulder, her eyes growing wet. Emma's daughter seemed just as sweet as her mother. "It was really nice meeting you."

"After you," Liam said, standing back to let Posey pass. She went down the hall, past the kitchen and grabbed her backpack from where she'd dropped it earlier.

"See you around, Liam," she called.

"Hang on," he said, and she jumped. He was right behind her. She turned warily.

The whole aging-rock-star-still-dead-sexy look...it worked. She wondered what he looked like with his shirt off—tattoo, maybe? She'd be happy to check...centimeter by centimeter...with her tongue.... *Enough, Posey!* Guys like Liam—the last thing they needed was yet another ego massage from yet another swoony woman. Besides, she'd pined over him enough for several lifetimes.

But still. It was hard not to get a little...aroused...when he was staring at her like that.

"You want to go to the movies tomorrow night?" he asked, and Posey was so shocked she actually choked.

"What?" she managed.

"The movies? Tomorrow?"

"Um...I, uh...um...what movie?"

He narrowed his eyes just a little, and Posey's nether parts gave a long, happy squeeze. *Get his clothes off,* those parts advised. *We're lonely.* "Does it matter?" Liam asked.

The words had the effect of ice water. "Actually, yes, Liam. Why? Do you think your mere presence is enough? Because I have to tell you, God's Gift, you're not really all that anymore."

Slowly, slowly, his mouth pulled up on one side, and Posey could feel those treacherous parts about to stage a mutiny. "What movie would you like to see?" he said in a scraping, low voice, and the effect was the same as if he'd said, *I am going to smear you with honey and lick you clean, Posey Osterhagen.*

"I...I don't know...what's, um...playing?" she muttered.

"Have you seen blah-blah-blah?" Liam asked. There was a roaring in her ears that drowned out his actual words. She couldn't take her eyes off that mouth. That was a really good mouth, that was. Oh, yeah. His upper lip was just a little fuller than his lower, and she wondered what kind of kisser he was, what it would be like to have that mouth on hers…or any part of her, really, her elbow, her toe, because she had a feeling that Liam's mouth would make her—

"Great. I'll pick you up at seven," he said.

Oh. Apparently she'd just agreed to go out with Liam Murphy. Liam. Declan. Murphy. Had. Asked. Her. Out. Holy Elvis Presley. Was this a date? An actual romantic date? Or was this two old sort-of friends just hanging out? Should she ask? Did it matter? Could she shove him to the ground and eat him for supper?

"Bye," she muttered, then fled before she did something utterly stupid.

CHAPTER TEN

"THAT'S GOING TO fall down and kill you someday," Henry muttered, staring up at the belfry. He looked at Posey and sighed, then jumped back abruptly. "Oh, God! There's a cat. I forgot you had cats." Henry was afraid of cats, something Posey and Jon found hilarious. "Why am I here again?"

"You're not here. Jon is here," Posey said. "I need advice. And the bell is safe. Mostly. But don't stand under it, okay? Mom and Dad would kill me if their precious perfect got a boo-boo at my house. Shilo, you move, too, buddy." They went down to the kitchen, where Shilo collapsed at Henry's feet with a thud that shook the room, then stared up at Posey's brother with adoring, red-rimmed eyes.

Henry sighed, picked up a bottle of wine, shook his head and replaced it, as if deeply saddened that his sister bought such uninspired booze. "You're welcome to buy me better stuff, Hen," she said.

"I should buy you a better house. This place is a death trap. Could you move this cat?"

"Meatball, go. Henry doesn't like you. And this place is not a death trap! It's great! It has character."

"And too many animals. How many do you have, Posey?"

"One dog, three cats. They came with the church, like angels, right, Sagwa? Try not to show fear, Henry. They feed off it." Posey giggled as her brother's face paled.

"Can we stop talking?" Jon asked. "We're getting ready for a date, and your sister's hair is a challenge to even the most gifted hair gods. Thank you. Now. We want to look nice, but not like we're trying too hard. Good thing I brought my tools." He unpacked a blow-dryer and rounded brush from his little case.

"So, who is this guy again?" Henry asked.

Jon sighed dramatically. "Do you listen to nothing I tell you?" he asked. "His name is Liam, he's a widower, totally hot. Better than that poser you were dating a while back, sweetie."

"You were dating someone?" Henry asked.

Jon looked at Posey and shook his head. "Ignore him. Now. I'm thinking sort of a Natalie Portman look, right?"

"What does he do for a living?" Henry asked.

"Motorcycle mechanic. Custom bikes, repairs, all that manly stuff we know nothing about," Jon answered. "Posey, tilt your head, honey."

"Motorcycles are good for my business," Henry said. "I did the coolest amputation on a Hell's Angel last week, did I tell you, Pose?"

Jonathan turned on the blow-dryer to full power. "La la la la, don't tell amputation stories, honey, how many times have we discussed this? Posey, what are we wearing?"

"Does everything have to be first person plural?" Henry asked. "Is that in the manual for how to be gay?"

"Well, sweetheart, if there's a manual, you should read it. You're gay, after all. Not that you can tell, sadly. Posey, he dresses like a straight, color-blind computer programmer, and it breaks my heart. Tilt."

Tonight wasn't a date, of that Posey was pretty sure. Or maybe it was, and she just didn't know it. If he'd said, "Posey, I find you very attractive and would like to spend more time with you," then she'd know. If he'd said, "I'm bored out of my skull and I asked you because you were standing in front of me and I have no feelings for you whatsoever," then she'd know that, too. If only men were more straightforward.

The heat of the hair dryer was making her ears itch. She wasn't sure this was a good idea. She wasn't sure she even liked Liam. Lusted after, yes, she'd covered that. So did every female around, clearly.

But.

You don't turn down a date with a guy who makes your knees buzz just by looking at you. The guy who held your heart in his fist for two formative years.

And maybe…maybe he did like her. Oh, crap, she sounded like she was fifteen again. Not good. Not good at all.

"Okay, your hair's…well, it's fine. It's good." Jon stood back and looked at her hair, frowning. "You don't have any hair glue, do you?"

"I don't even know what that is," she said. "And what happened to not trying too hard?"

"What are you wearing?" he asked. Henry checked his messages.

"Just jeans and a sweater," Posey said.

"Which jeans? Which sweater? We are doing makeup, aren't we? Come, child, look up. By all that's holy, how old is this eye shadow?"

"Old," Posey admitted. "Bush administration."

"Herbert Walker, or just Walker? Well, if it's bad, you'll be the first to know. Blink."

"Don't make me look like a child prostitute, okay?"

"You sure?" Jon said, rolling his eyes. "Honey, please. Don't forget who dressed up as Kate Moss for Halloween and looked like her twin."

"Damn, I missed a shattered elbow," Henry muttered, staring at his iPhone. "I love shattered elbows." He glanced up. "So, Jon and I are thinking about adopting a baby," he said, and Posey bolted out of her chair.

"Guys!" she said. "That's great! Oh, my gosh, I'm gonna be an aunt! At last!"

"You sound just like Mom," Henry said, grinning. "Well, we've just started looking around at different agencies and stuff. But we're ready. Right, Jon?"

"Totally ready," he said. "Sit back down, Posey. So, yeah, we're thinking it doesn't have to be newborn, right? But let me ask you, because Henry here doesn't have normal feelings…do you ever feel adopted?"

"I *am* adopted," she said.

"Right. But…I don't know. Do you wonder about your birth parents?" he asked.

"I don't," Henry said.

"I know you don't. I've been married to you for ten years. Do you, Posey?"

"Yeah, I think about them," she said. "Sometimes I see someone who might look like me, and I wonder if it's a long-lost cousin or something. I wish I knew the circumstances, you know? Henry at least knows that."

"The tragic orphan, yes."

"Right. So it would've been nice to know why my birth mother chose adoption. But otherwise, no. Max and Stacia are my parents."

"Are you done interrogating my sister?" Henry asked. "There's a call for an amputation, and I'd really hate to miss it."

Jon sighed. "Another night alone with a gourmet dinner and *Dexter* on DVD."

"Sounds like heaven to me," Posey said.

"Nonsense. You'll have so much fun on this date." He kissed her cheek and attempted one last time to flatten the cowlick on the back of her head. "Call me later, I'll be up. And dog, don't even look at me. Do you know how much these pants cost?"

"And take down that bell, Pose," Henry added as they left. "It's gonna kill you someday."

The bell was, in fact, Posey's prized possession. But she *wasn't* sure it wouldn't fall off, no matter what she told her family, all of whom viewed her house as riddled with opportunities to die. Still, the clock had lasted for more than a hundred years. Chances were it would last a little longer.

The makeup was starting to sting. Guess that three-month warning meant something after all. She went upstairs and washed it off, then took a long look in the mirror.

She would never be fat, that was true. Her roomy 32-A had become a 32-B somewhere in her twenties, and she was grateful. She wasn't unattractive, though she wished her hair would behave a little better. She kept it short, because it tended to curl when it grew, making her head look huge and giving her an overall lollipop appearance. But on a scale of one to ten, she was—maybe—a six, six and a half.

Gretchen was a ten.

Liam was a forty-nine.

Why had he asked her out? No one dated anymore, did they? They filled out computer forms, met and either moved on or got married. And Liam Murphy…he just didn't seem the type to date. He seemed like the type to press a woman against a wall, kiss the bejesus out of her and shag her into the middle of next week, though. Uh-huh. Oh, yeah.

At that very moment, the doorbell rang, and Posey jumped.

The doorbell was the only thing that seemed to hit her dog's protective instincts, and he barreled down the stairs, baying his hollow, echoing bark, then hurled himself against the door like a narcotics agent on a bust.

"Shilo! Down! Down, boy! Easy!"

Shilo took this as an invitation to jump against her, which caused Posey to stagger. "Down!" She managed to wrestle her dog off her, adjusted her shirt, and opened the door.

There he was, Hottie McSin. The details didn't matter—in fact, her vision was already blurry with lust—but the overall picture said *Do me.* Shilo seemed to agree, flopping on his back, paws stretching over his head. "Hi," Liam said, and she practically came on the spot. There was a wall right *there,* for heaven's sake. Just in case he wanted to push her up against it and—

Shilo whined, his tail whacking against her foot. Aware that she should greet her guest, Posey opened her mouth. "Yes. Hello." Her voice was husky, and she was positive he could read her mind. She swallowed hard. "Want to come in?"

"Will that thing eat me?"

"Maybe. Come on in and let's see."

He grinned. *Stay cool, Posey, stay cool,* she warned herself. *Do not have an orgasm just because he's here.* But come on! The man was *beautiful.* His jaw was dark with five o'clock shadow, his black hair rumpled, that faint look of reserve on his face. Posey wondered what he'd do if she ripped his shirt open and licked his neck. Seemed like a good idea to *her,* that was for sure. Shilo licked his chops as if echoing his owner's thoughts. "So," she said, then cleared her throat. "Um…want the tour?"

"Sure."

She led him through the house, careful not to touch him. Or look at him. Or have an orgasm. "So, this is my house. It used to be a church." Her dog woofed approvingly.

"Yeah, I got that," Liam said. He looked up at her vast ceilings. "Is that a catwalk?"

"Yep."

"Can we go upstairs and see it?"

Upstairs. Where her *bedroom* was. "Sure," she squeaked. "Shilo, stay." Her dog obliged, collapsing to the floor for some personal grooming.

She followed Liam upstairs, trying hard not to reach out and touch his—

"Are you doing this work yourself?" he asked, gesturing at the half-finished floor, where her cats lay around like throw pillows. Meatball lifted his head, then resumed his nap.

"Um…I hired out for some things—electric and plumbing and stuff—but yeah, I did a lot myself. I'm good with a saw." *That's great. Very hot. I'm sure he's incredibly turned on.*

"Is that a bell pull?" he asked.

"Oh, don't touch that!" She gave him a shove, and he stumbled back, giving her a baffled look. "It doesn't work. It's a little…iffy. Um… When's the movie?"

"Seven-thirty. You ready to go?"

"Yup."

Unrequited lust made for crappy conversation. As they rode along in Liam's car, Posey decided silence was better than making an idiot of herself. Besides, her brain churned with questions. Why was she here? Was this a date? Would he kiss her? What if he did in fact kiss her? Holy Elvis Presley, did he think they were going to have sex tonight? Where would Shilo and the triumvirate sleep? Was Liam Murphy hiding some deep, unspoken attraction for her? Did she have pajamas without holes or cartoon characters?

They got to the movie theater. Liam bought tickets, and Posey forced herself to go through the motions of polite conversation. Yes, she wanted popcorn. The large, please. Yes to Milk Duds. Yes to the ginger ale. Thanks.

She couldn't stop the surreal feeling. It was like a dream…so odd, too unbelievable. There was Kylie Duchamps, an old classmate, staring openmouthed as her tween-age daughter texted. A woman Posey didn't know was giving Liam the eye as he paid for their snacks.

"Hi, Mr. Murphy!" came a breathy voice. A girl about Nicole's age blushed to the roots of her hair.

"Hi, Caroline," he said easily, and the girl burst into giggles. Liam smiled and handed the popcorn to Posey.

"Thanks." She dumped in the Milk Duds so they'd soften and ooze some chocolate onto the popcorn. And people thought she wasn't a good cook.

"So, Mr. Murphy, can Nicole, like, come over sometime?" the giggler asked.

Kylie Duchamps appeared at Posey's side. "Hi, there!" she said. She'd been a cheerleader in high school—in other words, not someone who'd ever spoken to Posey, other than to call her Anne Frank. "Is that Liam Murphy? I heard he was back! What's he doing here?"

"I believe he's here to see a movie," Posey said.

"OMG! With you?"

"Yes." There should be a law that no one over the age of fourteen could say *OMG* without a public stoning. Except Jon, of course.

"That's… Wow." Kylie had been one of the slutty, popular girls, so pretty and confident back then. Since then, Kylie had packed on a few extra pounds, her once-cute features looking rather piggy in her puffy face. Sometimes, life *was* fair. "Weird, huh?" Kylie added.

"What's weird?"

"Ma-a-ah," bleated the child, who was a mini-me version of her mother. "I don't want to miss the previews! Come on!"

Kylie ignored her. "It's just that it's strange that he's with *you*—Liam! Hi! Long time no see, stranger!" She threw herself at Liam and hugged him fiercely. "You look great! It's so good to see you!"

"Ma, can we go?" whined Kylie's daughter. "Come on!"

Liam gave Posey a rather amused look. "Do I know you?" he said to Kylie, disentangling himself from her tentacles.

"As if! Of *course* you do! We went to *high school* together? Duh!" Clearly Liam had a wormhole effect on the former cheerleader, because she reverted into the tortured Val-speak that she'd affected back then.

"Oh. Sorry."

"Kylie Duchamps? Well, I'm married now. And a *mother,* if you can believe it!"

"Ma-a-ah! Come *on!*"

Liam nodded. "Nice to meet you. Cordelia, you all set?" He took her by the arm and led her away from Kylie and her irritable child.

"Sure you don't want to catch up?" Posey said, trying to ignore the sweet, strong tingle Liam's hand induced. This had to be a date. He was touching her. Right? Didn't touching constitute intent? Also, he'd bought her all this food.

"Very funny. I can't tell you how many times that's happened."

"What? You running into some girl you slept with?"

"I didn't sleep with that one," he muttered.

"You sure?" Posey couldn't help grinning.

"Shush." He held the door for her (very date-ish), and she went into the theater, which was one of those stadium types, and lurched to a stop.

Ah. So *that* was why she was here.

Nicole Murphy sat four rows up next to the boy Liam had threatened at school the other day. At the sight of her father, her face went from bright and happy to horrified disbelief. "Dad! Are you serious?"

"Let's sit here, Cordelia," Liam said, loping up the stairs to the fifth row.

"Dad! No!"

"Oh, hi, sweetheart. Didn't know you were coming to this show. What a coincidence." His voice took on a harder edge. "Tanner." Liam sat directly behind the boy.

So. Not a date. A stalking mission to ensure the chastity of his daughter. Super. She should've known.

"Excuse me," said a man behind her. Right. She was blocking the stairs. With a sigh, she headed up to Liam. Who was an idiot.

"Hi, Nicole," she said. "Sorry. I didn't know this was a reconnaissance mission."

"Whatever," the girl mumbled.

"Hi," Tanner said, turning around to smile at Posey. "Nice to see you again."

"You have beautiful manners," she answered, which caused Nicole to smile and her father to growl. "Tell your mom she did a good job with you."

"Thanks, I will," Tanner said. "Hope you like the movie, Mr. Murphy."

"I won't be watching the *movie,*" Liam said pointedly. He dug in his pocket and withdrew a miniature bottle of Purell and held it out next to his daughter's head. When he didn't withdraw it, she snatched it from him, poured a little onto her hands, and handed it back without looking at her father.

"I want to be adopted," Nicole said, rubbing vigorously.

"I'm adopted," Posey offered.

Nicole turned around to look at her. "Really? That's so cool! Would you adopt me?"

"Sure," Posey said. "Do you like dogs? I have a Great Dane."

"Absolutely!" she said.

"Done deal, then."

"Very funny," Liam said, rubbing Purell into his own hands. "Want some?" he asked.

"I'm good," she answered.

"I so cannot believe you're here, Dad," Nicole said. "Tanner, I am really sorry."

"No worries," the kid answered.

"It's a free country, Nicole," Liam said.

"Not if you're me," she grumbled, turning back around. "I'm, like, under surveillance."

"True."

The lights went down, and Liam reached over for some popcorn. "Get your own," Posey said, leaning away.

"Wow. That's not very nice."

"Well, neither is taking me to spy on your kid, Liam!"

"*Thank* you!" Nicole said. The previews began.

"Look," Liam whispered, and against her will, Posey's entire side tingled. "She's fifteen years old. Bozo there's a senior. Do the math."

"What math?" Posey asked.

"The sex math."

"You're an idiot," she muttered, shoving another fistful of popcorn into her mouth. Why try to be delicate when all Liam was looking for was a beard? Or whatever the term was?

"You really gonna eat all that by yourself?" Liam said, eyeing her barrel of popcorn.

"Yes, Liam. I have a very fast metabolism. I have to eat a lot. If I don't, I'll turn into a bag of bones. Now shut up and watch the movie."

She sat there in the dark, fuming. She was mad at herself, too—not just him. She should've known it couldn't really be a date. Should've smelled something. Shouldn't have read into him touching her arm, or giving her that hot look when he asked her, because let's face it, the man oozed hot looks. He probably looked that way at his dentist. His proctologist. She wasn't special—not to him, at any rate. She was nothing but a desperate woman dumb enough to go to the movies with him.

At least the flick wasn't too bad. Sci-fi freaky thing about nature gone wrong. At one point, when the hybrid alien creature tore out someone's throat, Nicole gave a little shriek, and Tanner put his arm around her. Liam kicked his seat, and when Tanner looked back, Liam said, in a very soft, somewhat scary sing-song voice, "Get your arm…off my kid." And even though he was being a jerk, Posey couldn't help the slight thrill she felt at the protectiveness in his voice. Papa Lion protecting the pride. Tanner glanced at Nicole, who sighed the sigh of a martyr, and obeyed.

When the alien hybrid had been killed (though not before it secretly gave birth to the sequel), the lights came back up. "Well, that was fun," Liam announced. "Nic, since we're going to the same place, I'll save Tanner some gas and drive you home."

"Dude, I don't mind," Tanner objected.

"Dude, you can call me Mr. Murphy, and I'm not letting you drive her anywhere," Liam said. "Do you know the statistics on teenage accidents?"

"Said the man who tore through our quiet countryside on a motorcycle when he was your age," Posey added.

"Dad! You drove a motorcycle in *high school?*" Nicole's eyes were wide. "How did you, like, keep all this secret?"

Liam turned his head very slowly to look at Posey. "Thanks."

"My pleasure," she said, tipping the popcorn bucket to her mouth for the last few kernels.

"Tanner, I'll take my daughter home. Nicole, thank Tanner for the movie."

Nicole straightened her jacket. "Tanner, thanks for putting up with my idiot father, who's, like, ruining my life, and if you never want to speak to me again, I totally understand."

"I think you're really cute," Tanner said, and Posey had to give the boy props. He was brave or stupid or, being a teenager, both.

"She is really cute," Liam agreed. "Also underage. Got it? I'll press charges so fast, you'll be picking up soap in the state prison before you even blink."

"Dad! Please!" Nicole's face turned bright red.

"See you in school," Tanner said. He leaned forward as if to kiss her on the cheek, but Liam punched him on the shoulder, stopping him.

"Drive safe," he said, and the boy got the hint and went off, leaving Posey, Liam and Nicole standing there.

"I am *so* not going home with you," Nicole hissed. "You *humiliated* me. I can't *believe* you came tonight! Can't I even go to the *movies* with a *boy?*"

"You did go to the movies with a boy," Liam answered calmly. "And now you're going home."

"I'll walk," she said.

"Then I'll drive alongside you until you get into the building, then call Mrs. Antonelli and ask her to keep an eye on you."

"I hate you," Nicole said bitterly, then glanced at Posey. "Sorry."

"How did you get here?" Posey asked.

"Dad dropped me off," she muttered. She pulled out her phone and clicked on it. "Gross! Dad! Jeez!"

"What?" Liam asked.

"Caroline Connors posted that you were hot! That's disgusting!"

"So disgusting," Posey echoed.

Nicole's fingers were flying, and she muttered as she typed. "Ew. That's my dad you're talking about. And he's a jerk."

Ten silent minutes later, they pulled up in front of Liam's building. "I'll wait for the light to go on," Liam told his daughter as she got out of the car. "And I'll be back from her house in twenty minutes."

Just in case there was any doubt that he was actually interested in her on any level.

Posey maintained her silence until the light on the fifth floor went on and Liam pulled away from the curb. "Think you might be a little overprotective, Liam?" she asked tightly as they turned on Bank Street.

"Yep. Show me a father who isn't."

"My brother-in-law says Tanner's not a bad kid." At his questioning look, she added, "I asked him yesterday."

"He's probably not. But what if he is? And come on, Cordelia. What eighteen-year-old boy doesn't want to get laid?"

"Just because he wants to doesn't mean he will. And Nicole's not stupid. I'm sure you've talked to her about all this stuff."

"I did," he acknowledged.

"So I guess what you're really afraid of is that Tanner is just like you, and all sorts of nice girls will be tricked—"

"You know what?" Liam snapped, not looking at her. "When you're a single parent raising a teenage girl, you can give me a lecture. Okay?"

"Sure. And when you're looking for someone to come spy on your daughter, ask someone else." She stuffed her hands inside her pockets and glared at the dashboard.

"What are you complaining about?" Liam asked. "I bought your ticket. I bought your silo of popcorn. You seemed to like the movie."

"Liam…" Posey took a sharp breath and held it and said nothing more. What was she going to tell him, anyway? That she'd thought it might be a date? That she was insulted that he'd barely spoken to her, that (maybe) he'd asked her to the movies because he knew she wouldn't have plans?

He pulled up in front of the church and threw the car in Park. "Look," he said sharply. "I'm sorry you had a crappy time. I just… Whatever. I'm trying to keep an eye on Nicole, and I figured you wouldn't mind coming, since you seem to like her."

Posey didn't answer, not sure what to say.

"But I'd appreciate it if you kept stories of my idiot years to yourself," he added. "Nicole doesn't need to know what a shit I was."

"You weren't a shit," Posey said. But then again, he had been. Ask any of the girls he slept with and dumped. Ask her. What about making fun of a girl because she was skinny, telling her prom date she was completely unattractive? That was pretty shitty.

Then again, ask her about that little striped cat. Ask her how it felt to float through the halls after he'd said hi in front of everyone.

Liam was looking at her, his face unreadable. "I'm sorry," he said.

"Okay. You better get back." And before either of them could say anything more, she jumped out of his car and ran into her house, unlocked the door and went in, only to find Gretchen lying on her sofa in her pajamas, eating Posey's last pint of Ben & Jerry's Peanut Brittle ice cream. In other words, completely at home.

CHAPTER ELEVEN

"HI. WHERE WERE you?" Gretchen asked. She tore her eyes off the television screen—one of her rivals from the Cooking Network—and gave Posey a fake smile, running her eyes up and down in the Scan of Judgment Posey so well remembered.

"Gretchen! What are you doing here?" Posey asked. Shilo lumbered over to greet her, then, getting a whiff of popcorn, began inhaling her clothes for leftover molecules. "How did you get in?"

"Your parents gave me a key. I thought it would be nice for us to spend some time together," Gretchen said. "I've missed you."

"Seriously, Gretchen."

"I figured I'd crash here for a while. It'll be fun! Like a big slumber party or a sorority. Come on, Pose! We haven't hung out in ages."

"By hang out, do you mean…you're staying with me? Really?" Posey asked, sitting down.

"Sure. I love Max and Stacia, but they can be a little *too* interested, you know?"

"Uh, yeah, I do. Since they're my parents and all."

"And they were *so* happy when I told them how I wanted us to catch up and spend some real time together." Another smile. "So. Where were you?"

"The movies."

"Alone?"

"With friends." She'd rather cut out her eyeball than let Gretchen know she'd been with Liam. You don't just hand a loaded weapon to an assassin, after all. With a sigh, Posey sat in the bishop's chair, Shilo's nose glued to her knee.

"Cool. Cute place, by the way," Gretchen gestured around the great room. "You have such…interesting taste."

"So you just decided to move in, huh?" she asked.

"I'm hardly moving in, Posey. It'll just be a few days. Maybe a week. I thought it would be fun."

If Posey knew Gretchen, she was just about to whip out the Parents Pity Card.

"After all," her cousin said, "we haven't really hung out since my parents died."

Bingo.

It had been a horrible year for everyone, but, of course, mostly for Gretchen. However, she'd taken her misery out on Posey through constant jabs and insults, minor thefts of Posey's treasures—the little heart necklace from her dad, Oma's blue crocheted blanket. Posey understood, but it hadn't been easy.

But family was family.

"You're right," she said, albeit reluctantly. Shilo put his massive head on Posey's lap, commiserating. "Sure. You can stay for a while. I do know what you mean about Mom and Dad."

"Great!" Gretchen clapped her hands and turned the sound back on. "Is there anything to eat?" she asked. "Other than ice cream?"

"Um…you're the chef, Gret," Posey said.

"And the guest," she replied, not looking away from the TV.

Posey paused. "Okay. I'm sure I have some cheese and crackers or something."

"That'd be fantastic," Gretchen said. "If you have some extra virgin olive oil and French bread, bring that too, okay? But only if it's extra virgin."

"I have a frozen French bread pizza," Posey said sweetly. "Close enough?"

Gretchen gave her another once-over. "It'll have to do."

A WEEK LATER, POSEY was ready to burn down the church with Gretchen inside.

"Seriously? It's really that bad?" Elise asked on Day Six of the Barefoot Invasion.

"Well, the restaurant's only open Thursday through Sunday until Memorial Day," Posey answered. "She has a lot of time on her hands."

"So what does she do all day?" Mac asked in a rare complete sentence.

"She looks at magazines, takes long showers and makes a big mess in the kitchen. But there's still never anything to eat." Posey took a sip of her coffee. "She leaves towels on the bathroom floor, tissues on the coffee table, glasses everywhere. Supposedly, she's making plans for renovating Guten Tag, but I never see any sketches or anything. Oh, and she's started calling my parents Mutti and Papa. That might be the last straw." Especially since Gretchen had reminded Posey—twice—that Stacia was genetically identical to her own mother. As if Posey didn't know that already.

"Does she, like, know Derek Jeter?" Elise asked. "They lived in the same building? In New York? Susan Lucci, too. I love her? From *All My Children?*"

"According to Gretchen, she knows every celebrity ever born, and they all want to date her."

"I don't think I'd want to date a famous person," Elise said, giving Mac a doe-eyed look. "I'm, like, drawn to the blue-collar type?"

Mac muttered something and fled to the back room.

"Posey, what did you do to that man? Beat him with a stick? He's like an abused dog."

Both Posey and Elise turned as Vivian Appleton came in. "Hi, Viv! I was going to pick you up!" Posey said.

"I took a cab. I'm allowed to do that, am I not? The Vultures wouldn't approve—there go six more dollars of their inheritance, and still I refuse to die. Well. What's the matter with you, young lady?" She sat in the leather chair next to the front desk and put on her glasses to better stare down Elise.

"That guy? The abused dog, right? Mac. I totally love him," Elise whispered.

"He's rather old for you, dear."

"I don't even care. From, like, the first day I came in here? I just fell so hard, right? I mean, sometimes you just can't help it? But he hardly even talks to me?"

"Perhaps it's because you end all your sentences as a question," Viv observed.

"Do you think so?" Elise bit her thumbnail.

"No. Don't bite your nails." Vivian surveyed the interior of Irreplaceable. "Older, unattractive men are generally good husbands," she said regally. "The gratitude keeps them in line. Keep trying, my dear. Wear something a bit more form-fitting, too. That looks like it's made out of a trash bag."

"Seriously? You think?"

"I'm always serious."

"You're like this wise old woman or something?" Elise said. "Oops, I mean, you're like this wise woman. Not a question, right? Posey, tell her about your cousin! I bet she could totally help you out!"

Posey rolled her eyes and gave Viv the nutshell version.

"You lack gumption," Vivian pronounced when she was done. "Kick her out. She sounds like a parasite."

"Right?" Elise said, her mouth half-open in admiration. "I totally agree."

"It's not gumption," Posey said. "It's my parents. They have this fantasy of Gretchen and me being close as sisters, and they're thrilled that we're bonding. Except we're not. She just lays around like a big blonde slug with giant boobs."

Vivian snorted. "Yes, she was blessed in that department, as I recall."

"Don't tell me you watched her show."

"Once or twice. Not that I like German food. Does anyone?"

"I do," Posey said, just in case her mother was lurking. One never knew with Stacia.

"How loyal of you. Are you taking me to lunch or not?"

"I am. Where would you like to go?" she asked.

"To L'Auberge," Viv answered. "I'm in the mood for French after all this talk of Germany. I lived through that war, you know. Your parents may be nice people, but I will never eat at their restaurant."

"L'Auberge. Okay." Posey hesitated. To get there, they'd have to take Route 149, which led right past The Meadows. Did Viv want to see her old home? It might be just the thing for her to see it again, and see how much Posey loved it, too.

"We'll go the long way," Vivian said, reading her mind. "It's a nice day for a drive."

CHAPTER TWELVE

"ALL RIGHT. MY assistant will call you when it's all drawn up." Allan Linkletter stood up, offered his hand. Liam shook it, but when it seemed time to let go, Allan hung on a little longer, his grip tightening. "So. Funny that we're on the same baseball team, isn't it?"

"I guess," Liam said. Allan still hadn't let go of his hand.

"You met my wife at Rosebud's afterward. I didn't realize you slept with her in high school."

Well, shit. What was the appropriate response here? "Um...who's your wife?"

"Taylor Bennington?"

Liam tried not to wince. He *definitely* remembered Taylor from the old days. Funny, she hadn't mentioned she was married the other night. "Taylor Bennington. Right." Should he smile? Congratulate Allan on getting her to the altar? Taylor had been quite...talented, as he recalled. A little scary, but talented.

"It was her first time, she said." Allan's grip tightened.

A memory of Taylor unbuckling Liam's belt—with her teeth—flashed to mind. First time, huh? Somehow, he doubted that. "You sure you want to be my lawyer, Allan?"

The other man shrugged and finally released his hand. "The past is the past. As long as it really is the past, because if the past becomes the present, the future won't look too good for you."

The speech reminded Liam of an English class on tense, but he had to give the guy credit for putting it out there. Allan was around five foot six, and it didn't look like he spent much time in the gym. As if reading Liam's thoughts, the shorter man said, "I know people." Then, realizing that a lawyer in New Hampshire wasn't quite as mobbed up as he'd like to be, he added, "Okay, I don't know anybody. But I love my wife."

"I'm not looking for a girlfriend. Or anything." Especially one who was married, no matter what she used to do with her teeth.

"Great!" Allan said. He smiled, punched Liam on the shoulder and walked him to the door. "I'm definitely interested in that bike, so I'll drop by this week."

"Cool." Apparently Liam's past with Allan's wife didn't prevent the lawyer from wanting a custom-made bike to celebrate middle age.

Liam went to the bank of elevators and pushed the button and sighed.

At least that was done. Last will and testament, updated to include the value of the garage, plus another hefty life-insurance package. Advance directives, updated. Guardianship...well, it had always been the Tates. The only other option would be a stepmother, and Liam didn't see that happening.

About a year after Emma's death, he'd had an uneventful relationship with a nice enough woman—Paige, who owned the florist shop down the street from the garage where Liam worked. Uneventful was just what Liam was looking for—they'd had dinner once or twice a month, had sex afterward. It was fine. Emma had been the only one since senior year of high school, and being with someone else...all those differences, the feel of her hair, the way she smelled, the way they fit...it was a little weird. The sex was nice...it was sex, how could it not be nice? It just wasn't...special.

They broke up amicably enough when Paige told him she was looking for a little more, and Liam couldn't blame her. She was young, wanted a family…normal enough stuff. It's just that he couldn't do that. No hard feelings.

The doors to the elevator opened, and Liam went in. His own elevator was bad enough; the lawyer's office was on the twenty-third floor, and it was an older building. The ride up had been painfully slow. Swallowing, Liam pressed the button for the lobby and waited. Some sappy song by Neil Diamond, made worse by the Muzak-ization of it. Oh, right, this was the one they played at the Sox game he'd dragged Nicole to last weekend to get her to start speaking to him again.

Suddenly the elevator gave a lurch, and Liam's hands flew out to the walls. Shit! But the elevator continued on, though Liam thought he detected a lower note to the gears. Did he? Or was that just paranoia? After all, how many elevator cables snapped these days? Not a lot. You hardly ever heard about that kind of accident.

Still, his heart had that uncomfortable flopping feeling, and his chest was tight. He tried to breathe slowly. *Calm down, idiot,* he told himself. *You're fine. This is no time for a panic attack. Breathe in, hold it, breathe out, stop sucking in air, you're going to hyperventilate.* He knew the drill. And he had to get past these…events. Not cool to wig out when you were the only parent left.

Maybe he should get off and take the stairs, even if they were only at the eighteenth floor. Better than staying in this casket-waiting-to-happen. Liam swallowed thickly.

The elevator stopped, the doors opened and there stood Cordelia Osterhagen, looking at her phone. She took a step forward, then saw him and stopped. "Oh. Hi," she said.

"Hi." The doors pinged. "Getting on?" Liam asked, holding his hand on the door so it couldn't close. His chest was tight still, but he wasn't hyperventilating. Not yet, anyway.

"Yeah." She stuffed her phone in her jeans pocket and came aboard. She wore sturdy-looking jeans and several layers of flannel, that lush mouth of hers the only feminine thing on her. Well, that and the hint of breast coming from under the layers of flannel. Was she humming?

The elevator started moving again. Crap. He'd missed his chance to get off. "You know this song?" he asked, wiping his forehead with his sleeve.

"Everyone knows this song. It's my favorite song, as a matter of fact, so if you're gonna make fun of it, don't."

"Neil Diamond. Huh."

She gave him an evil look and hummed more loudly.

See, you can do this, his brain told him in a confident voice. *You've hardly thought at all about the cable snapping, haven't pictured Nicole sobbing over your casket and then going to live with Tates, who really couldn't be happier at getting their grandchild all to themselves and turning her into a—*

A grinding shudder ripped through the elevator, which screeched, then slammed to a stop. *Shit!* It was happening.

Then the lights went out.

"Oh, bieber," Cordelia said.

Liam tried to breathe in. Didn't seem to be working.

Okay, okay, just because he'd pictured this exact moment…nope, couldn't happen. The cable had not snapped. Not yet, anyway. But the air was definitely being used up.

"Well, this is not good," Cordelia said. "I have an appointment in twenty minutes."

"Don't talk," Liam choked out. Because that would use air. And if there were no lights, then there was no air in the ventilation system—*Don't take me away from my baby*—and they'd suffocate up here in the pitch black. Already his lungs were desperate for air, heaving in his chest. His legs were suddenly weak, and he leaned back against the wall, the inky blackness smothering. What about Cordelia? Was she suffocating, too? "Cordelia? You okay?"

"Of course I'm okay. Hang on." He heard her clothes rustle. Then a light came on. Fantastic. She was the type who carried a keychain flashlight. Good girl. It didn't alleviate the oxygen problem, but at least he wouldn't die in the dark.

She shined the little beam onto the panel. "Think I should push the emergency button?" she asked.

"Yes! What are you waiting for?" he croaked, sucking in what felt like the last of the air.

"Chill, Liam. We're only stuck. It's not like the cable's about to snap or something."

Why would she say that? Was she psychic? Why would she mention the cable snapping? Was it a premonition? The elevator shuddered again, and Liam's legs gave out. He sank to the floor.

"You don't look so good," Posey said, aiming her light at his face. It seared his retinas, and he closed his eyes and held up his hand. "Liam? You're white as a ghost."

"Push the damn button," he ground out, pulling in another breath. His chest felt like it was in a vise, and he couldn't inhale deeply enough to get sufficient air. A rasping sound came from his throat.

"Holy Elvis! Are you okay?"

"The button, Cordelia, the button!" Finally, she pushed the thing. A bell rang, then went silent. Not reassuring. Not one bit. Cordelia dropped to her knees beside him. "Liam?" she asked, shining that stupid light into his face yet again. Her eyes widened in horror. "You're all clammy! Does your chest hurt? It does, doesn't it?"

It did. And apparently he was rubbing it with one fist. She grabbed his wrist and gripped it, the flashlight clattering to the floor. "No, no, no," she muttered, yanking her phone from her pocket. "Hello? We're stuck in the elevator in the Mirren Building, and I think a man's having a heart attack! I can't tell… No, he's down…and I— Okay, okay!"

"It's not…" But what if it was a heart attack and not simple, choking panic? The vise on his chest clamped down harder. "Cordelia, I—"

"Don't worry, I'm here." She shoved him to the floor with surprising strength, thunking his head against the floor, and if he'd had the air, he would've told her to knock it the hell off, but—

"Oh, please, don't die, don't die," Cordelia chanted, ripping open his shirt. She put her ear against his chest. "Bieber! I can't hear anything, he's gasping! I think he's dying!" Her phone clattered to the floor, and she was suddenly straddling him, her knees pinning his arms.

"Cordelia," he managed, and— Oof! What little oxygen remained in Liam's chest was suddenly pushed out as Cordelia began pushing on him. *Hard.* "Cord— Oof!" Crap! That hurt!

"Hang in there, Liam! Think of Nicole! Hey! 911 people! I dropped the phone, hurry up, hurry up!" She pushed down again, and a searing pain lanced through Liam's right side.

"Stop," he grunted. She was killing him.

The elevator lurched, then rumbled, then began descending again. "Thank you, God!" Cordelia said, giving him another compression. The pain in his side flashed light behind his eyes, and Liam managed to wrench his arm free grab and her wrist. "Stop fighting, Liam!" she said, wrestling with him. "Help is on the way!" Another chest compression, another white-hot pain down his side.

Then the doors opened, Cordelia barked, "He's having a heart attack!" and the paramedics descended.

CHAPTER THIRTEEN

"No sign of a heart attack," the doctor said. "Looks like you just cracked a rib."

That's right, Posey thought. *Rub it in.*

"*I* didn't crack a rib," Liam said, his words running together. "She did. She broke me."

"It *looked* like a heart attack," Posey snapped. "Go back to sleep."

He'd dropped right off after the first shot of painkiller. Men. Such wimps. *She'd* broken two fingers last year trying to move a fountain with Mac, wrapped them with electrical tape and got back to work.

"It *wasn't* a heart attack." He sounded like a grumpy toddler.

"I know, Liam! But if it had been, maybe I would've saved your life, okay?" She turned to the doctor for some female solidarity. "He was clammy, rubbing his chest, couldn't breathe. Err on the side of caution, I figured."

"Panic attacks can look a lot like cardiac issues, you're right," the obviously brilliant woman said.

"See?" Posey said, looking at Liam. His eyes seemed to be moving in opposite directions.

"You broke me."

"Oh, sac up and stop whining."

"Some nurse you make. Why don't you just stab me?"

"Don't tempt me."

"Are you two married?" the doctor asked.

"No!" they snapped in unison.

"Okay," she said, holding up her hands in surrender. "Well, Mr. Murphy, we have a consult coming in, and then you'll be able to go home, okay? Just rest for now." She looked at Posey. "He'll need someone to drive him, obviously."

"I'll take care of it," Posey said.

"You should," Liam said. "You should do a lot more than drive me. You should be my servant."

"Oh, for the love of Elvis," she muttered.

"Here are the follow-up instructions," the doctor said. "Call his primary physician if you have any questions. You're free to leave after the consultation, okay? Good luck."

Posey glanced at the sheet, which advised limited activity until he felt better (which she guessed would be never, based on the total wimp he'd been thus far). There was more information on panic attacks than cracked ribs.

A panic attack is a sudden episode of intense fear that develops for no apparent reason and triggers severe physical reactions. Panic attacks can be very frightening. When panic attacks occur, patients may think they're having a heart attack or even dying.

"Exactly," she murmured. Still, she did feel a tiny bit guilty. Okay, a *lot* guilty. Liam had tried to tell her that's what it was, she could see that now, but being too busy breaking his bones, she hadn't put two and two together. So much for her seventh-grade CPR class.

But if he'd known it was a panic attack, one could assume he'd had them before.

She glanced over at the patient, who was asleep once more, his head turned slightly to one side. He needed a shave. His hair looked even blacker against the white pillow. Her eyes lingered on his mouth.

Hard to believe she'd actually straddled him in the elevator and ripped open his shirt. Too bad she hadn't enjoyed it more.

Great. She was getting turned on. Apparently CPR was quite the aphrodisiac. Trapped in an elevator with Liam Murphy—it hadn't exactly been the stuff of erotic fiction, had it? A man clammy with panic, trying to fight off the woman who was cracking his ribs. So, he was claustrophobic, she guessed. Or was afraid of elevators. Or both. Maybe it had something to do with Emma's death.

The poor guy.

Posey stood up and went to Liam's side, pulled the blanket a little higher on his chest. He had a tattoo on his shoulder (of course he did, it was required by the Bad Boy Book of Beauty)…a Celtic knot of some kind. Strong, manly, blue-collar hands.

Liam's eyes opened. "You broke me," he murmured.

"So, why are you having panic attacks?" she asked gently.

"Mr. Murphy? I'm Brenda Lutz, the social worker on duty." A stout, gray-haired woman came into the room. "Just wanted to check on how you're doing." She looked at Posey. "Hello. Are you the wife?"

"No, just a friend. I'll step out for a few, how's that?"

"Stay," Liam muttered.

"He's pretty out of it," Posey explained. "They gave him some painkillers for his rib."

"Which she broke," he added, eyes closed.

"Cracked."

"I see." The woman turned to Liam and raised her voice, as if he were deaf, not drugged. "Okay, Mr. Murphy, well, the main thing is that even if it feels like you're dying, even if you can't breathe or it feels like your heart is going to stop, chances are it's not. Okay?"

"Okay," he murmured.

"Panic attacks and anxiety syndrome are very serious problems, Mr. Murphy. They can be very distressing. Sometimes even debilitating. Terrifying. Many times they go away, but some people never stop having them. They can't work, can't sleep, can't eat, they get no joy out of life—"

"Hey, thanks for the pep talk," Posey said. "He's had a little stress lately, but he'll be fine. Thanks. He'll call if he needs you."

The social worker took a breath, frowned. "Fine. I'll leave my card, in case he wants to se me privately."

"I'll make sure he has it." *Nice job, lady. In case he wasn't freaked enough.*

"Thanks for ditching her," Liam murmured.

"Okay, big boy. Let me get you home. Come on. Put on your shirt."

He sighed and sat up (groaning, of course, just in case she forgot who broke him), then pulled off the johnny coat, and Posey stopped feeling her legs. Irritation? What irritation? *Mommy.* Body like a Greek god, this guy, complete with washboard abs and thickly muscled arms…. Jeans were still on, alas—apparently ruling out a heart attack didn't require a complete strip-down. Pity. She handed him his shirt.

"What's wrong with these buttons?" he asked, looking down.

"They're…missing. Come on, you look great."

An orderly wheeled Liam to the exit (the wheelchair did not staunch the guilt, either) and told Posey he'd wait while she got the truck. Shilo was sprawled across the front seat, sound asleep. "Sorry, pal," she said, hefting up his front half so she could get in. Starting the truck, she sighed. This had not been a good day. Gretchen had felt the need to cook last night—not a bad thing, but she'd decided to film herself, narrating what she was doing as if she were filming an episode of *The Barefoot Fraulein.* Part of this apparently involved some weird new-agey music that made Shilo whine and tremble, which made Jellybean and Sagwa growl, which made Meatball hiss…so all in all, not restful.

This morning, she'd had a panicked call from the owner of the barn in Chelmsford—the historic district had decided at the last second to be interested, and the owner needed Posey to give a statement to his lawyer, which was why she was at the Mirren Building in the first place.

Then she'd broken God's Gift, which, despite her intentions of saving his life, was not a happy feeling.

Well. Time to get the poor lad home. She pulled up to the entrance of the ER, and the orderly helped Liam in. Shilo, accustomed to riding (or sleeping) shotgun, whined from the truck's small backseat.

Liam fell asleep yet again on the way home. His hand was just inches from her thigh…that nice, masculine hand. Dante's hands had been soft—softer than hers, that was for sure. Dante was a good-looking man, that was certain—but it was a polished, put-together attraction, rather than the raw appeal Liam possessed. She glanced at him again. Sooty lashes. Ridiculous. He was much prettier than she was.

"Stop staring," Liam muttered, not opening his eyes, and Posey jerked her attention back to the road.

When they reached his place, she got out and opened Liam's door. "Time for bed, tough guy," she said, and he got out carefully. He stood there a minute, not quite steadily, and she slid her arm around his waist—his lean, warm waist.

"You doing okay?" she asked, trying not to think dirty thoughts.

"Mmm-hmm," he said, leaning into her, and those dirty thoughts surged. Even through her layers of flannel, she could feel the heat of his skin. Glancing down, she saw that beautiful torso again. Perfection. Utter masculine perfection. Except for the rib she'd cracked.

"Back in a few, Shilo," she said, her voice a bit unsteady. Shilo gave a snore in response. Liam seemed to be getting heavier as they rode up in the elevator. "Your hair smells pretty," he said, and her girl parts gave a warm squeeze.

Mrs. Antonelli's door remained mercifully closed, though Posey could well imagine her on the other side, watching through the peephole. "Got the keys, Liam?"

"In my pocket," he said. His eyes were closed.

Feeling quite perverted, she reached into his pocket. *Do not cop a feel,* she warned herself. It was difficult to avoid, but she tried. She unlocked the door. Déjà vu all over again, except this time, Liam was the one who was, er, incapacitated. She steered him down the same hallway he had carried her a few weeks ago, into a different room this time. His room.

The bed was covered with a dark brown comforter, very manly, and you could tell it was a guy's room because it lacked all those touches a wife would've given it. On the night table was a photo of Nicole, a gorgeous black-and-white shot of her on a swing. Another black-and-white photo of Nicole on the beach sat on top of the dresser. Aside from that, the room was pretty stark.

Liam pulled back the covers and collapsed on the bed with a groan. Posey pulled off his shoes and covered him up. She was tucking in Liam Murphy, the stuff of many a teenage fantasy. Maybe she'd go home and write about it in her Hello Kitty diary, then watch Luke Perry movies…or she could remember that she was thirty-three years old and wise up.

"Can I get you anything?" she asked. "Want me to call your daughter or leave her a note or something?" She paused. "Or I could stay and tell her when she gets home."

"You can go. But don't tell Nicole."

"Tell her you cracked a rib? Because I think she'll be able to see that you're uncomfortable, Liam. Since you're such a baby and all."

He smiled faintly, not opening his eyes. "I'll tell her about the rib. Maybe. Just not the panic stuff."

"Have you always been scared of elevators? My brother's afraid of cats."

"I'm not scared of elevators," he said, eyes still closed. "I'm scared I'll die and she'll be all alone."

The words caught her heart by surprise. Posey opened her mouth, closed it, then tried again. "You won't die, Liam. I mean, you will, of course, we all will…but not for a long time."

"Except I almost did. I laid down my bike last fall."

"You… Does that mean you were in an accident?" He nodded. "Were you okay?"

Liam finally looked at her, his eyes bleary. "Yeah. But it was close, you know. The cop said he expected a… What's that word? When people die?"

"A fatality?"

"Yeah. 'Cause my bike was all…you know. Wrecked."

"What happened?"

His eyelids were apparently too heavy to keep open. "I was on the freeway. Some guy in a Porsche tried to…" His hand flopped. "You know."

"Pass?"

"Yeah. That's it. Pass. And next thing I knew, I was lying on the ground in the breakdown lane, and my bike was all—" he made a twisting motion with his hands "—crushed. But I got…" Another hand gesture.

"Thrown?"

"Yep."

"Were you wearing a helmet?" she asked.

"I'd be dead without a helmet," he murmured. "Even so, concussion and stuff. But I'm not gonna tell you that, because I'm not telling anybody about that."

Posey bit her lip. "Okay. I won't know about it then."

"Good. Because it's a secret."

Or it would be without the truth serum that had apparently been administered along with the painkillers. He shifted and winced a little.

Crikey. Imagine being in a near-fatal accident and not telling anyone. Maybe—just maybe—he didn't have anyone to tell.

That thought sat in Posey's brain for a beat or two, throbbing. Imagine living with the fear that if anything happened to you, your child would have no one. He'd said that's why they'd moved back to New Hampshire…to be closer to Nicole's grandparents. He just hadn't said, "in case I die."

There was a strange ache in Posey's chest.

"Can you get me a pillow?" the patient asked.

"There are two right next to you."

"You have to be nice. You broke me."

"I'm very nice, Liam, and I didn't break you, I cracked you. Just one bone, too, so let's not exaggerate. You have two hundred and five other bones that are perfectly fine." Nevertheless, she walked over to the other side of the bed and got a pillow.

"Oh, so now you're a doctor? How come you didn't know I wasn't having a heart attack, then?"

"Shush. Here's the pillow, Princess Precious."

"Can you tuck it under my rib? The one you broke?"

She sighed loudly and pulled the covers down—there was that beautiful, rippling torso again, hello, gorgeous—and leaned over him, as there really was no avoiding it. Tucked the pillow against his side, trying to channel an angel of mercy and not a lustful reprobate.

"How's that?" she asked.

Apparently it was pretty good, because his hands were in her hair, and he pulled her face down to his, and he was kissing her—Liam Murphy was kissing her!—and it was so shocking and so warm and so utterly… His lips moved against hers, deepening the kiss. It was like being filled with light and heat and a melting weakness, oh, Elvis, it was amazing. Her hands were on his chest, his bare skin warm and perfect and so… God…it was so…so…

Over. It was over. Lips no longer on hers, hands no longer in hair.

Posey pulled back a little. His eyes were closed, lashes a dark smudge on his cheeks. "Liam?" she whispered.

There was a little smile on his mouth—the mouth that had been kissing hers. Otherwise, he was incommunicado. "Liam?" she said again, more loudly this time.

Nada. He was out cold. Down for the count.

She straightened abruptly. Face was burning, joints buzzing with adrenaline, chest filled with helium. Liam Murphy had kissed her.

And he'd fallen asleep in the middle of it. She didn't know whether to burst into song or kick something.

CHAPTER FOURTEEN

"COME ON, COME ON. This way. No time to lose. We don't want the blue-hairs to take our spot," Steve said.

A bit unclear on what that meant, Posey followed her date. That's right, a date. She wasn't about to sit around and wait for Liam Murphy to remember that he'd kissed her and either apologize or ask her out. It had been five days since The Kiss. Once his unconsciousness had been verified with a poke to the uncracked set of ribs, Posey had given him maybe thirty seconds to rouse, debating on kissing him again (because, man! That had been quite a kiss!) or smothering him, because obviously it hadn't been quite a kiss for *him*...just a reflex or something. Whatever. Their paths hadn't crossed since, and that was *fine*. Because even if he was worried about his daughter being left alone, and even if Posey couldn't deny that he had the thickest eyelashes she'd ever seen, and even though her girl parts still yowled like her cats during a full moon at the thought of that kiss, it didn't mean that he wasn't a jerk. He was. Because only jerks went around kissing women in medicated stupors and then did nothing.

"Oh, fantastic. Here we go." Steve steered her to a row of slot machines and pretty much shoved her onto a seat. "Good luck." With that, he spread his coat, her coat and her backpack onto three other slot machines, swiped a card and began punching buttons.

"Okay, so I just..." Posey's voice trailed off. Steve was engrossed already, muttering, staring at the screen.

Steve was Elise's cousin—Elise had dozens, apparently, and Steve had moved back to the area recently. "You *might* like him?" Elise had suggested in her singsong voice. "Right?"

"Is he a good guy?" Posey'd asked. "He's not a serial killer or anything, is he?" Such high standards. But *that kiss* had solidified her resolve to stop being distracted by Liam Murphy. And given the number of times she had relived that bleeping kiss, she needed distraction. Quickly.

"Um...no? Not a serial killer, of course not. He's a good guy...I think. It's been a while since we really hung out? Like...when we were twelve. But yeah. I guess?"

It wasn't exactly the glowing recommendation Posey was hoping for...but heck. Everyone had flaws, right? One date. What harm could there be in that? Elise had found a picture of Steve, and he was very cute, and what more could Posey want, right? Not a serial killer, quite cute. Someone, call a priest.

She and Steve emailed, then talked on the phone. She'd been hoping for a walk or a meeting in the park—the weather was gorgeous, and Posey had been weeding at The Meadows for two hours that afternoon, but Steve suggested something else. So here they were at the new Indian casino—Revenge on the White Man, as Posey thought of it. They'd exchanged the briefest of pleasantries, but it was now clear Steve wanted to get to work.

The casino was filled with a strange, discordant melody as hundreds of slot machines were played at once. There was a bitter smell in the air, too, from the smoking section. No one was dancing, not like on the casino commercials, and there didn't seem to be a lot of happy, well-dressed younger people. No. A woman with pink-tinged hair sat to Posey's left, her oxygen canister taking up another slot machine. Apparently you could play more than one at a time.

"Hi," Posey said. The lady didn't answer, simply adjusted her sweatshirt, sucked in a deep breath of oxygen and swiped her card, which hung around her neck like an ID badge. Clearly, she was experienced.

Four or five seats down was a tiny, ancient man with a walker, and next to him, a woman wearing a thick red wig, her gnarled hands punching the buttons with surprising force.

Posey reached into her pocket for a quarter, inserted, pulled the crank and lost. Six minutes later, the twenty dollars she'd brought for gambling purposes was gone. "I guess I'm done for the night," she said aloud. Neither her date nor the old lady replied.

"So, Steve, how is it being back and all?" she asked, getting up and leaning against his slot machine. "Elise said you just moved back from Texas, was it?"

"It's pretty good." He gave her a quick smile—that was nice; he remembered she was here—and pulled the crank again. "Wanna be my lucky charm?"

"Sure."

He pulled the crank again. Lost again. He glanced at her, pulled. "You done already?"

"Yeah. Amazing how fast you can go through twenty dollars."

"Twenty bucks? That's all you brought?" He gave her an incredulous glance, then lost again, reached over and pulled another lever. Lost again. Pulled, lost, cursed. Pulled, lost, cursed. Posey sighed. The good news was she didn't seem to have a gambling problem. Bad news was that Steve did.

Sure enough, he cursed again. "I don't believe it!" he blurted, staring at a message on the screen in front of him. "My credit card is maxed out again. Perfect." He smacked the screen of the slot machine, shoved his hands in his pockets and sighed.

Steve was not going to be the father of her children, that was clear.

"This really sucks." He glanced at her again. "Do you have a credit card?"

"Um…yes."

"Want to front me some money? Just a hundred or so."

"No, thanks."

He sighed. "Okay. Wanna get a room?"

Posey blinked. "No, I'm good." Elise would be hearing about this, that was for sure.

"Well," Steve said, checking his phone, "I guess we can…I don't know. Walk or something. I'm broke."

Dante of the Booty Call was looking better and better. At least he fed her.

"Why don't we just go our separate ways, Steve?" Posey suggested. If she left now, she could get a pizza before Angie's closed. Settle in, watch a movie…

"Aw, man! Posey, can you…uh, stand right here and don't move, okay?" He hunched down, pretending to tie his shoe, and glanced around Posey's hips. "Crap. Let's go. Come on, hurry up!" With that, he grabbed her hand and jerked her past the oxygen-tank lady, one hand shielding his face as if he were Lady Gaga dodging the paparazzi.

"Steve, stop! What are you doing?" Posey glanced over her shoulder. "Holy Elvis! Are they here for you?"

Two uniformed police officers and three or four burly casino security men were pointing and talking into radios. Posey jerked to a stop. "Are you under arrest?" she yelped, wrenching her arm free.

"Steven Aubrey, you are under arrest," called the female officer. "Stop or I will use this Taser before you can say Charlie Sheen."

Steve stopped.

"Unbelievable," Posey said. "Can you believe this?" she asked the oxygen-tank lady. No answer, but there was a tinkle of coins.

"Gotcha, you bastard," the old lady said, scooping up her winnings. "You must be my lucky charm," she added, giving Posey a smile.

"My date's being arrested," Posey told her.

"She let me borrow it!" Steve called. "She's senile. She forgot, that's all!"

"Did she forget you hocked her engagement ring, too?" the cop said. "Hands behind your head, scumbag."

Steve hesitated, then bolted, but the tiny man swung his walker out, tripping Steve. He went down at the feet of a security guard, who calmly stepped on the back of his neck.

Posey felt a nudge at her side. "Ma'am? Hands behind your head, please." It was the female cop.

"Wait, wait, wait," Posey said, obeying. "I barely know this guy. His cousin fixed us up. Fun date, don't you think?"

"Are you aware that he stole his grandmother's car and jewelry?" the officer asked.

"No! Jeesh, Steve! That's really low."

"She doesn't know anything," Steve said, his words muffled by the carpet. "We just met." The second officer slapped on some handcuffs.

"You know how to pick 'em, sister," the officer said.

"Tell me about it," Posey muttered.

"I thought my mom's podiatrist was bad, but you win."

"See, I would love a podiatrist. Think of the foot rubs. Can I put my hands down?"

"Sure." The officer took her name and phone number, but Posey was quickly cleared. Cleared! How many dates had required her being cleared? Still, it would make a good story—Vivian would love it, as would Jon. Her parents...not so much. Then again, they didn't have to know.

Steve apparently had life yet in him, because as they hauled him to his feet, he twisted away and broke into a staggering run. Just ahead of him was a Japanese family—mother, father, toddler in stroller—and though his hands were cuffed behind his back, Steve grabbed the handle of the stroller, as if he planned to drag it behind him as a hostage or something. The mother screamed, grabbed the stroller back, and all of a sudden, Steve was on the ground, convulsing, the toddler smiling at the excitement.

"Bull's-eye," said the female officer, blowing a kiss to her Taser.

"Now I know what I want for my birthday," Posey murmured.

"I shouldn't enjoy it as much as I do," the officer said, "but come on. He grabbed that kid, he had it coming. I should've aimed lower."

As Steve was led/dragged away, Posey rifled through her backpack, pulled out her phone, and called Elise. "Your cousin was just arrested."

"Oh, man! Again?"

"Elise! What do you mean, again?"

"Well, right? I mean...he said he had a new leaf? Whatevs."

"He stole your grandmother's car. And her jewelry."

"So not cool. But seriously, Gran should know by now, right?"

Posey ground her teeth. "Elise, next time you fix me up with someone, let's do a background check first, okay?"

"Right? That's a totally good idea. I'm gonna write that down." There was a pause. "Background check...Posey. Got it."

"See you tomorrow."

"Posey? Mrs. Appleton called. And she was kinda lonely."

Well, dang it. Poor Vivian. She usually got blue after the Vultures visited—Countdown to the Grave, as Viv referred to it. The relatives would gather round, talk in overly loud voices, tuck blankets around Viv's legs and stare at their watches as if hopeful her heart would give out any second. Posey wished she'd been with Vivian instead of watching her date resist arrest (though she had to admit, it was kind of fun to see a guy tasered, and what that said about her emotional state was nothing good).

By the time Posey had given her statement, it was getting late, and she was starving. She got a massive chocolate-covered pretzel from the food court and began making her way back toward where she thought the exit was. No clocks in here, of course, and no windows. No fun, either, from the looks of it. Even the high rollers' lounge looked grim. Posey paused, looking in. A two-grand minimum bet. Holy Elvis Presley.

Hang on.

A familiar figure was seated at a table off to Posey's left.

Gretchen.

She was sitting on a stool, dressed to kill in an emerald, one-shouldered dress. A man in a suit was with her, and they were clearly engrossed in a heated debate. Was Gretchen dating him? He put his hand on her arm, and Gret pulled back. "Don't you know who I am?" she said. "Get your hands off me! This is a Stella McCartney, I'll have you know!"

"Gret! Hey!" Posey yelled. "How you doing?" She pushed into the lounge, immediately out of place in her engineer boots and jeans. Gretchen looked up, then glanced back at the suit.

"Do you two know each other?" the man asked.

"I'm her cousin," Posey said. "Is there a problem?"

The man folded his arms. "Not if you have three thousand dollars."

"I'LL PAY YOU BACK," Gretchen said tightly, as they drove home.

Posey flicked on her signal. "I don't understand, Gret," she said, glancing at her cousin. "How can you place a bet if you're broke?"

"You're so naive, Posey." Gretchen turned her head and looked out at the landscape.

"Right. But I'm also solvent, and I just wrote a check for three thousand dollars!"

"And I *said* thank you, didn't I?"

"Gret...you have to tell me about this."

"Fine. Can it wait till we get home, at least?"

And so, half an hour later, Posey sat on the couch, clad in her fleece monkey pajamas, Shilo's granite-like head in her lap as the dog crooned his appreciation for the belly rub she was administering. Gretchen came in from the kitchen and set a tray down on the coffee table. *She* was wearing what looked to be a midnight-blue satin peignoir (how Posey even knew the word was a mystery, but it looked like what a peignoir should look like, in her mind anyway, all long and flowy and expensive).

Posey picked up a mug—homemade cocoa—and took a sip, then dipped her finger in and offered it to her dog for a taste.

"Can you taste the Kahlua?" Gretchen asked. "And I used unpasteurized milk. Creamy, don't you think?"

"Yeah, it's great," Posey said. "So. About the three grand."

Gretchen sat down on the couch and arranged the robe around her. "Right. Well." She sighed. "My money's tied up in this fund, and I'm temporarily a little short on cash."

Shilo's tail began thumping against the sofa. "You're broke?" Posey asked.

"*Broke* is such an ugly word." Gretchen took a sip of her cocoa and didn't meet Posey's eyes. Jellybean, who had always been something of a traitor, leaped up next to Gret and began purring.

Posey said nothing. She seemed to remember Stacia saying that Aunt Ruth and Uncle Ralphie had left Gretchen quite a nest egg...that Gretchen would never have to worry about money if she was smart. "What happened to your parents' money?"

"That took care of cooking school and my year in France. And my car." Gretchen had bought a Mercedes two-seater convertible for herself upon graduating high school. Even so, she should've had some left over. "And some jewelry and um...my wardrobe."

"What about your salary?"

"See, that's the big myth, that we get paid so much. Most of the real money comes from endorsements and product lines. But if you want to sell yourself, you have to look the part. The wardrobe allowance they gave me was laughable. And to live in Manhattan—well, if you want to live anywhere decent, that is—it costs money."

Gretchen had lived in a glittering apartment in one of the sleek and shiny Trump buildings along the Hudson River. As Elise suspected, it was littered with celebrities.

Shilo stretched, hitting Posey on the side of the head with a massive paw. "So you were spending more than you were making," she said.

"Well, yes, Posey, I suppose if you put it that way, I was. Look. I'm a celebrity, okay? There are certain expectations of me that you don't understand. All those appearances, all those…things."

"Like opening that Kmart?"

"People expect a television personality to look rich. You have no idea, Posey. So, yes, I spent more than I made. Big deal. Everyone does it. Even Donald Trump declares bankruptcy once in a while." She flung her braid over her shoulder and took a defiant sip of cocoa.

Posey said nothing. There was no arguing with Gretchen when she started comparing herself to the rich and famous. After a minute or two, Gretchen sighed. "Look, Posey, I know you think I'm a big phony. And I was stupid, I admit that. I started playing blackjack—I dated this guy who had a share in a casino in Atlantic City, whatever, and at first I won. It was *amazing.* You have no idea what it's like, winning a thousand dollars, or even two." Her face took on a soft, dreamy look. "There's such a rush. I mean, you walk in with what, four, five grand, and you can double your money in an hour."

"I'm guessing you wouldn't be broke if it was that easy," Posey said.

Gretchen ignored her. "One time, Pose, I won seven thousand dollars in one night."

"How long did it take you to lose it?"

Slowly, Gretchen seemed to come back to earth. "That's the thing," she admitted. "You get hooked. You lose six rounds, then you win one and you think 'Oh, I'm on a roll now, I'll get it back,' and then even if you do, you can't help wanting more."

Sensing that someone needed a kiss, Shilo rolled off the couch and went over to Gret and licked her knee. For once, she didn't push his big head out of the way, just reached out and gave him an awkward pat. Jellybean, disgusted that Gretchen's attention had gone to a lowly canine, jumped off the couch and stalked away.

"I didn't quit the Cooking Network," Gretchen said, so quietly Posey almost couldn't hear. "They fired me. I'd borrowed money from a not-very-nice person, and when I couldn't pay it, he went to the network and said he'd make it public. So they paid it, but they fired me."

"How much was it?" Posey asked.

"Twenty-five thousand."

"Oh, Gret." Posey closed her eyes. "I'm so sorry." That dopey show had been everything to her cousin.

"Don't be sorry," she said, a hard edge to her voice. "They didn't know anything. Marketing practically ignored me. I was, like, how am I going to get a million viewers an episode if you put me in this slot? Against Rachael Ray, who gets everything handed to her on a silver platter? And who's gained fifteen pounds this year alone? Don't get me started on that scrawny tramp, Giada."

"Okay, let's just skip over all of the glaring hyperbole and let me ask you this," Posey said. "Gret, if your whole life has collapsed because of a gambling problem, why were you at the casino tonight?"

"Because! You think I like living here with you in this freezing-cold house? Listening to Max and Stacia tell me—me!—how to make a linzer torte?"

"Whoa! Stop right there, princess! I don't recall inviting you here, and as for my parents, you should be kissing their feet and scrubbing their toilets. So don't go there, okay?"

Gretchen looked at her hands. "I just want to get my life back in gear," she said in a quieter voice. "I thought if I could win a few thousand dollars, I could…start over."

"Where'd you get the money to gamble?"

Gretchen didn't answer for a minute. "From your parents. From what they gave me for the renovation."

"Gret! You can't do that!"

"Well, I did! It was stupid, but you don't understand!"

"How much did you take?"

"Two grand."

Posey took a deep breath, held it, then exhaled slowly. "Okay. I'll pay that back, too. But here's the deal. You're going to pay me back. All five thousand, because guess what? You cleaned me out, Gret. I'm not rich, you know."

"Really? I couldn't tell." She cocked a perfect eyebrow.

"And guess what else, Fraulein? You can start by helping out around here. Painting, window glazing, moving some of this stuff…"

"I don't know how to paint. Or glaze a window."

"Well, how about this, Gretchen? You can learn."

CHAPTER FIFTEEN

SIX TWENTY-THREE on Wednesday night of a long weekend. He could work. Or eat. He could make dinner, then eat, then work. Also, maybe watch some television.

Nicole was at yet another sleepover, as school was closed tomorrow for a teacher-development thing, then on Friday as well for Founders' Day Weekend. It was her third sleepover since they'd moved. This was either good, in that she was making friends, or very bad, in that she might at this very moment be guzzling vodka and doing Ecstasy with a bunch of boys, after which they'd get in a car and all end up dead.

Granted, he'd dropped her off twenty minutes ago, spoken to both Emily and Chris Carlisle at length, ensuring that both parents would be home all night. They seemed perfectly responsible, but still. He'd left his phone number (home and cell), and his address, just in case. Nicole had given him the Slitty Eyes of Death, followed by a hard elbow to the ribs, which still hurt a little, thanks to Cordelia Osterhagen trying to kill him.

And by the way, that whole hospital aftermath...that was oddly vague. The pain meds had knocked him flat, but there was something he should remember there. He and Cordelia had bickered at the hospital, he remembered that. She drove him home with the giant dog...but something else had been flitting at the edge of his brain for days now. Irritating.

Well, at any rate, Nicole had promised to text him at nine and eleven and call in the morning, then threatened suicide if he dared to call the Carlisles to check up on her. "Bye!" she said. "Have fun! Get out of the apartment, okay? You're not dead yet."

So here he was. In the apartment. Home alone, a widower picturing his child's misdeeds...not so much fun. Work held no appeal; he'd just come from there to take Nicole to the party. No. He should get out of the house, be with other people. Life was changing, and Nic was right. He wasn't dead. Not yet. He picked up the paper and got lucky.

A little while later, Liam pulled up in front of the adult education building. The ad had said walk-ins were welcome, so here he was. Granted, learning to design a website wasn't high on Liam's list of priorities, but he guessed the garage wouldn't hurt by having an Internet presence. Besides, it sure as hell beat out singles cooking or, God forbid, ballroom dancing.

Speaking of, there were the dancers. And oh, crap, there was Taylor Bennington of the talented teeth. Her face lit up at the sight of him, and Liam gave a terse nod, then continued down the hallway.

The smell of garlic slowed him down. A chorus of laughter came from that room, and Liam glanced in. People were paired together, chopping and tasting, and the smell was fantastic.

Cordelia Osterhagen was in there, opening her mouth for a spoonful of whatever her partner—a man—was feeding her, and Liam had an abrupt flash of Cordelia over him, and he could practically feel her mouth on his, that lush, beautiful mouth—

"Hi there."

Liam jumped. A man in his thirties stood in front of him. "I'm Jonathan White, your daughter's home-ec teacher? We met the other night at Rosebud's."

Liam nodded, offering his hand. "Nice to see you again." This guy was related to Cordelia somehow, he remembered.

"Nicole is such a great kid. I wish I had twenty of her. You hungry? Want to join us?"

"I'm starving, actually."

"Come on," the teacher said, smiling. "We eat at the end of the class. If Posey doesn't cut off someone's finger, that is."

"I wish I could take credit for that," Cordelia said, turning. "But it was just luck." Her smile fell as she saw Liam, and her face flushed. "Oh. Hi."

"Hey," Liam said. Oh, yeah. There was something about that mouth, all right.

"Gang, this is Liam, the dad of one of my students. You don't mind if he hangs out, do you? We always have too much food as it is."

"Hi, Liam!" Kate Ellington called, and Liam gave her a smile. She was with an older man who couldn't seem to take his eyes off her rack, not that Liam could blame him. It was nice there.

"Let's put you with Ginny, shall we?" Jon said, leading Liam over to a woman in her fifties.

"Oh, wow, thank you, Jon, I owe you," she blurted.

"Hi. Liam Murphy," he said, shaking her hand.

"Wow," she repeated. She wiped her hands on her T-shirt, which showed the werewolf kid from the vampire movies. *Team Jacob,* the shirt proclaimed. "I'm Ginny. Hi. Yeah. You are gorgeous."

"Nice to meet you," he said, grinning. They were next to Cordelia, who was studiously ignoring him, and her partner, a rather odd-looking man wearing a fur hat with earflaps.

"My ribs are doing just fine, thanks for asking," Liam said to her.

"Of all the cooking classes in all the world, you had to walk into mine," Cordelia muttered.

For the next half-hour, Liam flirted with Ginny, who was full of sighs and giggles. The class was actually kind of fun…they were making a Bolognese sauce, and the smell was thick and spicy. Liam was a pretty fair cook himself, but it was nice, being out with grownups. People joked and laughed and swapped insults. Everyone except Cordelia, Liam noticed, who seemed awfully quiet. When they all sat down to eat, pushing two tables together, Liam made sure he was across from her.

"I'd think you were already a pretty good cook," he said, taking a bite of the pasta.

His foot touched hers accidentally, but she jumped as if he'd slugged her. "Excuse me?"

"Since your parents own a restaurant," he said. Granted, people didn't really go to Guten Tag for the food, but still.

"Um, right. I cook a little." She didn't look at him, and Liam smiled.

"She's lying," the teacher said, coming over and putting his arm around her. "She's my sister-in-law, and even though I've been with her brother since the dawn of time, I can say that Posey here has never made me anything more than a Newman's Own pizza."

"Which was excellent," she retorted.

"Well, I'm sure she has other skills," Liam murmured, and bam, her cheeks went nuclear. She shoveled in a bite of pasta and chewed, still not looking at him. She wore two flannel shirts, but both were unbuttoned a few, and Liam could see a little camisole thing underneath it. Girl clothes, in other words, and Liam had the sudden urge to peel off those layers of flannel and see what lay beneath.

Well, well, well. Granted, it had been a while, but here he was, picturing Cordelia naked. Might be a nice little package under there. Compact. Petite. The word *spitfire* came pleasingly to mind. As if reading his thoughts, Cordelia laced her hands together and stretched out her arms, cracking her knuckles and staring at him with narrowed eyes. The Slitty Eyes of Death, Osterhagen-style. Liam grinned at her and took another bite of the spaghetti Bolognese.

"It sure has been nice meeting you," Ginny said, and Liam stood up.

"Same here," he said and kissed her on the cheek. "I had a great time."

"I'm going to relive that for quite some time," she said, and he laughed and kissed her again, then took his seat once more.

Most of the people were trailing out, he noticed. Jon was leaning in the doorway, laughing with a student. Only Cordelia and he were still eating—she might pretend not to notice him, but here she was—and Liam realized he really didn't want to go home just yet.

"Do you have plans tonight?" he asked.

"N— Um, yes."

"No, you don't."

She narrowed her eyes again—pretty eyes, now that he noticed. Brown. He'd always liked brown eyes. "What makes you so sure I don't have plans, Liam?"

"Do you?"

Another blush. "Jon, we're having drinks tonight, right? At Rosebud's?"

Jon paused, his eyes going from Posey's face to Liam's. "Uh…yes?"

"Mind if I tag along?" Liam asked.

"I… Posey?"

She set down her fork and glared up at him. "Okay, Liam, fine. I don't have plans other than going home and watching a movie with my dog and cats. Okay? Happy now?"

Liam cocked his head and studied her face. "Are you mad at me?"

"Nope."

"You seem mad."

Jon's phone rang. "Oh, there's Henry. Bicker away, young lovers. I'll call you tomorrow, Posey. Nice seeing you again, Liam."

"Same here. Thanks for letting me stay."

They were the only ones left in the room. She was clearly pissed, but why? And why wouldn't she just tell him, since he'd asked and everything? Women. They were the least straightforward creatures in the universe. "So," he said. "Back to your bad attitude. Are you always this grouchy?"

She shoveled in a huge bite of pasta. "No," she said thickly. "You just bring out the worst in me." She pursed her lips, and there it was again, that not-quite memory.

"So, how about it?" he asked. "Want to grab a beer? Or a coffee?"

Her face flushed. "Liam, I'm betting at least two dozen women have come on to you since you got back to town. I bet women have to take a number just to stand close to you. Why don't you call one of them?"

"Why don't you want to go out with me?"

"On a date? You want to take me on a date, Liam? Because don't forget, this is a singles cooking class, and only desperate people sign up for these things. I've never been married, I'm thirty-three years old, I have three cats, my mother already has an entire roomful of toys for my unborn children. You really want to take me out for a beer? Because you know I'll read into this and start shopping for a wedding dress."

He bit down on a smile. "Is that a yes?"

She tossed down her fork. "It's a no."

Well, color him shocked. He wracked his brain for a memory of the last time he'd been turned down and came up empty. "Okay. I'll walk you to your car."

"Truck."

"Whatever."

The smell of rain was in the air, and a damp wind blew from the river. Liam sighed. Guess he'd be sitting home alone after all tonight. Well. At least he'd gotten out a little.

Cordelia's hair fluttered in the wind, and she hugged her thick jacket more closely around her as they approached her truck.

"Liam," Cordelia said abruptly, then stopped. She sighed and stuffed her hands in her pockets. "Do you really want to get a beer with me, or are you just jerking my chain?"

He looked down at her; she was staring at her truck door. "I'd love to get a beer with you, Cordelia."

"Why?"

He hesitated a second. "Because I'm a lonely widower who doesn't want to go back to his empty apartment and stare at the walls."

She folded her arms and scowled at the pavement. When she looked up, her expression wasn't nearly so fierce. "Okay. But only because you pulled the widower card."

"At least it's good for something."

Then she smiled, just a flash, and something moved in Liam's chest. Something warm, and something he hadn't felt in a long time. "Meet you at Rosebud's," she said.

Then she jumped in her truck. Turned the key. He heard the click of a dead battery.

"I'll drive," he said, grinning.

"Shoot," she said. "I need a jump." She glanced dismissively at his car.

"My battery won't have enough juice for a truck that size," he said.

"I'm aware." She pursed her lips, and he found that he *really* wanted to get that beer with her.

"How's this?" he said. "I'll come back tomorrow and jump it with the truck from the garage. I can drive you home tonight. Good enough?"

"Okay," she said after a pause.

"Great," he said, and as he opened the passenger door of his car for her, Liam found that he was smiling.

As he started the car, however, Liam glanced at the dashboard clock—crap. It was 9:20.

He'd missed Nicole's call. "Hang on one second," he said as Cordelia buckled herself in. He dug his phone out. No missed calls, no messages. He typed a quick note. *Having fun? Text your dear old dad.* Waited a beat—Nicole, like every teenager he knew, practically had her phone implanted in her palm. She'd answer back within seconds.

Except she didn't. "Come on," he muttered.

"Problem?" Cordelia asked.

"Um…not yet." He'd call her. She hated when he called, but she'd missed their check-in, so she'd have to deal.

"Hi, you've reached Nicole Murphy's voice mail! Sorry I'm not around, you know what to do."

"Nicole, it's your father. Call me," he growled.

"'Nicole, it's your father,'" Cordelia mimicked in a low voice, smiling. "I bet she knows your voice by now."

"It's not funny," he said. "She's at a party. They said no boys were coming, but you know what? I bet there are boys."

"Why don't you call the parents?"

"Good idea."

Unfortunately, the Carlisles seemed to have an unlisted number. Very suspicious. He should've asked for their number when he dropped Nicole off. He'd left his numbers, sure, and obviously Nicole had her own phone. Why hadn't he asked for the Carlisles' number? Furthermore, why hadn't they offered it, when he was reciting his own? Huh? Because maybe they didn't want him to know it, that's why. That's what you'd do if you were a drug dealer, right? And drug dealers relied on children getting hooked, and Nicole was in fact a child and therefore a potential client for a drug dealer, and even if that was a little far-fetched, you never knew.

"We're just gonna swing by their house, okay? Just to check on them," Liam said, the tires screeching as he pulled out of the parking lot.

"Great. Another fun night stalking Liam's daughter," Cordelia muttered. "Can you let me out at the corner? I left something on the stove, I just remembered."

He didn't answer. Best-case scenario, Nicole was simply being a teenager, forgetting to check in with him, even if that rule was carved in stone, damn it. Worst-case scenario? Vodka. Ecstasy. Boys. Cars. Dismemberment and/or death.

They turned onto Lighthouse Avenue, where the Carlisles lived—okay, yes, they screeched onto Lighthouse Avenue. "For the love of Elvis, slow down," Cordelia said, clutching the dashboard.

Liam didn't answer, too busy sweating. The downstairs curtains of the house were drawn. On every window. That was not cool. In fact, it was really, really suspicious. He stared at the house, his hands clenched around the wheel.

"So…you going in?" Cordelia asked.

"What? No. I'm just… I'll just check."

"What do you mean, check?"

Liam opened the car door. "I'm going to…look. Because if they're doing something illegal in there, I want proof."

"Illegal? Liam, you're… Come back!"

He barely heard her. If there were boys in there—and oh, if there were boys, Nicole would be in such trouble she would never see the stars again, because he'd ground her for the rest of her life. If it was worse—a bong, maybe (hell, every party *he'd* been to in high school had a bong), or worse, some kind of crack paraphernalia…

He felt a hand on his arm. "What are you doing, idiot?" Cordelia asked.

"I'm just gonna climb this tree and take a look."

"Are you *insane?* You're going to spy on a bunch of teenage girls? You want to talk illegal, Liam? Climb that tree, and I'll call it in myself."

"Well, I'm not just gonna knock on the front door and ask if they have any drugs in the house, am I?"

"Liam, your kid forgot to call you. Relax."

"Right," he snapped. "Relax. I don't know those people, and yet my little girl is inside. And she's all I have. I have to keep her safe." There was that damn tightness in his chest again. He rubbed it with his fist, stopping when he saw Cordelia notice.

"Liam," she said in a gentler voice. "She *is* safe. She's at a sleepover. I'm sure it's completely innocent. Let's not have the choo-choo jump the tracks here."

"Really?" he said. "She's safe? Innocent? Then why didn't she check in? Is she even in there? Why isn't she answering her phone? Why do the Carlisles have an unlisted number? The curtains are pulled. Isn't that what drug dealers do when they're cutting up drugs?"

"Okay, crazy pants, you know what?" She sighed. "I'll climb the tree, and if there are boys or kidnappers or ninja assassins, I'll let you know. Okay?"

Liam gave a reluctant nod. "Okay. That's a good idea."

"No, it's not. It's a terrible idea, Liam. But at least you won't get arrested. I've already had one date this month get hauled away in handcuffs. Give me a boost, idiot."

Climbing a tree on a windy April night to spy on a sleepover party…well, it was different, Posey had to admit that. She'd also admit that climbing trees was pretty fun. So was spying, if you got right down to it. And she had to hand it to Liam—she could see right into the bonus room window from here.

"Okay," she said, glancing down at the world's most neurotic father. His face was clenched with worry, and her heart gave an unwilling tug. She looked back across the street. "There are four girls. Does Nicole have green Hello Kitty pajamas?"

"Yes."

"Well, she's there. Looks like they're playing Wii. Golf, I think. Or bowling. And oh, here comes a woman…forties…has a big bowl of something…is it needles?"

"Are you serious?"

Posey grinned. "Nope, seems to be popcorn. Should we call a SWAT team?" She looked down at Liam again. He was staring at the house, arms folded across his chest, the breeze ruffling his dark hair. "Can I come down now?" she asked.

"Yeah."

Taking care not to slip, as the branches were damp with the fog, Posey climbed down from the tree, making a mental note to climb one again when it wasn't night and they weren't spying on people. She jumped down the last few feet and brushed off her hands.

Liam was still looking at the house. "I'm sorry," he said, his voice low. He didn't look at her, but his expression was...well, miserable. Remembering his admission last week about his accident, his fears over Nicole's well-being, her heart gave a tug.

"It's okay." She punched his shoulder. "She's a good kid. And you seem like a good dad, in a neurotic, insane kind of way."

"Right."

"Oh, come on. I'm sure a lot of parents envision the worst."

"True enough."

"They just don't...run with it the way you do."

He looked at her then, a slight, self-deprecating smile in his eyes. "Thank you for climbing up there."

"You're welcome. It was kind of fun."

His smile grew, her girl parts meowed. Danger, Posey. "Well, it's pretty damp out here. We should get going, huh? I think I'll skip that beer, okay? You could just take me home. That would be great." Posey took a step toward his car, but Liam stepped in front of her, blocking the way. "What? You want me to climb up again?" she asked.

"No."

He was looking at her...at her mouth, specifically. Posey's stomach gave a warm squeeze. "So, let's get going, okay?" she said, her voice a little loud in the cold night.

He nodded but didn't move, just studied her mouth, then finally raised his eyes to hers. "Did I kiss you the other day?"

She sputtered, her face suddenly blazing with heat. Looked at the Carlisle house, the car, the tree.

"Did I?"

God, that voice. Low and smoky and such a turn-on! She cleared her throat. "Um...sort of. Yes."

He didn't answer. Risking a glance at his face, she saw that he was smiling. Just a little. She licked her lips. Mistake, because his gaze dropped again to her mouth as if...well...like he might...

"How was it?" Liam asked, and her knees threatened to give out.

"Um...you know. You were medicated. I've had better." Her voice was breathy now. If he stepped on her foot, she might well conceive a child.

"Can I give it another shot?"

Holy Elvis Francis Aloysius Xavier Presley! "Um..."

He stepped a little closer, enough that she could feel his warmth. "Doesn't seem fair that you remember and I don't, that's all," he murmured.

"Life is often unfair." Her voice sounded brisk, despite the wobbly knees, so at least there was that.

"Can I kiss you, Cordelia?"

Her brain barked out an admonishment...something about his track record, his current stable of interested women, his...his...his eyes were just beautiful, it should be against the law, the way he looked at her with that faint smile. If she took half a step toward him, they'd be touching.

"Okay," she said. "Get it over with." She jammed her hands in her pockets and waited.

Liam closed the small distance between them, and he was so warm, she could've melted right into him, that heat was so welcome, so wanted. His hands cupped her face, his smile fading as he studied her, and Posey's eyes fluttered closed—yes, fluttered—she couldn't seem to help it. Then his lips were on hers, softly, gently, and she had to clench her fists inside her pockets to keep from grabbing him by the belt buckle and throwing him to the ground right there. Oh, Elvis, it was the world's most perfect kiss, soft and warm and so...affecting, heavens...his mouth moving gently on hers, their lips fitting together like they'd been made just to kiss each other.

Then it was over, and Posey forced open her eyes. He was looking at her, that light still in his eyes. She swallowed, rather loudly. "Not bad," she announced. "It's just that with all the hype, I don't know. I guess I expected more."

Liam burst out laughing, so surprising her that she jumped back. "I really like you," he said.

"My life's work is done, then," she said, hoping he didn't notice that she seemed to be shaking.

"So…take you to your house?" he asked, opening her car door.

"Just driving me home, big guy. Don't get any ideas."

"I wouldn't dare."

Posey was somewhat surprised she could form sentences, as her brain was roaring with white noise. Her limbs were flooded with a hot buzz, and her heart clattered in her chest as Liam started the car and pulled into the street.

"You going to the parade this weekend?" Posey heard herself ask after a mile or five.

"I guess so," he answered, turning onto South Church Road. "Does Guten Tag still go all out?"

"We sure do."

He pulled into her small driveway, and Posey had the car door open before he came to a full stop. "Okay, see you soon," she said, bolting.

"Uh…good night," she heard him call.

She practically ripped the church door off its hinges, slammed it closed behind her and slumped to the floor as her wobbly legs gave out. From the great room, Shilo woofed twice before collapsing back in front of the woodstove. Gretchen had said she'd be working late, thank goodness. Meatball gave a little squeak of welcome, and wind gusted around the steeple, the only sound other than the roaring in her ears.

Now that she was safe, the reality of that kiss sank in. If he could make her feel this much with one chaste kiss, then what—

A knock on the door made her jump. "Who is it?" Her dog, purchased for protection, gave a snuffling snore.

"It's Liam."

Posey scrabbled up off the floor and opened the door a few inches. "Yes?"

His expression was wry. "You forgot your purse."

"Oh. Thanks."

He handed her the battered leather backpack. "Have a good night," he said, turning to go.

"You, too. Um, Liam?"

He turned back, and without further thought, she'd grabbed the front of his leather jacket, yanked him inside and kissed the stuffing out of him. One hand was gripping his damp, soft hair, and the other was inside his coat already, and she felt him smile against her mouth, and thank the heavens, he was kissing her back, pushing her against the wall of the little foyer (oh, the wall!), his strong, solid arms wrapped around her tight and sure. He slid one hand down her back, pressing her against him, and his heat and strength, his mouth on hers, was un-bleeping-believable; she was panting already. He dragged his mouth off hers, then kissed her neck, and Posey's knees buckled.

Then Liam pulled back, kissed her lightly on the mouth once more, and looked at her, his eyes narrowed. "I have to say," he murmured, running his thumb along her lower lip, "I'm a little surprised."

"Mmm," she managed. His weight was the only thing holding her up.

"I wasn't even sure you liked me."

"Who says I do?" she managed. He grinned, and without her explicit permission, her fingers tightened their grip on his shirt.

"Do you like me enough that I can I come in and stay for a little while?" he asked, leaning against her a little more purposefully. Elvis! One lean, and she was halfway to the moon.

She didn't answer. Waited for a reason to say no.

None came.

"Want me to go?" he whispered before kissing her jaw, trailing a finger down her throat.

"Nope," she said, her voice calm.

"You sure?"

"Yep," she said. Now or never, Posey. She grabbed his hand and towed him through the great room.

"Shilo, you remember Liam," she said as they passed her dog, who snuffled in response before resuming his power nap. Through the kitchen strewn with Gretchen's detritus. Don't let him change his mind. Don't let him overthink this.

At the top of the stairs, Posey pushed open the door to her bedroom, then stopped abruptly, dropping Liam's hand. Then, even though it wasn't easy, she forced herself to really look at him.

Liam Murphy. With her. Despite aeons of adolescent yearning and a goodly amount of more recent lust, Posey had never actually believed that anything like this would really happen. That he would choose her. That he would look at her the way he was, intently, seriously.

Then he reached out and touched her lips, gently, almost reverently, and that's what did her in.

Before he even kissed her again, she was in love.

Again.

CHAPTER SIXTEEN

LIAM SQUINTED AT the clock, the only thing illuminating the room: 12:13 a.m. He'd fallen asleep for a few minutes. Not that he hadn't earned a nap, he thought with a grin. He might've been a little out of practice, but yeah, he could say that things hadn't been half bad.

In fact, things had been pretty flipping fantastic.

Reaching over, he was a little surprised to find the bed was empty. After that Olympic round of sex, he'd expect her to be out cold, too. Well, there was something…a cat, apparently, because it mewed softly, then jumped down. But no human.

"Cordelia?" he said. No answer. Too bad, because he had quite the urge to kiss her again. And not only kiss her, either. He'd been right about what lay beneath all that flannel. Well worth finding. Lean, but not scrawny, everything in proportion. She was small—but in a nice way. Not underfed, just…nice. She was strong, too, and he hadn't been afraid of hurting her or being too heavy. Her skin was surprisingly soft and sweet, and the way she smelled was like an addiction, that orangey, clean smell. And man, that mouth of hers… The girl could kiss, and when her legs had wrapped around his waist…yeah. *Olympic* covered it pretty well.

Liam got out of bed, groped around for his jeans and pulled them on. Maybe she was taking a shower. Maybe he'd join her in there.

The bathroom was empty. Huh. He padded down the stairs, curious. Even though Cordelia didn't seem like the cuddling type, most women didn't bolt after sex, did they? Back in the day, he was the one itchy to leave. Which made him kind of a prick, he knew. Using women for sex, however willingly they'd offered themselves up, was not something he was proud of. Not anymore. When he was seventeen, back in his idiot days, sure. Amazing how fatherhood changed a guy's perspective.

One of the cats, the one with the big head, hissed at him and ran upstairs. Strange house, this old church. There was a light on in the kitchen, though Cordelia didn't seem to be there, either. But wait. A door was slightly ajar. Ah-ha. He could hear the telltale rattle of a food wrapper. Liam opened the door, and there stood Cordelia in the pantry, turned slightly away from him and clad in her bathrobe, hair all messed up, stuffing four or five Ritz crackers into her mouth, the giant dog staring at her, drooling impressively. "Hi," Liam said, folding his arms over his bare chest.

She jumped. "Urmph," she said, a few crumbs flying. A blush crept up her neck. She swallowed thickly and gestured with the crackers. Her dog took this as an invitation to gently remove the roll of crackers from her hand, then stepped delicately around them both, leaving with his booty.

Cordelia swallowed thickly, then shoved her hands in the pockets of her robe, an aging blue-and-green flannel thing that reminded Liam of something worn by his alcoholic uncle. Her feet were bare. And cute. "Hi," she said.

"I was wondering where you'd gone."

"Oh…just a…snack. Do you want anything?"

"No, I'm good," he answered. He stood there, looking at her. She made no attempt to leave the pantry. "You gonna stay in here all night?"

"Nope." Still blushing, she brushed past him—there was that nice smell of oranges again—and sat at the kitchen table. He joined her.

She was uncomfortable, that was clear. And man, she was cute. Those big brown orphan eyes, that little chin. She definitely looked like an elf, though Liam knew that most women wouldn't cherish the comparison. Her gaze made it about as far as his throat, then went back to his bare chest, then to his arms. She swallowed again, then looked at the sugar bowl.

"Everything okay?" he asked.

"Sure. Of course. What could be wrong?"

"I don't know. I wasn't the one hiding in the pantry."

"I wasn't hiding. I just didn't, um...want to wake you up."

"Thoughtful of you."

"My cousin will be home soon," she said, eyes on the sugar bowl.

"Want me to leave?"

"Oh! Um...well, you can if you want."

She still couldn't seem to meet his eyes. He suppressed a sigh. Why didn't women come with a user's manual? She'd practically mauled him in her front hall and now wouldn't even look at him. "Cordelia, I thought that was a lot of fun. Was I wrong?"

"Nope. It was fun. Very fun. Thank you." The blush flared again. She bit her lip—he wished she wouldn't, because frankly, he'd like to. He'd like to tug her up by the belt of that ratty robe, push it open and lift her onto the table and—

"Are you thinking about Emma?" she said, and Liam was so surprised that his head jerked back. "I mean, you must be. It's natural. It's fine. You loved her, she was your wife. I understand. It's all good."

Emma. Right.

"It's just...you know. You and Emma were together a long time. And, um, you must be thinking about her. About Emma." She finally met his eyes. "Are you?"

"Well, I am now. Since you keep chanting her name."

She nodded. "Were you before?"

"Before when? Upstairs before?"

Her face fired up. "Um...yes."

"No." Emma hadn't crossed his mind once. Well, that wasn't exactly true. Obviously, Emma was his main point of reference, the only woman he'd slept with for a lot of years. But not in an obvious way... just in the way that she was always there somehow or another. Now that Cordelia had brought it up, though...well, she was smaller than Emma. More, er, energetic. Her hair was short, and Emma's had been long.

Cordelia tugged the robe more tightly around her. "Cold?" Liam asked.

"No. Are you? Because your shirt is...missing."

Liam bit down on a smile. "I'm fine."

"Good." Eyes back on the sugar bowl, which apparently was like the Rosetta Stone or something for all the attention she was giving it. "Am I the first woman you've...um...been with? Since Emma?"

"No."

She nodded, pulled the robe tighter still, practically strangling herself with it.

"I had a thing with someone out in San Diego," he found himself saying. "About a year after Emma died. Kind of a friends with benefits situation."

"Right."

He was losing patience. "Cordelia, have I terrified you or something? You seemed like you were having a pretty good time up there."

"I was! I did! I just wonder about how you felt about it. Given, um...Emma."

"I wasn't thinking of Emma!" he barked, then lowered his voice. "You're the one who's like a dog with a damn bone."

"Well, Liam, I don't see how you can avoid it," she said in a huffy voice.

"I'm a guy, Cordelia! I think about whatever's in front of me."

"You don't have to yell at me, idiot," she snapped. "You're scaring my dog." Her dog was lying on his back, jowls drooping, the paper from the crackers under his ear. "I'm sorry," she continued, not sounding very sorry at all. "It's just…I've never been with a widower. And I remember Emma and how…nice she was."

Great. Now her eyes looked a little wet. Women. Extremely difficult. "She was nice. And I did love her." He paused. "But I was thinking about you," he said in a gentler voice.

"Really?"

Liam opened his mouth, closed it, opened it again. "Yes, Cordelia. As I said, I'm a guy. We're very basic. You're here, I like you, I'd like to be back in bed with you instead of in this freezing kitchen having this ridiculous conversation, but if you want to talk, fine. I think about Emma every day. She's part of me. My child's mother. Can't forget her. I wasn't comparing you, though. I was thinking of you. And that mouth of yours. I'm thinking of it right now."

There. That shut her up. Her cheeks blossomed with pink once more, and she blinked a couple of times. "Oh," she managed eventually.

"Speechless, huh?"

She grinned. Nodded.

Liam got out of his chair, stepped over the calflike dog and knelt down next to her. "Good." He leaned in close and kissed those ripe, pink lips, earning a quick intake of breath as a reward. "Now, if it's all right with you," he murmured, inhaling the smell of her, "I'd like to take you back upstairs and get you out of this disgusting bathrobe. What do you say?" He pulled back and looked at her.

She was smiling. "Sounds like a plan, biker boy."

LIAM JERKED AWAKE the next morning and glanced at the clock: 7:02. Sun streamed in through the windows, illuminating the rafters and a few cobwebs as well.

He had to get home; Nicole was due back at ten.

Cordelia was still sleeping, her hair standing up in odd little clumps, her lashes wispy on her cheeks. Elf-cute, there was really no other way to think of it. Her lips were slightly swollen, and he'd left a little beard burn on her neck. He'd have to shave first next time.

Next time. The thought made him pause.

Cordelia Osterhagen came from a nice family. Chances were high that she probably wanted to get married, have a couple kids, pick out a couch, the whole deal. All good things…just not with him.

Marriage hadn't been hell or anything…but it hadn't been easy. It wasn't the circumstances, the unexpected pregnancy. Those were actually their happiest years, when Nicole was little. But from the very beginning, he could sense it, the long, slow fading as Emma's heart slipped away a little further each year, as she fell out of love with the juvie mechanic who'd knocked her up.

Besides. There was Nicole to think of.

He got out of bed and pulled on his clothes in silence, then bent down and gave Cordelia a gentle shake. "Hey. I have to run. Nicole needs a ride."

"Okay," she said sleepily. Then she bolted awake, her head smacking his. "Ow! Sorry."

"It's okay," he said, rubbing the sore spot. "See you around?"

"Oh…sure."

He knew that look. *But aren't we in something here? Will you call me? When will I see you again? Didn't this mean something?* He'd seen that look on Paige's face in San Diego, and on the faces of a dozen girls back in the day, and now, seeing it on Cordelia's, he… Well, shit.

She pulled the covers higher and looked away. The awkward silence filled the room like carbon monoxide. Liam sat on the edge of the bed and pulled on his boots. "Last night was great."

"Yeah." She blushed, and he felt an uncomfortable pull in his chest. When she'd opened the door and jumped him, come on. A guy didn't just pass that up. Not when all the blood cheerfully fled from head to groin, rendering logical thought completely impossible. Then in the kitchen last night, he'd just wanted to…reassure her for some reason, even though she'd given him the perfect out, bringing up Emma and all.

"Cordelia, listen."

"You're not ready for a big relationship, you have a kid, you're still adjusting, a fling would be fine, but no commitment."

Wow. He smelled a trap. She didn't *look* mad, or like she was about to burst into tears, but women were tricky. "Um…well, in some ways, yes."

"Okay. See you around." She flopped back down on the pillows and closed her eyes.

He stood there, suspicious. Maybe she was about to bury a knife between his shoulder blades. Or maybe he'd just really hurt her feelings. Maybe she really didn't care if she ever saw him again. Or maybe…here was an odd thought…maybe she'd just used him for sex.

User's manual—so handy. "You free on Sunday?" The words seem to fall out of his mouth without permission.

She opened one eye. "Maybe."

"Want to do something?"

Her eyes stayed closed. "Something fling-ish that doesn't imply commitment?"

"Um…I get the feeling I'm being led to my doom. Can I take the fifth and just see you again?"

To his surprise, she laughed and sat up again, reached out and patted his knee. "Sure, biker boy. Now get out. I have to go to work."

He hesitated until she gave him an ungentle shove with her foot, then left, somewhat confused, mildly suspicious and…huh. And kind of happy.

CHAPTER SEVENTEEN

"OMG. You *slept* WITH him? Tell me everything. Every detail. Does he manscape?"

"What does that mean, Jon? I'm not gay, remember?" Posey smiled. She was feeling rather smug. And deeply satisfied. And still a little tingly. She'd slept with Liam Murphy (holy Elvis!) and he'd actually asked her out again, even if he'd been very clear on what he didn't want. But men always said stuff like that…at first. Right? And sure, in some cases, they continued to say it. But something told her Liam was different.

"Manscaping means does he have hair on his back? Tell me no. Please."

"No back hair. Tattoo on his shoulder, though. A Celtic knot or something."

"A little cliché, but we'll let it pass. Hi, Lorraine, would you be a saint and give me a little more coffee? It's so good today."

She and Jon were eating breakfast at Rooney's, the tiny little breakfast place on Miner Street. Generally speaking, you'd have to wait an hour to get a table on Founders' Day Weekend, but as Jon knew and was adored by all in the food industry, the beauty industry, the retail industry and the school system, he'd only had to wave to get them a table on the patio outside, as well as two cheese Danish, on the house.

"By the way," Jon said, "I'm getting you a Keurig for your birthday so you can stop drinking that swill of yours. Now, back to the dirt. Shovel."

"Oh, I love Keurigs! Thanks, Jon! Okay, dirt…" She took a bite of her omelet and chewed smugly, if a person could do that. "Well, I always had this nickname for Liam. God's Gift. God's gift to women, right?" She grinned at her brother-in-law. "And he is. It was worth the wait."

"The two-decade wait?"

"It's more like one and a half, but yes."

"He looks like he'd be a great kisser. Is he? Think he'd kiss me, just so I could tell?"

"No, I'm pretty sure he wouldn't, and *yes*, he's a great kisser, Jon. Like…legs shot out from under you kind of kissing."

"Oh, hooray! Now I have something to picture when Henry's at the hospital all night." Jon took a long sip of his coffee, looking at her over the rim of the thick mug, his hazel eyes kind.

She knew that look. "What?"

"Nothing."

"Something. You have reservations."

Jon winced. "Well, okay, as your best friend—and brother-in-law—and cooking instructor—I have questions, let's say."

"Shoot." She took another bite of the massive omelet, which didn't taste quite as good as before.

"Back in high school, he was kind of a slut, right?"

She gave a half nod. "A bad boy. He took what was offered, let's put it that way. Until he met Emma Tate, that is. The girl he ended up marrying."

"And Emma…what was she like?"

"Oh, you know. Squeaky-clean, super nice. She's the one who fixed me up for the prom."

Jonathan's eyebrows rose. "Ah. The prom. Where you had such fun?"

"My date stood me up. It happens." She took a sip of coffee.

"It seems like more than that, since you still refuse to chaperone. Anyway, back to the Taming of the Bad Boy. He meets the princess, and they lived happily ever after until she dies. Is that right?"

"As far as I can tell."

"Is he still—how did you put it?—taking what's offered? Still a slut? Because I'll beat him up if he is," Jon said, and Posey smiled.

"Home-ec teacher takes on mechanic. I like it," she said. "But no. I mean, I've seen women talking to him, but I think he's pretty focused on his daughter these days."

Jon nodded. "That's what I've heard, too." Jon had his thumb on the pulse, as a high-school teacher. "So, is this the real deal for you, Posey?"

Time for a mega-bite of home fries to stall. "Um...it's all new. Just Wednesday night, you know?"

"But you already look like you're in love."

"Please," she said, though she felt a telltale heat in her cheeks.

"Oh, dear," Jon said.

"It's just that...well, he's not exactly a stranger, right?" Her brother-in-law nodded encouragingly. "I had the biggest crush on him."

"Who wouldn't?" Jon said kindly. "Just try to be careful. I mean, if he feels the same way, bliss. But if not, we're back to the Dante situation."

"I wasn't in love with Dante," Posey said. "I mean, I wouldn't say I'm in love with...you know...the other one, either, but..."

But nothing. Since the moment she'd bumped into Liam in Guten Tag a month and a half ago, it had been impossible not to think about him. Even before last night, she'd felt a jolt of heat every time their paths crossed, every time she thought of him. She'd never been in love before, not really, unless you counted Ron, the Anderson Cooper fan. With Dante, she'd felt attraction, definitely, and she liked a lot of things about him, but the truth was, she hadn't known him well enough to feel more than that.

But since yesterday morning, she'd been walking around as if she was filled with a buoyant, glowing warmth. Every flash of memory caused a surge of heat so delicious that twice she'd broken off mid-sentence, causing Elise to ask if she was okay. Even Gretchen had noticed at the restaurant yesterday. "Posey, what's wrong? You're all blotchy," which of course caused Stacia to leap for a thermometer.

Yep. Felt a lot like love to her.

Jon chuckled. "Hello? Back to earth, sweets. Listen. I'm happy for you, hon, and I hope he deserves you. I never thought Dante Bellini was good enough for you. That pasta is like...well, okay, the food is amazing, and if you tell Ma I ate there, I'll deny it with my last breath, but Dante Bellini is a poser."

Posey put down her mug. "Speaking of Dante, I guess I should officially break up with him now," she said in a low voice. "In case there was any...doubt."

"Has he called you since you put things on hold?"

"Um...no."

"Well, something tells me he's not heartbroken. And here's your chance. He's getting out of his poser car right now."

Posey looked out the window, and sure enough, there was Dante's midnight-blue Audi, pulling up in front of Inferno.

"I'll get this," Jon said. "You go. Make a clean break, and here, take my bagel. I have to wear tights for the float, and God knows what I was thinking. You and your brother are freaks of nature. It's not fair."

"You have to wear tights?"

"Of course! Who do you think is playing the part of the prince?" He smiled proudly.

"Typecasting," Posey said. "Thanks for breakfast." She took Jon's bagel, smacked him on the shoulder and crossed the street. It was a gorgeous spring day, sunny, temp in the upper fifties, breeze light and salty. Perfect parade weather, if it held for tomorrow. Today was the sidewalk stroll, a band concert on the green and fireworks over the river. She, Mac and Elise would be staffing a little booth on the green, featuring some of the smaller pieces from Irreplaceable—a few stained-glass windows, some signs, ceiling medallions and a few other things that could be easily transported. They usually sold out, and it was nice, seeing the other merchants. Maybe Liam would be there with one of his motorcycles. She'd hoped for a phone call yesterday, but no.

Didn't matter (even if it did, a little bit). The birdies sang, the colors gleamed, the flowers smelled so sweet, the entire world seemed brighter. Amazing what a little some-some could do. Especially when the some-some had been so…well…heavenly? Would that be too strong a word? She pondered. Nope. Seemed to fit perfectly.

Oh, Elvis, the man could kiss! Sometimes, those bad-boy types, they didn't try that hard (or so *Sex and the City* told her). But Liam had taken his time, uh-huh. Long and slow and meltingly delicious… and fun. She'd been nervous and a little self-conscious, and practically dying of lust, let's be honest, but he'd made her feel…happy. And beautiful. Oh, sigh! And, in some strange way, like they were old friends, too. He smiled as they kissed, and threaded his fingers through her hair, and he told her she smelled like oranges. At one point in the wee hours, Liam had said, "Oh, God, do that again," and the memory of his smoky bedroom *do me* voice had her walk right into a lamppost in the here and now.

"I saw that!" Jon called, and she waved and opened the door to Inferno. Posey felt a rush of pleasure at the décor…there was St. Agnes of Rome holding her lamb, a gargoyle in the corner, the incredible walnut bar—that had been a delicate job, getting that taken down and reassembled, that was for sure. The overall effect was rich, intimate and tasteful.

From the kitchen came a crash of pans and some yelling (in Italian, which had kind of a hotness to it). "Hello!" she called.

The yelling stopped. "I'm so sorry, we don't open until— Oh. It's you." Dante came out of the kitchen, dressed in a white suit with a deep blue shirt.

"Hi, Dante," she said. "Got a minute?"

"Sure," he said. He pulled out a chair for her, and they sat down at a table. Posey looked at him—all dark pirate beauty—and smiled awkwardly. It was suddenly a little hard to believe they'd had a thing together. Not that she wasn't fabulous, of course (hey—if Liam Murphy slept with her…). But just that Dante's taste didn't seem to incorporate a woman in Carhartt. He wasn't smiling, and his was a face that was a little bit scary if it didn't have a smile.

"So, how are you?" she asked.

"Fine. And you?"

"Oh, great. Are you ready for the weekend?"

"Yes." Unlike Guten Tag, Inferno didn't participate in the parade. Way too tacky. Instead, they hosted a wine and cheese tasting on the town green, their tent lavishly decorated with grape vines and furnished with small tables. A far cry from the Goose Girl theme Stacia had chosen for this year's float.

Dante was looking at her with his glittering dark eyes. "So, why are you here, Posey?"

Was it possible that his coolness was to cover some hurt feelings? Granted, he was the one who hadn't wanted to take things to the next level, but maybe—maybe—he'd expected her to come back. She suddenly felt much worse.

"Well," she said, "you know how we talked about our, um, relationship? A little while ago?"

"Yes."

Her toes curled in her work boots. God, these talks were hard! Not that she'd ever given one, but heck. There should be index cards you could just hand out. "Um, well, I think that it's pretty clear that we want different things—" *also, I slept with someone else and am completely infatuated* "—and I just wanted to make things official."

"Official?" Dante's dark eyebrow lifted.

Posey looked down at the tablecloth. "I mean, we said we'd take a break, and we did, and I think we should just…call it quits. In case there was any gray area here."

He made a chuffing sound and leaned back in his chair, folding his arms over his chest. "Fine with me. Was there anything else?"

Ouch. She swallowed, then shook her head. "Nope. Nothing else."

"Then you have a good day." With that, he stood up and walked back to the kitchen and resumed his yelling.

Posey got up from the table, pushed the chair back carefully, and walked to the door, fighting the urge to bolt. Her skin crawled with...something. Shame. Dismay, maybe, because it was suddenly horribly clear that Dante had never wanted anything more from her than what he'd gotten.

Had she really imagined that he'd choose her as a girlfriend, or—yes, yes, she'd imagined it—wife? Had she really thought that a few sex dates would lead to a deeper relationship? Even though she was done with him, even though she'd initiated their breakup, she suddenly felt so...small. Hiding-in-the-bathroom small.

Dante Bellini had never had any kind of intentions toward her. She'd been available. She'd been convenient, she'd asked for nothing. She'd been easy, in more ways than one.

And tell me, said a small voice in the back of her brain—a voice that sounded distressingly like Gretchen's—*how are things with Liam any different?*

CHAPTER EIGHTEEN

STACIA SIGHED, SLAPPED down a giant ladle, spattering grease on the stove, and glared at Posey. "We have to discuss your birthday. It's only a few weeks away."

"I have to get changed, Mom. The parade starts in an hour."

Mother did not seem happy. Father, either, for that matter. Max was hiding in the office and had only grunted as she'd stuck her head in to say hello.

"Dinner, I was thinking. At home, since you and your brother never come by anymore."

"Ma, I was at your house Tuesday—"

"So us three, the boys, Gretchen. I'll make your favorite. Brathering mit Bratkartoffeln."

"Oh, goody." Posey tried not to wince. Somewhere along the line, Stacia had gotten the idea that Posey loved this dish, which consisted of an entire herring, deep-fried then pickled. It had been her traditional birthday dish for at least fifteen years, and Posey just didn't have the heart to tell her mother at this late date that she actually hated it.

"I refuse to go to some ridiculous ethnic restaurant," Stacia announced. The irony of her words didn't strike her, even as Otto came into the kitchen, dressed in lederhosen and green Bavarian hat. Guten Tag served breakfast on Founders' Day Weekend—eggs, fish, sausage and potatoes.

"Hey, Otto! You coming on the float today?" Posey asked.

"As luck would have it, my wife had her gallbladder out on Tuesday, so I have to swing home and take care of her," Otto said, giving her the thumbs-up behind her mother's back.

"You don't want to go, do you? Of course you don't. I don't know what she was thinking." Stacia huffed again, an indignant bulldog and queen of the non sequiturs.

"Sorry, Mom. Go where?"

"Inferno! As if I'd set foot in that place! Ever! Kitty McGrew went there last week, though why, I have no idea, we were supposed to be friends, but at any rate— Oh, you know Kitty's daughter? Ellen? Married. To a banker. That could've been you, honey. I honestly don't know how you manage to stay single. Are you a lesbian? Our son is gay, we can take it." Otto grinned, waved to Posey and slipped out the back door.

"Mom, I'm aware that Henry is gay, as I am his sister. And no, I'm not a lesbian." A brief and deeply satisfying flashback to just how straight she was made her knees wobble most pleasantly. But Liam hadn't called yesterday, either, or shown up at the sidewalk stroll. Which was fine. Sort of. "You were ranting about Inferno, Mom. Was there a point?"

"Right. Well, your cousin thought you might like to go there. For your birthday. And I said you'd rather die."

"I wouldn't. I'd rather eat at Inferno than die, Mom. Just for the record." Even in light of yesterday's conversation.

Stacia set a potato pancake in front of Posey (a little over-salted, but hey. Posey wasn't about to reject it). "I set her straight on that. It's one thing that you had to do business with that man—and I understand it was a lot of money for you, honey, so I forgive you—but *eat* there? Please. Poor Gretchen, she's so good-hearted, she just can't imagine anyone being snide or insulting like that Dante Bellini's been to us. Kitschy institution. I'll give him kitschy institution. Gretchen's just too sweet for her own good."

One had to wonder on which planet Stacia lived. "Dinner at home sounds great, Ma," Posey said.

"Good. Oh, you know what? I should invite Liam and that pretty daughter of his! Don't you think he and Gretchen would make the most wonderful couple?"

Posey swallowed her bite of congealing pancake without fully chewing it. "Um…I don't, actually."

"Well, you're nuts. They'd make beautiful children. Max! Get out here! Your daughter wants to see you!"

"Then she can come in here! Posey! Are your legs broken?"

"No, Dad, I'm coming." She went into the office, where her father was scowling at the computer.

"Do you know how to upload something?" Max asked. "I wish to God computers had never been invented!"

"Sure, I can help."

"Thanks." He gave her a grudging smile, then patted his knee. "You're not too big to sit on your old man's lap, are you?" he said.

"I'm almost thirty-four, Dad," she said.

"Fine. Stab in me in the heart, why don't you," he grumbled, so Posey sat, gave his cheek a smooch, and got to work. "What do you want to upload?"

"A picture of Gretchen," he said. "Seems like we should make more fuss over her, since she's a celebrity and all."

"Ah." Posey could imagine whose idea that was. She clicked through the folder to find the photo Max wanted. "So, how are renovation plans coming along?"

"Oh…she has a lot of ideas, your cousin."

"I hope you'll only change what you want, Dad," Posey said. "I mean, you're still adjusting to the new addition." A few years ago, there'd been a small fire at the Osterhagen home (candles left untended during some geriatric *amour,* which Henry and Posey still could not mention without wheezing hilarity). The result was that her parents ended up renovating, which caused great upheaval. They still went to the wall where the cellar door used to be, still seemed stymied as to where it went, six years after the fact. So an entirely new restaurant…it just didn't seem like them.

"That's the one she wanted," Max said, pointing, so Posey uploaded the photo to Guten Tag's home page, and there she was, Gretchen and her impressive Teutonic cleavage.

"Hi, Mutti. Hi, Papa!" Speak of the devil.

"Hi, sweetheart," Max said. "Posey's just helping me with the website."

"Oh. Hi, Posey, you look so cute today!" Gretchen flashed her blinding teeth. "Like you're about eleven years old, sitting there on Papa's lap. Adorable!"

"Why, thank you, Gretchen."

Gret smiled, then gave Posey a searching look. "Hey, how's the search for your birth parents going?"

Max bolted up from the chair, dumping Posey onto the floor, and there was a huge crash from the kitchen. A nanosecond later, Stacia loomed in the doorway, tragic confusion written all over her face. "What's this? You're looking for your birth parents?"

"No," Posey said, hauling herself off the floor. "I don't know what you're talking about, Gret."

"The book on how to find your birth parents? It was on the shelf in the kitchen."

"Oh, right," Posey said. "That book belongs to James. I keep meaning to give it back to him."

Gretchen looked wide-eyed at Max and Stacia, then at Posey, as if desperate to keep a terrible secret. "Oh. Right. Um…Mutti, I must've been mistaken. I'm sure it was James's book. Of course it is."

"It is, Mom." Posey glared at her cousin. "I'm not looking for anyone."

"If you want that information," Stacia began, her voice stentorian, "we wouldn't resent you. It's completely understandable."

"I'm not looking, Mom."

"You must want to know your roots. It would be fine. We know you love us," Max said, sounding as if he was reciting from a pamphlet on *When Your Adopted Child Wants Answers*.

"I'm *not* looking. James left his book at Irreplaceable a while ago, I brought it home and just forgot about it."

"I'm so sorry I brought it up. Posey, really. So sorry." Gretchen gave Posey a little wink, and Posey thought, for one deeply satisfying moment, how fun it would be to see her cousin fending off a couple dozen angry raccoons. Ever since the night at the casino, Gretchen had been more and more hostile—and clever. Nothing could be held against her, but it was malicious just the same.

"Well," Stacia said, still staring suspiciously at Posey, "it's time to get dressed for the parade. Come on, girls. Posey, where's that poor Brianna? Is she coming?"

"I'm here, Mrs. O," poor Brianna replied, rolling her eyes at Posey.

"Good. Your costumes are in the back. Gretchen, darling, wait till you see yours! It just came in yesterday!"

"I HATE YOU. I'M calling Big Brothers tomorrow and having you fired."

"Shush," Posey said. "At least no one can see your face. I'm the evil serving wench. Would you rather be dressed like me, young lady?"

"No. I'd kill myself if I was dressed like you."

Brie had a point. Posey's costume wasn't really a costume—it was just her waitressing outfit from the restaurant, the same one she'd worn when waiting tables at Guten Tag when she was seventeen. Ruffled white blouse (well, once-white, now yellowing). Green dwarf-embroidered vest that ended just below the bustline, ruffled skirt, green tights, painted clogs.

"It'll be fun, Brianna," she said. "You asked to come, remember? Beats sitting at home."

"No, it doesn't! I'm a goose, Posey! I'm dressed like a goose! You left the goose part out!"

"Sue me," Posey said. "Here, have a marzipan. They're not bad. Just suck on them long enough to soften the shell. The parade starts in ten minutes, so get in the spirit of things, kid."

"Hate you," Brianna grumbled, but she took a candy.

When Posey and Henry were three and nine, the Osterhagens decided to do a float for the Founders' Day parade. They'd chosen to depict Hansel and Gretel, Henry and Posey holding hands and waving, Henry dropping bread crumbs from time to time. It had been a big hit. From then on, the elder Osterhagens had run with the Brothers Grimm theme. After all, as Jon pointed out, it beat the other thing Germany was rather famous for: the Nazi party. The back room of Guten Tag was full of aging animal costumes—mice, horses, a wolf or two, and, yes, geese. Those roped into duty tossed bulletlike marzipan to the crowd, who had the tendency to flinch and shield themselves.

Getting out of float duty was akin to high treason, though just about every staff member came up with some dire emergency to dodge their duty. Henry always managed to be on call and was forgiven, as he was a brilliant surgeon. Only Jon and Posey really enjoyed it…and now Gretchen. In the past few years, Irreplaceable cosponsored the float; Posey had found an enormous sleigh from a decrepit Santa's Village in Lake George. The sleigh was mounted on a trailer and pulled by a stately old Farmall tractor driven by Mac. And this year, on the side of the float was something Posey had never seen, a banner that read *The Goose Girl by the Brothers Grimm and featuring the Barefoot Fraulein Herself, Gretchen Heidelberg! Brought to you by your friends at Guten Tag and Irreplaceable Artifacts*.

There were other floats, as well—the library had one shaped like an open book, the 4-H kids usually had one with a goat or a calf, and the marina always pulled some gorgeous sailboat. Rick Balin would sit on the deck, waving in boozy noblesse oblige, some unfortunate young woman shivering in a bikini next to him. Then there were the school bands, the Little League teams and a handful of veterans. But Guten Tag's float was something of an icon and always came last.

"Oh, man! This is so fun? Right? Thanks for inviting me, Mrs. Osterhagen!" Elise, also dressed as a goose, waddled up to Mac and honked at him. He swallowed and ignored her.

"If I see someone I know, I'm throwing myself in front of the nursery school float, and all those kids will have to watch me die," Brianna said.

"When you close your beak, no one will see your face. And please. I've been doing this since I was three years old. I have no sympathy for you. None. You asked to come, and here you are."

"Oh, Brie, you look so cute!" Jon leaped lightly onto the float. "Wherefore is my true princess?" he cried.

"He's hiding in an O.R. somewhere," Posey said.

"I wish I was in the O.R. I'd break a leg to get out of this," Brianna muttered.

"You're late, Jon," Stacia called.

"I had to get my hair perfect. And didn't I? Am I not the very picture of a proper Prussian prince?" He glanced at Posey and lowered his voice. "Speaking of gorgeous men, heard from you-know-who?"

"Nope," Posey murmured. "But it's fine. I think we have plans for tomorrow." Still, it would've been nice if he'd called. Dang it! She was just not the type to sit around mooning near the phone, yet that was exactly what she'd done last night. Loser.

Jon gave her a knowing look, then mercifully changed the subject. "Where did that banner come from?" he asked.

"Gretchen had it done herself!" Stacia said from the front, where she sat in her role as the queen. "Wasn't that so sweet of her? Now everyone will know a celebrity chef is working at Guten Tag!"

"Just in case they dodged that fact somehow," Jon said, winking at Posey and Brianna.

"So, what do we have to do, exactly?" Brie asked.

"Just wave and throw marzipan," Posey said. "Try not to hit anyone, though. It hurts."

"Could you be quiet, please?" Gretchen said. "We need to get into character."

"Is she for real?" Brianna muttered.

"I don't know the story," Jon said. "All I was told is that I need to look handsome, so here I am, handsome."

The float was just about to enter the official parade route, which wound for a mile and a half through town before ending at Memorial Bridge Park for the ceremonies. People from other floats milled around, kids dressed in their band uniforms scampered and warmed up, the Pedersen boys got ready to fire off the cannon that would mark the start of the parade.

Gretchen turned around from her seat on the front of the sleigh, where she sat with Max and Stacia. "The story is, Jon, that I'm the true princess, and Posey—"

"The evil serving wench," Posey supplied.

"Not quite, and I was getting to that," Gretchen said coolly. "Posey, my jealous maid, and I are on the way to the neighboring kingdom so I can marry the prince. But she steals my clothes and tries to pass herself off as me. In the meantime, I tend the castle geese, but the king—that's Papa, of course—the king can tell that *I'm* the true princess, and I'm reinstated and marry you, Jon."

"You lucky thing," Posey murmured.

"What happens to the maid?" Brie asked.

"Oh, I'm put into a barrel lined with nails and dragged through town until I'm dead," Posey said. "Fun, huh? Gotta make sure I read those fairy tales to my kids someday."

"Why isn't Posey the true princess?" Brie asked, her voice loud and defensive, and Posey felt a rush of love. Tough-girl act aside, Brianna was a sweetheart.

"It's really not my thing," she said. "I'd rather be the evil wench. More character."

"So Lady Boobs-a-Plenty got the job," Brianna said.

It was true. Gretchen's generous cleavage spilled out in levels not seen in New Hampshire since prostitution was outlawed. The true princess costume was low, tight and white, complete with sparkles, a staff and crown—Glinda the Good Witch, Vegas-style—and since Posey wasn't the dress-up type, she didn't really mind. Not much.

Max turned around and smiled. "Well, you're still my princess, honey."

"Aw. Thanks, Dad."

"Can we stop the chatter? Places, everyone!" Gretchen commanded. Elise waddled obediently to the back of the float.

"This is so awesome, right?" she said to Brianna. "Don't you, like, *love* being a goose?"

"If I had a gun—" Brianna began, but Posey snapped her beak closed.

"Okay, people, let's make this a great show!" Gretchen said, her voice loud, her smile ferocious. "Brianna, if that's your name, and Elise, would you mind honking once in a while? Not too loud. And in five, four, three…" She counted down on her fingers, going silent for two and one, as if the cameras were about to start broadcasting. The float rolled into motion. "Hello there!" Gretchen called. "So nice to see you! Happy Founders' Day! Thank you!"

"Can I whip this candy at the back of her head?" Brianna asked, her voice muffled.

"No," Posey said as Jon snorted. "Just toss it—gently—at the crowd."

Posey loved the parade, roles aside. She knew plenty of people, of course, and Gretchen's small fame had a couple of tweenie girls run out to the sleigh for an autograph, which Gretchen demurely gave. Brianna proved to have unerring aim, winging her classmates with the hard lumps of marzipan under the cover of goose. There were Kate and James, Kate blowing her nose loudly. Brie whipped about fifteen pieces of marzipan at James, and he gave her a peace sign in return. Kids yelled out to Jon, who responded by singing phrases of Gilbert and Sullivan. Elise was having a marvelous time, laughing and honking and occasionally leaning off the float for a glimpse of Mac's solid back. They passed a group of familiar faces—Vivian and her geriatric peeps. "Hi, Vivian!" Posey called, laughing as Viv covered her mouth in horror. "Laugh all you want." Vivian pulled out her phone, held it up, and Posey knew her picture would be on Facebook in seconds.

Unfortunately, a bank of solid gray clouds rolled in, dropping the temperature by a good five degrees. In her short-sleeved dirndl, which was thin with age, Posey was freezing. She looked enviously at the well-padded Gretchen, sitting snugly between her well-padded parents, and shivered.

The parade turned onto Miner Street, and people clapped and pointed at the Barefoot Fraulein, who was eating it up. "Thank you so much! It's so nice to see everyone! Happy Founders' Day!"

There was Inferno. The restaurant really was gorgeous, an old brick-and-stone building. The window boxes overflowed with trailing ivy and deep purple viburnum, and the paned windows gleamed. The staff wore all black. Max and Stacia studiously ignored the restaurant, waving to the folks on the other side of the street.

And there was Dante, just coming out of Inferno now, his trademark white suit a stark contrast to the black-clad staff. The sight of him caused a pang of anxiety in her stomach—that or the four pieces of marzipan she'd eaten. Again, the similarities between Dante and Liam leaped out at her. Two good-looking guys, neither of them interested in a real relationship. But she was on a float, and to compensate for the cold shoulder from her parents, she waved at the Inferno staff.

Dante folded his arms and shook his head. "Those geese look like they're on their last legs," he said, loud enough to be easily heard on the float. "I bet we'll be seeing them on Guten Tag's menu any day now." He grinned, and his staff guffawed with mean laughter.

Posey's head whipped around to look at her parents. Stacia's mouth hung open, and Max's face went white, then red. Gretchen stared ahead, her face red as well.

Posey looked back at Dante. They were almost past the restaurant now, and getting closer to Guten Tag. "You know, Dante," she found herself calling, a sweet smile on her face, "you might be able to get some decent spaghetti at Inferno. But you can never seem to have any fun." She let that sit a beat, then yelled as loudly as she could, "Zicke zacke, zicke zacke!"

"Hoi, hoi, hoi!" the crowd called back. After all, most of Bellsford had been to Guten Tag—once, at least—and if they hadn't had a gourmet meal, they'd had fun. They'd had a night to remember. They'd been treated like family.

"Zicke zacke, zicke zacke!" Jon yelled this time, and again, the crowd chorused back.

Posey stood on a sleigh runner so she could squeeze her mother's hand. "You guys okay?"

"Thank you, dear," Stacia said.

"Good job, baby," Max echoed. Gretchen had pasted a smile on her face and was waving robotically. Her face was scarlet.

Posey turned back to look at Dante. Even from half a block, she could see his look of contempt. "Love what you're wearing," he called, pointing to his chest.

Posey looked down at her own.

Oh, no. Her blouse was torn. A lot. The aging fabric had caught on the sleigh, apparently, and had split right down to the vest, the edges flopping out on either side. She grabbed the edges and pulled them closed, but the fabric tore right off in her hands. "Dang it!"

"Wardrobe malfunction," Brianna murmured. "Hey, at least you wore a bra."

Yeah. A graying, elderly bra with a safety pin. Posey had been forced to dig it out of the back of her drawer this morning, as Gretchen had forgotten to put their laundry in the dryer.

"Jon! Help me," Posey hissed, turning away from the crowd. Brie stood on her other side, shielding her. Elise, too, waddled close around.

"We should go to Victoria's Secret, right?" she said, cocking her head as she gazed at Posey's chest.

"Oh, boy," Jon said. "My kingdom for a sewing kit. Does anyone have a cape? No? Crap. Okay, just stand here, and um…don't move a muscle. Only about a mile to go, right?"

Gretchen and the Osterhagens had resumed their royal duties and called out to their friends and acquaintances, unaware of Posey's distress. No one was wearing anything that could be used to cover her up.

"Hey. Cordelia."

Posey looked up, and there was Liam loping out from the sidewalk. He shrugged out of his leather jacket and handed it up to Jon.

A warm, buttery sensation rolled through Posey's legs. He was *saving* her. Unfortunately, that also meant he'd seen her rattiest bra, which was less than optimum, but still. "Thanks," Posey said faintly.

"You're a prince, Liam," Jon said, handing over the coat with a pointed look. "A true prince."

"Liam! Come join us at the beer garden after the parade, dear," Stacia commanded from her perch up front. "Bring that beautiful child of yours."

"Will do," Liam said. He winked at Posey, then headed back to Nicole.

Liam's jacket was heavy and still warm. It smelled like him, and it felt better than any clothing had ever felt in the history of the world.

"Well, if you weren't in love with him already, I'll bet the farm you are today. I know I am," Jon whispered, waving to some students who were calling his name.

"He totally saved your ass," Brie said, sounding mildly surprised. "And your boobs."

THREE HOURS AND five speeches later, Founders' Day was officially over. Guten Tag's beer garden was full, Otto had returned from his wife's bedside and was playing polkas on his accordion, and Posey had yet to take off Liam's jacket. Given her druthers, she would never take off Liam's jacket. If possible, she would be buried in Liam's jacket.

Not that Liam would notice. He was too busy glaring at Tanner Talcott, who was sitting at the next table with Nicole, talking about his English class while Nicole listened and glowed. Officially, Liam was sitting at Posey's table, though he'd barely seemed to notice her since arriving. She, however, couldn't stop her brain from chattering away. *Hey, Liam, thank you for your jacket. By the way, I actually have several very attractive bras, which I'd be happy to show you later. Also, thank you for the sex, which was sock-knocking, even though I am totally playing it cool. Oh, and are we on for tomorrow? Remember you asked me if I was free on Sunday? I still am, and tomorrow is Sunday, but I haven't heard from you since you left my bed the other morning.*

James and Kate arrived, and a round of hellos was exchanged. "We loved the float, didn't we?" Kate announced, plunking herself down next to Posey. "It was the best float in the whole parade. James, tell Posey how much we loved their float."

"So, so much," James said, cocking an eyebrow.

"You know, I just sat down and right away, I have to pee," Kate announced, hauling her bulk out of the chair. "James? Want to come?"

"I'm good, Mom," he said, closing his eyes.

"Hey, I have your book," Posey said as Kate lumbered away. "You left it at Irreplaceable a few weeks ago."

"Oh, the birth-parents thing? Cool."

"Liam! Liam, sweetheart, over here!" From the other corner of the beer garden, Stacia waved imperiously.

"Excuse me a second," he said, his first words since arriving. He stood up, said something to Nicole, glared at Tanner, then made his way across the rooftop garden. A rather stunning brunette stopped him, putting her hand on his thigh and smiling up at him, and Posey had to drag her eyes off the little tableau.

Wednesday night seemed like aeons ago.

She glanced at Brianna and James, both of whom were watching Tanner and Nicole.

"The golden couple," Brianna muttered.

"Totally," James agreed. "Too perfect for the rest of us."

"You guys are great, too," Posey chided.

"Yeah. Dare to be different, right, James?" The two teenagers rolled their eyes at the dopey adult. Hey. It had been worth a shot.

Gretchen's laugh cut across the crowd, and Posey looked up. Liam had made it to the Osterhagens, and Gret was fluttering her fingers over her boobage, just in case Liam hadn't noticed it jutting out like the prow of a ship. He smiled, Max said something, and they all laughed.

"I have my DS downstairs in my backpack," James said to Brianna. "Want to play 'Dragon Master'?"

"Sure," Brianna said. "Is that okay, Posey?"

"Oh, yeah. You two have fun. I'll tell your mom where you are, James."

"Don't feel you have to," he said, grinning.

The two left, and Posey offered a quick thanks that James had become Brie's friend. Brianna, she knew, was lonely. Her family situation, cheap clothes and the fifty extra pounds she was packing didn't make high school easy. James seemed happy enough, despite Kate's constant attempts at symbiosis. And hey. Kate was doing a great job. James was gentle, wry and kind. Not your average teenage boy, and God bless him for it.

Well. Posey looked around. Here she was, alone at a table for eight. At least there was a giant plate of potato dumplings in front of her. But just as she felt the initial squirmings of awkwardness, Henry and Jon came over. "How are we?" Jon asked, setting a beer in front of her.

"We're fine," she said. "How was the hospital, Henry?"

"Oh, it was fantastic," her brother answered. "Total BKA. Gorgeous." At her look of confusion, he added, "Below the knee amputation. It was a crushing, right, so it was a mess, and not to blow my own horn, I did an amazing job. Want to see? I took pictures." He fumbled in his pocket and withdrew his iPhone.

Posey duly admired the photos—she was used to it, after all—while Jon shielded his eyes.

"So, how was the float this year?" Henry asked.

Posey and Jon exchanged a look. Posey went first. "It was… Well, it was…"

"Sort of a Chagall nightmare theme," came a voice. It was Liam. He set a glass of soda down in front of his daughter, then made his way around to Posey's table and sat next to her. Their knees bumped under the table, and Posey felt her cheeks burn.

"A Chagall nightmare," she said. "Aren't we cultured."

"I lived in L.A. I'm incredibly cool," he said, his eyes dropping to her mouth, and her toes curled in her silly shoes.

"Oh, dear. Mom's gesturing," Jon said. "Come, Henry. We're needed."

"I just sat down," he protested.

"Come! Be a good son. See you two later." Jon leaned down to kiss Posey's cheek. "Don't eat dumplings in front of him. That detachable jaw of yours is scary," he whispered and then pulled his partner away.

Liam stared at his kid, and Posey tried not to stare at him. But it was hard. He was undeniably the best-looking guy on earth, and she couldn't really blame the women who cut glances his way, or waved or called hello.

"Thanks again for your jacket," she said after a minute or two had passed. "I'll give it back to you tomorrow."

"Sure," he said, nodding at someone.

Posey realized abruptly that her regular clothes were downstairs, and she could change right then and there…indeed, she should've changed already, but clearly part of her wanted to hang on to the jacket, because apparently she was still the dopey teenager she'd been fifteen years ago.

"Dad? Can Tanner and I take a walk around the block?" Nicole asked.

"No," Liam answered.

"Daddy, it's broad daylight, and downtown is mobbed. Totally safe. Right, Posey?"

"True enough," she said, earning a smile from the girl. Tanner wisely stayed silent.

Liam cut his eyes to Posey's. She smiled. He didn't. A little chilly, those eyes. Then he looked back at his daughter. "Fifteen minutes. And bear in mind that I can see halfway around the block from here, and yes, I will be watching. Got it, son?"

"Yes, sir, Mr. Murphy. Fifteen minutes." Tanner practically knocked his chair over, he got up so fast.

"I'll be watching," Liam repeated.

"Thanks, Daddy!" Nicole fairly skipped away, and Liam took a slow, deep breath.

"Good boy," Posey said.

He grunted, then stood up to peer over the wall of the beer garden. "Great," he said after a minute. "They're holding hands."

"How sweet," Posey couldn't resist saying.

He gave her a murderous look, then sighed. "By the way," he said in a low voice, "I'd rather not have Nicole know we're…hanging out."

Hanging out. Horrible term, meaning absolutely nothing. "Of course not," she said, looking away.

"So, what else happens this weekend?" Liam asked.

"There are tugboat races tomorrow," Posey said. "Sunday." As in Sunday. As in *You free on Sunday?*

"Cool." Another few beats passed. Men. As perceptive as cement walls.

"Your mother's definitely trying to fix me up with Greta," he said, and Posey felt a nearly painful burst of love. He got Gretchen's name wrong! So sweet!

"Well, Mom thinks the entire world should be married," Posey said. Then, aware that her statement sounded leading, she added hastily, "But not everyone's meant for…you know."

There was another silence. "I think I'll go wait for Nicole," Liam said, standing. He looked down at her, almost as if seeing her for the first time today. "See you tomorrow? I could pick you up around noon."

Posey couldn't suppress a smile. "Sounds good."

He leaned down, and for a second, she thought he might kiss her, right here in public, but he just stuck a few bills under a plate for the busboy. "You looked cute on the float today," he said, and it was so unexpected that she was actually speechless. Then he smiled and left, and Posey sat there for a few long, delicious minutes, the glow in her chest nearly painful.

CHAPTER NINETEEN

"Have fun, sweetheart," Liam said the next day, kissing Nicole's forehead.

"Thanks, Daddy!"

"Don't go crazy with Grandma's Amex, okay?"

"I won't," she said.

"This is a shopping spree, sweetheart. You can get whatever you want," Louise said, giving Liam a cool look as she ran a hand over Nicole's hair.

"Within reason, Nic." He'd had to talk to her the last time there was a spree—they'd bought her a purse that cost eight hundred dollars.

"Darling, go out to the car, all right? Grandpa's waiting. I have to ask your father something." Nicole obeyed, regressing to age six and skipping down the hall. The elevator doors opened, and she blew him a kiss, which Liam caught. Baby Girl was happy today.

The second the elevator doors closed, Louise raised her chin, giving him the assessing, disapproving look he'd been getting since the first time he knocked on their door to take Emma to the movies. "Liam, George and I would like to talk to you about spending more time with our granddaughter."

Liam felt a tightening in his gut. "Well, you do see her quite a bit already. Dinner once a week, Sundays, the occasional sleepover. Seems like a lot to me."

"We'd like more. Every other weekend and at least once a week after school."

"That's...that's not gonna happen, Louise. I mean, we love seeing you—" a lie "—but Nicole has a lot of school things going on. And she and I do things on the weekends, too, so we'll just play it by ear, okay? But if something special comes up, you definitely talk to me."

"She's our only grandchild. Our only piece of Emma."

It wasn't a plea...it was an accusation, as if Liam had somehow caused Emma's illness. And no matter how much they loved Nicole, Liam would always be the kid from the wrong side of the tracks who'd knocked up their princess. If there'd never been a Nicole—if Liam had simply been their late daughter's husband—he doubted the Tates would have ever spoken to him again.

"I know that, Louise," he said, as gently as he could. "And we moved back here to be closer to you."

"We appreciate that, Liam. But we'd still like to have more time with her."

He nodded. "Summer's just around the corner. I'm sure Nicole would love to spend some time with you then."

Her face tightened. "Also, we'd like to buy her a car for her birthday. A Mercedes. Excellent safety record."

"Absolutely not."

"Why?" she snapped. "Liam, you never let us give that child anything! We wanted to take her to London last year, and you said no to that as well."

"You wanted to take her to London for a *month*. During the school year, Louise. As for the car, no. She won't even have her license until next fall."

"Fine. You're the father." She spit the word like it was a curse.

"Thank you," he said, forcing his voice to be pleasant. "If you could have her back by eight, that'd be great. It's a school night." If he said eight, they might make it before ten.

"Fine," she repeated in a tone that was anything but. Without saying goodbye, Louise turned and went down the hall.

Liam stood there, waiting till she was in the elevator, then stepped inside his apartment. Locked the door. Unlocked it. Locked it again. Then he went to the sink, slammed on the hot water and lathered up. Fifty-five seconds. It was never enough with the Tates. He'd moved across the continent and gave them pretty free access to their granddaughter, endured their crappy WASP dinners and veiled insults, but it would never be enough. And yet they were his backup plan for his child. Who wouldn't be a child much longer.

Hands washed and dried. Door locked. Jaw still clenched.

What time had he told Cordelia he'd pick her up? Well, how about now? Would now work?

Twenty minutes later, he pulled into her driveway, feeling slightly better. Cordelia's church stood alone, no neighbors, just a few thick stands of trees. Though the church could definitely use some work, it looked nice there in the sunshine, little purple flowers pushing through the earth in clumps. A nice place to live.

He knocked on the door, which opened almost immediately. The chef, what's-her-name, stood there, barely clothed. "Well, hello there, Liam," she said, sliding one hand up the doorframe.

"Hi," he said. He heard a deep woof, and the giant dog appeared, galloping straight at him, nose aimed for Liam's crotch, but the cousin grabbed his collar. The creature barked again, wagged its tail, knocking something to the ground, and offered an enormous paw. Some watchdog.

The cousin, meanwhile, looked like she was about to eat him alive. "So, how are you today?" she asked, giving him a slow once-over.

"Fine, thanks. Is Cordelia home?"

"She is. You guys are so cute," she said. "Come on in." She turned and walked inside. Liam followed, his eyes dropping automatically to check out her swaying ass, which was *very* nice, he had to admit, and outfitted for maximum attention—short shorts, even though it couldn't have been more than fifty-five degrees outside. Or in here. Not the warmest place, this church. "So, Liam, I didn't even know you guys were seeing each other, you naughty boy."

"We're friends," he said.

"Friends with privileges?" she said suggestively, sweeping her hair off the back of her neck, then patting the couch. "Sit down, sit down, relax."

He didn't, though the white cat with the big head took her up on it. Liam looked around. He hadn't seen a lot the other night, as Cordelia had practically dragged him up to her bed. Not that he was complaining. But there was lots of cool stuff here…an ornate, thronelike chair, a chandelier made of antlers, a statue of a scowling angel who looked ready to kick some sinful ass. "So, where is she?" he asked, feeling the cousin's eyes still on him.

"Upstairs. When she told me—well, I'll be honest, she was so cute and shy about it, you'd think it was her first date ever. Come to think of it, it might be. Anyway, I had to pry it out of her, because I *thought* that was you leaving our house the other day, and then when I saw you sitting together in the beer garden yesterday, I put two and two together."

"Genius," he said.

"Thanks," she purred. "So at any rate, she still dresses like a tiny lumberjack, no clue, as I'm sure you've noticed, so I gave her a little help. Poor Posey." She stretched hugely, arms over her head, arching her back. "You can thank me when you see her."

Piece of work, the cousin.

"Posey! Your date's here!" Also shockingly loud.

A door closed upstairs, and they heard footsteps. Tentative footsteps. Meanwhile, the cousin and dog both were eyeing Liam's groin. *Move it, Cordelia,* Liam thought. *One of these two is going to jump me any second.*

She came into the room, and the dog burst into furious barking. Liam flinched. "Uh…hi," he said after a moment.

"Hi." She scowled. "Too much?"

At the sound of her voice, the dog fell into a confused silence, punctuated with whining. "Shilo, it's me," Cordelia said tightly. He growled, disbelieving, then barked again.

"You look so cute!" the cousin exclaimed, clapping her hands.

Cordelia did not look cute. She looked—well, crap, there was no other way to put it—like a kid who'd gotten into her mother's stuff. That, or an underage prostitute. Her long, wispy eyelashes were coated with gunk, her eyelids smeared with purple. Hair was slicked down with some sort of product that made it look both greasy and stiff as the same time. Worst of all was her mouth, her beautiful, full lips smeared with oily red. If Liam tried to kiss that mouth, he'd slide right off. She wore an ill-fitting miniskirt and a shirt that was sheer (he had to give the cousin credit for something), revealing a black bra underneath. Tacky, but hot nonetheless. Just not…her. When Liam managed to look into her eyes, he saw that she was glaring at him.

"I liked you better before," he said. "Personally."

"Me, too," she said. "Back in a flash."

"I think you look great!" the cousin called. "Oh, well. So much for all my hard work."

Ten very long minutes later, she was back. Hair damp but in its usual clumps. Sturdy jeans, couple of layers of flannel and fleece, engineer boots. Much better. "All set," she said, grabbing her backpack. She barely looked at him.

"Have fun, kiddies!" the cousin said.

"Sorry about that," Cordelia said as they went outside. Her face was pink. "I had a delusional moment I could look like a…"

"Prostitute?" Liam suggested.

She shot him a glance, then smiled. "I don't know. Living with Gretchen, I kind of lost perspective. Since she's all flowy and shiny and stuff. She said I just had to get used to it, but I could barely see with all that gunk on my eyes." She had something in her hand—candy, it looked like, wrapped in wax paper, and she took a bite. That mouth of hers was even more distracting, now that she was chewing.

"Well," he said. "You have your own special thing."

She looked up in surprise, dropping the candy on the driveway. In a flash, she picked it up, gave it a quick glance, and took another bite.

"Really?" Liam asked.

"Shush. My college roommate sent me this fudge. It's from Z. Cioccolato. In San Francisco, okay? Best stuff ever." She held it out. "Want a bite?"

"Pass."

"Your loss."

Now her lips had just a little chocolate on them. Liam found himself getting a little…aroused. More than a little, actually. "So, your cousin lives with you?" he asked, trying to focus on something else.

Cordelia groaned. "For the moment. She's between mansions right now."

He laughed. "She looks a lot like your mom, doesn't she? More than you do."

She gave him an odd look. "I'm adopted."

"Oh, really? I didn't know that."

"Yeah. My brother, too."

"Well, that I did guess, since he's what? Vietnamese?"

"Yep."

"And what are you? Ethnicity-wise?"

"I don't know. It was a closed adoption. So, where are we going?"

Hint taken. "Um…" Right. He should've thought of that. It'd been a while since he'd been on…well, it wasn't really a date. Whatever. "Where do you want to go?"

She thought for a moment. "I have to check on something, and you might like to see it. Want to come?"

"Sure."

"Let me get Shilo. He can come with us, if that's okay."

"Sure."

She ran back into the church, opened the door and called her dog, who galumphed out, baying joyfully. "My truck?" Cordelia asked, as the pony-size dog whirled in circles next to her.

"We can take my car," Liam said. He opened the back door for the dog, who leaped right in, then seemed to fall unconscious. He was too big for the backseat, so his head drooped to the floor, nose almost touching.

"I thought you might have your motorcycle today," Cordelia said as she buckled up. "It's so nice out."

"I don't ride it much anymore," he said.

"Since the accident?"

He gave her a sharp look. "Who told you about that?"

She grinned. "You did, biker boy. When you were under the influence of pain meds."

"Right. After you broke my rib." He started the car and pulled out of her driveway.

"Cracked. And don't worry, you swore me to silence. Take a left at the stop sign."

"So tell me, Cordelia, have you always sucked at baseball?" Liam asked, and she punched his arm.

"I almost got a hit the other day," she said. "It was very close."

"Wow. So exciting." He grinned as she smacked him again.

"We can't all be perfect like you, Liam. Heard you had four hits against Oasis."

"It's true," he acknowledged.

"Good. Glad you're having fun. Go left here." He obeyed. "Where's your daughter today?"

His smile dropped. "With her grandparents."

"And how are they? With her, I mean?"

And so Liam found himself telling Cordelia an edited version of the Tates' demands, the endless stream of gifts and overindulgences. It was…nice, having someone to talk to. He'd made a few friends since moving—Allan the lawyer was a pretty good guy, but obviously it was a little weird with the whole Taylor-belt stuff. Rose, the bartender, had a killer Harley and brought it in for a tune-up and flirted without coming onto him, which was fun. The girls at the bakery were friendly.

But Cordelia…maybe it was his link to her parents, but she felt…safe. And she listened. It had been a long time since someone really listened like that.

"Up here on the right," Cordelia said, pointing. "Just pull in and stop, okay?"

An endless rock wall bordered a sloping lawn. There was a house up there, though Liam could only catch glimpses of it through the trees, which had started to bud out in earnest. A giant Victorian, from the look of it. Shilo, who'd been sleeping, perked up, pushing his giant head between the front seats to see where they'd stopped. A huge set of arching, wrought-iron gates with the words *The Meadows* spelled out on top marked their destination. Cordelia hopped out of the car, opened a metal box, punched in a code, and got back in the car. The gates swung open, and Liam drove in. Stone driveway. Very nice.

"You know the owner?" he asked.

"I do. Vivian Appleton. She used to live here before she got too old." Cordelia peered through the windshield at the house. "Man, look at those daffodils! They were hardly out last week!"

The house was massive and ornate, green with cream and blue trim. Dozens of windows, a huge set of double doors, curving front porch. And yes, hundreds, if not thousands, of bright yellow daffodils bordered the lawn, bobbing in the sun.

Cordelia leaped out of the car, opened the door for her dog, and ran up the granite steps that led to a stone terrace. "Come on," she ordered. "We'll go in this way. The front door sticks." Her dog, clearly no stranger to the property, trotted off, snuffling the air with enthusiasm. Liam followed her up the stairs. "It's empty, but it's gorgeous anyway. The owner's heirs are going to tear this place down, and I'm hoping to get the salvage rights."

"Tear it down?" he asked. "Are you kidding?"

Cordelia turned. "I know. Come on, come on. You have to see the inside." She typed in a code, then opened the door.

It was incredible. Everything about the house was ornate and...well, expensive, if in need of some care. The walnut staircase, the French doors, the leaded windows, plasterwork and ceiling medallions... it went on and on. Cordelia pointed out a few features, but she seemed almost as in awe of the place as he was, as if she were seeing it for the first time, too. The sun shone through a stained-glass window, pebbling the floor—and the dog, who'd come in with them—with color.

"Doesn't the town want to save it as a museum or something?" Liam asked, gazing out at the expansive lawns.

"Believe me, I tried. But you know how it is around here. Can't swing a cat without hitting some historical home where George Washington or Franklin Pierce had a snack. No money in the budget for one more." She ran her hand along a marble mantelpiece. "Vivian was hoping one of her nieces or nephews would want to live here, but nobody does. A developer made them a huge offer for the land." Cordelia sighed. "I get the impression Viv thinks that if she doesn't leave them the estate, they'll declare her incompetent, or just make her life miserable. Or just stop visiting."

"What a shame."

"I know." She was silent for a minute, then brightened. "Want to see the caretaker's house? A whole family used to live there, five kids, the caretaker and his wife, who was the cook."

The cottage was a short walk farther back on the property and was shaded by an enormous spruce. Diamond-paned windows, a stone fireplace, a snug little kitchen. "Viv tried living here for a while," Posey said, quite the tour guide, "but even that got to be too much once she had her stroke. Isn't it cute? Imagine being the family who got to live here."

It was so far from the types of places Liam had lived in as a kid that he couldn't. A bedroom of his own, rather than a ratty couch that smelled like beer or an air mattress on the floor. A yard full of trees and flowers instead of old car parts. Parents who made meals instead bringing home fast food...when they brought home food, that was.

"It's really nice," he said.

"Come on, I'll show you the grounds. They're gorgeous. I hope they'll keep some of the flower beds when they put in the McMansions."

They went back outside, Cordelia pointing out the occasional rare tree or telling him what would grow where later in the summer. The whole place was like a park, Liam thought—graceful old trees, a gently sloping lawn, rock walls edged with old flower beds, even a stream. They walked, not touching, the breeze gentle, the sun taking the chill out of the air. The dog trotted around, venturing off, then returning, nosing Cordelia's hand as if letting her know he was back. At the edge of the woods, two deer grazed. The dog barked once but didn't give chase.

Liam's phone buzzed. He pulled it out and looked at the screen. His jaw clenched.

"Problem?" Cordelia asked.

"No...well, the Tates just bought Nicole earrings. Two-carat diamond earrings. She sent me a picture." He held up the phone for Posey to see.

She whistled. "Wow. Pretty."

"Yeah," he said. "But see, I don't think a fifteen-year-old girl should be wearing five thousand dollars' worth of jewelry, which is exactly why they're buying these for her. I'll tell Nicole they're a bit much for high school, she'll get mad, the Tates will tell her she deserves them, I'll be the bad guy."

"I guess that's par for the course, being a dad."

"Yeah."

There was a little rock shed in the shade of some pine trees at the far end of the property. Cordelia fished out her keys and unlocked the door. "This was the pump house back in the day," she said. "And voila." She took out a blanket, spread it on the ground and sat down. "I come here sometimes for lunch," she added by way of explanation. Shielding her eyes, she looked up at him. "Have a seat, biker boy. You look tense."

He hesitated, then sat. The wind made a shushing noise through the pine trees, and a blue jay squawked. Cordelia was right. He was tense. His neck was so stiff it felt like he could barely move his head.

"Here. Put your head in my lap. Shut up, just do it." Her face was pink again. Liam gave her a long look and felt the beginning of a smile. Any time Cordelia did something that might be construed as suggestive or, perish the thought, *romantic,* she got all pink. Aside from punching him (twice), she hadn't touched him today, but there she was, blushing like she'd just popped the question.

For some reason, he found that ridiculously appealing.

He lay on his back and put his head in her lap. "Close your eyes," she said.

"So bossy," he murmured, obeying.

"Shush. Now just listen."

"To you? Do I have to?"

"To nature, dummy. You'll feel better."

The wind rustled. Far off, he could hear a Harley with cut pipes tearing through the countryside. Took a while for the noise to fade. Birds chattered and twittered and whistled and whatever else birds did. Somewhere, a crow was clacking. Liam heard panting, then a thud, and a warm weight was suddenly against his side.

"Shilo likes you," Cordelia said.

"I get the impression Shilo likes everyone," he said.

"You're right."

He put his arm around the dog, who rewarded him by resting his head on Liam's chest. He had to hand it to Cordelia…this was pretty nice indeed. The knots in his shoulders seemed to ease a little, and the sun was warm. He felt her fingers playing in his hair, and, shielding his eyes from the sun, he took a look. Sure enough, Cordelia's cheeks were burning pink. Grinning, he closed his eyes again.

"So, this would be a big job for you," he said, petting the dog's solid side.

"Oh, yeah. It would be a real coup. Every salvage operation in New England wants the rights to this place, and Vivian is having a ball, stringing us all along." There was a smile in her voice.

"So, salvage, that's kind of an unusual job," Liam said.

"I guess so," she said.

"Why do you like it?"

She didn't answer for a second. "Well," she said quietly, "when you salvage something, it's kind of bittersweet. On the one hand, you're destroying something—a barn, a home, a business, and it's sad, because there were so many stories that took place there, you know? When Mac and I take down a house, it's almost…religious. All those artifacts, all those stories, all the feelings that happened there. But you can save the pieces, give them a new life. A new story." She stopped abruptly. "Well. I sound like a dope. It's a job. An interesting job."

"You don't sound like a dope." In fact, her little speech had made his chest feel odd…not in the panic-attack way, but a warm pressure that made him feel a little wary…and a little drawn to her.

"Why do you do motorcycles?" she asked.

He looked at her again. "It's the only thing I can do."

"I doubt that," she said.

"Well, aside from being a gigolo," he said, sitting up and grinning at her. She didn't smile back. "I was kidding," he added.

"Mmm-hmm." There was a small hole in the knee of her jeans, and she started pulling at the threads. Not amused, obviously. "You shouldn't sell yourself short, Liam," she said quietly.

Not what he expected her to say. He looked away after a second.

"I have a present for you," she said and rummaged in her vast backpack. She pulled out a small object wrapped in cloth. "It's old," she added, handing it over. "I've had it for a while, and I saw it the other day, and…whatever."

He unwrapped it slowly. It was a brass medal, imprinted with the picture of an old-fashioned motorcycle. *Motorcycle Gypsy Tour, 1917.* "Where'd you find this?"

"In an old garage up in Tilton." She tore another thread from her jeans. "It's from the first Laconia Bike Week. You know, the big motorcycle rally up near Winnipesaukee."

"Yeah, I know what Laconia is."

"Oh, of course you do. Right. I just…figured you might like it."

"I do." He looked at her steadily. "This is a very good present, Cordelia."

Her cheeks brightened. "Glad you like it." The hole in her jeans was growing.

"I do." He set it aside and turned back to her. "Come here. Give us a kiss."

"You or Shilo?"

He laughed. "You can kiss your dog later."

"Well, then." She looked at him another minute, surrendered the attack on the jeans and just like that leaned over and kissed him into the middle of next week, all soft lips and sweet taste, and when she slid her tongue against his, it was like a bolt of heat straight to his groin.

"Thank you," he said against that mouth, pulling her onto his lap so they fit together more closely. His hand slid up to cup her breast—black bra, as he remembered, oh, yes—and relished the small softness against his palm, and kissed her again, that lush, sweet mouth. He could kiss her for a month and not get tired of it.

She pulled back a little. "I don't suppose you're living the bad-boy cliché and have something in your wallet?" she whispered. "Something that's not money?"

Liam laughed. "I actually do. I was hoping I'd get lucky today."

She smiled, and Liam felt that warm tug again, in his groin *and* his chest. "Lucky you shall get, in that case," she said, and with that, Liam relieved her of her fleece, and her flannel, and the rest of her clothes, and made love to her on the blanket, the pine trees shushing in the breeze.

The dog, he was happy to note, had found something else to do.

THEY SPENT MOST OF the afternoon at the estate, then hit a diner, where Cordelia put away a shocking amount of food before ordering two cheeseburgers to go for her beast. She fiddled with the radio on the way home, stopping on an old song from the 1970s. She sang along under her breath, looking out the window.

"Really?" Liam said. "Neil Diamond again? I thought you had to be over sixty to like that guy. Next you'll be telling me you're an Engelbert Humperdinck fan."

"Engelbert is very underappreciated, but Neil is an icon. Now shush, biker boy. This is a great song. 'I am, I said,'" she sang, a little more loudly. "'To no one there…'"

He laughed and found…well, it wasn't such a bad song after all.

When they got to her place, he walked her to the door. "I had a great day," he said, and it was true. Maybe the first day since Emma had died and when he wasn't with Nicole where he'd had a really good time.

"Me, too," she said, and there was the telltale blush.

Shilo (named after, yes, a Neil Diamond song, she'd told him) pushed his giant head in between them. "Go ahead, Shilo," she said, letting the dog in the house. "Um…you can come in, too. If you want." Her face was studiously neutral.

A warning bell clanged in Liam's head. Today had been great…but he didn't want her reading too much into it, not when he could offer her so little. "I should probably go."

"Okay. Well, thanks for lunch."

"Thanks for the medallion. And the shag." *And for making me relax, and feel better, and finding me a one-of-a-kind gift, and taking me to your favorite place. And by the way, don't fall in love with me, Cordelia. No one's ever been glad they did that.*

"You're welcome."

"See you around, then." He almost hated saying it, the casual dismissal, but it wouldn't hurt to remind her. This was a no-commitment fling. Friends with bennies. Nothing else.

He could tell by the look on her face the message had been received. "Hang on a sec. I almost forgot." She went into the house and returned a second later, his leather jacket in her hand. "Thanks for this."

Liam hesitated. "Keep it for a while. I have a couple." *Why'd you do that?* the smarter part of his brain asked.

"I do have a coat of my own, you know," she said, giving him an out.

"Well, hang on to it anyway." He was an idiot. But the idiot was rewarded with a smile.

"Okay, biker boy. See you around."

He wanted to kiss her. Instead, he reached out and punched her lightly on the shoulder. "See you around."

CHAPTER TWENTY

"I'M DEFINITELY IN love," Posey said one night. Jon and Henry had invited her to dinner (well, Jon had, and Henry was present). Posey was lounging on the camel-backed Victorian sofa she'd found for Jon several years ago, which he'd had re-covered in a luscious gold-and-blue hydrangea print, and the boys' cute little Colonial was redolent with the smell of lime and cilantro. "I'm pretty sure he is, too."

After three weeks, she and Liam had settled into a pattern. They'd see each other a couple of times a week—the nights that Nicole spent either at friends' houses or with her grandparents. They were dating, no matter what he did or didn't call it. He took her out to dinner one night in Portsmouth. One Sunday afternoon they rented a boat and motored slowly through the estuary, looking for herons and osprey. One time, he'd spent the entire night, when Gret was visiting a friend and Nicole was with her grandparents. They'd fooled around, eaten, fooled around again and then watched movies till she fell asleep, her head on his lap in the great room, Meatball and Jellybean snuggled against her belly, Shilo sprawled on her lower half. If that wasn't heaven, waking up to Liam Murphy stroking her hair and *Iron Man 2* on the telly, what was?

And if Liam wasn't quite in love, he was close. He certainly seemed happy; that was one of the best things about their times together, the teasing insults and smiling kisses. He even seemed less tense regarding Nicole. One night, she brought him up to the belfry, and they'd sat there, holding hands and sipping wine next to the jammed, rusted gears and big iron bell as the peepers chorused from the swamp behind her house. How could that not be love?

"Sorry, pet. It's not love until you go public," Jon pronounced. "You need romantic intention stated out in the open. Like if he was here, spending time with the most important men in your life, it would mean something. Right, Henry?"

"What?" Henry said, glancing up from a book—*Traumatic Amputations in Nonsterile Settings*.

"Meeting each other's families, going public with love. Remember? We held hands when Max and Stacia came down for Parents' Weekend. We were walking across the quad, Posey, all these families everywhere, and your brother took my hand. That's when I knew it was real."

"Knew what was real?" Henry asked, frowning.

"Never mind," Jon sighed. "Posey, has Liam kissed you in front of other people yet?"

She pretended to think about it. "No. But we ran into each other at the bakery yesterday, and we talked."

"About what?"

"Um…the baseball game," she admitted. "He had five hits in one night. Stubby's won, seventeen to six."

"Who were they playing?"

"Curl Up and Dye."

"Well, that explains it. But seriously, who gets on base five times in one game?"

"Well, not me, that's for sure," Posey said.

"Anyway, back to the public displays. Does he call you sweetheart or kiss you or lick your neck?" Jon asked.

"No. There was no licking." Not then, anyway. She smiled.

"Then I'm not sure we can say he's in love. Not yet. Or he is, but he's not brave enough to show it."

"Who are we talking about?" Henry asked.

Jonathan huffed. "Posey, do you see what I have to put up with? I work all day, I come home, I expect my partner to listen to me, but no, I could be standing here on fire and he still wouldn't notice."

"Henry, say something nice to your honey," Posey commanded.

"Jon, you're the best," Henry said.

"More, please," Jon said haughtily.

"You're a great dresser, our house is a showplace, the food you cook is fit for the gods. You're so understanding and compassionate, and I thank God every day that we found each other," Henry murmured, his eyes drifting back to his book.

"Wow," Posey said, closing her mouth. "I never knew you had it in you, bro."

"I wrote it down for him," Jonathan explained with an affectionate cuff to Henry's head. "So how's Gretch the Wretch acting these days?" He refilled Posey's wine glass. "Is she wild with jealousy that you're bagging the hottest guy in town, present company excluded?"

"Jon, this is my sister," Henry said. "Please, let's not talk about her sex life."

"What do you think we've been talking about for the past half hour?" Jonathan said. "Go back to the ripping and tearing." He turned to Posey. "Is she?"

Posey took a sip of her wine, which, while indubitably much, much more expensive than her own swill, didn't seem to taste much different. "She's not, actually. She's been pretty busy."

Gretchen's lack of interest was indeed kind of odd, especially after the way she'd acted that first day, tarting Posey up while channeling a Victoria's Secret supermodel. But since then, she'd been very nonchalant. Posey was often asleep when Gret came home, so their interaction was limited (mercifully). Maybe it was as simple as that.

"She's a wolf," Henry said, eyes back on his book. "Beware, Posey."

"I concur," Jon said. "By the way, please chaperone the prom with me, Posey. Himself here won't do it."

"It's true, I won't," Henry murmured.

"Oh, Jon, no. Sorry, bud. It's just not my thing."

"Not her thing," Henry echoed, eyes still on his book. "She had a very bad time at her prom."

"So, tell me about it!" Jon asked. "Pig's blood as you were crowned?"

"I wish," Posey said, rolling her eyes. "My date dumped me for someone else. Not unheard of."

"Some guy made fun of how skinny she was," Henry supplied, still reading. "She probably only weighed about ninety pounds back then. He called her a bag of bones, said she was built like a ten-year-old boy—"

"Hey. Savant. We don't need a trip down Memory Lane, okay?" she said, taking a healthy slug of wine. Brothers with perfect memories were so annoying.

"—and the mean girls made fun of her. She hid in the bathroom first, then walked, in the pouring rain, mind you, to a 7-11, whereupon she called her heroic older brother, who took her out for pancakes and covered to their parents." He turned a page and continued reading. "Oh, look at this. A shark bit this guy's arm half off, and the medic had to stitch up the artery right on the beach or the surfer would have bled out. Now *that* would've been a great day. I am *never* that lucky."

Jon looked suitably horrified. "I don't know which of those stories is worse," he said. "Your prom or the shark bite."

"The shark bite is worse, Jon," Posey said.

Jon shook his head briskly. "Well, how about this? Come with me, and I'll be a perfect date, and we can expunge the writing from the tomb or whatever. You'll have a great time. Please. Please, Posey, please! It'll be fun, I promise. Don't make me go alone and fend off passes from the Latin teacher. She wants to convert me, whether to being straight or a Lutheran, I'm not sure."

"Nah. Sorry." She took a sip of wine.

"I signed you up already."

"Unsign me."

"I'll cook for you. For a week." He put on his best puppy-dog face.

Posey mulled it over. Now that she was with Liam, the prom of long ago didn't seem so awful (over-looking the fact that he was sort of the cause of it). Jon was right. She could put those memories behind her. *And* have her brother-in-law cook for her. "Two weeks."

"Done."

"Can you make that chicken thingie? With the ham in it?"

Jon smiled. "It's called chicken cordon bleu, pet, and of course I can! Latin Teacher, *tu es non* getting some from this gay man. Who's ready for dinner? And Henry, please pretend you noticed the centerpiece, okay?" He pointed to a lush arrangement of deep red peonies, curly twigs and ivy set in a gleaming silver bowl.

"It's nice," Henry said.

"Nice? Nice? I want a divorce. Sit, sit."

But Jon's words about Liam had made Posey squirm a little later that evening as she sat on the couch with Shilo and Jellybean, watching television. Jon was her best friend, after all, and a guy, and her brother-in-law, so he had the triple crown of truth going for him. Liam, while undeniably enjoying Posey's company, seemed careful to…well, to keep a little distance. She had yet to be invited to his house, for example. And he only saw her when Nicole was otherwise occupied.

Except for the jacket. He wanted her to keep his *jacket*. Granted, the fact that she had it right next to her at this very moment made her a tremendous loser, but please. The coat was battered and leather and dead sexy and smelled like Liam, and if she couldn't have him right here at this very moment, she did have the Official Bad Boy Jacket of Hotness. Not bad. Plus, a marathon of *The Pickers* was on.

As Posey was practically drooling in envy as the show's hosts visited an old amusement park, the back door opened. She hit Mute and was just about to call out hello, when Gretchen spoke. "Okay, be quiet," she said (not quietly). "My housemate's probably asleep."

Housemate, right. Way too uncool to say *cousin,* as in *I'm staying with my cousin because I have a gambling problem and blew through all my money.* There was a rumble of a male voice, then Gretchen's sultry giggle.

Well, this was fun! No *wonder* Gret had been pleasant lately. She was getting a little some-some herself. Posey would just tiptoe upstairs. Unfortunately, they were in the kitchen, where the stairway was. Maybe she'd just stay put after all and let *them* creep upstairs.

Another giggle. "Come on in the living room," Gretchen said.

So much for hiding. "Gret? Is that you?" she called.

"Oh, Posey! I figured you'd be asleep by now." Gretchen's head appeared in the doorway. Her hair was tousled, and she was flushed. "Um…I have a guy with me," she whispered.

"Hi, guy," Posey called, grinning. Shilo's tail thumped.

The guy appeared.

Posey's smile dropped like lead. "Oh. Uh…Dante. Hi."

Clearly, he felt as awkward as she felt now. He gave her a stiff nod. "Posey. Nice to see you. I…I wasn't aware you two lived together." No. Dante had never been to her house, something that had bothered her when they were involved.

"It's temporary," Gretchen said hastily. "We're a very close family."

"Oh. How nice."

A couple of things were clear to Posey—one, Gretchen had no idea that Dante had had a thing with her. And two, somehow or another, Gretchen had forgiven Dante that nasty comment from the parade.

"Dante, could you pour us a glass of wine?" Gretchen asked, putting her hand on Dante's chest. "There's a gorgeous cabernet on the counter."

"Sure. Uh, Posey, one for you, too?"

"No, thanks."

"Very well," he said, retreating to the kitchen.

Gretchen sat in the easy chair, crossing her long legs. "Posey, I know this looks bad," she said, her voice low. "But we ran into each other at the farmer's market two weeks ago, and the truth is, I told him off. He called to apologize, and we ended up meeting for a drink. I know it seems like I'm sleeping with the enemy, but I really, really like him."

"Okay, but Gretchen, I should—"

"Please don't tell Max and Stacia." She tucked a strand of long blond hair behind her ear. "I just…I just don't have a lot of good things in my life these days. And even if it's early, it feels…special. I really fell for him, Posey. I bet you feel the same way about Liam." She gave Posey a smile—a genuinely excited, sweet smile, and Posey's heart sank slowly to her stomach.

"Um, sure, Gret. I mean, you're an adult. And the whole restaurant rivalry thing is silly."

"Exactly! Oh, Posey, I knew I could count on you. Thank you. And listen. I haven't said a word about you and Liam, because I know Mutti would go nuts planning the wedding and all that. So this is kind of fun, right? We each have a secret beau. Secret for now, anyway."

Posey's toes curled in discomfort. Of all the times for Gretchen to want to be friends…

"We'll get out of here. I thought for some reason you'd be at Liam's tonight, and he wanted to see where I lived… Anyway. We'll go to his place. It's gorgeous, by the way. House on the water in Midnight Cove."

Posey tried not to cringe. Granted, if she could erase the Dante chapter from her life, she would. But not telling Gretchen…that didn't seem right. Then again, maybe some things should be left to wither and die. Especially things that meant nothing.

"Dante, babe, never mind about that wine," Gretchen called, rising gracefully. "Let's head over to your house, shall we?"

"Good idea," he said, returning to the great room.

"Just let me run upstairs and grab some things," Gretchen said. She shot Posey a grateful smile, smoothed her skirt and swished out of the room.

Alone with Dante. How fun. Posey unmuted the TV to cover any conversation and looked over at the King of Slick. "Ironic, you two together," she whispered.

He eyed her warily. "She doesn't know about…our thing."

"So I gathered."

"I'd like to keep it that way."

"I bet you would."

"Are you going to tell her?" he whispered. "Because I'd really prefer that you didn't."

Posey's jaw clenched. "Well, Dante, you smug bastard," she whispered back. "I don't really care what you prefer. She's my cousin. So I'll sleep on this, and if I feel I should tell her, I will." Shilo put his massive head on Posey's lap and groaned in adoration.

"I don't see how that would serve anyone," he said. "You and I were hardly in a serious relationship. It really doesn't matter in the grand scheme of things."

Oh, that stung. "You know nothing about women," Posey whispered. "And you're a jerk, too."

"Posey," Dante said, his voice low. "Look. Maybe you're right. But this thing with Gretchen is… Well… it could be serious. If you tell her now, that would be the end of it."

From upstairs came the sound of running water. Posey disentangled herself from Shilo and stood up and folded her arms. "Listen up, Dante. If I tell or don't tell, it has nothing to do with you and your feelings and your whatever. You don't matter at all. She matters. So if I think she should know, I'll say something. If I don't, I won't. But I don't give a rat's ass about what you think. Clear?"

"So clear."

"I'm all set!" Gretchen breezed back into the room, hair perfect, a different outfit now. She held a small satchel in her hand.

"Oh, Louis Vuitton!" Dante said. "Very nice!"

Posey snorted. They might be perfect together.

"See you tomorrow, Posey," Gretchen said, beaming at her, and for just a second, Posey could see what it might be like to have Gretchen as a friend, to have a cousin who truly was as close as a sister.

CHAPTER TWENTY-ONE

"So Elise," Posey said a few days after learning about Dante and Gretchen. "Say you had a very, um... A fling with a guy. Slept with him a few times, it didn't work out. No hearts broken, not a big deal. Then a friend of yours started seeing him, but she didn't know that you and he had been together. Should you tell her?"

Both Ask Amy and Dr. Joy had said no...well, they'd said no in similar cases that Posey had found on the web. Posey was hoping for further validation.

"You should *totally* tell her!" Elise said.

"Really? Because I was thinking— I mean, this person was thinking that if the fling really didn't matter and would only hurt the person to know about it, then telling would just be mean."

"But seriously?" Elise said. "I mean, say I'd slept with Liam? Like, wouldn't that matter to you?"

Posey paused. "Did you sleep with Liam?"

Elise laughed. "No? Of course not! I haven't even, like, met him. Anyway, you should tell. Want to get lunch? I'm starving."

"Sure. Where you calling?"

"China City?"

"Okay. I'll have two egg rolls, some sesame noodles and the General Tsao's chicken. Fried rice, too. Pork, okay?"

Maybe she *should* tell Gretchen. One thing was for certain: it was very strange, being friends with Gretchen. Suddenly, clothes didn't litter every surface, and the kitchen was cleaned up. Not only that, Gret was being...sweet.

"Hey, I made you and Liam some goodies," she'd said that very morning. "You know, in case it's your night." She smiled—nicely. "You two serious?"

Posey grimaced. "Um...I'm not quite sure. I think so."

"You make a great couple. Okay, gotta run. Sauerbraten tonight. Takes some prep, let me tell you. Hey, what do you think? The food's better these days, isn't it?"

"Oh, definitely," Posey said. Then again, she wasn't exactly renowned for her palate.

"You know, I found a can of sauerkraut from 1996," Gretchen said, laughing. "I said, 'Mutti, are you trying to kill us?'"

For once, Gretchen's co-opting of her parents didn't feel like theft. It felt...natural. Gret's parents were dead, she really did love Max and Stacia...let her call them Mutti and Papa. No harm done.

On Sunday, when Guten Tag wouldn't open until five, Posey drove to her parents' house for lunch. Gretchen was going to drop her bombshell, and she'd asked Posey to be there as an ally.

Her parents lived in a classic American neighborhood, the kind that had been great at Halloween, when Posey would end up with an entire pillowcase of candy (most of which Stacia would purge, looking for razor blades or rat poison). The addition still made her wince a little—not because it was ugly, but because her parents' fooling around had caused the fire that destroyed the bedroom, and what kid wanted to think about that? Putting such thoughts aside, she ran up the steps to the front door.

Henry and Jon were already there, and Gretchen was in the kitchen, wrapped in one of Stacia's aprons.

"It smells fantastic in here," Posey said.

"I thought we'd have something a little different today," Gretchen said, setting a giant bowl on the table, and though Stacia scowled suspiciously at each piece of ziti, the rest of them fell upon the food like a Biblical horde of locusts. Twenty minutes after they'd sat down, most of the food was gone, though Posey had managed to nab the last of the pasta, to Henry's chagrin.

"My God, Gret, I had no idea you could cook like that," Jon said, sinking back into his chair.

Max leaned back and loosened his belt. "I don't generally like Italian food," he said, "but that was delicious."

"Wonderful, darling," Stacia said. "Almost as good as the spaetzle you made last week. And the Wiener schnitzel! Amazing."

"So, what's new, Gretchen?" Posey asked. May as well get things moving here.

"Well," Gret said, flashing her a grateful smile, "I have some news. Some happy news."

"Are you pregnant?" Stacia asked, getting a snort from Jonathan.

"No, no, not pregnant."

"Sweet!" Henry said, phone in hand. "Someone got his foot caught in a lawn mower. Four toes severed! I have to run. Sorry!" Posey's brother bolted from the table, face alight with joy.

"Henry is not normal," Posey said.

"Hush," Stacia chided. "Your brother's a genius. Those hands? So gifted."

Posey shot Jon a look. *It's true,* he mouthed, winking.

"Anyway, Gret, as you were saying," Posey said.

"Right." Gretchen took a deep breath. "Well, I've been seeing someone, and while I wasn't sure we were going to have a lot in common, it turns out we do. And we're moving in together."

Stacia gasped and covered her mouth with her hand, expression joyful. "Is it Liam?"

Gretchen glanced at Posey. "No. It's…it was surprising to us both, but…well, it's Dante Bellini."

"Holy sh—oot!" Jon blurted. "Wow! That's brave."

Max said nothing. Stacia's face was thunderous. "For a second there, I thought you said Dante Bellini," she said rigidly.

"I did," Gretchen's voice was small.

"I think it's romantic," Posey offered. "Kind of a Montague-Capulet vibe." No one said anything. "Romeo and Juliet?"

"Well, it's not," Stacia said. "Gretchen Katarina Heidelberg! Your parents would be—"

"Stop, Mom," Posey interjected. "Look. Dante owns a restaurant, a lot of people like it, he has made some…uninformed comments about Guten Tag, but he's hardly a criminal. Gretchen wouldn't be dating him if he was, right, Gret?"

"Right," she said. "Um, Auntie, Uncle Max, he's very nice, really. And I—"

"I cannot believe I just ate Italian food!" Stacia trumpeted. "I feel unclean."

"Okay, okay, calm down," Max said, patting his wife's hand. "Grettie's an adult, sweetheart. And Posey's right. Mr. Bellini there might be a bit stuck-up, but Gretchen likes him. Which means we have to."

Stacia shook her head. "I don't know if I can," she said, a Wagnerian note of disaster creeping into her voice. "He's been so unkind."

"Right, Mom," Posey said. "But you know how you were telling me how sweet Gretchen is? How she sees the best in people? Well, maybe she makes Dante want to be a better man." Jon made a gagging sound, and Posey kicked him under the table.

Stacia gave a little shrug.

"And didn't Opa disapprove of Dad?" Posey said.

Stacia shot Max a glance. "Well…a little bit."

"Maybe if you just gave Dante a chance," Gretchen suggested.

"Well, I'm certainly not closed-minded," Stacia said, and Posey had to bite her lip. "I suppose if you like him, sweetheart, then he can't be too horrible. No matter how it seems."

"Thanks, Mutti," Gretchen said. She caught Posey's eye. *Thank you,* she mouthed.

* * *

LATER THAT AFTERNOON, Posey lay on the bed in the guest room, watching as Gretchen packed her stuff. The big suitcases were out—Posey's church would be hers once again. And the cats could reclaim their afternoon napping spot.

"No offense," Gretchen said, "but I cannot wait to get out of here."

Posey rolled her eyes. She always loved how people stuck in the words *no offense* right before they insulted you.

"I mean, seriously, this place is just not me. Maybe when you're done with the renovations, sure. Oh, Posey, you should swing past Dante's house! I'll give you the tour. You've never seen anything like it."

Posey swallowed. "Maybe sometime."

"You want this bracelet?" Gretchen asked, tossing a sparkly blue thing on the bed next to Posey. "It never looked good on me."

"Um…sure. Thanks," Posey said. She couldn't imagine wearing it, but it was a nice gesture.

Gretchen zipped up the suitcase. "I think that's it," she said briskly. She went to the bureau and handed Posey an envelope. "Here. Half of what I owe you."

"Hope you didn't win this at the craps table," Posey said.

"Not funny," Gretchen said, checking her teeth in the mirror. "No, that's from my pay."

Posey cocked an eyebrow. "You're paid pretty well."

"Well, I *am* a celebrity chef, Posey," she said. "My name alone has brought in a ton of new business."

Ah, Gretchen. She may have softened a little in the past couple of weeks, but she was still Gretchen. She looked at Posey in the mirror, then turned around and sat down on the bed. "Posey," she said slowly, "there's something I think I should tell you. It might upset you. But after living here, and especially after the past couple of weeks when we've gotten closer, I feel like I should say something."

"What? I have no sense of fashion? I already know that."

Gretchen didn't laugh. "This is serious."

The sun was bright outside, and the sound of wind chimes could be heard over the springtime birdsong…a sharp contrast to the somber look on Gret's face. Posey sat up. "What's the matter?"

Gretchen took a deep breath. "Posey, you never tried to find your birth parents, right?"

"Right."

"Why not?"

Posey took a deep breath. "Well, Max and Stacia are my parents. I mean, I wondered about my biological parents, sure. I'm glad they gave me up. But even if I wanted to find them, it was a closed adoption. I can't contact my birth mother, she can't contact me."

Gretchen looked at her steadily. "Posey…she actually did."

Posey blinked. "What?" She shook her head. "No, she didn't."

"She sent you a letter."

"No! She didn't. What are you talking about, Gretchen?"

Gret took a deep breath. "Okay, this might make me look like a sneak, but…well…" She shook her head briskly. "It was when I was living with you guys senior year. A few weeks before we graduated, Aunt Stacia got a letter. From an attorney. She was really upset, and I thought…I thought it might've been about the accident or something."

All that pasta from lunch suddenly felt like cement in Posey's stomach. "My mom wouldn't keep something like that from me."

Gretchen looked at the floor. "I waited till everyone was out, and I know I shouldn't have, but I thought it was about my mom and dad. So I snuck into their room and found the letter. It was in the drawer with all her girdles. So…I read it. Well, I read part of it. As soon as I realized what it was about, I put it back. And I swear, I never looked at it again."

"What did it say?" Posey asked. Her voice sounded high and strange, and her heart was clattering in her chest.

Gretchen squeezed her hand. "Well, your birth mom was in college when she got pregnant. There was some stuff about her and your father. And some family medical history."

"Anything bad?"

Gretchen shook her head. "I don't remember the specifics, but no. Normal stuff."

Posey closed her mouth and forced herself to swallow. "Anything else?"

Gretchen was quiet for a minute. "I only read a few lines. Maybe I should've told you a long time ago, but if Max and Stacia didn't want you to see it...I don't know. It wasn't really my business. But I just thought you should know."

CHAPTER TWENTY-TWO

LIAM WAS A LITTLE torn. Nicole had canceled her afternoon with the Tates, claiming too much homework, and while he didn't mind the fact that he wouldn't have to see his in-laws today, he'd been planning on seeing Cordelia while Nic was out. He could cancel—Cordelia wouldn't mind—but since Nicole was indeed in her room surrounded by books, maybe he'd go anyway. Nic was always telling him to get a life, after all. And it wasn't like they were doing anything together right now.

And he did want to see Cordelia.

He hadn't expected her to be so…fun. Or sweet. She was unpredictable; one minute she'd be cheerfully insulting him, the next, looking at him with those big soft eyes. She baked cookies the other day, which was just so not her that he could tell it was a big deal.

"How are they?" she'd asked.

He chewed assessingly. "Not the worst I've ever had."

Her eyes narrowed, and before Liam saw her move, she'd snatched the cookie from his hand and tossed it in the trash. "No more for you, ingrate."

Liam looked at his now-empty hand. "Really?" He grinned. "Who's gonna stop me?"

"I am. You want another cookie, you have to come through me."

They'd ended up doing it on the kitchen table.

And that was another thing. Liam hadn't expected the sex to be so, well…mind-blowing. Here he was, a good month into seeing someone—granted, no strings attached—and was feeling a little bit like a randy teenager, walking around with a goofy smile on his face.

The only problem was that he suspected Cordelia might be getting a little…attached.

He walked down the hall and knocked on his daughter's door. "Nic, how much longer are you gonna be?"

"Dad, this paper is killing me! Can you, like, stop interrupting?" She glared at him from her desk. Audrey Hepburn posters had replaced Edward the Vampire, he was happy to see, and the clock from Sweetie Sue's glowed above her bed.

"Well, I just wondered if you wanted to do something later."

"No. This will take the rest of the day. I may as well just chain myself here and, like, work until I pass out, and you can just throw some raw meat in here. This teacher is insane! She thinks we have nothing better to do than study!"

An excellent teacher, clearly. "Okay, well, I thought I might run out for a couple hours," he said.

"Do it. Leave me alone, or I'm going to fail everything."

"You okay here by yourself?"

"Dad!" The three syllables of doom, followed by a huffy sigh. "I'm not six years old, you know."

"Just asking. If you wanted me to stay, I would."

"I don't." She must've realized she sounded like a twit, because she gave him an apologetic glance. "Sorry. It's just this is a hard class."

He smiled. "But you're smart. You'll do great."

"Thanks," she grumbled, then looked up at him hopefully. "So, Daddy, any thoughts on the prom?"

"Plenty. You're too young."

"I'm sixteen years old, Dad."

"You're fifteen years and eleven months old," he corrected.

"Grandma and Grandpa don't think I'm too young," she countered. "They said they'd buy my dress, too."

"Not helping your case," he said.

Her face fell. "Fine. You're the boss." She turned back to her computer. "I'll just slave away at this and, like, never have any fun, ever, because my father won't let me be normal and have a boyfriend, not that Tanner even *is* my boyfriend, because he hasn't even kissed me yet."

The threats must be working. Liam's opinion of Tanner went up a thousand points. Nicole sat back down at her desk and started tapping away on the razor-thin laptop the Tates had just bought her. She really was a good kid, and she did work hard.

"What's the paper on?" he asked.

"The themes of patriarchal suppression in *The Crucible.* Ironic, isn't it?"

He narrowed his eyes at her. His child was now officially smarter than he was, and he didn't like it. "Not funny."

"Oh, it was funny, Dad. Get out of here. I have to call Tanner and tell him you're gone so he can, like, bring over the drugs and the gang members."

"Even less funny. No visitors. I'm telling Mrs. Antonelli you're alone."

"Okay," she said. "Where are you going?"

"Thought I might take my bike out."

Nicole nodded, unaware of the monumental impact of this statement. "Wear your helmet," she said, turning back to the screen.

"I'll call you."

"I'm so sure." She made huffing noise, then turned back to her computer. "I love you, Dad," she added.

There it was, that shocking wave of love. She was the best kid in the world. It was a gorgeous Sunday afternoon, and she was doing her work, toughing it out. She'd been through hell, watching her mom die, and yet here she was, pulling in decent grades, playing lacrosse, on the debate team (her calling, he thought). And even though she was mad at him, she still told her father she loved him.

"You can go to the prom," he said.

There was a beat of silence, then her shriek split the air. "What?" She leaped up. "Daddy! Are you kidding? Don't answer that! Oh, Dad, thank you!" She threw her arms around him and kissed his face repeatedly.

"There will be a million rules and regulations," he said, laughing. "Maybe a tracking device."

"I don't care! Oh, Daddy, you're the greatest!"

"Tanner and I will be having a long, long talk," he added.

"Of course you will," she said, disentangling herself from him. "Daddy, thank you."

"Okay. You're welcome." There was a lump in his throat. "I'll call you in a little while, okay? And I'm buying your dress. Not Grandma and Grandpa."

Liam's mood was mixed as he walked toward the garage. On the one hand, it had felt great to give Nicole what she wanted. On the other, he was letting her go to a prom with a teenage boy, which felt more dangerous than if he'd fed her a lump of glowing uranium.

But if Emma had been alive, she probably wouldn't have objected to Nicole going to the prom. Emma had been queen of high school, after all. They'd gone to their prom, of course—Emma had been in a silky ivory dress with a low back, her skin so smooth under his hand as they danced. The rest of his prom memories were foggy, but he knew he'd had fun. Especially *after* the prom...the exact type of fun he didn't want his child to have.

Time for a subject change. A pretty big deal lay immediately ahead of him. The motorcycle.

He unlocked the garage and stepped inside, the smell of oil and metal as familiar as the smell of Nicole's hair. There was the Triumph, the same make and model as the one he'd wrecked.

The last time he'd ridden a motorcycle, he'd almost ended up dead. A concussion and bruising so bad he'd hurt for a month. But if he didn't get on a bike now, he probably never would. It was a beautiful spring day, he had a…friend waiting for him. He grabbed an extra helmet and strapped it on the back.

He wheeled the bike outside, locked the garage once more, and straddled the bike. So far, so good. Helmet on, check. He took a deep breath; the choking panic was still at bay—for now. But his heart was thumping, and his knees buzzed with adrenaline. He turned the key, and the engine purred to life.

And then, just like that, Liam flexed his wrist, and he was gliding down the street, free. No fear, no wave of dread, just him doing what he'd been doing for more than twenty years. It was like meeting an old friend after a long, long time apart. Strange, how easy it was, like he'd never stopped, never crashed.

Cordelia was lugging something to her truck when he pulled up. She shielded her eyes and walked over to him, frowning. Her face was a little pale. "Hey, Liam. I…I kind of forgot we had plans." Then she tipped her head and smiled, and it was like someone turned a light on inside her. "Are you on a motorcycle, Liam Declan Murphy?"

"Seems like it," he said, grinning. "In the mood for a ride?"

"Sure," she said. She ran into the house, then emerged again, shrugging into the leather jacket he'd let her keep.

"How've you been?" he asked.

"Just dandy." She pulled on the helmet, then slid on behind him and said nothing more, just wrapped her arms around his waist, and off they went. He drove on the back roads, the full-blown beauty of spring around them, the trees so green it seemed that they were underwater. They passed tumbled stone walls and lawns full of flowering trees, a pond so blue it almost hurt his eyes. The air was soft and sweet, the sun warm, the purr of the Triumph low and tight.

After about half an hour, Liam pulled over by an old cemetery. He turned off the bike and took off his helmet. Cordelia did the same, running a hand through her short hair, looking away.

"What do you think?" he asked, grinning at the world in general. "You love motorcycles now?"

"Yep," she said, and her voice was a little funny. Still a little pale, too.

Oh, boy. He took a deep breath. "You okay?"

She nodded.

"Are you pregnant?"

"No! No," she said. "Um…I'm not pregnant. No. I just got some news, that's all." And then her face got kind of scrunchy, and she looked away and swallowed.

"Come over here," he said, leading her to the edge of the cemetery. Whatever it was, he felt an abrupt sense of protection—almost like the urge to beat up whoever had made her cry. Because, yes, there were tears in her eyes, and he felt it like a punch in the lung.

There was a granite bench under a tree; the leaves were so bright green they glowed. The breeze rustled overhead, and a blue jay streaked in front of them.

She wiped her eyes and pressed her lips together.

"Tell me," he ordered.

She took a shaky breath. "My birth mother wrote to me."

Was that good? Bad? "That's big news," he said.

She nodded, two more tears sliding down her cheeks. "Yeah." She sighed and leaned back, looking up at the sky. "It's just…" Her voice dropped to a whisper, same way Nicole's did when she was teary. "It's old news, too." She swallowed. "I guess my birth mother sent me a letter when I was in high school, but my parents never told me. Gretchen did. Today. She read the letter back then. I'm definitely the last to know here.…" She bit her lip again. "And I'm kind of stunned, I guess." Her voice broke. "I never thought she wanted to meet me, and all this time, maybe she did."

Not knowing what else to do, Liam put his arm around her, and she leaned into him, resting her head against his shoulder, her goofy hair soft against his jaw.

Then she wriggled out of his grasp and walked off a ways, into the cemetery. "Sorry," she called over her shoulder. "I'm not the weepy type most of the time."

"You don't have to be sorry," he said. "It's a lot to take in."

He followed her, figuring she'd want to talk—women usually did. She didn't say a word, however, and Liam wasn't quite sure what to do, other than wish for that useful manual. "So, do you think you'll try to find her? Your birth mother?" he asked eventually.

She glanced at him. "I don't know. I don't know if her information is still current, or—heck, I haven't even seen the letter. My mom might have thrown it away." She stopped in front of a small marble headstone, its words erased by time. "I just feel so bad—she must think I blew her off, you know? If she sent that, what, fifteen years ago?"

"Do you want to meet her?"

She shrugged. "I don't know. Maybe." She knelt down and brushed off some lichen. "Every once in a while, I run into someone who's scrawny and has hair like mine, and I wonder, is that my relative? It'd be nice to see where I came from."

"Sure," he said. Of course, maybe it wouldn't be. Maybe her birth family was a mess, like his was. Maybe her mom had been a drug addict, and her father was in prison. You never knew.

"When I was a kid," Cordelia said, "people would constantly ask my parents if I was adopted. They'd never ask about Henry, because it's pretty obvious, but it seemed like someone was always asking about me."

"Well, people are idiots."

She shrugged. "I understood. I mean, I'm white, but I don't look anything like Max and Stacia, God knows. They're these big, strapping farmhand people, and I look like Anne Frank. It never bothered Henry—he's not bothered by much. But it always bothered me."

"Audrey Hepburn, I was thinking," he said.

"What?"

"Not Anne Frank. Audrey."

She paused, gave him a feeble grin. Still, it was something. "You get a sticker for that. Even if it's wildly untrue." She sighed. "It's just…see, when Henry was about five, my mom got pregnant. But they lost the baby, and it was a girl."

When Emma had been pregnant, she'd had a little bleeding. Turned out to be no cause for alarm, but that night in the E.R. was one of the worst in Liam's life. Funny how precious something became when you thought you'd lose it. He could only imagine how wrecked the Osterhagens had been.

"So you felt like that's why they adopted you?" Liam asked.

She gave a small shrug, her eyes still on the grave. "That *is* why they adopted me. And I'm glad they did…I just always felt a little bit like the consolation prize. And then there was Gretchen, constantly reminding them of the baby they lost, since she looks so much like my mom."

"Come on. Your folks are crazy about you."

Another ghost of a smile crossed her face. "Yep. That's true, too. But the other thought is still there." She moved on down the row of graves. "So now…you know, learning that my birth mother reached out…I don't know. There are all kinds of adoptions. The birth mother can stay in touch, all sorts of visitation arrangements. But mine didn't want that, and I totally understood. I pictured all these scenarios over the years…she was really young, or a drug addict, or maybe she was…raped. But now I find out that maybe she did want to see me…" Her voice broke again.

Cautiously, because she looked like a loaded spring, Liam went up behind her and slipped his arms around her, pulling her back against his chest.

"Don't be nice to me," she whispered, though she didn't move away. "I might cry if you are."

"And here I thought a hug would help," he said, holding her a little closer. "I really need a user's manual where you're concerned. Want me to pull your hair? Would that be better?"

She gave a shaky laugh. "Sorry I'm so…unfun today."

He turned her around. "Cordelia," he said firmly. "Don't be a dope."

"Such a sweet-talker, you."

"You just told me not to be nice." He tipped her chin up, glad to see she wasn't crying anymore. "What do you want to do? Want me to take you home? Take you to your parents' house so you guys can talk?"

She pursed her lips, thinking, and even though he was trying to be princely, a bolt of lust shot through him. That mouth was really something, and sure enough, he found he was kissing her, gently, her soft, full lips such a surprise coming from that wiry little package.

"I don't want to go home just yet," she said, blushing. Her arms were still around him.

"You want to talk some more? I have a teenage girl. I know all about feelings and crying and mushy stuff."

She laughed, and that warm thing in his chest squeezed. "Nah. I have to think about this a little more, but I'm done talking."

"Come on, then," Liam said. "Cemeteries don't generally cheer people up. Back on the bike, woman. I know just the place."

Twenty minutes later, they pulled up at their destination, and when Posey saw where they were, she gave him a big smile, the first he'd seen from her that day. "Jimbo's Batting Cages, huh?"

"That's right," he said, slinging his arm around her shoulders. "Time you learned to put some wood on ball."

"That sounds vaguely dirty," she murmured.

"We can only hope," and he gave her a kiss and was somewhat amazed at how great it felt to cheer her up.

WELL, LIAM HADN'T managed to teach her to hit, Posey thought, but it had been very fun (and yes, vaguely dirty) to have him stand behind her, his arms enveloping her as he tried to get her to swing at the right time, her bottom pressed most comfortably against his groin. Yep. Dirty. Who knew batting practice could be so much fun? As an improvement on her swing, it was worthless. As foreplay, much better. And he'd made her laugh, and that was really something, given how churned up she'd been feeling.

"Okay, try it yourself a few times. I have to call my kid," Liam said, stepping out of the batting cage. Seemed a lot lonelier in here without him. The next ball came. She swung. Missed. "You are the worst hitter I've ever seen," he added, smiling.

"We all have our talents, lunkhead," she said. Another pitch from the machine. Another miss.

"Hey, honey, it's your father," Liam said into the phone. So sweet. He gave Nicole the paternal interrogation—Posey was standing just feet away, it wasn't like she was eavesdropping. But it was…warming, Liam asking Nicole how was her paper going, had she checked in with Mrs. Antonelli, did she eat the leftover chicken and not just M&Ms. Posey's chest swelled. Liam was a good father, that was clear, and there was little more appealing than a man who was a loving dad.

Liam glanced at her a couple of times as he talked. "Mind if I grab dinner while I'm out?" he said into the phone. He had yet to mention her—Posey tried not to notice, but, yeah, her name had not come up, she was pretty sure. Not that it mattered, not really. "Okay, baby," Liam said finally. "See you later. Love you." He put his phone back in his pocket and looked at Posey once more. "Here it comes…you can do it…swing!"

Posey swung. Missed. "Okay, enough humiliation. What's the plan, Big Papi?"

"How about some dinner?" he asked.

"That would be fantastic," she said. "I'm so hungry, I'm about to gnaw off your arm."

They found a nice little place on the water, ordered some fried clams and scallops, a beer for him, a white zinfandel for her. "No whiskey sours?" Liam asked. "Because you were a lot of fun that night."

"Well, same to you on pain meds, you big baby."

He grinned. She smiled back. Goofy in love, that's what she was. Dang. Or huzzah. She wasn't quite sure.

They talked about ordinary things—she told him about the one-sided romance between her coworkers, he told her about Nicole wanting to go to the prom.

At the word *prom,* Posey felt that old twist of…betrayal. The complete and utter dashing of expecta-tions. But it was clear Liam had no knowledge of the impact of Posey's own prom, and it was better to keep it that way. "So, will you let Nicole go?" she asked.

"I said yes today." He took a long pull on his beer, clearly not convinced that his decision was a good one.

"Well," Posey said briskly, looking out the window, "proms can be very formative."

"Exactly what I'm hoping to avoid. Some idiot boy breaking her heart." The irony of his statement was lost on him; he gave her a half smile and a shrug. "Anyway. Enough about my kid. How are you doing? Feeling a little better?"

Her heart softened. "Yes. A lot better, actually."

"Good." Liam smiled fully, making her knees tingle. So he'd said a crummy thing back in the olden days. He was clearly a great guy now.

The waiter approached, slipping the check on the table. "I'll take this whenever you're ready," he said, gliding away.

"Let me get it," Posey said, grabbing the check. "You were a prince today. You deserve payment."

"Yes, I was a prince, and no, I'm paying." He reached over and took an end of the check.

Posey didn't let go. "Don't make me wrestle you, Liam," she warned. "We both know who would win, and you don't want to be embarrassed in front of all these nice people."

"No, no, let's wrestle," he said, and with that he leaned over and kissed her, a soft, full kiss, his fingers sliding through her short hair, and Posey felt herself melting against him, against his mouth, toward his heat.

Then he pulled back and tugged the check out of her unresisting fingers. "Sucker," he said, grinning.

"Jerk." She straightened up and slid him a glance, still a little flustered from that kiss. "Thanks for dinner, biker boy."

"My pleasure." He stuffed a couple of bills into the leather check holder and continued looking at her. His eyes were smoky. Maybe they'd have time to zip back to the church, have a tumble, before he had to get back to—

Oh, bieber. Oh, no.

George and Louise Tate were standing at the maître d's desk.

Staring at the two of them.

"Liam?" she whispered. "Um…the Tates are here."

His smile vanished. "Oh, crap," he muttered.

"I'm so sorry," Posey said, biting her lip. Dang it! Right when they were out in public—public, you know, with kissing and everything, meeting all of Jon's criteria—there were his dead wife's parents, frozen in dismay.

"No, no. It's… Well, let's go say hi."

They stood up and approached the Tates.

"Hi," Liam said, offering his hand to George. George didn't take it, and Posey had to force herself not to cringe. "Uh, George, Louise, this is Cordelia Osterhagen."

Louise Tate stared at her like she was a severed head on their doorstep. Posey swallowed. Her cheeks were on fire, her hair was, doubtlessly, a mess… "Hi, Mrs. Tate, Mr. Tate," she said, a little too brightly. "I remember you from church, way back when." She paused, lowering her voice. "I was so sorry to hear about Emma. We were friendly in high school, and she was—"

"Thank you," Mrs. Tate interrupted stiffly. "Liam, who's with Nicole?"

"She's at home, working on a paper," he said.

"Alone?" Mr. Tate asked.

"Yes. She's almost sixteen, George." Liam's hands were jammed in his pockets. The Tates said noth-ing. "Well, have a nice dinner," Liam said. "Talk to you soon."

"It was nice to see you again," Posey added, then kicked herself. It wasn't nice, certainly not for them.

"Tell Nicole we'd like to see her twice this week, since we didn't get to visit today," Mrs. Tate said, ignoring Posey. Her tone was ice-cold.

The sky was red and purple outside, and the lights of the Piscataqua River Bridge glittered in the reflection of the water. "I'm really, really sorry about that," Posey said quietly as they walked to the parking lot.

"Don't apologize. You didn't do anything wrong. It's fine." His voice was normal, but of course, it wasn't fine. He was tense as they drove home, the ride not nearly as pleasant as it had been earlier. His back was stiff and straight, his movements overly cautious.

When they pulled into her driveway, Liam walked her to the door, despite her protestation that he didn't have to. From inside, Shilo began barking in joy, his baying voice bouncing off the forty-foot ceilings.

"Okay, well, thanks, Liam. For today. You were really great," Posey said. She took a deep breath. "Sorry about the Tates and the kissing and stuff."

He shrugged. "I kissed you. And don't worry about it. But I should get back to Nicole."

"Sure, sure. Okay."

They stood there another minute, the silence growing awkward. Then Liam reached out and pinched her chin. "Good luck with the family stuff," he said. "And you know, you can call me. If you want."

"Thanks."

"I mean it."

"Thanks even more, then, biker boy." She stood on her tiptoes and kissed his cheek. "Now, shoo. Go home to your kid."

Instead, he wrapped his arms around her and held her tight for a long minute, and it was so unexpected that Posey felt her eyes prickle with tears. She kissed his cheek again. "You're a good guy, Liam Murphy," she whispered. Then, a little embarrassed at the proclamation, she pulled back. "Go on, git," she said. "And thanks."

Inside, with Shilo licking her face and wagging so hard he knocked over an end table, Posey found that she was still smiling. Even with the Tates ending their night on an off note, Liam had really come through.

Nope. That had not been cool. The joy of riding his Triumph was gone as Liam made his way from Cordelia's back into town. The Tates hadn't wanted him with Emma, but they sure didn't want him with someone else. Not now, anyway. And of course, they'd busted him at the very moment he'd been picturing Cordelia naked and underneath him. Bad enough that he'd deflowered, then stolen, their precious daughter. Now he was—in their minds, anyway—cheating on her.

Liam pulled into the garage, figuring the walk home might cool him off a little, give him time to figure out how to make this okay. The thing was, being out with Cordelia had been pretty fantastic. She'd been upset, he'd made her feel better, they'd had fun. It had been a long time since he'd felt so... well, so good. *You're a good guy, Liam Murphy,* Cordelia had said.

It wasn't something he'd heard a lot in his life.

Enter the Tates, almost on cue to remind him just how not-good he really was. Not only was Nicole left alone—Liam, the negligent father, was out with another woman. The warmth from being with Cordelia evaporated as he walked through the quiet streets of Bellsford. He hadn't heard the end of this, he was quite sure.

He opened the door of the apartment building and ran up the five flights of stairs. Heard the sound of the Ramones and smelled popcorn. Nicole must've finished that paper. Good girl.

Then Liam opened the door, walked into his apartment, and found Tanner Talcott and Nicole sitting on the couch, entwined around each other, kissing like a meteor was about to hit the planet and end life as they knew it.

CHAPTER TWENTY-THREE

"YOU CAN'T GROUND me for kissing someone!" Nicole yelled.

"I already have grounded you!" he yelled back. It had been three days since Nicole had aged him fifty years—three days of whining, sobbing and yelling—and if he could magically turn her mute, he'd do it in a heartbeat.

"You're so unfair! I'm sixteen years old, almost! I should be able to kiss my boyfriend!"

"You weren't grounded for kissing that boy! It was for breaking every rule I have! You were home alone, Nicole! No guests! You know that! Let alone a horny boy who just wants to get into your pants!"

"Our clothes were totally on! Maybe he doesn't just want to get into my pants, Dad. Maybe he loves me!" She burst into tears and threw herself into a chair.

Emma, you really screwed me by dying, Liam thought irrationally. *I don't know how much more of this I can take.* He took a deep breath. "Stop crying, Nic," he said in a calmer voice. "I'll drive you to school."

She cut him a glare. "I'm taking the bus."

"Get your stuff and get in the car, Nicole!"

There should be some drug for fathers of teenage girls. Something that calmed your heart so it didn't practically rip through your chest. Something that could soothe the fury your daughter could inspire, the absolute terror that something unspeakable would happen to her, the almost murderous sense of protection. Something that would give you the words to tell her that no one would ever love her as much as dear old dad, and if she just listened to him, she'd have a much easier time of things and be safe from boys who ruined her life.

Liam would bet his left nut that George Tate had wished for the same thing.

They rode to school in silence. When he pulled into the parking lot, she didn't get out right away, just sat there, staring straight ahead. "I still get to go to the prom, right?" she asked, her voice defiant. "Tanner already bought the tickets, and they were, like, really expensive."

No. You don't ever get to go out with that boy again. Do you know how hard it was for me not to kill him the other night? Prom? Are you serious? Are you out of your mind? Absolutely not. Never.

But nearly sixteen years of fatherhood had taught Liam one thing—sometimes, it's best not to answer right away. "Have a good day at school, and I'll pick you up at 2:30. I love you, even if I'm really, really mad, Nicole. And I know you're mad, too, but you're grounded for your own good."

Nicole answered with the Slitty Eyes of Death and got out of the car.

It was not with a light heart that Liam went to work. The smell of oil and machines, the faint bite of soldered metal, the cool echo of the garage that usually welcomed him failed to work its magic today. Usually, he loved coming to the garage. It was the one place he really knew what he was doing. When Liam was six years old, his father had asked him to help him take apart an engine. The car had been stolen, but Liam didn't know that and probably wouldn't have cared if he had. Father-son bonding times were few and far between. Dad may have been a mean drunk, but when he was sober, he'd been great with an engine. Liam had been hooked.

And now he had his own place, and work was going great. He was even hiring a kid from the vocational school. The bakery women had ordered a matching pair of custom bikes (who knew there was so much money in pastries?). They loved the design he'd made for them; he was just waiting for their down payment to get started. Right here in front of him was Jimmy Spencer's Harley, which had a burned-out clutch. Liam could fix that in his sleep. Wires, connections, components, all fixable. After that, he had three custom gas tanks to make. He picked up a wrench and got to work on Jimmy's bike, took off the housing and started disassembling the clutch plates.

Everything was so logical here. If you put something together the right way, it worked. The spark plugs didn't just decide that the rules of mechanics didn't apply to them. They didn't just say, *You know what? We're not firing up today. No, there's no reason. We just don't feel like we should have to. Screw the distributor and its stupid wires. We don't care. Maybe we'll care tomorrow. Maybe not. We'll let you know. Or we won't. We might hate you tomorrow. Count on it, in fact.* No, if the spark plugs didn't work, there was a good reason for that. Not like fatherhood.

And not like marriage.

That was another thing. His wife had left him a long time ago. Long before she got sick. She might've lived in the same house and slept in the same bed, but she hadn't really been there, not when it was just the two of them. He could tell in the way she listened to him, her mind elsewhere even if she made the right response, in the way she distanced herself from him just a little when they were out in public. He could tell in bed. What had once been that kind of soul-to-soul connection dwindled into a pleasant physical exchange, until all Liam had was the mother of his child and the woman who slept on the other side of the bed.

And then she'd died and taken even that and left him with a daughter. A daughter who seemed determined to ruin her life the same way her mother had.

"Damn it!" Liam yelled, throwing a wrench across the garage, where it clattered against the wall.

"Dude, chill," came a voice.

He straightened up, then closed his eyes. Red-faced Rick Balin. Again. The blowhard came in three times a week at least and thought nothing of wasting Liam's time.

"What can I do for you, Rick?" he asked. "I'm pretty busy."

"Dude, I'm ready to make a commitment, right? And nothing but the best, okay? I can afford it."

"Sure," Liam said tightly. "Come on into my office."

Rick wanted the best, all right. He looked through some of Liam's basic designs, adding features like a kid in a candy store. An S&S motor, Italian leather seat, custom-cut aluminum alloy wheels. Shortened handlebars, which Liam would send out to be chromed, to accommodate Rick's rather stubby arms. A turn here, a swoop there, more chrome here. He wanted the whole thing to be powder-coated a bright orange.

The price tag would be just over sixty grand.

"Not a problem," Rick said. He suppressed a burp, then leaned back and gave Liam a self-satisfied grin. "A man's gotta treat himself right, know what I'm saying, dude? And hey, I work hard. I deserve it."

Liam looked away, his eyes settling on the Gypsy Tour medallion. There was no doubt about it. He hated Rick Balin. It was more than the fact that the guy was an obnoxious, lazy, entitled pain in the ass…there was something else. Something visceral.

"Get out," he said.

Rick blinked. "What's that?"

"Get out, Rick. I'm not selling you anything. There are enough idiots on motorcycles in the world. I'm not gonna add one more to the roster. Buy your midlife crisis somewhere else and get out of my garage."

"Dude—"

"Now." He stood up, and Rick shrank back in his seat—well, shrank back as much as a three-hundred-pound man could.

"You're making a mistake," Rick said as Liam grabbed his beefy arm and towed him toward the exit.

"Doesn't feel that way," Liam said.

"You can't do this to me! I'm the president of the Downtown Merchants Coun—"

Liam closed the door in his face.

It should've felt good. It *did* feel good, even if he'd just flushed a year's worth of tuition payments down the toilet. But Rick...he was like that kid who'd called Liam no one from nowhere. Someone who felt entitled to everything.

Something flashed in Liam's memory...something from high school, something to do with Rick... but then it was gone.

He had the sudden urge to see Cordelia, and without further thought, he flipped the Open sign to Closed.

VERY, VERY CAREFULLY, Posey set the porch railing in place on the model house she was building, then held it as the wood glue set. Of all the models she'd built, The Meadows was most involved—try making stained-glass windows that were half an inch high. But she loved it; it was such a contrast to salvage, where everything was taken apart. Now she was building something. From the tiny slate shingles on the roof to the turned balusters of the porch, the model would be an almost exact replica. Vivian would love it.

She glanced over at Shilo, who happened to be sleeping on a black-and-white cow-skin-covered couch, meaning he was almost invisible. He was snoring, having exhausted himself by hiding from Al the UPS man earlier that morning.

She was pretty tired, too. Thoughts of the letter had been keeping her up at night. What had her birth mother wanted? Was she heartbroken because Posey never answered? Did Posey have biological siblings out there somewhere? And why would her parents keep that from her? How would they react when she brought this up, because really, how the heck could she not bring this up?

"Hey."

At the sound of Liam's voice, Posey jumped, knocking the railing askew. "Dang it. Hi, Liam," she said, feeling her face warm. She straightened the railing and looked up at him. There was Elise, standing behind Liam and grinning hugely, mouthing the words *Oh, my God!* as her hands fluttered in excitement. "How are you?"

So hot! Elise mouthed.

"Great."

He didn't look great...well, he always looked pretty great, actually. At the moment, though, he looked clenched, his mouth grim, jaw tight, hands stuffed in the pockets of his jeans. "Want to grab lunch?" he asked.

This was a first. Well, this was two firsts, in fact. Liam had never come to Irreplaceable, and he'd never asked her out on an impromptu date.

Unfortunately, his timing sucked. "I can't. I'd love to, but it's... Um, I have plans."

At her words, Elise began humming "Happy Birthday."

"Elise," Posey said tightly, "could you...check the register or something?"

"Totally," Elise said, pointing at Liam's ass with another *Oh, my God!* She obeyed, however, practically skipping to the front of the store.

"So...yeah. I have a lunch thing. Sorry," Posey said.

"Should've called, I guess." He paused. "Everything good with you? Family-wise?"

"Oh, sure." She gave a little shrug.

Liam glanced around the barn. "This is quite the place."

"Thanks," she said, feeling the familiar sense of pride as she followed his gaze. His expression was somber. "Everything okay with you, Liam?"

"Sure. Just...do you remember—"

At that moment, the door opened. "Come on, birthday girl!" boomed Kate. "I took an entire day off for this. I tried to get James to come, because they have stuff for guys there, too, back waxing, manly manis…they actually do a scrotal wax, can you believe that? Not that I want that for my son, but come on! Wouldn't that be a son of a bitch?"

Ah, her delicate friend. Kate finally seemed to notice Liam. "Oh, hi, biker boy. How's it hanging?"

"Kate," Liam said, grinning. "How's it hanging with you?"

Kate gave him an unabashed once-over. "I'm taking the birthday girl here to a spa. Nose to toes. Buffed, polished, oiled…whatever the hell else they do there. I tend to fall asleep, personally. But I can guarantee she'll smell like something other than polyurethane. Thank me later. Come on, Posey, our appointment is in twenty minutes."

"Happy birthday." Liam looked down at her, a faint smile in his eyes.

"Oh…thanks."

"What did you get her, Liam?" Elise asked. "I'll totally keep it a secret. Is it, like, jewelry?"

"Okay, okay, that's enough," Posey said, mortified. "He didn't know it was my birthday, and he's not getting me anything." *Because one doesn't announce to Hottie McSin that it's one's birthday, because one may be trying very hard to pretend that this relationship is casual, and birthdays shouldn't be brought up, since that could be construed as begging for a gift and/or acknowledgment of a special event in one's life.*

"Have fun," Liam said in a low voice. "Can't wait to smell you later."

Oh, Elvis. Posey's knees gave a significant wobble.

"Princess! Come on! You know I hate to be late! Those waxings take a while on me," Kate barked. "Oh, and Liam, I'm so glad you and Posey are getting it on. I think that's very cool."

Posey's face actually hurt from blushing. "Okay. Sorry about lunch," she managed.

"Not a problem."

The memory of his smile made her feel wriggly for quite some time.

CHAPTER TWENTY-FOUR

LIAM THREW HIS TOOL BAG in the trunk of the car. Half a day's work, gone but for a good cause. He could make the work up. Maybe (though not probably)…maybe Nicole would want to come down to the garage and do her homework while he worked. They could order pizza. She used to love being near him when he was working; she'd never be one of those women who couldn't fix her own car, that was for sure. But she hadn't been down in a while.

Liam pulled into Granite State Custom Motorcycles and muttered a curse. A shiny black Mercedes was parked right in front of the door, the Tates sitting in the front seat, their expressions as cheerful as cadavers.

"Come on in," he said, holding the door for them.

"No need, Liam," George said, getting out of the car. Louise did as well, joining her husband at his side. "We'll make this brief."

Liam looked at Louise, whose lips were pressed together. "What is it?"

George cleared his throat. "We're filing for custody of our granddaughter."

Liam's mouth dropped open. "Are you crazy?"

"She needs a stable home after all she's been through," Louise said, her face tight with hatred.

"She *has* a stable home!"

"Without a parade of women traipsing in and out of her life," she added viciously.

"Okay, hold on." Liam held up his hands. "I— Nicole doesn't—" Sweat broke out on his back, sticking his shirt to his skin. "You can't just take her away from me. She's my child."

"Look, son," George said, "we're not trying to take her away."

"You're filing for custody, but you're not trying to take her away? Bullshit, George."

"You can still visit whenever you want."

"First of all, are you insane? Absolutely not! And secondly, she wouldn't—" *She wouldn't want to leave me,* he was about to say.

Except maybe she did.

"You were out gallivanting around the countryside on a motorcycle with some *woman*," Louise hissed, her voice like a razor, "and that child was alone! No wonder she called her boyfriend! No wonder she was afraid! And she told us about how you grounded her, which is utterly and completely hypocritical, given that you'd just rolled out of that tramp's bed—"

"Stop it! Stop!" Liam barked. "First of all, I was gone for maybe four hours, and Nicole is almost sixteen. Mrs. Antonelli was right next door, and Nicole knew that. Secondly, Cordelia is an old friend. And yes, we've been seeing each other a little bit here and there. But that doesn't make me an unfit parent—"

Louise snorted. "Your track record speaks for itself," she said, folding her bony arms across her chest.

"My track record? Would that be raising your grandchild and taking care of your daughter for the last year of her life? That track record, Louise?"

"How many women have you slept with, Liam? Do you honestly think that we believe you were faithful to our daughter? How many of your old conquests have you seen since you've been back, hmm? I bet quite a few of them would love to come to court and talk about your habits."

"I *never* cheated on Emma," he said hotly. He turned to his father-in-law. "George, this is crazy. You can't take my daughter away from me." His voice cracked.

"We have concerns about your stability," his father-in-law said. "And I'm not just talking about women. Our lawyer has taken a statement from a social worker at the hospital regarding your...problems."

"What are you talking about?"

"Mental health professionals can testify in cases regarding the stability of a parent," Louise said. "Did you think we wouldn't find out about your panic attacks? I am on the board of that hospital. What else are you hiding? Are you a drug addict, like your mother?"

"My God," Liam breathed.

"Look," George said. "We're not taking her away. We're just providing her with the things you can't. Stability, a woman's influence, a good...ah, moral code."

"No judge would ever—"

"We'll see." George Tate opened the car door. "You'll be hearing from our lawyer."

NICOLE DIDN'T SEEM to notice anything different when he picked her up from school. She ignored him as best she could as they drove home.

Liam had been fighting off a panic attack since the Tates left, and no amount of hand washing seemed to be helping. On the one hand, he could cheerfully murder them both. Whether or not they had a legal leg to stand on, they sure had a lot of money to throw at this and make his life utter hell. The bit about the social worker...he didn't even remember a social worker, which might be a problem. What had he said?

He was a good father. Wasn't he? He'd never tried so hard at anything as he had with raising Nicole.

On the other hand—this was the thought that had his heart heaving—what if they were right? What if Nicole needed more than he could give her? She loved him, he loved her, God knew, but was that enough? Was he enough? Would Nicole jump at the chance to live with her grandparents? What if this was her idea? If it was, then he really was no one from nowhere, because the only good thing he'd ever done was be a father to Nicole.

"I need to talk to you," he said, setting the keys down on the table.

"I have *homework*," she said defiantly.

"Do you want to spend more time with Grandma and Grandpa?" he asked, and his voice was a little hoarse.

"Right now? Totally."

He tried not to flinch at her words. "Nic, do you want to live with them?"

Nicole's mouth dropped open. "What?" Her face turned bright red, whether with guilt or surprise, Liam couldn't tell.

"Grandma and Grandpa came to see me today. They want you to come live with them."

Her expression didn't change for a second. Then her beautiful blue eyes were suddenly swamped with tears. "You're sending me away? Because I kissed Tanner? Are you really that mad, Daddy?"

Liam leaped across the kitchen and folded her against him. "I'm not sending you anywhere, baby," he said, almost ashamed at the relief flooding through him because of his daughter's distress. "I already told them no." He kissed her head. "I just wasn't sure if you wanted that."

"No!" Nicole sobbed. "I want to stay with you! I'm sorry I broke the rules!"

"Honey, this isn't about that, okay? But they just think that it would be...good...if you spent more time with them."

"Why?" She pulled back and looked at him, her face wet with tears.

He could say it, he knew. Tell how her grandparents were filing for custody, how they thought he was trash, a womanizer, an unfit father, had never been good enough for their daughter. In this moment, if he told her all those things—and all those things were true—he could do some serious damage to the Tates' relationship with their precious granddaughter. She'd never look at them the same way again.

He touched the tip of her nose. "They just love you so much, sweetheart," he said gently. "And they miss your mom, and you remind them of her."

Nicole's face scrunched up. "I know," she whispered. "But I want to stay with you. Even if you're a hard-ass."

Thank you, God. Liam felt the sting of tears in his eyes as he hugged his daughter again.

"I don't want anything else to change," Nicole said into his shirt. "Losing Mommy was hard enough. I like it just the two of us. That's the way I want it to stay."

"Me, too, baby," he murmured, breathing in the smell of her hair. "Me, too."

He wouldn't give the Tates any more ammunition. He wouldn't leave Nicole any room to screw up again.

He'd stop seeing Cordelia, and though the thought caused a hollow echo to roll through him, all that mattered was here in his arms.

CHAPTER TWENTY-FIVE

"So what do you think, Viv? Do I look like a girl?"

Vivian squinted through her bifocals. "Well, it's nice to see you in a dress, even one so ill-fitting."

"The saleslady said it was supposed to be loose."

"She lied."

Posey looked down at herself, the landscape unfamiliar in the sheath dress. But she wanted to look a little nicer these days. She certainly was feeling more…womanly, having a boyfriend and all. Especially one who complimented her. Was the dress a little Audrey Hepburn–inspired? Probably. She might like Liam to see her in it (or out of it).

"You might be right. Anyway, I was at the spa today. I didn't think I'd like it, but it was kind of fun. And don't I smell great?" She offered her forearm to Vivian, who frowned and turned her head away. "Well. I smell great, take my word."

Sitting down next to Vivian, she sighed. The spa had been fun, but now she had to see her parents and the thought of the letter from her birth mother burned in her mind.

"What's the matter with you?" the old lady asked. She'd gone psychic, apparently.

Posey hesitated. "Did anyone in your family ever keep a secret from you?"

"Of course. It's the nature of families. Why?"

"I don't know." She paused. "Why didn't you and your husband ever adopt, Viv?"

"Aren't we personal," Vivian murmured.

"You don't have to tell me."

"I'm aware of that." Vivian gave her a lethal look, then turned her face away. "Ernest was against it," she said eventually. "I wouldn't have minded, but he was a bit of an ass about the subject. Anyway. It's your birthday, if I recall."

"How did you know?" Posey asked.

"A little bird who won't stop talking told me. That girl needs finishing school. You both do. Here." She handed Posey a box.

Well, knock her over with a feather. Vivian Appleton was not a sentimental person. In all the time Posey had known her, she had never given a compliment, let alone a gift. "Are you dying, Viv?" Posey said.

"We're all dying. Open it."

"This is so sweet. Thank you!"

"Thank me when you open it," the old lady said, sitting a little straighter.

Posey untied the ribbons. "It's the thought that counts."

"I never believed that expression, did you?"

Posey laughed and opened the box. Her breath caught. "Oh, Vivian! It's beautiful!"

It was an antique butterfly pin, wings sparkling with tiny, multicolored crystal beads. The butterfly's body was gold, and it seemed to be smiling, the black jeweled eyes glittering.

"It's not worth much," Vivian said, looking away. "But it was mine when I was a girl. My aunt gave it to me for my tenth birthday. It reminded me of you."

So uncharacteristic, all this thoughtfulness! "I love it." Posey fastened it to her dress, then leaned over and kissed Vivian's soft, withered cheek. "Thank you, Viv."

The old lady stared straight ahead. "I signed with Down East Salvage this morning."

The words hit Posey like a slap. She opened her mouth, but no words came out. Down East Salvage? The thought of The Meadows being taken down was horrible enough...but those gorillas at Down East... how could— They wouldn't— Oh, bieber, she was going to cry. Realizing that her mouth was still open, she closed it and sat back against the couch so she wouldn't have to look at Vivian.

"They offered me ten thousand more than you did," Vivian said, her tone brisk. "It would've been foolish not to take it."

Posey's throat was too tight to answer.

"I have the right to dispose of my property as I see fit, Posey," Viv snapped. "I have my nieces and nephews to think of, you know, and they wouldn't appreciate me—"

"It's okay," she said, taking Vivian's hand. If she looked at the old lady now, she'd start bawling. "I understand." She bit her lip to control the trembling of her mouth.

How could Viv's Vultures just...erase a place like The Meadows? Pretend it never happened and slap up a bevy of soulless McMansions, and that gracious, beautiful house, built in the time of Mark Twain and parasols, of lemonade on the porch in the summer and sleigh bells on harnesses in the winter, would be gone.

Down East Salvage would strip the house down in days. Posey had seen them work—they used chainsaws, for the love of Elvis, and backhoes. Those beautiful gardens would be torn up, thousands of bulbs and plants crushed or thrown away. Down East would cut down the elm tree, she'd bet her life they would, never mind that it was three hundred years old. They would desecrate the entire place. They didn't love The Meadows the way she did. They hadn't been there twice a week for the past two years. They hadn't made love out by the pine trees.

Posey would've taken months with that house. She and Mac would've lovingly removed every feature, from the marble fireplace in the dining room to the copper tub on the third floor. She would've cut out the lead-paned windows with her sharpest, smallest saw and coaxed them from the walls. Every doorknob, every light-switch plate, every heating grate would've been wrapped carefully until Posey found them new homes, where they'd be loved and appreciated. And when the beautiful shell of the house finally had to come down, Posey would've stood guard until it was done and paid her last respects.

Down East would use Dumpsters. They'd hire high-school kids, and they'd throw things out the windows into *Dumpsters*. She'd seen it happen on their job sites before.

"I have to get going," Posey said when she could trust her voice.

"Yes. You have a birthday engagement, I suppose," Vivian said.

"Dinner with my family." She swallowed. "Thank you for the pin. It's beautiful."

"Go. You'll be late, and it's so inconsiderate." With that, Vivian fished out her phone and began texting.

Posey tried not to think about The Meadows on the drive to her parents' house.

But it was hard.

The whole week had been hard. She hadn't seen her parents since learning about the letter.

Max and Stacia had always given all the right lip service on the rare occasions that the subject of birth parents came up. But Posey knew. If she'd ever said, "Hey, I'd like to find my birth parents," they'd take it like a knife in the heart. Who, after all, had done the real work of parenting, staying up when Posey was sick, helping her with her science homework, taking such pride in her depiction of the turnip in Farmer Smith's garden?

So she'd done nothing about the letter, aside from telling Liam. And, it must be acknowledged, Liam had been incredible. All that upset, all that churning, and he'd somehow made her feel...happy.

It was too bad about the run-in with the Tates. She wondered how that was going.... He hadn't called her, but tomorrow was Wednesday, usually the night they saw each other.

She pulled up in front of her parents' house. Was her letter somewhere inside? How exactly would she ask about it?

"Look at you! You're beautiful!" Jon announced as he answered the door. "Come in, birthday princess. Everyone's here except Gretch the Wretch, even Brianna, OMG, you should've seen her face when she found out we were having pork knuckles for an appetizer. And listen, I tried to bring chicken cordon bleu and scalloped potatoes, but your mom said your heart was set on herring, so we're stuck with the food from the Fatherland." He paused for breath. "Why the sad face?"

"I didn't get the rights to The Meadows," she said, and you know, that was the thing about family. They hugged her and patted her shoulder, and Jon made her a vodka gimlet, and Mom set a plate of pork meatballs in front of her.

"They're stupid if they didn't hire you," Brianna said, and Posey smiled. Brie was nothing if not loyal.

"Agreed," murmured Henry.

"Well, it's your birthday, so be happy," Dad said, squeezing her shoulder.

"Thanks, Dad," she said. He might've kept a secret for the past fifteen years, but he was her dear old dad nonetheless.

The door banged open, and there was Gretchen, dressed to kill in a slinky pink shirt and tight black skirt that clung to her curves. She gave a rather formal nod. "Hello, all."

"Sweetie, have a seat!" Stacia said. "You look exhausted!"

"Is four half-days a week just too much?" Jon murmured to Posey.

Gretchen allowed Max to get her a drink. "Well, don't just sit there," Stacia commanded, ever the gracious hostess. "Get into the dining room. *Essen und geniessen!*"

"Come again?" Brianna said, examining a pork-liver ball at the end of a toothpick.

"Eat and enjoy," Stacia said. "Come on, sweetheart, while it's hot!"

When they were all seated around the dining-room table, Henry tapped his glass. "We have an announcement, and Jon said I was the one who should tell you." He glanced at his partner and smiled. "Okay, here goes. Posey, we have a birthday present for you, but you'll have to wait a little while before it gets here."

"I hope it's big and expensive," she said.

"It's expensive, but still pretty little. We pick it up in Guatemala next month." He paused. "It's a niece."

There was a moment of silence. Posey covered her mouth with her hand. "A niece? Oh, guys!" She lunged up from the table to hug them both. Max and Stacia followed suit, engulfing the boys in hugs and sobs.

"She's thirteen months old," Jon said damply, "and her name is Elisabeta Rosa Josephina Juarez, soon to be Elisabeta Rosa Josephina Juarez-Osterhagen-White."

"Rolls right off the tongue," Brianna said, buttering another piece of bread.

"We're going to call her Betty," Jon continued.

"Betty White?" Brie said, grinning.

"Who better to be a role model? Anyway, she's at Our Lady of Angels Orphanage right now, and we have a picture and everything. And of course, Posey, you'll be godmother."

"I can't believe it. I've waited so long for grandchildren," Stacia said, sinking back into her chair in a happy daze.

Henry handed Posey a picture, and her eyes filled with fresh tears. The baby had dark hair, long enough for the barrettes and ribbons Jon was sure to employ, and huge dark eyes. She was chubby, her expression solemn, and Posey's heart swelled with love. "She's so beautiful. Hi, Betty." She grinned up at the boys, then looked at Brianna. "Pretty cool, don't you think?"

"Oh, yeah. So cool."

"Don't worry. I won't ditch you."

Brie cut her a glance. "Feel free."

"Sulk all you want, you're stuck with me. You can help change poopy diapers and everything."

"I'm counting the hours." But she gave Posey a grateful look and didn't make gagging noises when Jon described the mural of unicorns he was going to paint in the baby's room.

Only Gretchen didn't seem terribly interested. She duly admired the photo, then passed it on. Nor did she say boo during the entire dinner, or even sing "Happy Birthday." Something was definitely up, and a warning wriggled down Posey's spine like a cold fish.

Brianna's mother picked her up right after coffee and kuchen were served, and Posey was happy to see Tina give her daughter a kiss. Home life had taken a turn for the better, according to Brie.

The family slumped around the living room in the usual high-carb, high-fat coma that Osterhagen meals induced. Stacia was still clutching the photo of Betty, murmuring about getting some baby things down from the attic.

"So," Max asked, patting Gretchen's hand, "you're awfully quiet. Everything okay, sweetheart?"

She took a deep, measured breath, as if about to give a speech. "It's nice that someone finally noticed, Papa." She looked at Posey.

Ruh-roh, Posey thought. Something was about to hit the fan.

"I had a little surprise last night," Gretchen said, ice dripping from her voice. "Dante happened to mention that he and Posey had been lovers. Isn't that funny?"

Posey's stomach contracted, the three helpings of potatoes threatening to revisit her. "Um…Gret, maybe we should talk privately," she murmured. She glanced at her mother, whose face had frozen in horror.

"No! I think we should talk now, Posey!" Gretchen slammed her hand down on the armrest. "You were sleeping with my boyfriend and you never said a word!"

"More coffee, anyone?" Max said, bolting from his chair into the kitchen. No one else moved.

"She wasn't sleeping with Dante!" Stacia protested. "She would never do such a thing!"

"Really?" Gretchen demanded. "Tell them, Posey."

Posey glanced at her mother, then at the boys. Jon grimaced, Henry shrugged. "Okay, yes," she said. "Dante and I had a very brief, uh, relationship. Which was over before he even met you, Gretchen."

"And you never thought to mention it?"

"No!" Stacia gasped. "Posey! Dante Bellini? How could you?"

"Do you think I would've taken your leavings if I'd known?" Gretchen's face was mottled with fury.

"Time for us to go, don't you think?" Henry said. "Happy birthday, sis."

"Want us to stay?" Jon murmured.

Gretchen turned on him. "No! She doesn't get her little fan club to cheer her on, Jon! Go home! You're not wanted here."

"Watch yourself, young lady," Max said sternly from the kitchen. His head popped into the living room. "But she has a point. No reason for you to stay, fellas."

"Exactly, Pop. See you soon." Henry took Jon's arm and towed him out of the dining room.

"We're thrilled about the baby," Stacia said automatically.

"Congratulations," Posey called.

Jon pulled a face—dismay and sympathy—and slipped out after Henry.

Silence fell over the living room. Stacia shredded a napkin, staring at the photo of Posey as Turnip as if wondering where that sweet child had gone. Max lingered in the doorway, his gaze bouncing between the three women.

"I can't believe you lied to my face," Gretchen said, her lips tight.

"I didn't lie," Posey said, glancing at the picture of Pope Benedict. *Lies of omission are still lies,* she could hear him whispering in his creepy bad-guy voice. "I mean, I didn't say anything because I didn't think it mattered, Gret. That's all."

"How could it not matter?" she hissed.

"I'm so disappointed, Posey," Stacia announced. "I'm stunned. Shocked. Horrified."

"Okay, Ma, I get that. Look, Gret. It wasn't— It didn't have anything to do with the present."

"Well, I think it's disgusting," her cousin said. "Dante crawls from your bed into mine, and you crawl from his into Liam's, and I'm sorry, Posey, I guess I'm not like you, but I think that's vile."

"It wasn't like that!" Posey protested.

"Liam? Now you're sleeping with Liam? Oh, Posey, are you a sex addict?" Stacia asked. Max flinched and retreated once again, running the water to drown out the conversation.

"Ma, I'm not a sex addict! Come on! This is me, remember?"

"That's right," Gretchen snapped. "Posey who can do no wrong. Well, guess what? *This* was wrong. How dare you? You get everything, don't you, Posey? You always have to have everything—Henry, Jon, a niecey-poo on the way, that fat kid who follows you around like a dog."

"Don't you dare—" Posey began.

"And now I find out you had Dante first, and I can't take any more." With that, Gretchen stormed out of the house, slamming the door. A second later, they heard the sound of a car peeling out of the driveway.

"I can't believe what I've heard," Stacia said, wringing her hands. "I'm stunned. Max, I'm stunned. Get me a sherry."

Well, this birthday would certainly be memorable.

Max came back into the room and handed his wife her little cordial glass, then sat next to her, a wall of Teutonic solidarity. "You've upset your mother," he said, his voice gentle but still stern.

"*I've* upset my mother, Dad? How about Gretchen has upset my mother?" she said sharply.

"We'll deal with her later," Max said.

"How could you keep this a secret? How could you even be with that man in the first place?" Stacia asked, tossing back her drink in one gulp.

Ironic, that Stacia now had a problem with secrets. Posey took a deep breath, then another. "Okay, let me explain. First of all, I always thought it was kind of ridiculous that you had such a grudge against Dante."

"Oh! Now you're taking his side?" Stacia cried.

"Ma, calm down. He has a very successful restaurant. And so do you, in your own way. There's room in the world for both."

Stacia harrumphed.

"And secondly..." Posey's voice trailed off. "Okay, secondly, it's not like men are beating a path to my door. When he...asked me out—" *made a pass* "—I was flattered, you know? He's a good-looking, charming guy. So we saw each other—" *slept together* "—a few times, and it just petered out. That was it."

Stacia lifted a disbelieving eyebrow.

"Gretchen was so excited about him that I didn't want to ruin things for her. Dante and I had a little talk and just agreed that some things are better left unsaid. I don't know why he told her, since it obviously didn't...mean that much."

Posey clutched a throw pillow against her stomach. In hindsight, it was clear that she'd felt almost nothing for Dante, other than some basic attraction and the hope that they'd see something in each other... something special. It had had little to do with reality. She knew that now—now that she'd felt the real thing.

"And yes, Liam and I have been dating," she added quietly. "For about a month."

"Another secret. And here I thought we were so close," Stacia sniffed.

Posey gave her mother a long look. "Speaking of secrets," she said, sitting up a little straighter, "I was wondering if you could tell me about that letter."

"What letter?" Max asked.

"The letter from my birth mother."

The blood drained out of both parents' faces, answering the question of whether Max knew about it.

"How did you find out about that? Did you find her?" Stacia asked, her voice shrill.

"No, Mom. Gretchen mentioned the letter. She read it when it first came."

"What do you mean, she read it? That was none of her business!"

"Ma, she thought it was something about her parents. Can we stick to the point here?"

"You said you never wanted to find them," Max said.

"I might've felt differently if I'd known my birth mother wrote to me, Dad! I can't believe you kept that secret! Didn't it occur to you that I'd like to know?"

"The letter wasn't to you," Stacia boomed. "It was addressed to me."

That stopped Posey in her tracks.

"It's true, honey," Max said gently. "It came through the lawyer who handled your adoption, and it was addressed to 'the woman who adopted my baby.' We would never have hidden a letter that came to you."

Posey exhaled slowly. "Okay. But it was about me, obviously."

Her parents exchanged a glance. "Yes, of course it was," Stacia said. "And we always agreed that if you ever said anything about wanting to find your birth parents, the first thing we'd do was hand you that letter. But you never did. So we didn't say anything." Stacia folded her arms across her massive chest and dared Posey to find fault.

Max came over and sat next to Posey and put his arm around her shoulders. As always, the smell of her dad was comforting, his big arm heavy and solid. "It was a tough time," he said. "Your aunt and uncle had just died, you were getting ready for college. We wanted it to be your choice to find her, not to have this letter just come out of nowhere. We figured if she wanted to write to you, she would have. So we kept it secret. Maybe it wasn't right, but...well, we thought it was."

Posey nodded. In her heart, she knew her parents would never do anything to hurt her. Not on purpose. "I'd like to see it now," she whispered.

Max and Stacia exchanged a look. "I'm sorry, Posey," her father said. "We lost it in the fire."

The letter, which Stacia coolly recounted with the help of an index card on which she'd noted the pertinent information, was more of a recitation of facts than anything. Posey's birth mother had updated the family medical history: Posey's maternal grandfather had diabetes. Her paternal grandmother had had breast cancer. Posey's birth mother's name was Clarice. She had brown eyes and brown hair. Her father's name was Paul. He had brown eyes and black hair. They'd been in college (English for her, art history for him) when she got pregnant. Clarice had not seen Paul since they graduated. She had felt compelled to write after eighteen years because the baby she'd given away was now the same age she was when she'd had her. She hoped that "the baby," as she called Posey, was happy and healthy.

And that was it.

"Nothing about wanting to meet me?" Posey said quietly.

Max squeezed her hand. "No, honey. Which is not to say that she might not want to meet you now, if you reached out."

"So all of a sudden, you want to meet her?" Stacia asked, her voice tight.

Posey swallowed. What she wanted was a stiff drink. And Liam, maybe. Liam definitely. "I don't know, Mom."

"Well, I hate to be the one to point it out, honey," Stacia said, "but she could've had any arrangement she wanted, and she chose a closed adoption. For whatever reason, she thought that was best."

"I know." Posey sat there for another minute. "I'm gonna go, okay?"

Her parents followed her to the door. "Are you going to apologize to Gretchen?" Stacia asked, her way of regaining the moral high ground.

"Not really high on my list of things to do," Posey said tightly, and with that, she walked out to her truck, her steps shortened by her dress. The new sandals were already giving her a blister.

At home, she changed into shorts and a sweatshirt and poured herself a glass of wine. A healthy glass, one guaranteed to induce a buzz. She sat on the back steps, rubbing her dog's head as he licked her ankle.

The sky was that sweetly painful shade of between, not quite dark, not quite light, the blue aching and melancholy. The birds quieted, a bat wheeled out from the belfry, and from the swamp, the frogs sang their nighttime song.

What a sucky birthday. Well, it hadn't all been bad. A niece was on the way, and that was…that was unabashedly wonderful. She fished her phone out of her pocket and texted Henry and Jon, apologizing for the drama and telling them she wanted more info on her soon-to-be niece and would stop by tomorrow.

But still. As the sky darkened, it seemed that melancholy wouldn't be put off. The Meadows would be ripped down. Gretchen was furious, her mother was furious and somewhere out there was her birth mother, who, one would assume, loved to read. Her birth father, who liked art and old things. They had dark hair and dark eyes, as did she.

Posey knew she was lucky. She had a brother and a brother-in-law and would soon have little Betty to spoil. She had Brianna as a surrogate sister, and she had parents who would lie down in front of a bus for her. She'd had everything she needed. She even had Liam, sort of.

But even so, even if she might never admit it out loud, it was hard not to feel a little lonely, picturing two dark-eyed people in their fifties who never wanted to meet her.

When the church bell rang, she just about leaped out of her skin, bolting off the back step, spilling her wine. Shilo jumped up, barking and running in a circle before dashing under the lilacs, and Posey stared up at the belfry. Her bell swung back and forth, right on time, and the deep iron tone rang out loud and strong into the night, reverberating in Posey's stomach, filling the air. Nine cavernous, unspeakably beautiful clangs marking the hour, the sound so rich and profound that it felt like it might lift her right off her feet.

As the last note finally faded from the night, Posey raced inside, charged up the stairs, out onto the catwalk and up the skinny stairs to the belfry.

There was a note secured with duct tape, right on the lip of the bell.

Happy Birthday.

It wasn't signed.

It didn't need to be.

CHAPTER TWENTY-SIX

"Bad choice," Mac muttered into his coffee cup the next morning. Posey had just broken the news about The Meadows, and the mood was glum.

"Right?" Elise said, blinking back tears. "I totally thought we had that one in the bag."

"Well, at least Viv won't have to see it," Posey said. "The salvage can only start after her death. It's in her will."

"She's lucky, then," Mac added. "We're the ones who're gonna have to drive past and see that poor place ripped apart. It's not right."

Quite possibly the longest speech Posey had ever heard from him. "I'm sorry, guys," she said.

"Seriously? It's not your fault, Posey," Elise said staunchly. "You were great, visiting that old grouch all the time. She totally led you on, making you think we had a chance. She took advantage of you, Posey."

"Well. She doesn't get a lot of company."

"No. Elise is right," Mac said, his voice hot. "You went above and beyond the call. And Elise—you were…" He seemed to lose steam as he looked directly at her. "You were…very…um…good." His cheeks flushed. "Back to work," he mumbled and headed for the back room, the flow of words clearly more than he could handle.

Elise sighed. "I wish I didn't like him so much," she whispered.

"I'm sorry," Posey said. Elise looked so miserable. "Maybe you should look around a little. Maybe for someone your own age."

"Whatevs," Elise mumbled.

The rest of the day was quiet. Somewhere during the night, Posey had decided to just let the issue of the letter rest. No point in dwelling on it—her biological parents were out there, always had been, and she was here, and she was fine. Her birth mother had put her up for adoption, and Posey was grateful. It would've been nice if Clarice—the word felt strange just to think—if Clarice had wanted to send her a letter, give some indication that she had some feelings for the baby she gave up? Sure. But she didn't, so that was that.

Posey paid bills, answered emails, worked up a bid for a house in Durham. They sold a grand total of two items—an old fire department light and a carved wooden pedestal. Since it was so quiet, she sent Elise and Mac home, watching with a pang as Elise stared after Mac's broad back. One of these days, the girl would give up and move on.

But speaking of relationships, it was Wednesday—Liam night. And at the thought of seeing him (possibly seeing him naked, which was always quite the thrill), and thanking him for fixing the bell, Posey's heart rose considerably. Maybe she'd even cook. Yes. She could do it. That class hadn't been for nothing, after all. She closed up shop and headed to the market for the ingredients for spaghetti Bolognese, needing to call Jon only twice with questions. Once home, she put on *Hot August Night*, muting the music only to hear the bell chime six times—the greatest sound ever, in her opinion. It rang at six in the morning, nine, noon, six in the evening and nine. She could hear it from Irreplaceable, even. Hopefully, no one would complain, though how someone could object to that sound was a mystery.

She showered, squished down her cowlick and opened her closet. She only owned two dresses—the sheath and the itchy one. Well. Shorts, then. But a girly shirt, a yellow tank top with a little stripe of satin at the edge. Bought in the juniors department, but hey. She looked kind of cute. Definitely female. Maybe she'd get her ears pierced, even.

Since they'd hooked up, Liam had called her every Wednesday afternoon to ask if she was free that night. Gretchen had warned her not to be too available, but Posey didn't really go for that kind of game playing (and what did Gretchen know about relationships?). It seemed dumb to pretend she was unavailable if she was dying to see him.

But Liam hadn't called today.

Maybe, she rationalized, he didn't need to, because this was their thing, their routine, and he was as comfortable with it as she was. She chopped an onion and added it to the frying pan with the garlic. It was starting to smell really good in here. Shilo whined, so she tossed him a little ball of ground beef. Poured herself a little wine. Checked her hair. Squished down the cowlick again, which only seemed to give it new life. Replayed "Kentucky Woman" and danced around with Shilo. Sautéed the beef. Added it to the sauce. Looked at the clock.

Quarter to seven.

Every time she heard a car on her street, her heart wobbled. Crikey, she had it bad. And maybe…it seemed, anyway…that Liam had it bad, too. While their sex life was undeniably fun, and smiling during kissing was becoming a habit, Liam also had a way of looking at her once in a while, or touching her lips, and his gaze would lose that laughing light, and he'd look…in love.

Those other Wednesdays, he'd been here by now. Which meant nothing.

No need to obsess—going slow was the way to go. That was what blew it with Dante. Not that Dante was nearly in the same class as Liam, of course. Dante was all surface charm. Liam…he had substance. He'd come from a ragtag upbringing by some not-very-nice people, yet managed to build a successful business. He'd been a devoted husband. He certainly was a loving (if neurotic) father. He'd come from nothing and made something of himself.

He'd become the man she'd imagined he could be all those years ago.

When the phone rang, shocking her out of her dopey-with-love reverie, she dropped the spatula, spattering sauce on her shirt. Dang it! But hello, here he was, and just the sight of his name on her caller ID made her heart actually flutter.

"Hello, God's Gift." She grinned.

"Hey, Cordelia. Any chance you can meet me at Rosebud's tonight?"

She looked around her kitchen—the first meal she'd prepared in, oh, a decade, unless you counted scrambled eggs. "Actually, I made dinner. Want to come here?" He didn't answer. "Spaghetti Bolognese. Smells wicked good."

"Uh…Rosebud's would be better. If you don't mind."

She hesitated. Not really what she had in mind for tonight, but… "Okay. Give me a half an hour?"

"Sure."

"See you then."

But he'd already hung up.

Posey stood there a minute, looking at the phone. A trickle of dread threaded through the earlier glow. But no, that was silly. Nothing to worry about. He wanted to eat at Rosebud's, what was the harm in that? And it was public, too—he'd kissed her in public over in Kittery, and now he wanted to be seen with her right here in town. It wasn't bad…it was the opposite. A very positive sign.

No reason to worry at all.

THERE WAS NO GETTING around it. This was going to suck.

Granted, Liam had once been master of the art of breaking up. No, that wasn't exactly true. He'd been master of the art of dumping someone. It hadn't been as classy as breaking up. Nope, back in the day, he'd been an idiot who'd slept with a lot of girls, and when someone else caught his attention or when a girl got too clingy or demanding or predictable, he'd say something brutally casual—*Yeah, about that… it was fun while it lasted.* The cruel pause. *Was there something else you wanted?* And then, because he'd been such a prick, he'd give that sleepy grin that made women of all ages blush, pinch her chin and wink at her from time to time, ensuring that she'd stay half in love with him—you know, just in case the urge struck. Why some brother or father hadn't beaten him to a pulp was a mystery, because if someone treated Nicole like that, he'd go after the guy with a car battery and a healthy set of jumper cables.

Until Emma, he'd never been in love. He'd been a player. A dick, in other words. And he was about to be a dick again. He'd chosen Rosebud's because he was a coward. There it was in a nutshell. Seeing Cordelia in public was very different from seeing her in her house, with that goofy dog and the battered-looking cats, the soft old couch where a person could really relax, the huge bed that seemed a place he'd like to stay for a week or so. He was fairly sure he couldn't go through with this if she cried, and he was also pretty sure she wouldn't make a scene in public. Booth in the corner, back near the pool table. Not real crowded on a Wednesday night. Private, yet public, and therefore safe.

Coward.

"Hey, biker boy!" There she was. "So, about the bell. You are a prince, Liam Murphy. I almost spit blood, I was so excited when I heard it! I can't believe you fixed it! I was sitting on my back steps, and when it went off, I jumped up, spilled my wine, broke the glass, and you should've seen Shilo, he was going crazy, running all around the yard, barking. It's amazing. Have you heard it ring? You probably did. It's the best sound in the world."

She seemed a little…sweaty. And tense. Trying a little too hard. She took a deep breath and slid across the table from him. "Thank you," she said more calmly. "It's the nicest present anyone's ever given me, Liam. Well, I take that back. My brother gave me a niece for my birthday. I just don't have her yet. But the bell is definitely second best. Really. It was…it was perfect."

The words were like a dull knife in his chest. "You're welcome," he said, looking into his Sam Adams.

"Hey, Posey! What can I get you?" Rose called over from the bar.

"Hi, Rose! Um…I'll have a glass of white zin, if you won't tell Henry."

"How is Henry?" The bartender grinned.

"Still gay."

"Sorry to hear it." Rose brought over a glass of pink wine. "Any food tonight, kids?"

"I'm all set," Liam said.

"Oh, um, me, too," Cordelia said, and he knew she knew what was coming, because when had Cordelia Osterhagen ever turned away food?

"Okay. Let me know if you need anything else," Rose said, gliding away.

So. Time to make the break. Liam took a sip of his beer. *Hey, it's run its course, don't you think? But it was fun while it lasted. Take care.* "How are things with you? Birth mother, all that stuff?" he asked, managing to glance up at her.

"You're breaking up with me, aren't you?" Her voice sounded oddly normal, and her hair was sticking up on the left. So ridiculously cute.

Get this over with, idiot. "Life's gotten a little more complicated recently," he said carefully. "I really can't be in a relationship right now."

She swallowed. Otherwise, she didn't move a muscle. "Is this about the Tates?"

"Yeah. Sort of. I need to focus on Nicole, and I…" He shook his head. He wasn't about to blame his daughter for this. "It's not really about Nicole, Cordelia. I can't… Look. You and I, we want different things. That's all."

"What…what different things do we want?"

He returned his eyes to his beer. Fascinating beer, Sam Adams. Nice color. Very…amber. "Listen, you're fun, and I like you, but I can tell you're getting…attached. I'm sure you want to settle down, have a couple kids, whatever, and that's great, but I'm not looking for that."

She was listening. She'd always been good at that. Liam forced himself to go on, his chest actually hurting. "This was supposed to be fun, and it has been, but…it's run its course."

Her eyes were huge, her mouth slightly open. Then she took a quick breath, pressed her lips together. Swallowed. Nodded. "Yeah, no. I understand." She took a sip of her wine. Her hands were shaking. She must've noticed that, too, because she folded them and put them in her lap.

If she'd thrown her wine in his face, that would be something he could react to. If she called him names, he could agree. Slapped him—hey, it wouldn't be the first time he'd been slapped.

"Liam," she whispered, "I don't need much." The words sliced into his gut like a razor. "I mean, I know you have to think about Nicole, and I wouldn't expect anything else. But I don't see why we have to...stop seeing each other. I can... I mean, what we have, it's...it's enough. We could just keep things the way they are, right?"

Liam looked at his beer, because it was too hard to look at her. "I'm sorry, Cordelia."

Because she deserved more, of course. She was the type who was meant to be married, to have a bunch of kids and animals, a big noisy family and a guy who loved her with all his heart. A guy she loved with all hers. And while she might be in the throes of a mighty crush on him—just as she'd been a long time ago—he didn't want to sit around and watch her learn, bit by bit, that he was no one from nowhere, and the only thing he had going for him was his daughter, and he had to protect that child, not just from the Tates, but from the Tanners of the world, from Nicole's own mistakes and the random accidents of life. He couldn't take his eye off the ball for even a minute.

"So that's it, then?" she whispered.

"I'm sorry if you thought something else," he said, trying to sound matter-of-fact.

"No, it's...it's okay." She sat for another minute. Her mouth quivered, and Liam hated himself more than he could ever remember. He looked down, not trusting himself to blow a perfectly effective break-up. In a few minutes, she'd be out of here, and he could go home and wash his hands and check on his kid and beat his head against the wall and do all those other fun things that made up his life these days.

"Do you remember that cat?" she asked suddenly.

He looked up. "What cat?"

"Joe. The little stray you fed back when you worked at Guten Tag."

He hadn't thought of that cat in years. But yeah, he remembered. "What about him?" he asked.

She looked at him steadily, her usually pixie-cute face solemn. "I always thought that said a lot about you," she said, her voice shaking a little. "That you took care of him. Fed him and tamed him until that lady adopted him."

And there it was, that completely baseless idea that he was somehow a hero. "He wasn't adopted, Cordelia," Liam said tonelessly. "He got hit by a car."

Her mouth opened. "But...you told me yourself. Some woman came around—"

"I lied. He got hit by a car, and I buried him near the Coast Guard station."

"He got hit?" There were tears in her eyes.

"Yeah."

"Why did you—"

"Hi, Liam, how are you?" Taylor "the Teeth" Bennington Linkletter swayed over to him and placed an oily kiss on his cheek.

"Hey, Taylor. You know Cordelia Osterhagen, right?"

"Mmm." She didn't even bother to glance at Cordelia. "So, want to come over to my table and meet some of my friends? We're having a girls' night out, and they're all wondering who this incredibly hot guy is." She dropped her voice to a 1-900 whisper. "They cannot believe I slept with you."

He looked at Cordelia. Maybe she needed one more nail in the coffin. "Yeah, sure, I'll say hi. We're done here, right, Posey?"

She flinched. "Yeah. Yup. See you around."

Liam put down a twenty and, without looking at Cordelia, went to the table of giggling, overper-fumed women, flirted briefly—no idea what the hell he said, but they ate it up—and, when Cordelia left, he counted to fifty-five then left the bevy of women and walked home, toward his daughter, toward fatherhood.

But the whole way, he thought about that dopey little cat, who didn't even have the sense to stay off the road. Taking care of that cat had been the highlight of his day back then, the idea that he could tame something that had never been shown much kindness. The first day Joe had taken food from him, it was like a small miracle. He remembered its rusty purr, the little bumps of its spine when he petted it, how quickly it fattened up on tuna fish and pork scraps. It was the closest thing to a pet he'd ever had. He'd wanted to take him home, but his uncle said no.

Then one day, when Liam was riding his battered motorcycle home, there was Joe, lying on the side of the road. He wasn't dead yet, but he was a mess, his back legs broken and bloodied, looking up at him with giant eyes and an expression of utter confusion. Didn't make a sound as Liam whipped off his T-shirt, wrapping the cat in it as gently as he could, then holding him against his stomach as he raced to the vet.

Joe died before he even got there.

Liam took him down to the marsh and buried him, still wrapped in his T-shirt, and damned if he didn't sit there and cry, harder than he had when his mother had died. He should've found a way to hide Joe in his uncle's garage, or made him a shelter or something, but no, he'd just let Joe stay in the alley, feeding him until that fucking car came by and hit him.

It was the look on the little cat's face that did it, as if shocked by the pain…but accepting it just the same. Like Joe knew cans of tuna behind the Dumpster were just too good to last. As if getting hit by a car, while horrible, was more the type of thing that happened to a stray cat who'd been alone most of his life.

It was the same way Cordelia looked tonight.

And even though breaking up with her was the right thing to do—he'd save her a lot of misery, and the Tates might get off his back, and he could focus on keeping Nic on the straight and narrow—even so, it felt like the best part of himself had died back there in that bar.

CHAPTER TWENTY-SEVEN

"He called me Posey."

"Well, that is your name, right? I mean, I haven't been calling you the wrong name your whole life, have I?" Kate asked, shifting in her La-Z-Boy. "God, these hemorrhoids are killing me."

"Sorry to hear it. Officially, my name's Cordelia."

"Right, right. I always forget that."

They were sitting in Kate's living room, Sunday night—five days and four nights after The Dumping. Posey had barely left the house since, but Kate had come over this afternoon and put her gym-teacher muscles to use, practically carrying her to the car. Back to Kate's house, where crappy wine and excellent ice cream were administered. Posey took a bite of Ben & Jerry's Super Fudge Chunk ice cream, then offered some to her dog, who licked the spoon agreeably.

"How much longer should I give you on the pity party?" Kate asked. "Not that I'm not enjoying myself, mind you."

"I don't know. A year? A decade?" Shilo sighed and put his head on her lap. The dog had been a trouper these past few days...the cats, not so much.

Someday, these feelings of rejection (there was no other word for it)...they'd be gone. This phase, this...ache would slowly lift off her heart. It was just that lying in bed this morning at 2:47, surely the loneliest moment God ever invented, she couldn't help the tears that leaked out of her eyes and slid into her ears. Shilo had taken it upon himself to lick them, so at least she had that.

Back in high school, she'd loved Liam from afar, and he broke her heart. First love, young love, crush—it was called crush for a reason, wasn't it, because it certainly had crushed her—whatever name you gave it, it had *hurt*.

But this time, she'd loved him up close. This time, she'd seen what could have been, had felt in little flashes and small moments what it was like to be loved by Liam Murphy. Just a little bit, and even the loss of that possibility, those sweetly tender, unguarded moments, hurt so much that it was stunning. And at 2:47 a.m., with a 140-pound dog and thirty-seven pounds of cat wedged against her, tears slipping out of her eyes, she cursed herself for not believing what Liam had told her from the start.

So she'd been dumped. Liam Murphy had dumped her, as he'd dumped so many women and girls over the years. And he'd called her Posey. Back in high school, it seemed that calling her Cordelia was a way to mock her...sort of like *you can call yourself whatever you want, but you still have that bulky, endless name.* But then...recently...the way he said her name, like it was so special and lovely, and Cordelia sounded less like the poor naive slob killed by her sisters in *King Lear* and much more like a Victoria's Secret model, inspiring slathering lust in every male within a thousand-mile radius.

"Don't you think so?" Posey asked, taking another bite of Super Fudge Chunk. "Didn't it sound like foreplay when he said it?"

"No more wine for you," Kate said. "And look. You can always adopt. Look at James and me and how happy we are. The foot rubs that kid gives? Amazing. James! Give Posey a foot rub!"

"No thanks, James," Posey called, turning her head. Ew. That ice cream–wine combo might not have been the best idea after all. "About James, Kate... Maybe a little less mother-boy time, don't you think?"

Posey offered another spoonful of ice cream to her dog. One lick of the giant tongue, and the ice cream was gone.

"Oh, save it. I already know. Signed him up for some mentoring thing. Big Brothers or the Boys and Girls Club or whatever. Guess who he got?"

"Whom? Whom did he get, Teacher. Please."

"I teach gym. We're not famous for grammar." Kate drained her wine. "He got that guy. Used to play for the Red Sox. You know the one."

"No, Kate, I don't know."

"The cute one with the sloping forehead. Looks like a hot Neanderthal? Matt Damon?"

"Do you mean Johnny Damon?"

"I don't know. Hockey's my sport. Anyway, James has a role model with a penis. I hope everyone's happy now." She shifted again. "I happen to think James is the best person on the face of the earth. I might be doing a great job."

Posey softened. "You are, Kate. He is. He's great."

Kate smiled. "Okay, let's talk this thing to death and then bury it. Liam the Sex God dumped you. You didn't see it coming, should have, are now miserable. What's next?"

"I have no idea. Back to the grind, I guess."

For the past couple of days, Posey had been living the cliché of pathetic female, and it was getting old. She'd skipped work—first time ever. Screened phone calls. Didn't turn on the computer and futz around on Facebook. She had, however, ordered three hundred and eleven dollars' worth of skin care from the Home Shopping Network.

But life was waiting. Her dad had called, wondering how she was doing. No word from her mother, though Max had made sure to say "your mother and I miss you" and all that. But seeing them was just too tiring to think about right now. The whole birth-mother thing… Nothing had really changed, except that her parents had kept a secret from her, and she knew slightly more than she once did about her biological mother and father. Still, it gave a throb every now and then, now that she had names and a few slivers of information. But it would fade. As for Gretchen's issues with Dante…who really cared? Posey had had enough of her cousin. The boys were getting ready for little Betty, and she didn't want to be Debbie Downer in light of all their happiness.

So she'd been cleaning, which was rather uncharacteristic. Not that the church was a sty or anything, but it was cluttered with stuff she thought she might want someday—a gilt Victorian mirror, a bank of post-office boxes, the statue of the elephant. She moved what she could onto the truck, called Mac for help—at least he would never ask her about her love life—and brought some stuff to Irreplaceable. The rest—the angel with the broken arms, the shabby little lead-paned window, the sundial with no dial—she took to the dump, and even though it was hard, she left it there.

Not everything was worth holding on to.

"Posey, the right guy will come along," Kate said with uncharacteristic gentleness. "Now, do you want James to give us pedicures? James! Come here, hon!"

The boy appeared in the doorway. "Mom, no. No pedicures. I'm establishing boundaries." He smiled at Posey. "Hi, Pose."

"Hi, James," she said. "You're a good kid."

"So I hear. I was eavesdropping."

"An underrated life skill."

"Tell Brianna I said hi," he said.

"Will do."

Eventually, Kate pointed out that the Bruins game started in twenty minutes and called Henry to fetch his sister. A few minutes later, he pulled up in his immaculate Volvo and honked the horn. "Thanks for the sympathy," Posey said, hugging her friend.

"You're welcome. Buck up, okay?"

"Does the dog have to get in, too?" Henry asked as she and Shilo went out to the car.

"Yes. Any other questions?"

"I guess not," Henry said, wincing as Shilo squeezed in the backseat, leaving a trail of drool on the headrest.

Posey closed her eyes. Kate was right—enough was enough.

"Heard you broke up with what's his name," Henry said, pulling away from the curb.

Posey opened one eye and looked at him. "Yeah."

"Sorry."

"Thanks."

"I heard about the other stuff, too. The birth-mother stuff."

This warranted the opening of both eyes. "Did you?"

Henry nodded, his perfect features as hard to read as ever. "How are you handling all that?"

"Did Jon tell you to talk to me, Henry?"

He cracked a small smile. "Actually, no. Look, I know you two are close, and that's great. But I'm your big brother. You can, um…well, whatever little sisters are supposed to do. Talk to me or whatever." He pulled into her driveway, turned off the engine and looked at her. "I just… I don't know, Posey. I don't know what I have to offer, aside from a free knee replacement." He cleared his throat and reset the odometer. "But you know…you're my sister. I love you. I'm proud of you. The guy who dumped you is an idiot, and you deserve better. If you need anything…you know." He glanced at her. "Okay?"

"Henry."

"What?"

"I love you, too."

"I know. Now shoo."

She kissed his cheek and went inside her strangely tidy house, made a sandwich and gave half to Shilo. Went upstairs to finish the model, which she'd brought home to paint. Played "Brother Love's Salvation Show" on her iPod over and over. When the bell went off at nine, she managed to ignore it pretty well.

"Boss! Hi! You look…great? Right? Good to have you back!" Elise gave her a peachy-scented hug, and when she pulled back, her eyes were teary. "Sorry," she whispered, fumbling for a tissue. "I thought he was, like, super nice."

"Thanks, hon," Posey said, touched at her reaction.

Elise blew her nose. "So I took your advice. Registered on Match.com last night." At that moment, Mac opened the front door. "'Morning, Mac!" Elise sang, not looking at him. Her voice wobbled.

Mac nodded and headed for the back room. Elise looked down.

Posey's heart twisted. What would it be like, to fall in love with someone who was pathologically shy? Who could barely look at you, let alone speak to you?

"Mac, stop," Posey said.

He obeyed, turning to see what she wanted.

The phone rang. "Irreplaceable Artifacts, good morning!" Elise chirruped into the receiver. Posey took the phone from her and hung it up.

She looked at them, her faithful employees. Her friends. "Mac. Elise likes you. She has for the past two years. Have you somehow missed this?"

Mac's cheeks flamed. "I…noticed."

"So?" Posey demanded. "Do you like her? She's beautiful, she's cheerful, she's got a huge heart. Any interest?"

Elise's mouth was hanging open, her eyes wide. For once, she didn't say a word.

"She's pretty young," Mac said, his voice barely a whisper.

"Right. How old are you, Elise? Twenty-eight?"

Elise nodded.

"And you're forty-two, Mac?"

He nodded.

"Elise, you like older men, I'm guessing?"

"Well," she whispered, blushing furiously, "I totally like this one."

"Would you like to go out with a younger woman, Mac? A beautiful, sweet younger woman who's been crazy about you since the first week she started here?"

His eyes went from Posey to Elise, then back again. "Um…okay."

"Seriously?" Elise breathed. "Oh, my gosh! Right? That's great! How about tonight?"

Mac swallowed audibly. "Sure," he said. He looked back at Posey. "Can I get to work now?"

"Yes. Please do," she said, smiling. Mac's blush extended all the way up to his bald head. He looked at Elise—it took some effort, but he did it—and said, very quietly, "See you later, then," and fled.

Posey held up a finger to Elise and trotted back to the shop. Mac was leaning against the wall, his shirt blotchy with sweat. "You okay?"

He nodded.

"You really want to go out with her?"

Another nod.

"Are you having a heart attack?"

He cut her a glance. "I think so."

Posey grinned. "I think it's love," she said, and Mac shook his head, but a little smile crossed his face. Assured that he wasn't about to drop dead, Posey went back to the counter.

"You're totally the best boss, like…ever?" Elise said, throwing her arms around Posey. "I thought I was gonna have to come in here naked and handcuff him to me!"

"Now, see, that would've worked, too," Posey said, smiling. "Now, go easy on him. Be gentle. He needs time."

"Time. Roger that." Elise beamed, and Posey's heart lifted at her friend's happiness.

"Okay, I have to run out to the candy factory and talk to the owner about what he wants to keep. And then I have an errand. I probably won't be back today." With that, she chose two aging wicker chairs whose cushions didn't smell too moldy and hefted them in the back of her truck, whistled for Shilo and went off.

WHEN VIVIAN ANSWERED her door a few hours later, her wrinkled old mouth fell open. "Posey! What are you doing here?"

"Hi to you, too," Posey answered, shifting the box in her hands.

"But…but I thought you…" Viv closed her mouth. "I thought our business had concluded," she said, enunciating carefully.

"Well, we're still friends, right?" Posey asked. "And it's Monday. Our day for lunch?"

Vivian blinked. "Aren't you angry that I went with Down East?"

Posey hesitated. "Well, not angry. Disappointed. But it's your property, as you said. Can I come in? This is heavy. It's a present, by the way."

Viv held the door wider, and Posey came in, the familiar musty smell of lavender and old lady greeting her. She put the box on the table, and, knowing Viv's old hands weren't strong enough, took out the gift.

Vivian stared at it for a long minute. Then her faded blue eyes filled with tears. "Posey…"

It was the model, of course. The Meadows in miniature and Posey's best effort to date. She'd even found an elm tree to put in the side yard.

Vivian bent down to look more closely. "This was my bedroom when I was a girl," she said softly. "I used to look out this window first thing every morning. There was the noisiest family of wrens in that tree." The old lady's mouth quivered, and she straightened abruptly. "Do you think the Vultures might… save it?"

Posey looked at Vivian, once a great beauty, once somewhat feared and revered in this town, once a beloved wife. A woman who'd never had a child and whose few relatives visited her only to ensure they were kept in the will, who would rip apart what was most precious to her. "They might, Viv," she lied. "They just might."

Vivian looked at the model again. "They won't," she said. "But they're family, and you forgive them, even if they are the human equivalent of hyenas. Because that's what you do, Posey. Forgive."

"I guess so."

"Well, I know so. And I'm older and far wiser than you." Her voice was sharp and familiar once more. "Thank you for this. It's quite accurate."

"Would you like to go out for lunch?" Posey asked.

Vivian looked at her, her eyes returning to the present. "Is that what you're wearing?"

"Yup. Care to be seen with me in public?"

Vivian's lips twitched. "I suppose. Where are we going?"

Posey smiled. "I thought we'd have a picnic."

DRIVING HOME that night, Posey found she was whistling. When Vivian had seen the model, that had been pretty great. But when she'd seen The Meadows…well. That had been even better.

Both of them had a good cry, sitting in the wicker chairs Posey'd brought, breathing in the scent of the peonies and lilacs. It had been wonderful hearing Vivian's stories about parties and games of hide-and-seek, snowstorms and holidays, the maid who'd fallen for the cook, how Vivian's husband had proposed under the chestnut tree.

"I'm glad you brought me, Posey," Vivian had said as they trundled slowly down the long drive of The Meadows. Her voice softened, and she swallowed. "But I don't want to come back again, dear."

"Me, neither," Posey said, taking her hand. "This was goodbye for us both." Vivian squeezed her hand, and if both women were teary-eyed, they pretended otherwise and chatted about the weather for the rest of the drive.

"See you next week," Posey said as Vivian unlocked her door.

"Try to dress like a woman," Viv said, and with that, she went inside, leaving Posey laughing in the hallway.

But it was hard to keep thoughts of Liam from seeping in. The way his hands felt on her skin. His low, smooth voice, the way her name rolled in his mouth like he was tasting it. The way he kissed her, as if she was the first woman he'd ever kissed, that slow appreciation, building into something deeper and more intense—

"Okay! Shilo! What do we want for dinner?" Maybe she'd pop a Stouffer's French bread pizza in the oven, since her deal with Jon didn't start till after she'd chaperoned the prom. Great. Another thing to look forward to.

As she pulled into her driveway, she saw Gretchen sitting on the back steps, long legs crossed, a good three-quarters of her breasts heaping out of her neckline as if for inspection. Shilo galloped over, and before Gretchen could move out of the way, gave her a slobbery kiss.

"Ew! Disgusting!" Gretchen said, scrambling up.

"Well, you're just sitting there like a big piece of raw meat," Posey said. "So. Here to set fire to my house, Gret? Since you like ruining things and all?"

Gretchen gave her a contemptuous look. "Dante and I are back together," she said.

"Oh, let me break out the champagne, by all means."

"Well, I thought you should know," Gretchen sniffed. "Since it affects you."

"No, it doesn't, Gretchen. Dante and I had a two-second fling. In hindsight, I think he's a superficial, shallow ass. Which makes him perfect for you, by the way."

Gretchen crossed her arms, which made her boobage surge even more.

"Could you cover those up?" Posey couldn't help asking. "They scare me." Her stomach growled, so she walked past her cousin and went inside. Alas, Gretchen followed.

"Look. I'm sorry I ruined your precious little birthday dinner, okay? It was…bad timing. But you know what?" Her voice took on that familiar edge—the one she only used with Posey. "I couldn't take it anymore. There you are, always having everything. Your parents fawning all over you, your brother telling you you're going to be an aunt, and the godmother, too, of course, God forbid anyone else gets any recognition in this family."

"Oh, please. You're the prodigy, the television star, the Barefoot Fraulein, remember?" Posey yanked open the freezer, tore open a box and shoved the pizza in the oven.

"You need to turn it on first," Gretchen said, condescension dripping.

"Thanks for the tip. It's so great having a professional chef around."

"Fine. I won't say another word. Cook away."

Posey slapped on the oven. "As for poor, ignored Gretchen, give me a break. Look around my parents' house. There are more pictures of you than me. It's not my fault you threw your career in the toilet, Gret."

Suddenly Gretchen's eyes flooded with tears. "That's not what I'm talking about, Posey," she said. "You don't know what it's like to be an only child. Or an orphan. All our lives, my parents compared us, right? I know that! I know I was the golden girl, and you were the ugly duckling."

"Wow. We're really bonding now."

Gretchen wiped her eyes. "No, Posey. I'm serious. No one ever expected anything from you."

"Can you please leave?"

Gretchen waved her hand dismissively. "I didn't mean it like that. But Posey, come on. You…you could flush a toilet and your parents would be on the phone, telling everyone how wonderful you were. Whatever you did, no matter what it was, they acted like you'd just walked on the moon. What do you think my parents would've said if I told them I wanted to be a junkyard owner?"

"It's *not* a junkyard."

"Whatever. What if I wanted to be a doctor or a pilot or a park ranger! I *had* to be a chef, Posey. My parents owned a restaurant, and I was going to follow in those footsteps. They drilled that into my head from birth on. A German chef, no matter the fact that I love Italian food. Or French. Or Thai!" She flopped into a chair.

"Still not feeling sorry for you, Gret. Your parents loved you, and come on. They died when you were seventeen. You could've become a mortician and they wouldn't have known."

"The thing is, Posey, I had a role in the family. You and Henry…you could be whatever you wanted. The truth is, I've been jealous of you my whole life. You had freedom, you have a brother and you've always known exactly who you are."

Posey's head jerked back in surprise, but Gretchen kept talking.

"Me…I've been programmed since birth to be the Barefoot Fraulein, and that all came down in flames." Gretchen's face scrunched. "And your parents didn't die! I don't have anyone."

"My parents love you like a daughter, Gretchen."

Gretchen snorted. "No, they don't, Posey. You're their little girl. I'm just the niece."

"Are you serious? They're so proud of you."

Gretchen wiped her eyes and gave Posey a pitying look. "Right. Only because they have no idea what's happened to me. I have a gambling problem. My career's dead, no network would touch me with a ten-foot pole, Guten Tag is the best I can do. My parents would be so ashamed." She began sobbing in earnest, covering her hands with her face.

"Oh, Gret." Posey went over and, after only a nanosecond of hesitation, hugged her. "I don't think they'd be ashamed, not at all. You made some mistakes, that's all."

"I had to live with my *cousin*," Gretchen continued, and Posey rolled her eyes and released her.

"I didn't realize I was quite so repulsive, Gret," she said. "So sorry you had to suffer."

Gretchen sighed and wiped her eyes with her fingers. Then she opened the fridge—ever entitled—and took out a bottle of wine and poured herself a glass. "Want one?" she asked.

"Sure," Posey answered, sitting at the table. Shilo flopped at her feet with a groan and offered his belly, which she rubbed with her foot.

"So, here's the thing," Gretchen said quietly, handing Posey a glass of wine. "When I finally found something that was good and exciting and fresh… I mean, I can't tell you how it felt, the first time Dante kissed me, Posey. Like the whole world was new. You have no idea."

"Oh, I do." At Gretchen's dark look, she added, "Not with Dante, though. I never— We never had a real connection."

"When I found out you were with him first, Posey, I just…lost it. I just felt like… I don't know. The runner-up. Again." She paused. "I'm sorry I outed you to Max and Stacia."

"On my birthday," Posey added.

Gret sighed. "Yeah. Bad timing." She took another sip of wine. "It's just been hard," Gretchen whispered, tears falling once more. "My life came crashing down around me, and coming back here, seeing you so…adored, your parents, the boys, that chubby kid—"

"Brianna."

"Whatever. You're lucky, Posey. You love your job, everyone likes you, and you have that god in your bed at night." She blew her nose.

"Actually, we broke up," Posey said.

Gretchen's face brightened. "Really?"

"Don't look happy, you pain in the ass."

Gret grimaced. "Sorry. I am, Posey. He seemed like he really liked you."

"Well, not enough, I guess."

Gretchen's perfect nose wrinkled. "Your supper's burning," she said.

Sure enough, smoke was coming out of the oven. "Crap," Posey muttered, looking in. Dang, she'd forgotten to take off the plastic wrap.

Gretchen grinned. "You said you didn't want help," she said. "Don't worry. I'll whip something up."

A half-hour later, Posey was eating the best omelet of her life—herbs and some exotic cheese left over from Gret's month here—laughing as her cousin told a story of her own cooking disasters on the air. "No wonder that stupid show didn't get any ratings," Gretchen said thoughtfully. "I just don't think America really wants to know how to deep-fry pork rinds."

"More for us," Posey said. "Even if they do take ten years off your life per serving."

Gretchen smiled. Then she gave Posey a long look. "Think we can be friends? Even if you are a weird little junkyard dog who dresses like a man?"

Posey smiled. "You bet, Gret. Even if you are a pretentious diva obsessed with her own boobs."

They clinked glasses and sealed the deal.

CHAPTER TWENTY-EIGHT

"DAD? ARE YOU OKAY?"

Liam looked up from the strut he was installing. "Oh. Hi, Nicole."

His daughter didn't come down to the garage much...certainly not since the cold war that began when he grounded her. The past two weeks had been filled with Nicole either ignoring him or whining that, seriously, he *had* to lift the ban on Facebook, texting, cell phone and friends, which only made him more and more tense.

His daughter gave him that baffled look she'd perfected around age twelve. "Dad, I've been standing here for, like, ten minutes." Her voice echoed off the walls of the garage.

"Sorry. What do you need?"

"I just thought we could hang out."

He looked down, not sure he wanted her to know how much he'd missed her. "That'd be great." Why the lessening of hostilities, he had no idea, but such was the way of the teenager. The knot that had been living in his gut lately loosened. "You hungry?"

"Not for any of that crap you have in the vending machine." She gave him a pitying look—*fathers, such idiots*—and took an apple out of her backpack, along with a thick red book and a notebook.

"Geometry?" he asked.

"Physics. It's easy, though."

"Because you're smart."

"Thanks, old man." She smiled—Emma's smile—and it caught him in the heart. When Nicole had her first fever at four months old, she would only sleep if he rocked her, and even so, only in fifteen-minute installments. On the third day, Emma had come in from school, seen them both dozing in the rocking chair and said, "That baby is holding you hostage."

Hadn't stopped since.

Liam had received the letter from the Tates' lawyer this week, gone to Allan Linkletter, who assured him that the odds of him losing full-time custody of his child, who was almost old enough to be emancipated in the eyes of the law, were very small.

They just weren't small enough. The Tates had a lot of influence in the old-boy world around here. Liam could afford a good lawyer, that wasn't an issue, but what if the judge was an old crony of George's? What if Liam had slept with the judge's daughter in high school?

Just last night, Liam had bolted awake from a recurring dream...Nicole calling him from far, far away, asking if he'd come get her. In the dream, he'd jumped on the Triumph and headed toward her, only to realize he didn't know where she was. Then the dream changed, and it was Cordelia he was supposed to pick up. But she'd been waiting a long, long time, and by the time he got there, she didn't remember who he was.

It felt like he hadn't smiled in a lifetime. The slow evaporation of his wife's love, the wasting sickness and endless, bleak months that followed, Nicole's grief, then the accident and all its consequences...and now this. Now his damn in-laws and all their drama.

That little window with Cordelia seemed impossibly bright. The idea that a couple of weeks ago, he'd had someone to kiss, someone who made him laugh, someone who fell asleep against him as they watched a movie on the couch...someone who had told him not to sell himself short...that seemed like it had happened to someone else.

Best not to think of it.

"You have a game tonight, right, Dad?" Nicole asked.

Ah, crap. "That's right." A game against Cordelia's team, no less. So much for not thinking about her.

"Can I come and watch?" Nicole asked.

"Sure."

"Daddy, you seem sad," Nic blurted, her own eyes filling.

"Oh, no, honey. I'm fine."

"Do you miss Mom?" Her voice sounded so small.

"You bet." He missed her, all right. He'd been missing her for a long, long time.

"Tell me something nice about her," Nicole said.

It was something he'd done the first year or so after Emma died. Every day, he'd tell Nicole a story about her mom. The sweet things, the funny things, the *normalcy* that, before marriage, Liam had only ever seen on TV—pancakes on the weekends, family movie night, dinner together, every day. No matter how mundane the story, Nicole loved hearing about her mom—the way Emma insisted that they all floss nightly. The hot-water bottle on which she'd drawn a smiley face. The way she'd leave notes under Nicole's pillow if she had to go away on business.

Then, when the story was over and Nicole was in bed, Liam would write that story in a notebook, his hand cramping, his head aching from the effort of keeping the letters where they should be. But when the day came for Nicole to leave home, he'd give her those notebooks, and she could take a piece of her mother with her, recorded in her dad's careful handwriting, like a shield against the world.

"Okay." He took a deep breath and told Nicole about seeing Emma for the first time. How the light shone on her hair, how her laugh floated across the courtyard. He couldn't take his eyes off her, that beautiful, perfect girl who seemed to glow from inside, and when she'd finally looked over at him, she smiled, and all the other sounds fell away.

Nicole's face was glowing when he finished. "That's so romantic, Daddy," she said softly.

Liam didn't answer. He'd described that meeting a hundred times, and while he'd told his daughter what he'd seen and heard, he never did tell her how it felt. Because when Emma Tate had met his eyes, it felt like every bad thing Liam had ever done—the fights and suspensions, the petty crimes that had landed him in juvie, the many girls he'd led on and slept with, the beers and the drag racing—all of that was about to be forgiven. That this perfect, radiant girl was some kind of angel about to change the soul of no one from nowhere, to see him as someone worthwhile, more than the hot guy with the bad rep, one small misstep away from being just like every other loser his family had ever produced.

But Emma didn't change him.

Nicole was the one who'd done that.

But still, that moment—that golden moment of seeing the girl who'd become his first love—it had been...amazing. A shimmering, perfect moment.

Another memory came to him—Cordelia's face as they sat on the blanket under the pines at the old estate. Her big, dark eyes had been soft...and trusting, too.

Nice job, idiot. She sure as hell won't ever look at you that way again.

"Dad?"

He cleared his throat. "Yes, babe?"

"You can say no, but...I just want an answer, okay?" Nicole squeezed her ring finger, her signature for nervousness. "The prom's this Saturday."

Ah. Hence the thaw.

"Dad, it's okay if you say no. I screwed up, I know it. And there'll be other proms. I just need to let Tanner know one way or the other."

No. Don't grow up. Stay with me. You're all I've got.

"I want you home by eleven," he said, his voice uneven. *If you're not home by eleven, I will call the police, the fire department, the National Guard and the SWAT team. I will find that boy, and if his hands are on you, I will rip off his head and drink his blood. I will bury his body where even the vultures won't find it, and I'll—*

"Oh, Dad," she breathed. "Really? I can go?"

"Yeah. Do your homework."

Liam turned back to the strut and tapped it gently into place. The lump in his throat didn't go away.

JUST BEFORE THE game on Tuesday, Posey girded her loins and went to her parents' house.

"Oh, it's you," her mother said by way of greeting. "I thought you forgot where we lived, it's been so long. Not a phone call, not a visit. I thought you were in the hospital. What's it been, a month?"

"It's been two weeks, Mom," Posey said with weary patience. "And I did call. Twice."

"Messages on that machine don't count."

Where was the more amenable parent? "Is Dad home?"

"He's at Guten Tag. Come in. Are you hungry? I just made bockwurst."

"Got any cake?"

Stacia narrowed her eyes. "Yes. Have you eaten supper?"

"Mmm-hmm."

"Liar."

Posey smiled, and her mother relented enough to step back from the door and let her in. Two minutes later, she was sitting at the kitchen table, eating apple kuchen.

"Gretchen and that horrible Italian man are back together," Stacia announced.

"I know."

"Well, I guess I'm the last to know everything." She sat heavily, the cutlery rattling as her bulk hit the chair. "So. How are you?"

"I'm okay, Mom."

"Still with that Liam?"

That Liam. Funny. "Nope, not anymore."

Stacia frowned. "Why?"

"Oh…he's got some issues to deal with. His daughter. Stuff like that."

"Well, he's an idiot if he doesn't want you."

Posey's eyebrows lifted. "I thought you wanted him for Gretchen."

"We did. I did. I don't know. I pictured you with…someone else."

"Who?" Posey asked.

Her mom sighed. "I don't know. Someone perfect. A prince, maybe. A prince who also cured cancer." She smiled reluctantly. "No one's ever good enough for your little girl. You'll see someday."

Motherhood seemed far, far away. But she could picture feeling that way toward Brianna. Yes. Brianna's future boyfriend would have to watch his back. Made her understand where Liam was coming from. But she wasn't here to talk—or think—about Liam. She said nothing else, knowing the best way to get her mother to talk was to wait her out.

The fridge cycled on with a wheeze. A catbird sang from the clothesline. And…bingo.

"Posey, listen," Stacia said, her pale eyes suddenly wet. "I—I have to tell you something. A couple of things, really." Her hands twisted together, and she gave her head a little shake. "We—your father and I—we had a daughter before you. When Henry was five. She came too early, and they couldn't save her. She only lasted an hour."

Stacia's face scrunched up, and without a thought, Posey got up and wrapped her arms around her mother's solid shoulders.

"I'm so sorry, Mom," she whispered, tears slipping out of her eyes. Even though Posey had known this fact her whole life, Stacia had never spoken of it. For a long moment, she just hugged her mom, breathing in the smell of baking and Suave shampoo. "I'm so, so sorry."

"We named her Marlene," Stacia said thickly.

"Beautiful."

Stacia nodded. "She was. She was beautiful, Posey. And I still think of her. Every day." She wiped her eyes and cleared her throat. "Sit back down, honey. I'm not done."

Posey obeyed.

Stacia looked at the table, her finger tracing the pattern in the painted enamel. "We adopted you two years later. And you were perfect and healthy and beautiful, too, but I was so afraid of losing you, too, in any way. I had nightmares about you drowning, or being kidnapped, or forgetting you on the ironing board."

"The ironing board?"

Stacia shrugged. She was quiet for a long moment. "With Henry," she said eventually, "it was different. Oh, I loved that little boy, but you know how he was. How he still is. Completely self-sufficient. Sometimes I used to think that if he fell out of a tree and cut his head, he'd just stitch himself back up and wouldn't even mention it to me."

"I know what you mean," Posey murmured.

"But with you, I was so scared. All the time. Maybe it got in the way of me being a good mother, I don't know."

"Oh, Mom. You're a good mother. A great mother."

Stacia blew her nose again. "Mostly, though," she continued, her voice rough, "I was afraid that your birth mother would show up one day and ask for you back. And she'd be so much more than I was… she'd be young and pretty and fun, and you'd want to be with her. And you'd leave me."

The words cut Posey's heart right in half. "Mom! I would never leave you! I love you. How could you think that?" She gripped her mom's hand. "Since it's true confessions time, I'll tell you one of mine."

"You broke Glubby's antler, didn't you?"

"Oh…um, yes. Sorry about that." Posey smiled, then grew serious. "No, what I wanted to say was that I always thought… I was always afraid that every time you looked at Gretchen, you wished she was yours."

Stacia jerked back. "Gretchen? I mean, I love her, she's my sister's child…"

"Well, it always seemed like she could do no wrong. The German chef, your twin sister's daughter. The way she calls you Mutti…constantly reminding me that I'm adopted. She's the real reason I hate to cook. Because I didn't want to be compared to her and come up short."

Stacia shook her head. "Oh, honey. It's just that sometimes you love a kid just because they need it. Not because they deserve it, not because you really like them…just because they need love. And that's Gretchen. The truth is, she drives me crazy half the time. Your father and I were so glad when she moved in with you, we got a little romantic on the couch."

Posey grimaced. "Feel free to keep that to yourself, Mom."

Stacia smiled, then grew serious. She squeezed Posey's hand, her grip almost painful. "I'm sorry I never told you about that letter," she whispered. "It was selfish of me, and that's not what a mother is supposed to be. If you want to find her, you go right ahead. I'll help you." She wiped her eyes and looked at Posey, her face blotchy. "Do you?"

Posey didn't answer right away. "Maybe. I'm not sure." She looked into her mother's face, that strong-boned, handsome face, and noted, maybe for the first time, the web of wrinkles under her mother's eyes, the heaviness of the skin. "And maybe she'd be great. But she'd never be you."

Stacia looked down at the table. Nodded. "There was something else in that letter, Posey," she whispered.

Her heart twisted. "What? Am I a twin or something?"

Stacia managed to smile. "No. Oh, honey, I wish I'd kept it in a safer place. I'm so sorry about that."

She sighed, then looked at Posey. "You don't know this, but your birth mother...she was the one who picked your name."

"What? What about Great-Aunt Cordelia?"

"Who's that?" Stacia frowned.

"Gretchen said we had an aunt..." Leave it Gretchen to tell her some idiotic story. "Never mind. My birth mother picked my name?"

Stacia nodded. "The social worker who handled the adoption told us that even though we didn't have to keep your name, the birth mother hoped we'd think about it." She stared at the table, lost in memories. "And we were so grateful to her for giving us her baby, that we did. We didn't really love it, to be honest. When Henry called you Posey, it just seemed to fit better, and I have to tell you, I was relieved. Cordelia. It's not even German."

"Was there something about my name in the letter?" Posey asked. A sudden weight pressed on her heart, as if she knew what was about to come.

Stacia took her hand. "She said her favorite play was *King Lear.* By William Shakespeare."

"I know," Posey said. "I read it in college."

"Well," Stacia said, her voice now a whisper. "She said she picked it because Cordelia's the daughter the king sends away."

Posey swallowed and pressed her lips together.

"But," Stacia said, her eyes filled with tears, "she's also the daughter he misses for the rest of his life."

Cordelia. Not a great-aunt who was blind in one eye. Not the naive girl murdered by her evil sisters. Cordelia, the precious, beloved daughter.

What a gift to have such a name.

"I'm so sorry I didn't tell you," Stacia said, her eyes streaming. "Please, honey. Please forgive me. I should've told you the other day. I should've told you when the letter came, and I didn't, and I'm so sorry. Please tell me you still love me."

Posey gave her head a little shake. How could Stacia have not told her this? How could... And yet, Stacia had fed her and bathed her and soothed her and read to her. She'd baked goodies every day; she had never missed a teacher conference or track meet. She'd walked her to school, driven to Boston to find clothes that fit, told her she was beautiful, smart, funny, gifted. She thought Posey was the best turnip that had ever been.

"Oh, Mom," Posey said, slipping out of her chair and kneeling next to her mother. She put her head in the soft, familiar lap, felt Stacia's hand on her hair. "Of course I love you. I loved you since before I could say your name. Nothing—and no one—could ever change that." She smiled and looked up into her mother's face. "Let's not even talk about those dumplings you make."

Cordelia. The best name ever.

The only time she'd ever loved her name before was when Liam said it. Now, though...now everything was quite different. Cordelia Wilhelmina Osterhagen. Sounded rather regal.

Stacia had stuffed her with some cold sausage and cheese, as well as a couple of boiled potatoes, but as Posey headed for the baseball field, she felt light. She may not have gotten The Meadows, she may never weigh more than a hundred and seven pounds or really need to wear a bra. Her house might in fact be past redemption, and her hair would never behave. She seemed incapable of attracting a man who saw her as a potential wife, and her truck's muffler needed fixing.

But her mother loved her. *Both* her mothers. And Max, and Henry, and Jon and Brianna and maybe even Gretchen and a whole host of other people.

She was blessed. It wasn't a word she thought often, but today, nothing else would do.

Cordelia. What a great name.

"Hey, guys," she said, as she got to the dugout.

"Hey, Posey," Bruce answered, stretching out his arms.

"Today's your day," Jerry said.

"Well, you're a minister, so you have to be optimistic," Posey said, punching him fondly on the shoulder.

"Get ready for some heat," the good reverend returned. "Lift thine eyes and watch as I smite mine enemies with my mighty curveball."

"You go, Rev," said Kate. She thumped Posey on the back, causing Posey to stagger forward. "You done sulking?" she asked in a lower voice.

"Yes," Posey answered.

Jon gave her a hug. "How are you, sweetheart?" he asked.

"Looking forward to my niece," she said.

"And the heartbreak?" His eyes were full of sympathy.

"I'm really okay," she answered firmly.

Stubby's Hardware began trickling into their dugout, and Posey felt Liam before she actually saw him. Her skin tingled, and heat rushed to her face. Yep. There he was, dark and beautiful, his face somber. He looked over at her, and their eyes locked, and even across the baseball diamond, she could feel that tug, that warm, almost uncomfortable pulling. Then he gave a nod and turned away. Kylie Duchamps, who had recently joined Stubby's team, stumbled (probably faked it, Posey thought), and sure enough, Liam reached out and grabbed her elbow. Kylie gave her patented hair toss and whinnied with laughter.

It was okay, Posey thought. That empty spot in her heart would fill in. She'd get over Liam Murphy. She would.

"Batter up!" the umpire called.

A typical game, a beautiful spring afternoon. Posey glanced at the stands—there were her parents, and Stacia gave her an almost shy wave, though it had been fifteen minutes since they parted. They sat with Shirley Schmottlach, who waved merrily (she often brought a flask of peppermint schnapps to these games), and Brianna and James, whose heads were almost touching as they looked at something on James's phone. Nicole Murphy was there as well, sitting next to Henry, who was reading, as usual.

"Hi, Posey!" the girl called. Nice, that Liam's daughter came to see her dad play. She seemed like such a good kid. Then again, with her parents, how could it be any different?

Posey waved to her cheering section. She didn't look at Liam. Not a lot, anyway. It was a little difficult to avoid, since she was the catcher. "Hey," he said as he came up to the plate in the top of the first.

"Hi, Liam." Her voice was pleasant. Hopefully, her face mask hid the blush that was burning its way up from her chest.

The first pitch came, Liam swung. Fly ball…Jon only had to open his glove to catch it. In the two games they'd played against Stubby's, Posey had yet to see Liam pop up—his batting average was even higher than Bruce Schmottlach's. But he was already trotting back to the dugout before Jon had even tossed the ball back to Jerry.

Liam lined out to first base out in the third inning, grounded out in the fifth, and popped out again in the eighth. First-pitch swings, all, and Posey knew it was his way of getting out of her vicinity as fast as possible.

Posey herself struck out in the second, the fifth and the seventh. Those batting lessons from Liam, while arousing, hadn't done squat. Still, each time she went down swinging.

"You'll get there, sweetheart," Max said, lowering his large video camera.

"Any decade now," Brianna called, getting a grin from James.

"Nice swing, Posey," Nicole added. Yep. Great kid.

"Thanks, guys!" she said. There weren't a lot of other parents here, that was for sure, and Posey grinned as she walked back to the dugout. Not many people with a .000 batting average had a fan club, but she did.

Still, her heart ached every time she caught a glimpse of Liam. She tried to ignore it.

By the bottom of the ninth inning, the score was 14-1, Stubby's. Liam was the only one on his team who hadn't scored. The reverend's curveball wasn't quite the mighty sword he'd envisioned, whereas José Rivera was pitching for Stubby's and looking about as good as Mariano, his famous third cousin.

Kate had belted a solo homer in the second, but that was Guten Tag's only run of the night. But José was tiring, and Jon had singled and Bruce walked. Two outs, and Posey was up.

As she walked to the batter's box, she saw Kylie packing up her gear. Indeed, most of Stubby's assumed the game was about to end, chattering and shuffling and checking their phones. Only Liam still sat on the bench, arms folded over his chest. He glanced at her, and the corner of his mouth pulled up just a little. Then his gaze dropped to the ground.

"Come on, Posey!" called Nicole.

"You can do it, sweetheart!" said her mother.

"Swing away, Merrill!" yelled Jon and Kate.

Posey settled into her stance. Bat up, knees bent, back foot planted, just as Liam had shown her, same as she'd been doing for the past four years. The handsome yet evil Derek Jeter had what—three thousand hits? More? Surely she could get just one. She took a practice swing, tapped her cleats, and got ready, staring at José, who gave her the full power of his third-cousin stare, then brought his glove up to his face. The wind-up. The pitch.

She swung, and something went wrong, because her arms reverberated and the bat was heavier than normal, there was a loud *thwack,* and a roar, and Stubby's entire team turned away from her.

To watch the ball fly over the outfield fence.

Her mouth hung open, the bat dangling from her buzzing hands.

"Posey, run!" Jon shouted as he came down the third-base line.

And so she did, trotting in a daze to first base…and then second, where Emily Rudeker slapped her butt, and then to third, and her team was cheering and jumping up and down as she came home.

A home run. Her first hit, ever, was a three-run homer.

She was slapped and pounded and generally roughed up as her teammates whooped and hollered. In the stands, her fan club, as well as Nicole, were on their feet, Stacia crying, Henry grinning and accepting high fives (not that he'd been actually watching, Posey guessed), her father jumping up and down, the camera still in his hand. She grinned up at them, realized she was laughing. Amid the cheers of her teammates, she walked—floated, really—back to the dugout and sat down, dazed and utterly thrilled.

"Well, well, well," Kate said, clobbering her on the back. "I expect to see that on *SportsCenter* tonight. That was one amazing hit, pal."

Looking across the diamond, she saw Liam. He hadn't changed position, but his eyes were on her, and there it was again, that locked-in feeling. Then he started clapping, quietly, and smiled. That was it, but warmth flooded Posey's chest as if he'd just presented her with a dozen red roses.

She tipped her baseball cap and smiled back.

The next batter grounded out, and the game was over, Stubby's 14, Guten Tag 4. Even so, the moral victory was clear, and Stubby's agreed to buy the first round.

When Posey had been congratulated yet again, when her parents had hugged her and Max had taken several dozen pictures, when most of the people had trickled off, Posey saw Liam and Nicole walking off the field, heading in the direction of their apartment.

"I'll see you guys at Rosebud's," she told her gang, then broke into a run and caught up with Liam.

"Hey, Posey, that was an amazing hit!" Nicole exclaimed, scooping her hair off her neck in a gesture Posey remembered Emma doing.

"Thanks, Nicole," Posey said. She glanced at Liam, whose eyes were on his daughter.

"Your dad said it was, like, your first hit ever," Nicole said.

"Sad but true. Hey, do you mind if I have a quick word with your father?"

"Sure! Dad, I'll catch you at home." She gave Posey a wave and walked away, all lithe grace and beauty.

Posey watched her go. Abruptly, her heart began slamming against her chest.

"That was a great hit," Liam said, his eyes glancing off her.

"Whatever," Posey blurted. Suddenly, looking at Liam was hard. A car passed, and down the street, a mother pushed a pink-clad baby in a stroller, a Golden Retriever walking like a guard at their side.

She took a shaky breath and looked into those green, clear eyes. "Okay, look. I understand you have a daughter, Liam, and she'll always come first, and it shouldn't be any other way." She bit her lip and shoved her hands in her pockets. "When you broke up with me, I said I didn't need much. But I do. I love you, Liam. I loved you when I was a kid, and I love you now."

"Posey—"

"No!" she blurted. "It's Cordelia. You always called me Cordelia."

"Okay. Cordelia, I just don't think—"

Posey's hands flew up to stop his words. "I'd wait as long as you needed, as long as Nicole needed. But I know you feel something for me, and I love you, and I've never felt this way about anyone, ever. I want to be with you. I want you to pick me. I know Emma will always be your first love, and that's fine. But don't just...don't just let me go."

He folded his arms across his chest and looked at the sidewalk. Posey swallowed. Her hands were shaking. "You won't be sorry, Liam. I'm worth it."

"I know that," he said in a harsh whisper. "I do. But I'm not...capable of... Damn it, I have no idea how to say this. But you have this version of me in your head...and it's just not true."

"Yes, it is!" He flinched at the force of her words. But once she'd said them, a feeling of calm settled around her. Her heart slowed, her hands stopped shaking, and she reached out and put her hand over his heart, feeling the steady thump. "Liam," she said softly, "I bet I know you better than anybody. And I love you. There's no one—no one—I'd rather be with."

He looked at the ground, and she knew it was over. "I'm sorry, Posey. I really am."

With that, he walked away, and Posey stood there until he turned the corner and disappeared.

CHAPTER TWENTY-NINE

"WELL, IT WAS THE whole do-or-die thing," Jonathan pronounced, taking up the blow-dryer. "You said it all, gave it your all, went all out. No regrets. Sounds like you were amazing. Hold still."

Oddly enough, Posey had been feeling...well, not horrible. It was hardest at night in the church with the animals doing their best to let her know she was loved, Shilo's cementlike head on her belly, the cats purring at her side. But she had tried. Said everything in her heart, and if it wasn't enough, then it just wasn't. She was lucky on every other front in her life, and this echo, this empty cavern in her heart...it would fill in. She knew that. She did.

Posey winced as Jon applied a medieval-tong type of instrument. "Is that burning smell anything I should be worried about?"

"You're fine. You'll be OMG cute, trust me. Henry, doesn't she look cute?" Henry grunted. "Betty's going to adore you, Posey," Jon continued. "Ten more days till we're fathers! Ten days, Henry!"

"Ten days!" Henry chorused back, finally looking up with a smile.

"He's in a good mood today. Some bozo with a table saw lost a thumb yesterday, and guess who reattached it? Happy times, right, darling?"

"So happy," Henry said. "You look pretty, sis. Jon will be the luckiest boy at the prom."

A knock came at the door. "Come in!" Jon shouted, then lowered his voice. "That's my other appointment. Um...it's Nicole Murphy. They couldn't fit her in at Curl Up and Dye, but luckily, she has the best home-ec teacher in the world. My curse. I do everything so well." He fingered a lock of her hair and hit it with some spray. "I hope you don't mind, Posey."

"No, no. Of course not." She looked up as Liam's daughter came into the kitchen. "Hey, Nicole!"

"Oh, hi, Posey! Are you Mr. White's date?"

"She's in love with me and begged me to take her," Jon said, pulling a face. "Very awkward, but what can I do? She's family."

"So, you're going with Tanner?" Posey asked.

The girl's face lit up. "Yeah. My dad finally relented."

She was so lovely, it was as if the room glowed. For a second, Posey felt such a wave of grief for Emma—who would never see this moment, who had been so good to Posey, who had died so horribly young—that tears came to her eyes. "You're even prettier than your mom," she said, her voice a little husky.

"Thanks, Posey." The girl's face softened.

"There we are, darling, you're done," Jon said, and Posey got out of the chair, the unfamiliar fumes of hair spray giving her a little rush.

"So, Nicole, how's Mister Jonathan doing your hair?" she asked.

"An upsweep?" Nicole said. Jon squinted at her, then nodded.

"Old-school Hollywood, none of this tangled-ponytail business, don't you think, precious?" Jon began brushing her hair, asking Nicole about her dress, the flowers Tanner would bring her. Henry poured Jon some sparkling water and handed it to him, then sat on the counter, watching the beautification.

"You seem good these days, big bro," Posey said.

"Can't wait to be a daddy," he said.

"Can't wait to be an aunt." She squeezed his arm, happy to see him exhibiting normal human emotions.

"Did you have fun at your prom, Posey?" Nicole asked.

Though the question was completely normal, Posey froze. "Oh...well. Sort of."

"She did not," Jonathan retorted. "Some horrible boy made fun of her, ruined the whole night. Her date dumped her, and she had to walk home in the rain. It was so *Carrie*. Minus the killings and fire and blood. But just as bad in its own way."

"Oh, my gosh!" Nicole exclaimed. "You poor thing!"

"It wasn't *that* bad," Posey said, her face burning.

"If you have any problem at all tonight, Nicole, my dear, you tell me, and I'll take care of it, okay?"

"You're so nice, Mr. White. I really appreciate you doing my hair."

"You're very welcome. Tilt, please."

Nicole tilted. "Why would a boy make fun of you? What a jerk! What did he say?"

The fact that Nicole's father was the subject of the conversation was making Posey's stomach knot. "Um...I don't really remember. You know. It was a long time ago. Kids. Teenagers. Whatever."

"He called her a bag of bones," Jon said. "So mean! You're petite, that's all, sweetheart. Nicole, wait till you see Posey's dress. So cute! I picked it out, of course."

"I can't wait," Nicole said, smiling sweetly.

"So, who was that jerk, anyway, Posey?" Jon asked. "Henry, you beat him up, right? Does he still live in town?"

Henry was looking steadily at Posey, and a horrid realization sliced through her. Henry *knew*. He'd memorized all the bones in the human body by the age of four. His IQ was 164, and he had a near-perfect memory. There was no way that he didn't realize that the jerk in question was the father of the girl sitting in his kitchen...and the guy Posey was in love with. He'd probably known all along.

"I don't remember," he said, putting his arm around her. "I'm pretty sure I didn't beat anyone up, though."

"Well, I would have," Jon muttered.

"Oh, man, look at the time," Posey said. "I better get going. Nicole, see you later. You already look gorgeous."

"I'll pick you up at seven," Jon said. "Bye! Nicole, dear, tilt your head the other way, now. Hold still, we're not done yet."

SHE WAS BEAUTIFUL. Liam's daughter was perfectly beautiful, and it was killing him.

"What do you think, Daddy?" She twirled around, her long blue dress swishing around her.

"You look twenty-five."

"Seriously? Thanks!"

"It wasn't a compliment."

She grinned in the mirror anyway, then applied some lip gloss. The ache in Liam's heart tightened. Emma should've seen this. She would've loved this moment. She would've known what to say; she would've been excited for Nicole, not filled with dread. She would've laughed at Liam's anxieties and made him feel better, because even if they hadn't been the best couple on their own, they'd always been good parents to this beautiful, magical creature in front of him.

"Hang on a sec," he said and went into his bedroom. In the back of the closet was a safe. Liam twisted the combination and opened the heavy door. The safe contained the usual items—the deed to this apartment, his garage, the life-insurance policy, a couple grand in cash—no son of a criminal ever really felt safe without cash.

And there in the back was a black velvet box. Liam opened it and took out the strand of Emma's pearls.

For a moment, the memory of her was so intense that he could smell her perfume, feel the soft skin of her neck, see the pearls glowing against her throat. He could almost hear her laugh.

The pearls were cool in his hand. For a second, he pressed them against his lips and let himself remember just how much he'd loved his wife. Once, the strongest truth in his life was that Emma Tate had chosen him. Those days…those had been burnished with gold, and even if the light slowly faded over the years, those days had happened nonetheless.

Liam cleared his throat and went back into his daughter's bedroom. "Here," he said gruffly. "Your mom wore these on our prom night."

Nicole's mouth opened. "Oh, Daddy," she whispered, and her eyes filled with tears.

"She'd be so proud of you," he said unevenly, fastening the pearls around her neck. "She thought you were the best thing that ever happened."

His daughter wrapped her arms around his waist and hugged him.

"Nic," Liam whispered into her hair, "I'm sorry for being such a jerk this past year. I just love you so much. When I look at you, I think of the little girl I held in the hospital. You were so pink and perfect, I couldn't believe I got to keep you. And you loved me so much…I don't want to lose that. I know you're growing up, and I'm so proud of you and the person you're becoming…but I'm so…scared that you won't need me anymore."

"Daddy! That would never happen!" She pulled back to look at him. "Oh, wow, you're going totally sentimental on me."

"I just want to protect you. I never want you to get hurt or be heartbroken." He swallowed. "I don't want you to make mistakes and fall for the wrong guy. I'd jump in front of a bus to keep that from happening. All I want for you is to be safe and happy."

"Are you crying, Dad? Are those, like, tears in your eyes?"

He gave her a mock scowl. "Give me a break, Nicole. My baby's growing up. It's hard."

She hugged him once more, the smell of her hair so precious it made his heart ache. She pulled back a little, then wiped her eyes with a tissue, careful not to smear her mascara. "Dad," she said firmly. "I *am* safe and happy. And like, chances are my heart *will* get broken someday, and I'll screw up plenty, right? But if that happens…" She turned to face him. "I know where to come."

He looked at the floor and nodded. Why were little girls allowed to grow up? And get smart?

"Daddy? You're doing a good job, you know. You're a really good father."

This would be one of those golden moments. He'd keep this moment with him till the last day of his life. "Thanks." It was the only word he could get out.

She planted a quick kiss on his cheek, then turned back to worship her reflection. "You're such a softy. Mom always said I should marry a guy like you."

His head snapped up. "What was that?" he asked.

Nicole slipped an earring into place. "She said to make sure I picked someone who'd take care of me the way you took care of her." She smiled at him in the mirror, oblivious to the fact that her words had just about knocked him down.

Emma had told their daughter to marry a guy like *him?* "When—when did she say that?"

"I don't know. Sometimes when you were going out on a date, and I'd watch her put on makeup, and I'd say how I couldn't wait to get married, and she'd say, 'Make sure you pick someone like Daddy.'" Nicole smiled at him and put in her other earring.

Liam, suddenly aware that his mouth was open, closed it.

"Oh, so guess what? I saw Posey, right? At Mr. White's house. He was doing her hair, too, because she's, like, a chaperone. And listen to this. When she went to her prom, some creep told her she looked like a bag of bones, and she got totally dumped and had to walk home! In the rain. How's that for nice, huh? I'd totally slap that guy. I'd give him a knee to the crotch, that's what I'd do."

Bag of bones? That phrase sounded…familiar. Those words…they meant something to him.

His daughter was looking at him in the mirror, waiting for a response. "Knee to the crotch. That's my girl."

"Do you like her, Dad? I got a vibe between the two of you the other night. After the game?"

Liam inhaled sharply. "Uh…yes. I do."

"Are you guys dating?"

"Well…no." He swallowed. Now or never. "Nicole, I thought you wanted it to be just the two of us. Remember?"

She frowned. "Oh, that! When you asked if I wanted to live with Grandma and Grandpa? Dad, come on. I was totally PMSing that day. You can have a girlfriend. As long as she's cool and doesn't go all Cruella De Vil on me. And don't even think about popping out triplets before I leave for college, okay, because I am so not the diaper-changing type."

Once again, Liam found his mouth was hanging open. "Oh."

She patted his hand. "Get a life, Dad. Do more than sit around and worry about me, okay? Posey's nice. Anyway, don't you love my hair? I wish I could do this myself. Mr. White is so awesome. I wish he could be my teacher for every subject. They're adopting a baby. Isn't that cool?"

The doorbell rang.

"Oh, my gosh! That's Tanner! Daddy! Go get the door! Go, go! Tell him I'm not ready." With that, she shoved him out of the room.

Mom always said I should marry a guy like you.

But those weren't the only words ringing in his brain.

Bag of bones.

Memory was dawning, the thick fog lifting over what was not a proud moment.

Nothing but a bag of bones.

But first things first. He had fatherly things to do. He opened the door, and there was Tanner Talcott, wearing a tuxedo, corsage box in hand.

Liam had been working at the garage before coming home this evening. He was dressed like the thug he'd once been—black motorcycle jacket, black leather boots, faded jeans, Orange County Motors T-shirt. Hadn't shaved today, or yesterday, now that he thought about it. He was a good three inches taller than young Tanner, and probably forty pounds heavier. He stepped a little closer to his daughter's date. Tanner took a half step back. Good.

"Ground rules, Tanner," he growled. Tanner paled. More good. "No alcohol. No smoking. No drugs. No looking at other girls. You can dance with my daughter. Your hands will avoid the danger zones, which are here, here and here." Liam gestured to his chest, groin and ass. "You can kiss her. Once. At 10:59 p.m. tonight, when you'll be standing here once again. I will be on the other side of this door, waiting for her. Am I clear?"

"Yes, sir," Tanner whispered.

"I was your age once, too," Liam said.

"I'm aware of that, sir."

"I know what you think about."

"I'm sorry."

"You can think it. You can't do it."

"Okay."

"I have many sharp tools in my garage."

"Yes, sir."

"We're clear, then?"

"Very, sir."

"Good!" Liam smiled, then grabbed the boy by the shoulder and dragged him in. "Nicole! Your date's here."

FORTY-FIVE MINUTES later, when the pictures had been taken and Nicole had kissed her dad and Tanner had shaken his hand and Liam had managed to let his child go, he got on his bike and headed across the bridge into Maine. When he pulled up in front of the Tate residence, he gunned his motor before shutting it off. Let them know he was loaded for bear, in other words.

George opened the door, frowning. "Liam. Is Nicole all right?"

"She's fine. I'd like to speak with you and Louise both, please."

"Well, we're having a dinner party. It'll have to wait."

"Now, George." Liam folded his arms across his chest. "Or I can come in and say it in front of your guests, if you'd rather."

His father-in-law frowned. "Fine. Wait here." He returned a long minute later with Louise.

"Liam," she said, her lips narrowing. "What is so important that it can't wait?"

"My daughter is," he said, staring at them both. "I have something to say. I know you didn't approve of me following Emma to California. I wouldn't approve of that, either, now that I'm a father. And I know you weren't happy when she got pregnant, and I know you told her to think about an abortion, and I know you told her to get me to sign away my paternal rights. And I know you told her not to marry me, and I know you probably told her to divorce me once we were married."

Louise's eyebrows rose, as if to say *So?*

"But you should know that I loved your daughter from the day I first saw her to the minute she died. I never stopped. I held her when she cried, I carried her to the bathroom when she was sick, I washed the sheets and made her soup and gave her morphine when the pain got too bad."

His in-laws' faces were frozen. "Son, we're aware—" George began.

"I'm not finished," Liam growled. "How dare you threaten to take away my daughter? The child I raised and read to and fed? How dare you even whisper that I'm unfit? Have you seen her? Talked to her? Don't you know how special she is?" His voice broke. "You should be thanking me. You should be kissing my goddamn boots. So if you want to try something in court, you go right ahead. I won't have to say a word. You'll bury yourselves, and you'll lose, and when you do, I wonder what Nicole will think about the people who tried to take her away from her father."

Louise looked like he'd slapped her. "Liam…we…" Her face collapsed. "We just miss Emma so much. When we saw you with that other woman…"

George put his arm around his wife. "We'll drop the suit. You're right, son. It was stupid of us."

The fight went out of Liam as if a light had been flipped off. "I know you miss Emma. So do I, believe me. And I know it wasn't easy to see me with someone else, but I'm allowed to keep living. And I know you love Nicole. But you can't come between us, and you have to stop trying. My kid. My rules."

George nodded, and to his credit, he looked ashamed. Louise fished a tissue out of her pocket and wiped her eyes. "Have you…told Nicole any of this? About…the things we said about you?"

Liam looked at her. The echoes of Emma were in her face—her nose, the shape of her eyes. "No, Louise," he said gently. "Of course not. And I never would."

"Louise? Is everything all right?" A tall woman, dressed in Barbara Bush wear—sweater set, plaid skirt, sturdy shoes—stood on tiptoe behind the Tates.

"Oh, yes," Louise said. "It's Liam. Our son-in-law."

"It's prom night," Liam said, smiling at her. He fished in his pocket and withdrew his camera. "I brought pictures of Nicole." He handed the camera to George. "You can look at these without me, since I have to run."

"Thank you," Louise said, her voice still tremulous.

Liam looked at her a long moment. "Give Nicole a call tomorrow. I'm sure she'll want to tell you all about it."

"Thank you, Liam," she whispered.

"See you soon, son," George said.

Then Liam walked back to his bike, which had never looked quite so beautiful, and slung his leg over it, pulled on his helmet and started her up.

One more stop, and then he'd be done.

CHAPTER THIRTY

PROM. POSEY WONDERED how many people would walk away from tonight with the memories they wanted.

Only about a third of the kids were dancing—well, if you could call it that. They looked more like salmon swimming upstream, all aiming for the stage, oddly in unison, as the band played what the lead singer had called a "classic" by Eminem. Shockingly, most of the kids seemed to know the words: *There's vomit on his sweater already, Mom's spaghetti...*

And people wondered why she liked oldies.

Jon was wandering through the ranks, pulling out the kids who weren't sober, putting in calls to their parents. A large majority of kids seemed to be trying too hard...shrill, forced laughter, exaggerated gestures, darting looks to see who was where and if he or she had noticed. And then there were those who seemed either bored or miserable. Sad, really, when you thought of how much effort and time went into preparing for the big night.

But there were the golden kids, and Posey was glad to see that Nicole was among them. She was one of the salmon swimmers at the moment; her face was bright and happy. Posey couldn't wait to tell Liam—actually, no. She wouldn't be doing that.

With a sigh, she looked around. Whitfield Mansion looked great. Same setup, same décor. Same cliques—the mean girls, the fringe kids, the smart-asses, the invisibles.

Well. Time to hit the loo. Posey made her way across the dance floor, stopped at a couple engaged in some pornographic moves, cheerfully told them she'd turn a hose on them if they didn't keep six inches between body parts, and continued on. The band's next song was another she didn't recognize, and more kids flowed out onto the dance floor. The music was so loud, Posey could feel it in her stomach, and the quiet of the bathroom felt like an oasis.

She realized abruptly that this was *the* bathroom. Huh. There was the last stall, where she'd hidden. May as well use that one. A long time ago, she'd had to bite her knuckle to keep from crying in here. Funny, how huge that moment had been at the time. Funny, too, how it was now just one of those things.

When she came out of the stall, she found she wasn't alone. A girl was wiping her eyes with the rough paper towels.

"You okay?" Posey asked.

The girl gave her a panicked look. "Are you in my class?" she squeaked.

Posey smiled. "No. I'm a chaperone. I'm thirty-four years old, actually."

"You don't look like it."

"Thanks. So. Having a bad time?" She turned the water on and washed her hands.

The girl's face scrunched up. "My boyfriend just broke up with me. Can you believe it? Like, it couldn't wait till tomorrow?"

"What a putz," Posey said, patting the girl's arm. "Want some advice?"

The girl gave Posey that classic teenage look—dubious that this relic of the last century could offer anything useful. "Sure," she said sullenly.

"Screw him. I mean, no, don't screw him in the...you know. But this is your prom. Your friends are here, you look gorgeous, the band is, um, great, and you'll never do senior prom again. So don't go crawling off and let him see how much he hurt you. Just put that away for now and go have fun."

"Right," the girl said, rolling her eyes.

"Well, crawling off to cry works, too. Your choice, sweetheart."

Posey had crawled off. But she never had again, had she? That night, miserable as it had been, had made her a better person.

The bathroom door burst open, and three girls, all pretty as swans, came in. "Sierra, he's such an ass! Don't hide in here, though! Come on! Pretend he doesn't exist. Ryan Joyce will be totally thrilled."

The girls were gone in the next instant, and for whatever reason, Posey felt...well...a sense of closure, an affection for her sixteen-year-old self, for the heartache of an unrequited, crushing first love. She'd really loved Liam back then. She really loved him now. And you know what? It was...good. Someday, maybe, she'd tell her grandkids about the bad boy with the leather jacket who took her for a ride on his motorcycle, and wouldn't they all think she was the bomb?

Well. Time to go back and return to chastity patrol. A glimpse in the mirror revealed that Jon's hairspray had not been up to the task of conquering the mighty cowlick, but so what? She looked like herself, and it was oddly reassuring.

As she came out of the loo, she could hear the lead singer of the band talking. "Okay, kids, we have a request, and maybe you've heard it, if you've ever been to a Red Sox game. Bear with us, we haven't played it for years, but the guy gave us a hundred bucks to do this."

Posey emerged into the ballroom. There was Jon, who waved to her. A few teachers were with him. Posey headed over, then bumped into Nicole. "Hi, honey, having fun?" she asked.

"Totally," Nicole said, looking at the stage. "How about... Oh. Oh, no." Posey looked, too, but even standing on tiptoe, she couldn't see what was going on—the salmon had not fled the waters, and the dance floor was rather packed.

Then the bass player started to play a very familiar phrase.

"Oh, no," Nicole said. "You gotta be kidding me."

Posey's heart crashed to a stop. Oh, she knew this song, yes indeed. No doubt about it. Her mouth was suddenly dry.

Then someone started singing.

"Nicole!" a girl in a pink dress shrieked, whipping out her phone. "Are you *seeing* this?"

"Oh, kill me now," Nicole said. She turned to Posey. "Um...I think this is for you. Tanner, move." She pushed Posey forward so she could see.

There, onstage, stood Liam Declan Murphy, leather jacket, five o'clock shadow, guitar in his hands. Singing "Sweet Caroline" by Neil Diamond.

Her favorite song. The same song that was playing in the elevator the day she gave him the CPR he didn't need.

His eyes scanned the crowd, and when they fell on her, he smiled, and when he came to the chorus, a fair number of the kids and pretty much all the teachers sang along with him.

Posey's eyes were suddenly stinging.

"Mr. Murphy, don't quit your day job!" someone shouted, and everyone laughed, including Liam. But he kept singing, doggedly, messing up some of the words, and when he came to the chorus the second time around, it seemed like everyone in the room was singing with him.

"I think you're hot, Mr. Murphy!" called a girl.

"Ew! Hello! That's my *father,* so shut it, okay?" Nicole said. She glanced at Posey and rolled her eyes. "Sorry for you, Posey. I told him he should go out with you, but I never pictured..." The girl gave her a closer look. "Oh, man, you're eating it up, aren't you?"

Posey gave a shaky laugh, nodded and wiped her eyes.

The song ended, and the kids gave him a good-natured round of applause, and he jumped off the stage.

"Back to something a little, ah, more contemporary," the singer said and counted off a beat to yet another song Posey had never heard of, and the salmon-jumping began again.

Then Liam was standing in front of her, and the sight of him was so overwhelming that she forgot to breathe.

"Want to dance?" he asked.

"Dad? Seriously? Not here," Nicole shouted over the music. "I'm embarrassed enough."

"Whatevs," he said, and taking Posey's hand, he led her through the maze of tables—there was Jon, grinning into his seltzer water and pretending not to see them.

In the foyer of the mansion, the music wasn't so loud. "Want to dance?" he asked again, and Posey couldn't quite answer. Apparently, he took this as a yes, because his arm went around her waist, and he pulled her close and moved in a slow rhythm that had nothing to do with the music, which was some god-awful song about wanting someone's body and their disease—blick—but somehow it was the most romantic, mushy moment of Posey's entire life. Holy Elvis, she might actually be crying from happiness. She could smell leather and fresh air, and his soap, and she looked up into his face and saw that he was smiling.

"That was the most pathetic version of 'Sweet Caroline' I have ever heard," she said, her voice shaking.

"You loved it," he said.

She shrugged, but couldn't help a smile. "You're right."

He stopped moving and pulled back a little, taking both her hands in his. His smile was gone. "Cordelia, you're not a bag of bones," he said, and her mouth fell open. "You weren't back then, either. I mean, you were a little thing, but I only said that because... Oh, crap." He sighed. "Rick Balin said he planned to, uh...sleep with you that night."

Posey took a quick breath. The truth was, sex had never even crossed her mind. She hadn't thought further than the prom itself.

"And I..." Liam shook his head. "I just said something stupid to put him off. It was an impulse or whatever. Because you were a good kid, and you didn't deserve some idiot like Rick trying to...you know."

So Rick had been planning to sleep with her—and Posey being barely sixteen, vastly inexperienced about the world of boys, and outweighed by probably a hundred pounds by a boy used to getting what he wanted...that could've been really bad.

Liam was looking at her solemnly. "I didn't realize he'd drop you like that. I just thought maybe... I don't know. I didn't think it through, and then I completely forgot about it. I didn't mean to ruin your night, and I'm really sorry."

"Oh...I... That's okay," she whispered. "It's actually a little...sweet, now that I know."

He grinned, and her knees went weak. "I am pretty sweet."

"Well, let's not go overboard," Posey said, though her heart was just as soft and mushy as all her other parts were becoming.

"Cordelia," he said quietly, his smile fading. "I seem to be in love with you."

The words were like sinking into a vat of warm caramel sauce. "Oh," she whispered. "That's...nice." If she died now, that would be fine. Completely fine.

A small smile tugged at the corner of his mouth. "Will you forgive me for being an idiot, then and more recently? Because that image you have of me...I wouldn't mind trying to live up to that."

She let those words, and all the others, sink in. The past was never what you thought, was it? Liam Murphy had been protecting her honor—awkwardly, perhaps, but there it was. He'd been looking out for her, because that was the kind of man he was, and always had been.

"So?" he said, his eyes warm.

"Yeah, well, I'll definitely think about it, Liam, and—"

"You should probably marry me." He smiled. "When Nicole's ready for a stepmother, yeah. You should marry me. I've never been so happy as I've been with you, Cordelia, and let's face it, you've been in love with me half your life, more, maybe, and of course, I am incredibly good-looking and—"

"My God, the ego." But she was crying, and laughing, and almost unable to take in what he was saying, her heart pounded so hard.

Liam's face grew serious. "I'll take good care of you, Cordelia. I promise." Then he was kissing her, the gentle scrape of his five o'clock shadow, the heat and softness of his lips, and she melted against him, heart utterly light.

"Lovebirds?" It was Jon. "I hate to interrupt, especially since I'm filming this for YouTube, but pay attention." Posey pulled back—with difficulty—and looked at her brother-in-law. "I've released you from chaperone duty. If you want to leave, you're free to go."

Posey and Liam looked at each other. "Nah," Liam said. "I think I owe you a decent prom."

And with that, he led her back into the ballroom. And danced with her.

And kissed her.

More than once.

Right in front of everyone.

EPILOGUE

Fifteen months later

IT SEEMED ONLY RIGHT that the first wedding at The Meadows in sixty-two years was Posey and Liam's. The old mansion was still standing, oh, yes. And would continue to stand for a long, long time, if not forever.

On the first day of fall, Vivian Appleton died in her sleep at the age of 102. On the bureau across from her bed was the model Posey'd made, and it comforted her to know Vivian had had it close, that maybe The Meadows, even in miniature, had been the last thing Vivian had seen.

A month later, when Allan Linkletter asked her to come to his office for the reading of the will, she hoped it was because Viv had left her the model. It wasn't worth anything much beyond its sentimental value.

She said hello to the Vultures, trying to be pleasant, despite the gleeful greed that glowed in their faces. "Took the old bag long enough," muttered one of the nephews, and Posey stifled the urge to kick him in the nuts.

Allan wasted no time in getting down to business. When everyone was seated around the conference table, he read the preliminary legalese, and then paused and cleared his throat. The Vultures all leaned forward.

"'To Cordelia Wilhelmina Osterhagen,'" Allan read, "'I hereby give the land, buildings and their contents of The Meadows, my property located at 1100 Shady Brook Road, Bellsford, New Hampshire.'"

There'd been a moment of silence. Then chaos exploded, the four Vultures squawking, swearing, sobbing as Posey sat there, wide-eyed and stunned into silence. Eventually, Allan explained that the Vultures had no legal recourse at all. The will was iron-clad, witnessed, and Viv's doctor had signed an affidavit that she'd been completely competent when she made the change. The Vultures didn't have a talon to stand on.

Vivian had also left Posey a very brief note: *You've been more family to me than those money-grubbing Vultures ever were. It was noticed.*

That was all. But that was everything.

It took a while to process—Posey *owned* The Meadows, a huge Victorian mansion on ten acres of land. What to do with it was another question.

At first she'd done nothing—being with Liam was new enough, and gently trying to become part of Nicole's life without causing the girl any undue stress. But Nicole had been very sweet…she seemed to view Posey almost as a big sister, and Posey was careful not to take sides when Liam and his daughter disagreed.

Liam's worry about Nicole had lessened from DEFCON four down into normal overprotective father range. His obsession with door-locking dwindled to just one check, and while he still had a thing about hand washing, it was just enough for Posey to mock him for scrubbing in before meals. Then again, the guy was a mechanic, so she couldn't really fault him there. And if he was still occasionally brooding and growly…hey. It had a certain hotness, and Posey was not objecting.

In the spring, though, Posey made the hard decision to sell the church, acknowledging that it needed more than she could give it, in both time and money. It was hard, especially leaving behind the bell, but a nice young couple had bought it and seemed quite gung-ho to fix it up the way it deserved. They'd also bought a dozen or so treasures from Irreplaceable Artifacts. She imagined they'd be back for more, in fact. Her perfect customers—taste *and* money.

So she'd moved to The Meadows—not to the mansion, but to the stone caretaker's cottage, which she had always loved. The only downside…the cats hated it. Twice, they'd made the mile-long trek back to the church, Meatball in the lead, followed by Jellybean and Sagwa, Posey in hot, panicky pursuit. The third time, the owners suggested that they keep the faithless felines, who clearly were more attached to the place than to the person who'd fed them all those years. Then again, they'd come with the church. Posey dropped by about once a week to visit, and sure, they seemed happy enough to see her…as happy as cats got, that was.

But Shilo loved The Meadows, as he always had, and it always made Posey smile to see her giant dog galloping sloppily across the lawns, jowls flopping, as he came at her first whistle.

And in the mornings, as she sat with her coffee on the small balcony of the caretaker's cottage, her hand on her dog's big head, Posey could still hear the bell, and it never failed to make her smile.

The Meadows was going to be a banquet facility…weddings, anniversaries, stuff like that. Posey thought Vivian would approve of filling the old mansion with parties again. But though she now owned the estate, party planning really wasn't her thing, and there was no way she was giving up Irreplaceable Artifacts. So she'd hired a person to get things going, a person who could handle both event planning and the catering end of things, a person who'd been looking for a slight change of career…and if that person was a pain in the butt sometimes, and if she tended to show off too much cleavage, that was probably okay. Gretchen had already managed to book six weddings for this summer alone. Seemed like her celebrity status was a good thing after all.

Gret was in the kitchen now, checking on the wedding food (some German, some other types, too). She'd dumped Dante almost as soon as they'd patched things up and was cutting a wide swath through the single men of New Hampshire.

At the moment, Posey was in her room, alone, though Stacia, Jon and Brie were due any second. In her hands was a note she'd received last month, something she'd taken out just because it seemed right to look at it again. In February, she'd decided to write to her birth mother, sending it through the attorney who handled the adoption. Nothing terribly emotional, just the facts. But she'd thanked Clarice for having her, and for giving her to Stacia and Max. She told her birth mother what a happy life she'd had, that she was a sister, and now an aunt, and that she'd be getting married soon to the man she'd loved her whole life. She'd signed it only "Cordelia."

Clarice had written back through the attorney. *I'm so, so glad to know these things, and I wish you every happiness in the world, Cordelia. Thank you for telling me.*

And that was it. But again, it was everything.

Well. Time to get girlified. Posey put the note in her night-table drawer.

Today she was marrying Liam Declan Murphy. From today on, they'd be living together, sleeping in the same bed, waking up together every morning. His daughter loved her, he loved her, and it was so utterly wonderful that the very thought brought tears of happiness to her eyes.

In just a couple of hours, her parents would walk her down the aisle of St. Martin's Church. Brianna was her maid of honor, and little Betty was the flower girl. Jon and Henry were ushers, as was James. And Nicole would stand up for Liam, which had made Posey burst into tears when they told her. Half the town would be there, everyone from Mac and Elise (who had moved in together), to the girls from the bakery, to her teammates on the softball team, to the Tates, even.

A knock came on the door. "Come on in, Ma," Posey called.

It wasn't Stacia. It was Liam, sticking his head in her room, and the sight of him—the black hair, those clear green eyes—still gave her a thrill. Her husband. In about a hundred and twenty minutes, her husband.

"Ditching me?" she asked, grinning.

"Hardly," he said, giving her that sleepy, bedroom-eyed smile that never failed to get the girl parts yowling. "I brought you a present."

"Is it food? I'm kind of hungry."

"Gretchen told me you had five pancakes for breakfast," he said, still not coming in.

"What's your point, biker boy?"

"You won't faint, that's all I'm saying. Plus, I know you have an Almond Joy in that drawer."

She narrowed her eyes. "So, what's my present?"

He opened the door fully. "Here."

It was a cardboard box, the kind with holes in the side. The kind used to carry animals. As if on cue, a small, striped paw stuck out.

"It's a kitten," Liam said, opening the box and lifting the little thing out. "Since your other cats dumped you for the new people."

"Oh, Liam," Posey breathed. The cat was tiny, a gray tiger kitten. Shilo lumbered over and gave it a sniff, his tail wagging, and the kitten squeaked and batted the dog's giant nose, earning a lick.

Liam set the little cat in her lap. Its fur was so soft and fluffy, and its eyes were wide and blue.

"It's a boy," he said, reaching up to tuck some hair behind Posey's ear. "I thought we could call him Joe."

* * * * *

DISCUSSION QUESTIONS

1. Posey sometimes struggles with feeling different from her family; her brother, who is also adopted, does not. What are some of the different ways you think adopted children deal with their experience? Is it possible not to think about it at all, as Henry appears not to? If you were adopted, would you want to find your birth parents? Did you relate to Stacia and her fears about Posey and her birth mother?

2. Liam returns to Bellsford and finds, somewhat to his surprise, that his past hasn't been forgotten. The ultimate high-school bad boy, he's now seeking redemption by trying to keep his daughter from her parents' mistakes. How do you feel about his parenting skills and ideas? Are his concerns valid? Have you ever returned to your hometown to be reminded about your past, even when you feel that it should've been put to rest by now?

3. The romantic theme of bad boy reformed by true love is examined in *Until There Was You*. But Liam and Emma's marriage was less than ideal, though the issue of divorce was never discussed. Do you think Liam's take on their marriage was accurate? Why do you think he still carries so much guilt over Emma? What are some of his deeply held beliefs about himself that turn out to be wrong? What about him has never changed?

4. Posey's physical appearance is a significant factor in this book, both when she was a teenager and even now, as an adult. Her chronic hunger, inability to gain weight and the fact that she doesn't resemble her family play a big role in how she views herself. How much effect do you think physical appearance has on self-esteem? Have your feelings about your own physicality changed over the years?

5. What did you think of the rivalry between Gretchen and Posey? Do you have a relative or longtime friend who pokes at your weak spots the way Gretchen poked at Posey's? Do you think family roles are as strongly defined as Gretchen believes? Can family rivalries ever truly be put to rest?

6. When Nicole tells her dad what happened to Posey at her prom so long ago, it has an electrifying effect on Liam. Why do you think that was? His grand gesture is more than Posey's favorite song—why do you think it worked?